Final Wishes

Shirley Welch
Dan Matney

Final Wishes

Copyright 2022 Shirley Welch and Dan Matney

All rights Reserved

DEDICATION

Shirley Welch and Dan Matney would like to dedicate this book to the seniors who inspired them to write about their lives and their stories: Judy, Jim, Rick, Marijke, Mary, Sherrill, Joe, Terri, Rose, Polly, Ingrid, and Ann-Marie.

PROLOGUE

"What they did to us. It was hell," Hanni said, her voice firm with conviction.

A hush fell over the room as ten pairs of eyes looked at the woman seated in the wing-back chair. Wrinkles covered her face, the layers sagging as if the force of gravity worked overtime. Today, her hair had been washed and curled, and now gray swirls touched her cheek. With her lips pulled tight, the lines in her face deepened. Her eyes, usually bright blue and filled with anticipation, looked watery with pending tears.

Across the room, Pastor Stan asked, "Do you need a minute to gather yourself?"

Hanni turned toward the voice. Her back stiffened. "No. I have never been better. I can remember. I need to go on."

On Pastor Stan's right, Skeeter felt a veil of depression cover the room. It wasn't supposed to be like this, either. It was Hanni's birthday, number 93, and Skeeter had brought a birthday cake to the Piney Center to celebrate the event. A table held the cake and a vase of flowers, paper plates, cups, a pitcher of lemonade, and helium balloons tied with colored ribbon. A half-dozen birthday cards lay on the table.

After the residents at the Piney Center gathered to celebrate her birthday, Skeeter had started the conversation with a simple statement, "Hanni, today is your day. What would you like to share with us about your long and happy life?"

She met the stares of those seated around her: Skeeter, Pastor Stan, Cecil, Richard, Jayne, Cordy, Layla May, Millie, Julia, and little Charlotte. All of those who did not know her when she was a child or the events of her life. All of those who would find out. Today. Because it could be her last day, and today her mind was clear.

Hanni began, "It was the winter of nineteen-forty-four. I was fourteen. My father and brothers had already escaped the Netherlands, but mother and I remained." She pushed an errant strand of gray-streaked hair off her cheek. "The Germans occupied our town, Utrecht. For the most part, they left us alone, but we lived with fear. One day, Friedrich Schmidhober arrived at our house and told us to leave or give him a room. A big German officer with a square chin, blue eyes, and broad shoulders, my mother couldn't refuse him, or we would be living in our barn and would surely freeze. He moved in, looking strong and smart in his pressed uniform and polished boots. He carried a crop whenever he came or went. I feared the whip more than him. With time, it would change.

"He took over my mother's bedroom, so my mother slept on a cot in my upstairs bedroom. At first, he acted like a guest in our house; as the months passed, we realized that Jews were being removed. He changed. He issued orders, withheld extra food rations, and he studied me. My best friend, Lettie, and her mother who were both Jewish, disappeared one day. Simply gone. No one knew where. Our neighbors, the Bettendorfs, hid a Jewish family in the attic of their barn. The Bettendorfs vanished, and the barn doors stood open. When I asked Schmidhober about them, he smiled. I learned the Bettendorfs had been dragged from their cottage in the middle of the night by German officers, taken to the train station, and were never seen again.

"Schmidhober became a man with hardliner Nazi ideals. He left my mother alone but not me. I was all bones, but he took me to my mother's bedroom and had his way with me. I couldn't fight him; I could not refuse him. I have never felt such hate, before or after."

Hanni picked up a water cup with a lid and straw. She brought the straw to her lips and sipped. "The dikes had been bombed; the fields flooded. Everywhere I looked the land was frozen. Food became as scarce as hope. When we ran out of ration coupons, we weren't allowed to ask for more. Schmidhober had plenty of food, but he wouldn't share it with us. I remember seeing chocolate smeared on his lips, and I could smell it, but he wouldn't give me a taste. My family owned several acres where we grew tulips. Thank goodness. Winter came. We ate tulip bulbs to survive."

Across the room, Cecil uttered a gasp.

Hanni looked in his direction as if to assure him what she said was true. With her cane on the floor, she adjusted her hips in the chair. "I am old, and my eyesight is almost gone, and my hearing picks up some things, and most days I don't remember my name, but today my memory is as clear as it was then. If you want to know, tulip bulbs are not hard to eat. They are sweet in flavor, and no, various colors do not taste differently."

Millie, Hanni's friend, whispered, "I'm sorry for what you had to endure."

Reaching for Millie, Pastor Stan gathered her hand in his. "We all are," he said, his tone of voice soft.

Hanni pointed her cane at Millie. "You were raised in Germany but I know your heart, Millie, and it was never tied to the Nazi bastards."

Cordy gasped. Layla May jerked. Cecil's jaw sagged open. Millie nodded.

Pastor Stan looked at Skeeter, who sat with the group of seniors every Monday, Wednesday, and Friday in the afternoons. She was twenty-five, too young to know much about that war, except what had been written in books, and for her, the Second World War had never come alive. However, Skeeter knew Hanni kept a photograph of a brilliant field of tulips by her bedside, a field of blossoms so big it stretched as far as the eye could see. She told Skeeter that before she died, she wanted to stand in her family's tulip fields. With Hanni's poor eyesight, bad hip, and with her journey with Alzheimer's disease, Skeeter knew the old woman's wish was unlikely to be granted. Still, today the seniors would honor their friend with a cake and cards and well-wishes; it was the best they could do.

Charlotte, Cecil's three-year-old blonde-haired granddaughter cast a wary glance at Skeeter and took several steps toward the birthday cake. Blond curls bobbed as she moved. Pausing, she looked over her shoulder to see who watched.

Aware that Charlotte's mother had stepped away to take a cell phone call, Skeeter leaned forward and gave the toddler a negative shake of her head. The cake, a white sheet of sugary frosting with rosebuds, was a super tease. Charlotte held Skeeter's gaze and froze. For the moment, the toddler's fingers would not touch the cake, but Skeeter guessed that Charlotte would not back away from the temptation of the cake.

Hanni continued, "My mother must have known what Schmidhober did to me, but she couldn't intervene. If she did, he would have shot us and buried our bodies behind the house and no one would have known or cared. My mother and I never spoke about what happened in her bedroom." She pushed a lock of hair over her right ear.

Millie asked, "How did you cope?"

Hanni smiled at her friend. "When I went into the bedroom with Friedrich Schmidhober, I became a different person than the one who resided in the remainder of the house. It was how we survived the war. We became someone else. Still, it was hell."

Pastor Stan wanted to steer the conversation away from Germans and war, even though the events were part of Hanni's life. "Yet here you are in America, Hanni, in Colorado. I believe you told me that you came here as a young woman. Is it true?"

Hanni's blue eyes sparkled. "Colorado was a world away from the Netherlands and German officers."

Layla May asked, "How did you get here?"

"By starving."

The room again fell quiet.

Hanni straightened. "The winter of nineteen-forty-five was harsh. The Germans cut off all food and fuel shipments to the Western provinces. Food was scarce. Many starved. We managed with our supply of tulip bulbs from the fields behind our house and sometimes we had sugar beets. Finally, the Allies arrived to liberate us. In the spring of forty-five, I traveled with one-hundred-eighty-six malnourished children between the ages of six and sixteen who were loaded on the vessels *Zwerver* and *Bona* and shipped to Yorkshire, England to a camp designed to help me and the others regain normal weight and health. Our final destination was the northeastern province of Groningen, where food remained plentiful. After six months, I joined my mother who had emigrated to Paris. I finished my education in Paris. I spoke fluent French and became a nanny for several years, but I longed for home, to see those tulips fields again." She sighed as if tired. "My brother convinced me to come home, and so I did. Imagine my surprise to find a handsome young American living in my bedroom!"

A commotion began in the hall leading to the social room at the assisted living wing of the Center. The director, a big man with wisps of hair circling the top of his head, escorted a man dressed in slacks with a soft green shirt and leather shoes. The seniors turned in his direction. "Good afternoon, folks," Harry Chamberlain began. He placed his arm on the shorter man's shoulder. "Joe's son came for a visit and left Joe in the dining hall. I found him napping in the physical therapy room."

Skeeter stood. "Oh, Joe," she said, "let's get you to a comfortable chair." The bent-over-man looked ancient and muddled. Skeeter pushed her chair closer to Cordy, a woman in her mid-eighties, who had a brain tumor. She grabbed a folding chair and brought it into the circle of seniors. "Here you go, Joe. Have a seat. We are celebrating Hanni's birthday today."

Joe looked over his shoulder. "Is Mary coming too?"

The director gave Joe a push toward the chair. "Not today."

Shuffling, he sat down with a little grunt.

"I'll be on my way," the director said. "Continue with your celebration."

Skeeter thought the director had the emotional correctness of a speed bump. He said nothing to Hanni and didn't realize he had interrupted a retelling of the most terrible happenings in her life. It would be difficult, now, to recapture the mood.

Watching the director leave, Skeeter sighed, aware that Mary was Joe's wife who had died several months ago. She turned to Joe. He smiled. Some folks wore a smile, Joe *was* the smile. Everything about him spoke understated joy, except when he talked about Mary. "We are celebrating Hanni's ninety-third birthday."

Joe held his smile. For living close to a hundred years, he had his original teeth and showed them when he grinned.

"Congratulations," he said. "I'm older than dirt. I've had one hundred and three birthdays. I'm a centenarian. So, it makes me somewhat of an expert on birthdays. My advice is not to have anymore."

From Joe's medical records, Skeeter knew he was only 97, but liked to tag on five extra years. Skeeter chuckled and the others laughed. She turned to Hanni. "Sorry about the interruption, Hanni. You left off about when you returned home."

Cecil tapped his fingers on his walker. "Are we going to have the cake soon?"

Over her shoulder, Skeeter shot a glance at Charlotte, who had inched closer to the birthday cake, and now the family dog, Bear — a huge brute of a dog with a black coat and a gray muzzle and who always accompanied the family — joined Charlotte, and the two of them looked like they had a game plan for the cake. Skeeter shook her head at the toddler, and in turn, Charlotte blinked and pretended Skeeter wasn't in the room. Bear inched closer to the table.

Cordy rubbed her hands over the back of a stuffed animal.

Layla May straightened and pushed her shoulders back, giving everyone in the room a perfect silhouette of her body. Today, the cream dress she wore hugged her figure and although she didn't need to enhance her femininity, she crossed slender ankles. She wore soft leather shoes in sparkling gold color. Her fingernails were painted bright red.

Hanni frowned. She gazed at her shoes and back to Skeeter. She nibbled on her lower lip and swayed. Her face had lost color and her eyes turned dull. "This is my home," she said. "All of those things outside go one way and then the other and if they don't, they find a way to do the other thing, and then they come back even if you go looking for them outside."

Skeeter glanced at Pastor Stan and both of them *knew*. They'd lost her to Alzheimer's disease. For this one glimpse on her ninety-third birthday, Hanni had been able to recall her childhood in Holland, the young woman she had once been, the hunger, the tulips, and the atrocities committed by the Nazis. Perhaps her memories had been sparked by the bouquet on the table, perhaps by painful recollections, perhaps by nothing in particular.

Now the window of clarity had closed, and Skeeter knew it could not open again, not today and perhaps not ever. *Who was the handsome American man in Hanni's bedroom?*

Turning her head, Skeeter saw Charlotte reach up and draw her finger through the frosting on the cake. The toddler glanced at Skeeter and quickly licked the frosting from her fingers. Her expression did not register guilt. Skeeter rose and headed for the table, taking no more chances Charlotte or Bear would sneak more of the cake. "Okay, everyone. It's time for the birthday cake."

For now, Hanni's story was finished.

CHAPTER 1

Three weeks earlier…

Skeeter tapped her three-inch heels beneath her seat. "Could you repeat the question?"

Across from her in the sterile office, Harry Chamberlain checked the job application on his desk. Lifting his head, his stare went through her, as if she were a spreadsheet with a red flag pointing out something offensive. "I asked why you applied for this job?"

She took a minute to calm the hammering inside her skull. She pointed to the application. "You can see I'm an information specialist. You advertised for an IT person in the newspaper." She studied Chamberlain. He wore his hair parted to the side, cemented with some sort of gel with wisps of hair curling over the top of a bald head. He was a man in his mid-forties who had an aura about him that said he knew everything, and she guessed he assumed Skeeter was a Millennial product and naïve about the world.

As if uncomfortable in her presence, he shifted. "Yes, I am aware of that, but I wonder if you will fit in our small mountain community?"

She leaned forward, disregarding his intimidating intensity. "I am twenty-five. I am adaptable."

He didn't meet her glare and ran his index finger over a section of her application. "You recently moved to Piney from San Francisco. It's a big change."

She tried to smile. "Yes, it is." His desk was clear of all papers except her application. Behind his chair on a shelf, she saw a picture of him with his arm around a girl who looked about ten years old. She guessed it was his daughter. In the photo, he towered over her and had to be over two hundred pounds. The girl had the same flyaway hair as her father. On the shelf was also a vintage leather ski boot, plus a stack of books about Colorado's mountains. Against the wall to the left of his desk rested several framed prints, yet to be hung on the wall. He held a pen. It looked as though it had come in a velvet-lined box and cost more than lunch at a nice restaurant.

He put the pen away in his top drawer and asked, "Can you adjust?"

Her resume included her education with a degree in Communication, plus years of work with several dot.com companies in the San Francisco area. She excluded from her resume the fact that she had worked with Vulnerability Exploitation Tool Metasploit, along with Wireshark, and moonlighted as a hack when material considerations required extra funds. What she didn't know was anything about retirement communities, but she had worked at different businesses where she had to learn as she went along. This was no different. "I'm like a chameleon. Adaptable, changeable, easy to adjust."

He didn't react to her reply. Pinching the knot on a maroon tie, he took a sip from a bottle of water. "Piney Center is both privately funded, plus funds from the state. Because of this, we have strict fiduciary requirements and regulations we must follow, and because we are a new facility, our governing board carefully watches us. The state also requires inspections, which we must pass to continue with funding."

She nodded since all of this was common sense.

He went on, "Our assisted living section has been open four months. We are fine-tuning. However, the Center has computer applications in need of creation. You are qualified." He paused as if deciding how to continue. Picking up a pencil, he twirled it between two fingers. Then he said, "The job is yours."

He made it sound as if he were doing her a favor. She digested the decision and decided she had not wowed the director, and because she was a good judge of character, she knew Harry felt uncomfortable with her, most likely because she was female and attractive. She also guessed a small mountain community must not have produced many applicants for the job. "When do I start?"

"Right away." Chamberlain went on to outline her duties at the Piney Center. "You will be responsible for computer hardware and software, also networks and servers, making sure they work consistently and correctly. You would be required to install programs, configure networks and databases, and provide assistance to end-users." After sipping from his water bottle, he added, "Your job will be two-fold. Half the day will be spent on the computer data information, and the rest of your day will be to engage with the seniors."

Skeeter sputtered, "What? The ad in the paper didn't include working with seniors."

With a nod, a wedge of hair fell on his forehead. "Yes, but you insisted you can adjust and adapt, and we are a new facility and need afternoon leadership, which entails social activities."

She sat back in her chair, assimilating the information that she would engage with people decades older than herself and had no idea how to do it. However, she needed this job.

Adaptability was her middle name. "Sounds good," she said, betting Harry Chamberlain did not adjust and adapt. He looked as rigid as a lamp pole.

Chamberlain tapped his finger on his desk. "Is there anything else I should know about you?"

She forced a smile she had practiced in a mirror since she was seven years old. She lifted the corners of her lips and showed several teeth, but the almost-smile also produced indentations on each cheek that gave off a perception of sincerity. "I once worked in a preschool," she said, lying. She felt bad for lying but didn't know what else to say. "I grew up in a semi-normal household in Northern California. I went to college in Southern California, which can be considered a different country entirely from Northern California. I lived in Seattle for a year but so much rain grew depressing. I gravitated back to the San Francisco area. I moved here to help my grandmother. She is a recent widow." She hoped this would be enough to qualify her as someone who could work with aging adults.

Chamberlain lifted an eyebrow. "Has she been to the Piney Center?"

Skeeter would not reply to anything close to the truth. Her grandmother thought she was seventy-seven years young and had a lot more living to do, especially where men in her life were concerned. "She is very active," Skeeter replied, "but her memory is beginning to fail, and it's another reason why I want to work here. I want to have a plan in place for when my grandmother needs more than I can provide."

Chamberlain beamed as if Skeeter had told him he won the lottery. "It's exactly what we tell people when we have informational events." He shook his head. "Most people are not knowledgeable about what resources are available for their aging loved ones. Caregivers aren't prepared; they feel trapped, both emotionally and financially. The Piney Center provides three levels of care: Assisted Living for those able to care for themselves but want to do less; our rehabilitation center provides short-term, skilled nursing after hospitalization, and we have a memory care unit specially-designed for those with Alzheimer's disease and other forms of dementia."

Voices grew louder from outside the office. Chamberlain paused with his windy explanation and looked up to see a man at his office door. The receptionist was next to him but quickly nodded and retreated. "We're in a meeting," Chamberlain said.

"Oh, yeah." The man entered the office as if he had rushed from somewhere, sat a guitar case on the floor, and stood next to Skeeter. "Hi." He extended his hand. "I'm Pastor Stan."

Skeeter looked up to see a middle-aged man, about six feet tall with thinning brownish-gray hair. He had nice blue eyes and dressed more casually than the director. She took his hand "Skeeter Rawleigh." She found his handshake to be firm but without crushing her bones, a good indication of a man's sensitivity.

Chamberlain adjusted the job application papers and placed them in a pile. "Miss Rawleigh is our new hire—"

Skeeter held up a hand. "Please, call me Skeeter. Otherwise, I think you are talking to my mother, who by the way, I haven't seen in several years, so it can be confusing."

Chamberlain pushed himself back from the desk. "As I was saying, Skeeter is our new hire. She will be leading our afternoon social time."

"Great!" Pastor Stan replied with enthusiasm. Then he stepped back to get a better look at the new hire. Decades younger than himself, she wore a calf-high black skirt and a flowing white blouse. He could tell she had blondish hair but it was pulled up on top of her head and the sweep of it made him stare at her neck. "We have music this afternoon," he told her, choosing the correct words with some difficultly. Her air of professionalism and intelligence left him groping for words, a strange mix to juggle while standing in Chamberlain's office. "I would be happy to introduce you to our group."

"It would be, ah, nice." She checked her watch. Her grandmother had a date with a guy several years her junior and Skeeter wanted to check him out. All of this was new to her — the death of her grandmother's latest husband, the escrow of the estate, what to do with the house, where Grandma should live, and most of all, the dating rules when seventy-seven.

Pastor Stan picked up his guitar. "The seniors are in the day room. It's down the hall to your right."

Nodding to Chamberlain, she followed the pastor out of the office and into the building's entry hallway. When they passed the receptionist's desk, Skeeter glanced down the corridor to the rehab portion of the facility where she saw several women in scrubs at a nursing station. "How many people are in the rehab section of the facility?" she asked as they walked along beige hallways, on tan carpets, and beige paint on the walls.

"Twenty-eight beds," he replied. "Because this is a young and vibrant community, both winter and summer, the rehab section caters to athletes with recreational injuries mainly from bike and skiing wrecks."

Turning a corner, they entered a room with several tables and chairs, all occupied by people who had passed through decades of living and now had slowed down and looked stagnant. Skeeter whispered, "How many live here?"

"Right now, we have eight."

Skeeter's heart rate increased when she saw the expectant looks on the faces of the seniors in the room as if she held the key to youth and could pass it along. She moved inside the room. It was airy with windows to the north which overlooked a walled-in garden with Primroses blooming in shades of purple and yellow. It was pleasant enough, she decided, even if it was filled with over 600 years of living.

Pastor Stan put his guitar down. "Good afternoon, everyone—"

A man, whose face looked more like a used baseball glove, interrupted, "Did you see Mary?"

Pastor Stan shook his head. "Not today, Joe," he replied.

Skeeter gazed at the pastor to see if he looked concerned Mary was not here. He did not change his expression.

The pastor lightly pressed on Skeeter's arm and guided her to a frail-looking woman who sat on the chair to their left. She looked as though she weighed under a hundred pounds and wore blue slacks and a matching top with an ivory-colored sweater buttoned most of the way, even though it was warm in the room. "Cordy?"

The woman didn't change her expression.

Pastor Stan bent closer and said, "Do you have your hearing aids turned up?"

Cordy reached inside her blouse, and from her bra pulled out hearing aids. She held them to the pastor.

"Put them on," he yelled at her.

She nodded.

"Okay, then." He moved toward the next chair where a silver-haired woman reclined and had a big smile on her face. "Hi, Hanni. This is Skeeter. She is going to join us for social time."

Hanni said, "There are things you can do with that when you know the little men are not in the attic, but sometimes it's best to do the other thing. My son is coming. The little men will know if it's a nice day." She nodded. "Besides the shoes are lined up in my closet."

Pastor Stan nodded, whispering to Skeeter, "Sometimes she has a good day, sometimes not. As her mind slips away, she has one wish, and it's to stand in a field of tulips. I haven't figured out how she can do it in Colorado."

Skeeter didn't know how to reply, wasn't sure if the pastor was clear with his thinking, and further wondered if this job was a good fit for her. "Nice to meet you, Hanni."

Pastor Stan moved on to a man with a walker. A guitar case sat beside him. "Hi, Cecil! Ready to sing?" He nodded toward Skeeter. "This is Skeeter, and she's joining us for singing."

To Skeeter, Cecil looked tall, perhaps over six feet with balding head and age spots on his forehead. He had clear aqua eyes and for a second, she saw a flash of recognition? Intellect? Curiosity? "Hello, Cecil," she said and smiled at him.

He beamed, working his jaw as if words were jumbled inside his mouth which he had to arrange before he could speak. He turned to Pastor Stan. "You got us a pretty one."

Pastor Stan agreed with Cecil, and hoped in time, Skeeter would find out what a brilliant mind was buried in the senior's head. He'd been one of the first people to learn how to program computers in the 1960s. Then a car accident landed him in a coma for months. His brain paths had a million places of memory interruption. However, music was buried deep in his brain and Cecil could strum his guitar with the best.

Pastor Stan moved on to a woman who had a service dog lying by her feet. The Pastor ran his hand over the dog's body. "Jayne, we have Skeeter with us today and she will be joining us for social time."

Jayne's head tilted toward the ceiling as she extended a hand nowhere close to Skeeter. "I hope she can sing better than the others," she said.

Next to her sat a woman with styled brown hair and who wore gold earrings and a dangling necklace which accentuated a fitted green dress. A fringed scarf of green tones wrapped around her shoulders. "Good afternoon Layla May," Stan said. He turned to Skeeter. "Layla is our resident who reminds us daily of manners and grooming. She was raised in the south but migrated to the Midwest and then to Colorado."

Layla May pulled her lips together. "Ah, Stan, you always have a nice-looking woman on your arm."

Stan smiled at Layla and made the rest of the introductions, finishing when he turned to a man with a more updated walker than Cecil's. Pastor Stan tapped the walker to get the man's attention. "Richard, this is Skeeter."

He put down a newspaper. She shook hands with a man with a crop of white hair and clear blue eyes. "Aren't you a ray of sunshine for a bunch of old people who have lost the glimmer of light!"

Pastor Stan laughed. "He's always poetic and knowledgeable." Stan pointed toward Skeeter. "She's the new IT person."

Richard smiled. "The last time I turned on my computer to get on the internet, my dear wife said, 'That's the microwave.' She's gone now and I haven't tried again."

Skeeter hid a little gasp. She had no idea what it would be like to live in a world where everything had changed and where a person needed another person to do the simplest things.

Pastor Stan sighed. "Richard was a travel agent for group travel, specializing in athletic events. He can recall going to sixteen Olympic Games. If you want a story, ask Richard."

Richard wore a baseball cap that had US Eisenhower monogrammed on the front. Beside his chair was a walker with a dark jacket hanging on the frame. "Pastor Stan and I are trying to figure out how to convince Hanni's son to return to Colorado. He and his siblings are estranged." Richard sighed. "It preys on Hanni's mind."

Stan glanced around the room, "I'm happy to see Hanni, but I noticed her mind is cluttered today. She's worried and wants her children to reconcile, besides wanting to see the tulips fields. I don't know how it will work out."

Skeeter had been in the Piney Center for only an hour, but she felt her energy drained by people who were stuck in the reality of ebbing health and family dysfunction. She wondered if she could do this job. Glancing at the pastor, who chatted with Cecil and who now had his guitar case opened, she wondered if the pastor would quiz her on her spirituality. She hoped not because at best, it was thin.

Looking over Pastor Stan's shoulder, she saw Cordy fumbling with tiny wires of what had to be her hearing aids. Skeeter knew nothing about hearing aids, but she did recognize the look of confusion on the woman's face.

Quietly moving to the side of Cordy's chair, she knelt and asked, "Do you want help?"

"They make these things so tiny you need a microscope to see them," she said as she tried to fit the hearing aid in her ear.

Skeeter took the device from Cordy and slipped it in her right ear. She did the same with the second one. Suddenly, Cordy's eyes turned bright as if a light had turned on inside her head. "Thank you, dear."

Pastor Stan looked over his shoulder. "Have her tell you about all the years she helped pilot a hot-air balloon."

Cordy laughed. "I always told my kids that most of my life I flew higher than a kite. They thought I was talking about drugs."

As he took his guitar from its case, Stan had to hide a laugh. "Let's start with 'Country Roads'. There's nothing better than singing about 'almost heaven'." Stan and Cecil stroked their guitars as they tuned them. Then Stan handed out folders to the various adults. "Here are your songbooks," he said.

Skeeter noticed Cordy and Joe opened the folders and flipped through pages. The others didn't open their books. Finding a chair, she sat and listened. For a minute, she thought about her situation, how three weeks ago she worked in a high rise in San Francisco and chatted with Millennials who wore hundreds of dollars in clothing, who drove fancy cars, and bought expensive wine and discussed their stock portfolios. How life had changed in a few short weeks.

She checked her watch. *Gad.* Grandma's date was due to arrive at the door in fifteen minutes. "Pastor Stan? Excuse me but I have a family obligation at home in a few minutes. I need to go."

Stan held his guitar against his chest and nodded. "Skeeter, it was a pleasure to meet you, and I look forward to working together"

She slipped the strap of her purse over her shoulder. "Me, too."

Stan added, "Wednesday we will be discussing the end-of-life wishes. It's part of our living history project."

"Oh, okay. I guess I'll have to think about it."

"Dying is all part of living," he added.

She smiled at him. "I'm still working on the living part."

CHAPTER 2

Skeeter hurried from the Center. The mid-afternoon sunshine hit her with a wave of warmth. Overhead, puffy thunderhead clouds dotted a blue sky that seemed fake. In San Francisco, the sky stayed a constant gray, a smear of chalk tones interspersed with tan colors from smog, and wisps of cotton-string clouds.

Her car roared to life when she tried the key, which gave her confidence that the rest of the day would go as planned. She steered out of the parking lot and headed east, up a two-lane road rising over swales. On either side, the high desert ground grew sparse sage, rabbitbrush, pinion trees, and juniper. To her right, where the valley remained broad and where Brush Creek tumbled to meet the Eagle River, cottonwood trees mixed with evergreen trees. Overhead a red-tailed hawk cruised on a current of wind.

Her grandmother, Beth — short for Elizabeth — lived in a two-story house set back from the road and snuggled up to the river. This had been Roger's house. It still belonged to Roger who had unceremoniously dropped dead from a heart attack. Beth had found him on the bathroom floor in his underwear.

Although considered short at five feet tall, Beth was the kind of woman that you met on the street and knew to move out of her way. She was a survivor and always recognized what she wanted. Her hands were tied with blue veins, crisscrossing over her able fingers, hands always able to take on another task. She had brownish-gray hair that shined in the sunlight. Although she had aged gracefully, wrinkles around her mouth were giveaways that at one time Beth had been a smoker.

Skeeter thought about her grandfather, a man who had died too early when Skeeter was only six years old. Devastated but resolute, Grandma Beth decided she would survive and find another man, and she did find another. He died, too. Grandma moved on to a third husband. This one had a mid-life meltdown and ran off with a yoga teacher. Beth got a divorce. On a celebratory cruise with friends after her divorce, she met Roger. It was a version of 'love at first sight'. He moved Beth from her hometown of Dublin, California to the Brush Creek house, which he had built with his second wife. Somewhere in all of his early marriages were step-siblings, but it was confusing, so Skeeter didn't try to keep it straight and Beth didn't either. Roger liked fly-fishing, golf, and nice cars. Beth was happy with hikes with the over fifty-year-old group of ladies, tending her garden, and she kept Roger eating healthy meals and made sure he went to various doctor appointments. The two of them played in bridge tournaments. With several husbands under her belt, Beth told Skeeter that she kept her finances to herself and Roger did the same. With Roger dropping dead, financial matters turned to the forefront, and Beth had asked Skeeter to come to Colorado to help her sort through the miasma of problems associated with the sudden death of a spouse.

Out of nowhere, two children from Roger's first marriage had contacted Beth. Although they were due to inherit most of their father's estate, they wanted to know who would inherit the house.

Beth didn't know and couldn't tell them. The children decided the house should go to them and hinted to Beth they would sue to get it. Anyhow, that was the gist of what Beth had related to Skeeter when she arrived.

All of this would be difficult enough, but she also learned that Grandma Beth had early memory loss. She had trouble recalling words that should be in her normal vocabulary, forgot plans which had been made, and began smoking cigarettes once again. Worst was Grandma's idea that life wasn't full if she didn't have a man in it, and she failed to remember she had outlived three husbands and divorced another. It was surprising to Skeeter that Beth found men of interest in such a small town. This guy she was going out with today, Bruce — actually Beth said it only was for coffee and not a date — lived on the outskirts of town, was semi-retired, and liked to attend the local wildlife exhibits.

Beth had told Skeeter, "He likes to meet people."

Skeeter had a feeling this guy saw dollar signs on the house along Brush Creek. Being a bedroom community of a popular ski area, real estate properties were a valuable asset. In a small town, it was no secret Roger had owned the house and now Beth owned it — or perhaps would own it if the kids from the first marriage didn't press a lawsuit.

Pulling in the driveway, Skeeter saw the faded red truck which belonged to Bruce. Cutting the engine, she slid out of her car. On her way inside, she peeked into the truck's cab. She spotted a gun rack mounted on the rear window, a pair of gloves on the seat, a steel thermos, and several newspapers.

The inside of the vehicle didn't tell her much. She headed to the kitchen entrance to the two-story house. The home had a master bedroom and office on the main floor with two bedrooms upstairs and a basement with a rock fireplace, pool table, extra bedroom with bath, and a small patio that overlooked the sloping grass to the creek.

Several cottonwood trees lined the creek bank and offered nice shade plus a roosting spot for red-tailed hawks.

She found Beth in the kitchen, standing next to a solidly built man. He had a goatee of white hair which suited him, a buzz haircut, and she noted he had two crooked fingers, probably from an old sports injury. He wore a blue polo shirt, tan pants, and dirty white sneakers. Skeeter introduced herself, and he offered a firm handshake with a hand that felt calloused as if he worked with cement or wood.

"I'm Bruce," he said.

Skeeter smiled at her grandmother, who was dressed in a plaid shirt and print pants and the combo screamed 'too much going on'. Once Beth prided herself on dressing immaculately, but now she had trouble figuring out what looked good with what. As Skeeter kissed Beth on the cheek, she got a whiff of stale cigarettes. "Looks like you are set for a nice afternoon."

Bruce said, "We're driving up to Sylvan Lake. There's going to be a talk at the Ranger Station."

Skeeter decided it didn't sound like much of a date. *He doesn't stand a chance with my grandma.* "Have fun." She placed her purse on the counter, spotted a pack of crushed cigarettes and a giant barbecue lighter, and sighed. "Bye, Grandma."

As they left the house, Skeeter stared at the huge lighter. Beth had assured Skeeter that she would quit smoking, so Skeeter had disposed of all lighters and matches in the house. With a frown, Skeeter figured Beth had forgotten about her promise to quit smoking and had found the barbecue lighter. *Another problem.*

***

The following afternoon, Pastor Stan went to the rehab portion of the Center to visit with a member of his church who was in the facility after surgery for a broken femur. He spent an hour there and next stopped to visit a member of the church who suffered from cancer that continued the relentless destruction of his body. The two prayed together and finally, Stan left. He hurried through the front doors, waving to Charmaine who guarded the reception desk.

Heading down the hall, a hum from the circulating air was all he heard. He found the bedroom door he needed, paused, and knocked. He waited. Knocked again. Finally, he heard a male voice, "Come on in."

Opening the door, Stan smiled at the gentleman seated in a rocking chair near the window. Richard sat tall in the chair, his shoulders square. His face was timeworn and wrinkled. Crow's feet lined the corners of his eyes, a testament to the hours of reading. Even with white hair, he appeared robust for eighty-some years old, even though body parts were failing him. "Hi, Richard. How was your day?"

"Come in and settle. I'll give you a five-second report about my day, which did not have a speck of interest. That's my report. I've rocked a thousand miles and daydreamed of beaches with sand the color of peach skin and with the soft music of waves coming ashore." He placed a book, *Three Days in January: Dwight Eisenhower's Final Mission,* on his lap.

Closing the door behind him, Stan found a chair. He looked at the perfectly made bed and to a stack of shirts all neatly folded on a shelf next to the closet. Richard had served in the Navy on an aircraft carrier and read extensively about politics and world affairs. "How's the book on Eisenhower?"

Richard ran a thumb over the side of the book. "Filled with information and useless facts. Eisenhower was one of only nine Americans to reach the five-star rank as General of the Army, the second-highest possible Army rank. Not many people are aware nor care."

Stan agreed and added, "I bet you were also thinking about Ellie."

Richard's blue eyes sparkled at the mention of his wife, deceased now six months. When she had passed away from cancer, Richard was no longer able to care for himself and thus had sold his townhouse and moved into the Center. His knees were bone-on-bone but his heart would not stand the anesthesia required for knee replacement. His hips weren't so hot, either. He told Stan, "Ellie was in my thoughts. I was thinking about the last disagreement we had. We were on a beach and the sun was about to slip beneath the horizon. Overhead palm trees rustled with a light breeze. I was hungry and wanted to go to dinner. Ellie wanted to stay. We got into an argument. It was so stupid. Eventually, I forgot about being hungry and looked at her and saw how beautiful she was even then when she had cancer and her head was bald. Most importantly, though, I didn't let my hunger get me into a heated disagreement with the person I loved the most. We stayed and enjoyed the sunset, and you know what? Dinner was especially wonderful."

"I'm glad to hear it. It makes me want to hug my wife a little tighter when I get home this evening."

Richard sighed. "I miss those quiet times with Ellie, and I miss world traveling."

"In the Navy?"

He shook his head. "After the years in the Navy, I worked years in the travel business." He spoke slowly, pronouncing each word with care.

Stan had heard all of this once, but he let Richard continue.

"With several partners, I opened my own business, specializing in sports travel." He gazed out the window at late spring snow covering trees and shrubs. He lifted his chin an inch or two. "I've been to sixteen Olympics. I've been to the Masters in Augusta too many times to remember, and I recall seeing Jimmy Conners play

John McEnroe at Wimbledon in 1982. What a match. Men in white. Wooden rackets. Strawberries and cream for a snack. Today, the game isn't the same."

Pastor Stan was not a sports enthusiast but recognized the names and knew for Richard, it had been one of the thrills of his lifetime. "Oh, the sights you have seen," he quipped.

"I've told my kids to travel while they're young and able. Don't worry about the money, just make it work. Experience is far more valuable than money will ever be. Both of my kids listened. They traveled the world. Now one of them lives in Atlanta and the other lives in Hawaii. I never see them."

"Good places to visit," Stan commented.

Richard chuckled and raised his hands as if giving up. "Yep, and look at me now. Stuck here. The only speed I feel is the back and forth of my rocker. Only my memories take me places."

"Travel isn't on your calendar?"

"Oh, I could do it. I would go. I could come up with the needed stamina." He pounded his knee. "My knees may hurt but it's a hurt I can live with. I hate my damn walker but it keeps me from falling over." Richard leaned forward and the chair rocked. "I don't want to die until I prove to myself that I can still handle international travel. Those long flights…. ha, it's easy. Those endless airport terminals. Phew. It's sissy stuff. Strange food. Bring it on! I thrived on all of it. I need someone to go with me." He pointed at Stan. "In case I drop dead in some off-beat European city."

The Pastor nodded. "I hear you, Richard. I'm not much of a traveler myself or I'd say 'let's go.'"

Richard pushed back in his rocker. "Remember you said that."

Pastor Stan got up. "I think for now you have to be happy with your dreams, but I will pray for you."

"Thanks."

Stan added, "Just so you know, I am afraid of flying. If we travel together, you will have to do the praying for me."

Richard kicked his feet hard; the rocker nearly went over backward. "You bet," he said.

Pastor Stan left Richard and shut the door behind him. He next knocked at Joe's door. After a second knock, he received no answer. Stan knew at age 97, Joe generally napped in the afternoon. Stan quietly opened the door. He saw Joe stretched on the bed with a throw blanket over his legs. His shoes were on the floor beside the bed, and Stan noticed a hole in the heel of one of his beige socks. Joe's fingers were knotty and formed the shape of a claw. When Stan first met Joe, he smiled with megawatts of sincerity. He had that type of effect on everyone. Today, he lightly snored, his lips parted. On the bed beside him was a photograph of a lovely woman with dark hair and a big grin; Joe's fingertips touched the edge of the frame. In the photograph, the young woman gazed at Joe who stood on her left. *Mary.* The light of Joe's life. She had died many months ago but now his memory faded. Joe believed Mary was alive and looked for her every day. Pastor Stan shut the door, silently leaving Joe to his dreams. Perhaps for Joe, dreaming was a better place to be.

CHAPTER 3

Wednesday, Skeeter arrived at the Piney Center with a thermos of coffee tucked under her arm. Harry Chamberlain greeted her, looking as professional as a supervisor could be dressed in a long-sleeved shirt and khaki pants. He guided her to a small office off the central social room. The walls of the room were painted tan, the rug was beige, and one picture hung on the wall which looked like a swatch of browns surrounding something to do with water. It almost looked as though the place was done in sepia tone. Skeeter tried tilting her head to see if she could make sense of the painting but it didn't help.

Two chairs sat alongside a long desk. A stack of metal file cabinets lined one wall. Harry pointed to a computer screen and keyboard. A binder sat beside the keyboard. He tapped it. "Everything we need you to do is outlined here."

Smiling, she set her thermos on the desk.

Harry added, "I asked Pastor Stan to give you a tour of our facility today before the social hour."

"Okay, thanks."

"We have a kitchen with a chef who prepares all meals. He can fix your lunch. His name is Larry, and he can be more creative than macaroni and cheese."

Skeeter nodded. "Thanks. I'll go meet him a little later."

With a nod, Harry backed out of the office. "Let me know if you have any questions."

Skeeter watched him retreat. Sitting at the desk, she turned on the Dell computer. While it warmed up, she adjusted the new office chair to her desired height and back angle. Taking out her cell phone, she checked her messages. She wanted to make sure Beth was okay and hadn't set the house on fire with the barbecue lighter. No message from Beth. She checked several other messages and deleted them. She looked for a message from the guy she had been dating in San Francisco for a few months but didn't find one. She admitted to being a woman who had difficulty committing to a relationship, especially now that she was 1,000 miles away. After turning off her phone, she poured coffee into her thermos cup, woke up the computer, and flipped open the binder with the list of projects she needed to do.

***

Pastor Stan poked his head in the office sometime after lunch. "How's it going?"

By that time, Skeeter's eyes were tired from staring at the computer screen. She had begun work, building a file about the facility's donor names and information, including past donations. It was slow going. A paper plate sat on the desk, littered with bread remnants and a few threads of honey ham, Swiss cheese, and limp lettuce. Only crumbs remained of the potato chips.

"Oh, hi. Good to see you." She closed the black binder. "It's going about how I expected. Not much has been done to set up the databases. Everything has to be done from scratch."

"How is your grandmother handling the loss of her husband?"

Skeeter stretched her arms over her head. "Becoming a widow is easy for her. She's been through this previously with her first two husbands."

Stan sat his guitar case on the table. "Still, it has to be difficult. Let me know if I can do anything."

Skeeter stood. "Thanks. Later this week, we are meeting with an attorney for the estate. I'm concerned about who owns the house, but even more worried about my grandmother's loss of memory." Taking in a deep breath before letting it out, she went on, "A year ago Grandma seemed only forgetful. Now she can't remember words she should know. I found her car keys in the refrigerator the other day, and she doesn't remember that she promised to quit smoking, and she's already going out with a new man friend. It's almost as if she doesn't remember Roger recently passed away."

Stan frowned. "I'm sorry to hear that. Perhaps the best thing is to suggest a visit to her primary physician."

"Yeah, I chatted with Harry, and he said the same thing. I'll make her an appointment. I've lived in California most of my life and have been out of touch with Beth except for phone calls. My mom was her only child. Unfortunately, my mom lives in New Jersey with a new husband, and my dad retired to Florida and, no one in my family has made the effort to stay connected."

"It happens with families," Stan offered, "but you're here now with your grandmother, and hopefully you will create lasting memories."

"I don't plan on relocating here, only helping Beth get situated now that Roger has died."

She managed a smile. "Harry said you would give me a tour of the facility before the afternoon get-together."

"Yeah, let's do it." He pushed his guitar case out of the way. "Let's head to the rehab wing of the Center. With twenty-eight beds, they are usually filled."

A half-hour later, they had covered the rehab facility, including the area for physical therapy. She met nurse Sherry and housekeeper Carmen and the physical therapy person and the occupational therapist and also ran into a petite woman with a big smile who was the registered dietitian. She made Skeeter think about the doughnut she had eaten for breakfast. By the end of the tour, she found the staff to be polite and professional. The west wing of the Center had two stories of apartments for seniors who needed assisted living care. The last stop was the memory care unit, where several of the seniors resided whose memory loss included a threat of wandering away from the Center.

"I take it you met the chef?" Pastor Stan asked.

Skeeter replied, "Yep, Larry. He's a nice guy. He was making cookies and the smell alone added a few hundred calories to my diet."

They swung by Skeeter's office for Stan's guitar and ended in the social hall. Eight seniors gathered around a long table, which had paper cups, a pitcher of water, and a plate of cookies, probably still warm. A mumble of conversations quieted when she and Stan joined them. Those seated at the table smiled at Stan and looked warily at Skeeter.

"I don't think they remember me," she whispered to Stan.

"It's common with folks with brain injuries or dementia, but don't worry, they'll remember eventually." Pastor Stan greeted everyone and said, "I think you all met Skeeter the other day. She is going to join us on social afternoons. To help her remember you, I'm going to tell her something about each of you." He placed his hand on the shoulder of each of the seniors while making light chatter.

When he reached Cecil, he said, "Cecil and I are members of the Senior Band. We both play guitar, and Cecil will probably brag he is a better singer than I am, but I will refute it by saying Cecil is a better fibber than me."

Skeeter watched as Cecil's smile grew big. He almost blushed.

Stan moved on to Jayne, pausing to pat her seeing-eye dog who sprawled over Jayne's feet. He added Cordy, Joe, Richard, Layla May, Millie, and Hanni. Stan settled in a chair close to Cecil. The two men shared a music stand and began to strum their guitars. Skeeter watched each person to see who followed along and sang or those who closed their eyes and dozed. To her surprise, most of the participants moved their lips.

After a slow rendition of "Puff the Magic Dragon", Stan put his guitar aside. "Today we're going to discuss our personal history." From the supply cabinet where they kept the music stands and songbooks, Stan brought out colored folders and pens. He handed one to each senior and gave Skeeter a pen and notepad. "Inside the folder, you will find a questionnaire. Do your best to fill it out with your name and members of your family. Answer whichever questions you can. We'll take ten minutes to fill out the forms. Skeeter and I will help you. Then I want to hear a verbal answer to the last question, which is: Do you have a final wish before your life ends?"

Skeeter felt a little shiver along her spine. She thought it almost impolite to ask the last question. However, she didn't see any resident who had changed expressions or seemed upset by the question. Now hunched over the table, the seniors began to write their answers. Skeeter saw Joe struggle to hold the pen, and she moved behind him and looked over his shoulder. His writing was more like a scrawl. The skin beneath his right eye twitched. He looked up at her. "At one time I worked a jack-hammer. My whole body shook. Afterward, I could thread a needle. Today I can't even write New York City."

Giving Joe a reassuring smile, she scooted a chair close to him. "Why don't you let me help?"

Joe sighed. "Okay, but when Mary shows up, she can finish for me." Skeeter glanced at Stan who slowly shook his head and then looked away. She took the paper from Joe and filled in his answers as he told them to her. She learned that Joe grew up in New York and his first job was when he was eleven, selling newspapers on the street for seven cents each.

When he came to the question about family, he lifted his chin and thought for a few moments, his blue eyes sparkling as if good memories had suddenly filled his head. "It's simple. I met my wife, Mary, in 1945 when I was in the Army. We didn't get to court long because I had to ship out. I was on a big destroyer in the middle of the ocean when the war ended. Ain't that something?"

Skeeter wrote his words for him and nodded, feeling the sense of pride Joe had as he told his story. "Then what happened?"

"I married Mary and we were together for 63 years, that's what."

"How about the rest of your family?"

Joe thought for a second. "Me? I was in the middle of nine children born into an Italian family in New York City, and I still can make a mean pasta sauce."

Skeeter wrote fast. "How about children?"

"We had a son and a daughter." He frowned. "My daughter died in an automobile accident before she turned forty, but my son lives close enough, and he can keep me in a fresh stock of sauce. 'Course, it isn't quite the same sauce, because I didn't make it. He doesn't put enough meatballs in it."

Skeeter chuckled. She couldn't remember her father ever cooking anything except hot dogs and hamburgers on the grill. "What did you do for a job?"

"I worked in a shipyard. Never changed jobs."

Skeeter nodded. "How about hobbies?"

"Heh, heh, don't get me started. My love is the Yankees. I have five thousand baseball cards, some signed. As a kid growing up in East Harlem, I saw Joe DiMaggio play twenty games of his fifty-six-game hitting streak in 1941. I can give you a replay of each game."

"Boy, that's a lot of baseball games."

"I wouldn't miss one. I had to walk five miles to the stadium and wore out my shoes going there."

"How did you end up in Colorado?"

"Ah, because of my son. He's retired. I'm so old, my son is now retired! Imagine.

He moved here. It was a dream of his, and he brought me with him. That's how I landed in Colorado."

Skeeter paused with writing, feeling a little emotional after hearing Joe's story. "It sounds like a wonderful life, Joe."

Pastor Stan tapped the tabletop with his pen. "Okay, I think you have finished with the questions." Cecil sat to his right. "This is when I'd like you to pay attention to what people say. You'll learn something. Sit back and listen. I want to start with you, Cecil. Tell us about the most important thing in your life other than when you married and had children, and end with what you still need to accomplish."

Cecil blinked. He worked his jaw and he fiddled with his guitar strap, taking a long time to gather his thoughts. "The most important thing in my life was surviving an almost fatal automobile wreck. More than anything I want to play my guitar with a band on stage. That's it."

"Nice, Cecil." With a nod, Stan motioned to Richard. "Your turn."

Richard didn't pause to think about his response. "The most important thing in my life was my final day on my aircraft carrier. It was a huge ship. I didn't want to end my time in the Navy but my family needed me. Then I traveled the world, not by ship but by airplane." He paused to take a deep breath. His jaw quivered ever so slightly. "I cannot envision my life ending until I go on an airplane again. Not a two-seater, either. I want to travel in a big jet. The feeling when the jet takes off is something I don't ever want to forget." He shook his head. "I need to do it again before I die. It hangs over me like an elastic band which keeps me from escaping my body, which is almost useless."

Stan drew his lips together. "That's deep, Richard."

Richard shrugged.

"Cordy? How about you?"

Cordy patted the collar on her blouse. "The most impressive moment of my life was being nine-hundred-feet in the air and wishing I could go higher." She beamed with a smile. "It was breathtaking. The silence. Then the sound of 'whoosh' when we let more fire into the balloon. I flew hundreds of hot-air balloon tours but never realized when I piloted my last ride. It draws me down, thinking about when I last flew in a balloon. I had my mind on what I had to do, and when we gently came back down to earth, I didn't understand it would be my final balloon ride. That's my end-of-life goal — to go in a balloon again."

Stan said, "It's a big order since we live in the mountains but God does move in mysterious ways. Let's pray it will happen."

Pastor Stan looked at Layla May. "Take the stage."

She lifted her chin a notch and said "I attribute my long life to whiskey and expensive clothes. My doctor says I wouldn't be alive without both." She raised her arms. "I'm still upright, and I can lift my elbows and wear a sleeveless dress without the skin on my upper arms flapping. It's great. What do I want before I die? I'd like to be on stage again, just once. I sang with a band. I loved the show. To have a spotlight on me. To have the audience gasp. To smile back at the viewers. I have no family, so it would be my last performance."

Stan inhaled and held it for a moment while everyone digested Layla's emotional statement. "Hanni?"

"Oh, Lordy. So many things of importance happened in my life. Sometimes they blur together and sometimes I can't remember any of them. My most memorable day was when the Allies liberated our town in Holland. It wasn't a moment of joy; it was a lifetime of happiness packed into one hour of one day. I wanted to hold it forever. I can't explain the feeling." She closed her eyes as if remembering. "Before I die, I want to stand in a field of tulips. I can see them now; my memory is so clear. The fields are so pure, the colors so vivid, the aroma of acres of tulips sweet, and pungent." She opened her eyes. "All colors, purple, pink, orange, white. Me in the middle." She sighed. "And I want my three sons to make amends and visit me together before I die."

Stan sighed, pleased Hanni's memory was sharp today, and she could share her memories. He hadn't been prepared for these emotional testaments to final wishes. He looked at Skeeter and saw the stricken look on her face. He couldn't stop the confessions of the final wishes of these seniors.

Millie went next. She rarely spoke and Stan wasn't sure if she would today. Then she began, "I remember the day of the competition. I took my horse over obstacles so big I thought we would both fall and die, but we didn't. I won a blue ribbon. It was the end of my life as a teenager in Germany. My father was in the diplomatic service and that's why we were in Europe. Although we remained in Germany, I was no longer a girl and horses became a frivolous thing. The war killed many things, and for me, it was riding horses. I survived the war but others didn't. If I could sit on a horse again, I could happily die."

Stan didn't know this background about Millie and figured there was more to her story and wondered if he would hear it. He hoped so.

"Jayne? How about you?"

She stroked Scout on the head. "I slowly lost my sight. I had time to prepare but for me, the most important day of my life was when I first read a book in braille. It completely erased all the worries I had about my new existence with blindness. Due to being blind, I never saw the ocean. I regret that. Before I die, I'd like to feel an ocean breeze on my cheek and waves on my feet."

Stan took a sip from his water glass. "I hope we can help you, Jayne." He looked toward Skeeter and the man beside her. "Joe? How about you? I forgot to ask about the best day of your life?"

Joe's shoulders rolled forward as he gave the question some thought. Skeeter placed her hand on his shoulder to give him confidence.

He sat up straight and said, "The best day of my life, before marrying Mary, was July 2, 1941, at Yankee Stadium when I saw Joe DiMaggio crush a home run over Red Sox pitcher Dick Newsome. He brought in two runs. I will never forget seeing the ball soar out of sight and the noise of eight thousand fans hollering." He smiled at Skeeter. "I'm an old man, and I'm ready to meet the Lord, but the last time I saw Mary, I forgot to tell her I loved her. I need to do it before I go." He smiled and touched Skeeter's hand as if to tell her he knew it would happen and everything would be all right.

Skeeter swallowed to ease her throat which had become dry. She had to wipe a tear from the corner of her eye, while inside she asked herself how she had become so emotional while listening to old people in an assisted living facility. What was wrong with her?

A commotion toward the entrance to the building turned heads. Several people came toward the social room. Against the glare of outside sunshine, it was difficult to see who it was. Wearing a knee-high pink dress, a toddler yelled something at her mother while dancing in a circle, while a big black dog with white muzzle hair pulled on his leash and escaped, running toward Cecil. Behind Charlotte and her mother, a man who looked like a younger version of Joe followed.

Cecil smiled. "Ah, yes. My daughter and granddaughter have arrived in a flurry of energy, and the dog always comes with them."

Leaning across the table, Stan gathered all the folders. "I think that wraps up our living history documents for today."

Charlotte climbed up on a chair and lunged across the table to reach the cookie plate. After turning in a circle, Bear lay down with a groan. Joe waved at his son, who padded across the room and sat in a chair next to Cecil.

Cecil studied the man. "Do I know you?" he asked.

Tony Sabattini nodded to Cecil. "Yes, we've met a few times. It is always good to see you, Cecil." Turning, he placed a hand on his father's shoulder. "Hi, Dad. It's good to see you. I brought you sauce."

Joe took the bag with the sauce from his son. "It better have plenty of meatballs."

Straightening the folders, Stan patted the pile and said to Skeeter, "I thought you might want to read through these to give you a better idea of the lives of our older adults."

Cecil frowned. "You make it sound like our lives are over, Stan."

"Nonsense. We're only in a different phase of life. "

Charlotte slipped back off the table and landed in her granddad's lap, smearing cookie frosting on his shirt sleeve, then bending over and licking it until it was gone.

Cecil adjusted Charlotte in his lap. "If it's the case, Pastor Stan, I thought you would ask us 'What is the dumbest thing you have ever done?'"

Skeeter raised an eyebrow.

"It didn't occur to me," Stan answered

Cecil nodded, working his jaw, his gaze locked on the pastor. "It shouldn't because none of us have peaked. There's plenty of room for dumb to happen."

Laughing, Stan handed the files to Skeeter. "Introduce yourself to Cecil's daughter, Julia, and then take these home. Read them. Everyone has a story. Next time we are together, we'll hear yours."

Skeeter glanced around the room at eyes glazed with age and memories. In the midst, Charlotte launched over the table to grab another cookie, as if she had hit some sort of toddler jackpot. Bear snorted, and Scout lifted his head to see who had been so rude, and Cordy began talking about men in the attic, and Richard asked Millie if she had toured the Louvre, and Cecil's daughter talked on her cell phone, and Layla May brought out a fashion magazine, flipping through the pages. Tony and Joe chatted, and Jayne blasted an audio e-mail from her cell phone.

Skeeter held the folders to her chest and watched and listened.

CHAPTER 4

Skeeter checked her watch. It was close to dinnertime. When she arrived home, she found Bruce's car in the driveway with Beth's car gone and wondered what it meant. Inside, she did not find a note from her grandmother, but she did remember her mentioning she wanted to show Bruce a local recreation trail she liked, and she guessed since the day had warmed nicely, it was where they headed.

Anxious, and feeling the slump from being indoors all day, Skeeter checked in the garage, saw Roger's bicycle, and figured that by lowering the seat, she could ride it. She changed into bike shorts and a short-sleeve top. After adjusting Roger's helmet to fit her, she clipped it under her chin and rolled the bike down the driveway. Ten minutes later, she cruised through the neighborhood, which included similar-looking homes to the one Roger owned with variations in landscaping to change up the designs. A golf course ran through the development. Farther to the south, she found a recreation path, turned onto it, and pedaled another three miles through pastures with thigh-high grass, big cottonwood trees, and an irrigation ditch alongside the path in places and in two places the path crossed Brush Creek. Off in the distance, sage-covered hills were dotted with pinion trees, and to her right soaring mountains reared to the sky. By the time she turned around, she felt lighthearted and much impressed with the raw beauty of the land. She could understand why Roger chose to retire in the town of Piney.

Once home, she gulped the remaining water in her bottle, and then went inside and chose a bottle of wine from the refrigerator. She checked her watch. She had been gone for an hour. Beth wasn't home. With a glass of chardonnay on the table and her laptop opened, Skeeter glanced at the back door, so she could close the computer quickly if her grandmother came into the kitchen from the side door. Roger's attorney had a scheduled appointment with Beth to take place in a few days, and Skeeter guessed her grandmother would not be prepared. Skeeter planned to go with her. Because she wanted to know something about Roger Sutton, she Googled him. Eighty possibilities came up. She filtered the list by adding Colorado. She ended up with three hits and narrowed her search to Roger Sutton who was 82. She opened her favorite people's search account, put in the password, waited for the screen to fill, and then added his name and location in Piney, Colorado.

People on the grid have nowhere to hide. Information services were always working. This website gave a brief biography of Roger Sutton but had not been updated to disclose he was now deceased. Twelve years ago, he had retired from the construction business. His business had been in Kansas and the information correctly listed him as living in Colorado. The website listed his present wife as Elizabeth Hurly Sutton, and he had two children, a daughter, Melissa Sutton Hamilton, living in Utah, and a son, George Sutton, living in Pennsylvania, both children were from the first marriage. Several grandchildren were listed. His net worth was stated at over half a million dollars. Skeeter knew the net worth information was basic, basic, basic. He was worth over half a million dollars, but he could be worth ten million. Still, he was not in debt and his credit rating was good.

Sitting back, Skeeter stared at the screen. Then she copied and pasted the information to a new Word Document. Next, she Googled Melissa in Utah and George in Pennsylvania. After copying their information to the Word Document, she sipped her wine. It had a little woody taste to it, which she liked. She glanced at the wine bottle label. Chardonnay from California.

Her thoughts turned to Steve. Although her choice in men had veered toward the more laid-back style of guys who wore Birkenstocks and techie jeans, Steve wore more traditional clothes for a city guy. They had dated a few months, but he didn't know how she liked coffee or was aware if she would rather do something active rather than visiting a museum, or if she preferred a thriller movie or drama. However, she wasn't sure she wanted him to learn those things. He should be everything a girl wanted in a guy, but she couldn't connect in a way that let her be who she wanted to be. He also was a fellow hacker, so she guessed he knew most everything about her even though she hadn't been the one to tell him. When she thought about him, it left her feeling as if she were walking on a balance beam with a load of pineapples on her head — nothing was right.

Back on the keyboard, she opened a real estate page and got an estimate on both Melissa and George's property. Nothing outlandish, she learned. George's two-story home had lost value in the past few years. A quick search of Roger's house on the top real estate website gave an estimated value of over $1,700,000, which was in the high-end range of homes in the area. Doing a little hacking, Skeeter found out who the mortgage lender was on Roger's house, and he carried a mortgage of only $100,000.

A brief search on the internet about a deceased spouse and Skeeter learned that in Colorado a spouse would inherit property not covered in a will. She figured this was the case with Beth and thanked her grandmother for making the union legal by marriage. However, she guessed George and Melissa would be disgruntled and may challenge the law. She made notes on her Word Document for when she and Beth visited Roger's attorney. Pausing, she sipped Chardonnay, gazing at the yellow liquid in the glass and wondering why Roger had not specified who would inherit his house. It appeared like an obvious mistake. For Beth, selling the house would mean Beth could afford to live almost anywhere, and in the future, it would pay for her to live in an assisted living situation similar to the Piney Center. The thought was reassuring but a niggling prick of doubt crept into her brain. She figured Roger's children would fight for the house.

Leaning forward, she typed the address for a fresh website. She added Melissa's name and Utah. She eliminated those which didn't fit, either too old or too young, and found Melissa Sutton Hamilton in Logan, Utah. She was 48 and related to Roger Sutton and had two children, ages 22 and 24. With a net worth of under $90,000, she was listed as married. Next, she entered George Sutton and Pennsylvania. There were two George Suttons in the state but one was eighteen. She pulled up the other George, who was 58. He was in the construction business in Johnstown. He had no children and was listed as related to Roger and divorced. His net worth was under $100,000.

Skeeter copied all the information to her Word Document, sent the doc to Roger's office printer, and hit print. She heard the machine wake up in the next room. Taking a sip of wine, she went to Roger's office and grabbed the document. This room doubled as a den and Roger's office. On the coffee table, Skeeter saw a pack of cigarettes and the damn barbecue lighter. With a frown, she returned to the laptop and closed the open web pages. She sat down and strummed her fingers on the kitchen countertop, thinking about Beth and Roger, and then Roger's children. She visualized Melissa and George with their father in Colorado, married to a woman they didn't know. Neither had much financial security. Skeeter had no idea what Roger had in his estate to leave his kids, but she guessed it was not a lot. *No wonder they want the house.*

She checked her cell phone. She had a text from a fellow hacker in San Francisco. He wanted to know how long Skeeter would be in Colorado. *Unknown,* she replied. She checked her e-mails and found one from Steve. She met him at an art gallery opening, which was hosted by a fellow hacker. Presently, Steve worked in finance. Occasionally, he took on hacking jobs to help support his dad, who had pancreatic cancer and no health insurance and was not expected to live. In his e-mail, Steve said he wanted to take his dad home for a visit to Canada but his dad was in too much pain to make the trip. Skeeter gave a generic reply and sat back, thinking about the seniors at the Center and their unfinished life projects.

With an empty wine glass, Skeeter went to the refrigerator for a refill. She grabbed the wine bottle and in so doing knocked a jar of pickles askew. She spotted a jar of something behind the pickles. Taking it, she read the label. It was a mid-tone face cover-up. She knew it was Beth's. It didn't belong in the refrigerator. With a sigh, Skeeter took the jar to the master bathroom and left it on the counter. She wondered what else Beth had misplaced?

She glanced in the mirror. Her eyes looked especially green in the fluorescent light and the blond streaks in her hair looked brighter. She found a hairband, pulled her blond-streaked hair back, and secured it in a ponytail, smiling at herself, thinking she almost looked like a teenager.

Hearing voices, she went to the kitchen. Beth put her purse and grocery bag on the counter and Bruce added her car keys. "We took

Beth's car today," he said. "We stopped at the grocery store on the way back." He sheepishly glanced at Beth. "It took us a while to find the car."

Her grandmother appeared unruffled, most likely unaware she had trouble finding her car. "It happens," Skeeter said in a calm voice.

Bruce touched Beth's arm. "Thanks for the nice afternoon. I'll be in touch."

"Bye," Beth said. After she washed her hands, she turned to Skeeter. "We'll have tacos for dinner." She took a box of taco shells from the bag, along with ground beef and other fixings.

Skeeter eyed the open pantry where she saw three boxes of taco shells. "We had tacos last night," she reminded her grandmother.

Beth waved her to be quiet. "Oh, no, we didn't. We had steak. Roger always wanted steak on Thursday night."

Skeeter didn't have the heart to tell her she was wrong, and she wondered if the stress from Roger suddenly dying had made the progression of her grandmother's mental loss go faster than it should. *I'll have to Google that. Or perhaps Harry can give me insight.*

As Beth put the groceries away, Skeeter heard another voice from the side entry. Then Pastor Stan followed Beth from the pantry to the kitchen. He gazed at Skeeter and said, "Hi. Sorry to bother you. I hope I am not intruding."

Skeeter smiled. "Not at all. Come in, grab a seat."

Beth pushed a hair off of her cheek. "I'm going to go freshen up before I start the tacos."

Skeeter pulled out one of the chairs at the kitchen island. "Is this okay?"

Stan slipped into the chair. "Thanks. Harry told me your address. I decided to stop on my way home. Hope you don't mind."

"Truly, you are the best thing to happen to me today."

He chuckled. "I'll tell my wife to see if she feels the same way."

Skeeter offered him some wine. He declined but was happy to have a glass of ice water.

"So, what brings you my way?" She studied his face to see if this visit was serious or might be on the lighter side. She decided on serious.

"I was at the Piney Center this afternoon. A member of my congregation is in rehab. He has cancer and is in the final days of his life."

This was out of Skeeter's realm; she wasn't sure how to respond but went with her gut. Steve had talked about his father's cancer, but she had barely paid attention since she couldn't relate. "I'm sorry."

Stan fiddled with a drop of water that had landed on the countertop. "David is a fine gentleman. I've known him for years, but I didn't know his oldest son, Peter, cut off all ties with his dad some years ago. As David slipped into his final days, I sensed that he was crossing to the other side and then coming back. He suffered. He was near tears. He had the type of pain I couldn't help relinquish. And why? Because he hadn't found a way to reconcile with his son."

A stagnant silence filled the kitchen. "I don't know what to say," Skeeter told Stan and sipped her wine to gather her thoughts.

"I am sorry to say I didn't know what to say to him in those moments. I did my best to bring him closer to God, but I felt as though I was lacking."

Skeeter couldn't look at Stan, feeling lost with this discussion.

Stan sighed. "I said what I thought was helpful. He closed his eyes to sleep, and I left him because I needed to go and be with someone who I could help. I knocked on Richard's door. Richard asked me into his room, and I found Richard in his comfortable chair with a thick book in his hands. We chatted. Being with

Richard lifted my spirits. We talked about a lot of his trips to foreign countries, and he recalled numerous insignificant facts which left me wanting to hear more. Then I heard a scraping in the hall, and Cecil came into the room, pushing his walker in front of him with those tennis balls not working to mute the scraping sounds. His idea of hurrying is to bend his head down as he saunters. We were happy to see Cecil, more than happy to have him stop pushing the walker, and told him to have a seat.

"Cecil sat on the bed and kicked at his walker. He sighed as if tired and then told us he wished he had more time to play his guitar. Then he asked Richard 'What are you reading. I hope it's something other than politics.'"

Skeeter laughed.

"I told Cecil we were talking about what is important to us."

Skeeter raised an eyebrow as if curious.

"Cecil worked his jaw, his eyes bright as a thought took form. He has a way that makes me look at him, anxious to hear what he has to say. It takes a while and I can't rush him. He told us it doesn't matter what you are passionate about. Maybe Dixie Cup covers. If you do it passionately, you are alive."

Skeeter said, "That is deep."

"I laughed and immediately thought about David. It was as if a light bulb went on inside my brain. I knew what I could say to David to make a difference. I got up and told Richard and Cecil I had to go. Richard nodded, so did Cecil. As I left the room, I heard Cecil ask Richard, 'What boring non-fiction book are you reading?'

"I hurried to David's room. I knew what I needed to tell him, but I also knew something was wrong when I saw the bright lights in his room, because when I left him, the blinds had been drawn, and it was dark. I saw his wife standing beside his bed with her shoulders slumped. I could hear her crying."

"David died?" Skeeter asked. "I'm so sorry. What did you say to his wife?"

"I told her God is watching over him now, and I also told her David was parched by the heat of life, including estrangement from his son, but also drenched by the rain of life, which included all the good years with his son."

Skeeter looked out the patio door to the rays of sunshine and the ruffle of leaves from a breeze. "I hope those words helped her. They are touching."

Stan didn't look at her. "Yes, but I missed the opportunity to make a difference in his last hours. I think he was tormented. I think he spent his last days on earth with the Angel of Death hovering over him, willing to take him since he was unrepentant and unwilling to reconcile with his son." Turning, he held Skeeter's gaze. "I don't want it to happen to our seniors who are still with us."

She tilted her head. "Are you asking me a question?"

He shook his head. "No, not a question. A statement. It's something I need to do and I think you'll see that you have to help me."

Skeeter heard her grandmother turn the television on in the family room with the volume turned up almost as high as it would go. *Help you with what?* she almost yelled Instead, she chose words carefully, "Grandma, turn down the television!"

The volume became lower but not by much.

Stan adjusted his voice, "The seniors in the assisted living part of the Center: Cecil, Richard, Hanni, Cordy, and the others. Each has something standing in the way of them making a smooth transition."

Skeeter swallowed to ease a dry throat. "Transition?"

"Death, Skeeter."

"Oh, man." She gulped the last of her wine. "Are you sure you wouldn't like a glass of wine?"

He slid off his chair. "Positive. I am high on life most of the time, except for today when I couldn't help David." He pointed at her. "You are a special person, Skeeter. I see it in you. You can help me with this. We, meaning you and me, are going to make sure each seniors' end-of-life goals are accomplished."

"Why me?"

"Because God brought you to me and the seniors. That's why."

Looking over her shoulder, Skeeter saw her grandmother take a cigarette from the pack on the TV table. She flicked the barbecue lighter and a giant flame burst in front of her face.

With his back to Beth, Pastor Stan patted Skeeter on her shoulder. "We can do it." With that, he returned the chair to its original position and turned toward the back door.

Skeeter smelled hair burning. "Grandma!" she yelled.

CHAPTER 5

Shortly after sunrise broke over the mountains to the east, Pastor Stan strolled into the Piney Center, said hello to the receptionist, picked up a folder she kept for him, and asked about any new arrivals. Satisfied he wasn't needed in rehab to console somebody; he made his way to the assisted living wing. Richard's door was closed. So was Cecil's. He found Hanni's door open. Poking his head into her room, he saw her seated in her chair, holding a picture in her hands. Dressed in a pale green shirt, a white sweater, and dark pants, a plaid lap blanket covered her knees. Oxygen tubing was askew on her face. Steam from coffee in a cup on her bedside table snaked to the ceiling.

Looking up, she smiled. "Hello, Pastor. Is it Sunday?"

He shook his head. "No, but it is a nice morning and I would like to share my coffee with you."

"Come in," she said, pointing to the end of her bed. The extra chair in her room was covered with a nightgown and robe. "Have a chair. Although it's a bed."

He made himself comfortable on the edge of her bed. "You look rested this morning, Hanni."

She adjusted the oxygen tube in her nose, grumbling to set it correctly. "It's about all I do," she replied. "Rest is overrated."

"How are you feeling?"

She leaned forward as if allowing him in on a secret. "I'm dying, Pastor Stan. One breath and then another, closer to death, and it's taking a darn long time. I'm not sure I have the patience."

Shifting uncomfortably, the pastor ran his free hand over the soft comforter covering her bed. "The journey of our life is not always clearly written." It was the best comment he could make. He pointed to the picture that she held. "What is your picture?"

Hanni turned the photograph toward Stan. "It's my son, Finn." A middle-aged man, perhaps fifty, stood against a rainbow field of tulips. She touched the photo, running her finger across his cheek. "It was the last time I visited him." With a nod, she tapped the photo. "I've lived for a long time. I'm ready to go say goodbye to this life. God has chatted with me about it, and I am fine with all of his plans, but something stands in the way."

He frowned. "What's that?"

Again, she touched the face in the photo. "Finn is in the way."

"I don't understand."

"I need Finn to end his estrangement with his brothers."

"Doesn't he live in Holland?"

She looked puzzled for a second, then nodded. "Yes, at home. My home. The fields of tulips."

"I still don't understand."

Hanni sat back and sighed, closing her eyes as if it would help her regain memories of what she wanted to say. "Money," she quietly stated. "My kids won't talk to one another over money."

"It's a shame, Hanni."

43

"I keep sayin' that but my son doesn't listen. He's as stubborn as my husband, God rest his soul. I married my husband after I came to America. He was from Texas or was it Nebraska? Somewhere hot in the summers. We vacationed in Colorado. I remember that. Francis—"

"He was your husband?"

"Yes, and Francis had a middle name but I can't remember it. He bought forty acres along the Eagle River, down the road a bit from the ski area. In those days it was hell and gone from the town, but Francis insisted. It was the stubbornness in him. He bought the property and built a cabin. We had our boys—"

"Three sons as I recall?"

"Yes, Finn and the other two." She frowned.

Stan wasn't going to press but guessed she could not recall their names. "Go on."

"Finn lives in Holland near the tulip fields. The brothers stayed in America, closer to me, somewhere other than Piney but close enough for one of them to visit. I don't remember where they are now." She waved her hands as if pushing fresh air would help her remember. "After Francis died, I lived in the house we built here until it was too much for me. My two younger sons sold the property. Today expensive condos have sprung up where we grew hay." She stopped and took a sip of her coffee, her skinny fingers next adjusting her oxygen tube. "Hot," she commented and remained silent. Stan wondered if her memory had shut down.

"And so, what remains the problem?"

"The boys didn't tell Finn about selling the ranch. They should have, but they didn't. He had been away for so many years and didn't make any decisions about the ranch, didn't do any work on it, either. The boys felt he didn't deserve anything from the sale of the land." Inhaling, she slowly exhaled, and her whole body gave the impression of being deflated. "Finn has been angry ever since. He won't talk to his brothers and won't come to visit me."

"Does he blame you?"

"No, but he won't talk to his brothers. I can't die until this is fixed."

Sipping coffee, he tasted some bitterness despite the sugar he had added. "How do you think this could be resolved?"

"I would happily die tomorrow if Finn would end his anger with his brothers. I also need to see those tulips fields one more time before I die."

Stan didn't have a snappy reply. "I'll pray about it, Hanni. Prayer is powerful." He reached for her hand. "Will you join me in prayer."

She stretched bony fingers toward Stan. He took them and her skin felt like cellophane. Enclosing her hands with his, he bowed his head and began a prayer for Hanni and her children.

***

When Skeeter swung into her office, she was surprised to find Pastor Stan. "Hi, she said. "It's early." She put files on her desk, sat down, and turned on her computer. A low hum filled the silence. "I hope you weren't here to visit someone who is dying. It's too nice outside to die today."

He grinned at her. "Wouldn't it be wonderful if we could choose when we die?"

She thought for a moment. "I can see all sorts of problems. Most likely there would be a sign-up sheet for the correct day and time. As a hacker, I would be asked to change it, and changes could get emotional and messy."

"Yeah—"

"Perhaps a caveat for choosing a date would be you couldn't die until you have won some victory for mankind?"

"Is your brain always so busy this early in the morning?"

"Yeah, I guess." She sat down and sipped her coffee.

Stan held up his coffee cup, which was empty. "Cheers! I had an errand here and stopped to visit with Hanni." He didn't continue.

Skeeter bent forward. "I detect a somber attitude."

"Meeting with Hanni was a bit of a downer."

Skeeter checked the morning's messages from Harry. "Before you tell me about it, I see Harry e-mailed me about Hanni's birthday next week." Pulling a file from the bookends on her desk, she opened it and pawed through papers. "Hanni Winslow. She will be 93 on her birthday and is in the middle to late-stage of Alzheimer's disease, and also has a bad heart." Skeeter turned to Stan. "What can you add to it?"

"It's what we talked about the other night at your house. Right before your grandmother burned her hair with the flame thrower."

"Yeah, I remember. I put the lighter in the trash but found it on the kitchen counter the next day." Skeeter sighed. "She's losing cognitive reasoning."

"Some of the time, Hanni has clarity. This morning, she was clear, and it was a pleasure to hear her thoughts, but it's troubling me. Because she's fighting death, it rattles my insides, and although she doesn't have a problem with meeting God, she has a problem with her oldest son. She is ready to make the journey, Skeeter, but her son, Finn, is holding her back. So is her longing for a final view of the tulip fields."

A month or so ago, Skeeter would have made a snippy reply or something humorous, but she could picture Hanni with the twinkle in her clear blue eyes and her slumped shoulders, and the vision left her heart heavy. She looked at Stan and saw a glimmer of hope. "What are you suggesting?"

"God frequently asks us to be a part of the answer to our prayers. If we're not willing to be a part of the solution, we shouldn't ask Him to help us. God asks us to give Hanni and the others what they need so they are ready to be with Him." He straightened. "Prayer is not saying a prayer and then waiting for God to act. Prayer is a process, and it often involves planning and working to see the answer come to pass. I haven't given up on prayer but I'm suggesting that we can take matters into our hands. For the first time in years, I feel that doing something proactive is a better way to serve God than only through prayer."

"I don't know," Skeeter said. Skeeter looked at the message on her computer about Hanni's birthday and rereading the words gave her mind time to settle her thoughts. She turned to Stan. "I wish I were as committed to prayer as you are, Pastor. I do pray but my prayers are rarely answered."

"God does answer prayers. You are an answer to one of my prayers."

"Me?"

"I have been praying for someone to help me meet the needs of these seniors. Your youth, energy and skills, are needed." Stan paused, "And, you may not know it, but God is also answering your prayers.

"What do you mean?

"You commented that traditional work has been unfulfilling. You want your life to count for something. God heard your prayer for purpose, and he sent you here to help your grandmother and these seniors. It will give you a sense of satisfaction that mere success will not." Stan paused again. "Did you need prayer to help you through a difficult childhood?"

Skeeter laughed. "No. I had a normal childhood and I prayed for the normal things. I lived in a one-story house with a nice garden and a swing set in the backyard. I had a mom and dad, no siblings, and we went to church. We had a white cat, named Sprinkles, which was a silly name for a white cat. I did all the normal kid stuff."

"I kind of thought you might say that."

"I was exceptionally smart. Normal girl kid stuff didn't interest me. Normal was not connected to me. Prayers asking for me to be normal weren't answered. Math was my friend. I skipped a few grades in math. I would hole up in my room and do the math Olympics. Girls my age were experimenting with makeup and discussing clothes. I started coding before I had a driver's license—"

"Coding?"

"Writing code. Developing software."

"Gad. I was lucky to understand algebra."

"For me, high school was a blur of accelerated math classes, Math Olympics, and after-school computer groups." She looked away. "Always curious, I experimented with ways to connect to the outside world anonymously. From online chat rooms, I leaned about phishing, cracking, and spoofing. I met coders and hackers who showed me how to find digital versions of textbooks and manuals. I practiced around the clock. By the time I was eighteen, I could support myself from stealing information, generating forged documents, and scamming anyone. About then, I gave up praying."

Stan wasn't sure he heard her correctly. "Hacking, cracking, spoofing? You mentioned hacking earlier. I'm not sure I know what it means."

"The computer club I belonged to introduced me to hacking. Hacking means gaining information from other computer systems. We learned how to do it in computer lab. I continued with it while I went to college in Los Angeles. My parents separated up about this time, which truly didn't affect me other than I had two different places to visit my folks. My dad is now in Los Angeles with a new girlfriend, who I like, and my mom is in New Jersey with a career that makes her happy and a new husband. After college, I wandered to Seattle, didn't like the weather but learned more about hacking, so I landed in San Francisco with all the dot com companies. For the past three years, I have been an Information System Analyst, which kind of means I am a paid hacker." She shrugged. "What I have been hired to do here is child's play. I was doing this when I was fifteen."

Stan squinted. "Did you do anything illegal?"

She managed to shrug and offhandedly said, "At one time, but not anymore, and I never stole anything with real money. I used Bitcoin. What I do now is not considered illegal, but it could be frowned upon. I have continued to do simple stuff."

"What's considered simple?"

"Do you need a new loan? I can change your credit rating. Or do you need traffic tickets to go away? Are you suspicious about your wife's e-mails? I can get you records—"

Stan held up a hand. "Good grief. Stop there."

She didn't meet his gaze. "Everything I hacked made people happy. Was it wrong?"

Shaking his head, he answered, "I wish my prayers did the same." He studied her. She had an intelligent presence about her and had the fresh looks of someone born thirty years after he was born. "Beauty and brains."

"Not all guys like brainy women," she commented.

"No boyfriend wanting your constant help?"

She laughed. "I've had boyfriends but no one who makes my heart sing."

"That's too bad."

She nodded. "I agree." She flipped through the papers in the folder she held. Each was intake information on the seniors in the assisted living portion of the Piney Center. Those seniors living here would not go home. For a few moments she thought about the morality of it; Piney Center made money by keeping people alive in their advanced years. Was it wrong to help the end-of-life wishes so older adults could die sooner? Or happier? She wished she had the religious beliefs Stan did to unravel these thoughts, but she also knew she had to follow his lead with this.

She had listened to the seniors' last wishes and had their folders on her desk and knew about Hanni's desire to see the tulip fields and for her children to be reconciled. However, she did not understand until now that it could prevent Hanni from dying. Sitting at a computer to plan, organize, and integrate cross-functional information projects was hardly stimulating and not creative. It was boring stuff and why Skeeter had veered into hacker territory when needed; it was more fun. Something in Stan's face, a little glint of mischief made her smile, and a prick of interest grew in her head. "How do you think we can help Hanni?"

His eyes brightened. "Hanni and the others," he corrected. "First, Hanni. I think we need a plan. I'm guessing I need to find Hanni's son. Go see him in person. A phone call won't cut it."

Skeeter arched an eyebrow. "And do what?"

"Not kidnap him. I'm betting he wants peace of mind and although angry and bitter, he wants to see his mother. Because I have attended seminars on forgiveness, I think I can help both of them. If I can find Finn, I'm pretty sure I can convince him to forgive his siblings."

"He's not next door; he's in Holland."

Stan rubbed the back of his neck. "I know, and it's a problem since I hate flying."

She bent sideways to catch Stan's attention. "I can't go. I have to look after my grandma, who by the way, appears to be slipping deeper and deeper into memory loss."

"I realize you can't go. I'm thinking of traveling with Richard."

"Richard? Our Richard?"

Stan nodded. "He's the logical one. He's a retired travel agent. He's been to Holland on various occasions, and if you recall, his final wish is to travel one more time. This trip would serve a purpose for Hanni and Richard."

Skeeter pushed herself back in her chair. "It's a lot to think about but it's worth considering. There will be expenses —"

"Yes, and more money than I have, and I don't think we can ask Hanni or Richard's family to fund this."

Skeeter picked up the folder with the papers filled out by the seniors. She flipped through the papers. "Cecil wants to play in a band. Cordy wants another ride in a hot-air balloon. Millie wants to ride a horse. Joe needs to talk to his wife who is dead. Jayne wants to see the ocean, and she's blind."

Stan nodded to each of the statements.

She locked stares with him. "You think we can do this?"

"I think we can."

She pointed a finger at him. "If you ask me to pray for these things to happen, I don't think it will happen, only because of my track record with prayer, but if you suggest we plan and execute events so these things occur, then I'll help to get it done."

"Let's pray and plan."

She thought for a moment and said, "Okay, I will pray we can make these things happen."

Stan slapped his palm on his thigh. "I love this life! I feel answers to prayer coming!"

Skeeter smiled, happy to see Stan smile, and watched his eyes brighten. Stan crushed his paper coffee cup and tossed it in the trash can. "Tomorrow is our day to sing. We've missed it the past few weeks. It's important. Research has shown singing provides an emotional and behavioral benefit for people with dementia, especially those with Alzheimer's."

"I didn't know that."

Stan nodded. "Key brain areas linked to musical memory are buried deep in the brain and are usually left untouched by the plaque that clogs the arteries. Better yet, music tends to unlock memories for older adults. Music is better than all the medicine you could give those with fading memories."

Skeeter thought about her grandmother. When the music played in the house, Beth tended to be in a lighter mood. "Wow. I didn't know it could make such a difference."

Stan rose, sighing, contented they had accomplished a lot. "Okay, I'll see you tomorrow."

Skeeter smiled in return while making a note to herself to research music and dementia.

After Stan left Skeeter's office a little lighter in his step, he slowed. *Wait a minute!* He put a hand on his hip. *What did I agree to do?* Skeeter told him that she veered off the edge of legal into some gray area he didn't even understand. He was a pastor and had a congregation that expected exceptional behavior from him. Could he amble into a shady area, did he want to, and should he? He shook his head as conflicted emotions left him off balance. Perhaps he was thinking too hard. What he wanted to do was to ease the transition to be with God for those who were struggling. He thought harder as he unlocked his car door, looked around at the pinon-studded hills with mountain peaks in the background. *Certainly, this is God's country. I am here for a reason.* Yes, he told himself, making a difference was the path to follow. However, when he slid into his car, a frown creased his brow, and he stared out the windshield as a niggling doubt crept into his soul. *Does the end justify the means?*

CHAPTER 6

That night Skeeter convinced Beth to bake chicken breasts in herb sauce and added steamed rice and a salad. It was a nice change from tacos. She had wanted to put the chicken breasts on the grill but couldn't find the barbecue lighter, and her grandmother claimed she had no idea where it was. As they ate, Skeeter glanced at Beth and noticed the wedge of hair near her right cheek was noticeably shorter. Beth had cut off the singed hair, and Skeeter hoped she wasn't hiding the lighter. Changing her thoughts, she asked, "Are you set to visit with Roger's attorney?"

Beth frowned. "I don't remember Roger having an attorney. Did Roger meet with him every week?"

Skeeter closed her eyes for a moment, warding off a tension headache. "No, Grandma. This was planned after Roger passed away. You're supposed to meet with Roger's attorney to go over his will."

Beth paused with a chunk of chicken on her fork. "I don't think it's necessary. Everything is fine."

"Everything is not fine, Grandma. Roger is dead, his ashes are still at the mortuary, and you haven't had a service for him."

"He didn't have many friends."

That you remember, Skeeter wanted to add. "Nonetheless, you should hold a memorial service for him. He had golf buddies and he volunteered for various organizations. His family may want to attend to say goodbye to their dad. Besides, the attorney needs to let you know what to do about the house."

"What about the house?"

Skeeter chose her words carefully. "This is Roger's house. Who owns it now?"

Beth frowned as if this was a fresh idea. "I have no idea. Roger should have told me about this."

"He didn't know he was going to die."

"It's still annoying."

Little drums banged inside her skull. Skeeter grabbed a notepad and a pen. "I'm going to write questions for you to ask the attorney about money for a memorial service, about the house, addresses for family, and any other important financial bequeaths in his will."

"Do I have to come with you?"

"Grandma! This is information about how your life will go on. Please, try to understand this."

Beth swirled a sliced plum tomato on her plate. "I'll go if you want."

Skeeter shut her eyes for a moment and sighed. "One other thing—"

"We need to shop for dinner tomorrow night. Tacos, I think."

"Grandma, get your mind off tacos. I want you to make an appointment to see your primary physician. I don't know how long it has been since you have seen him or her."

Beth sat back, a faraway look on her face. "I'm not sure I go to the doctor. I'm never sick. Roger was sick a few times."

"Where would you have information about your doctor?"

She glanced toward the TV room and Roger's desk. "Probably in there someplace."

"Could you look for the information after dinner?"

"Of course." She popped another tomato in her mouth. "These things are fantastic, whatever you call them."

***

Pastor Stan arrived early at the Center the following day, carrying his guitar and some new music sheets. He wanted to update the music books. He thought about his commitment to those living at the Center and how music had a positive effect on them. The songs they sang were a combination of folk songs, hymns, and a few vintage Western songs. Cecil joined him on guitar, and at times Stan had to challenge Cecil's ability on the instrument since he played with only one tempo. However, Cecil was a living testament to the power of music and how it resonated with him after a horrific brain injury. He was in charge of the songbooks, and that job gave him a sense of accomplishment. Stan enjoyed the good-natured banter between the two of them.

Today, Stan turned pages in the songbook to decide which song to sing. He laughed as he stopped at "The Cat Came Back." The song was about a yellow cat who wouldn't die. The owner tried unsuccessfully to end the animal's life but to no avail. Dynamiting and drowning attempts failed. He thought those at the Piney Center could relate to this cat because each of them had lived long lives which seemingly couldn't end. Even now Stan could hear Cecil pause in the way that made him look like he was chewing his words. Then he sang, "But the cat came back the very next day, the cat came back, they thought it was a goner' but the cat came back."

Other songs were favorites: "I'd Like to Teach the World to Sing", "County Roads", "This Land is Your Land", "Puff the

Magic Dragon". Stan skipped in his songbook to "Clementine". The song was written in 1884 but remained a favorite. Jayne could manage a crying lilt in her voice with this song. It was close to a melancholy twang.

When they finished the song, Layla May once said, "After Clementine falls into the foaming brine, he kisses the little sister. So much for true love."

Millie had added, "Typical man."

Chuckling, Stan turned to his laptop computer and found a search engine. He wanted to check the validity of the benefits of music for folks with dementia. He read about the power of music, especially singing, to unlock memories and kick start the gray matter, an increasingly key feature of dementia care. Music reached parts of the brain other methods of communication could not. The auditory system of the brain was the first to fully function at 16 weeks, which meant that humans were musically receptive long before anything else. So, it's a case of first in, last out when it comes to a dementia-type breakdown of memory.

Stan turned from his laptop reassured that music was a positive impact on the people in the memory care unit. When moods changed, smiles appeared, and memories become sharp. He had witnessed a non-verbal octogenarian move her lips when singing in the afternoons and was determined to continue with the music and also hoped to find a way to make Cecil's wish to play for an audience come true.

Stan heard the squeaking sound which accompanied Cecil's walker. Cecil rounded the corner, grinning when he saw Stan. Cecil had his guitar case balanced over his walker, plus a sort of saddlebag on his walker that carried his songbook, extra Kleenex, a water bottle, his notebook, and too much other stuff. Stan patted a metal chair next to him. A music stand stood between the two chairs. "How's it going?"

Cecil pushed his walker to the chair, turned in a circle, and then backed up to the chair until the back of his legs touched metal. "I'm alive," he drawled and lowered into the seat. He sighed. "I need to engineer a better design for a walker."

Stan glanced at Cecil's walker, which had dissected tennis balls on the front legs to keep the metal from scraping the floor. A previous owner had put various stickers on the rails, one advertising Nude Skiing, and another a gospel concert. When Stan offered to scrape off the Nude Skiing sticker, Cecil told Stan it was the name of a band and not to bother.

It wasn't worth arguing with Cecil. In his younger days, Cecil had instructed military personnel on the use of computers back in the early 1970s. From there, Cecil worked for Martin Marietta. His IQ was off the charts. Then the automobile accident left Cecil in a coma for several months with a severe brain injury. Cecil's brain still worked, if slowly, and his wit remained, but sometimes his memory failed him. Music, however, never failed. To Pastor Stan, Cecil was a work in progress. Once a believer in God and a higher power, his college years at Berkeley, divorce, car wreck, and brain injury had left him angry with God and an avowed atheist. For some reason, Stan and Cecil were friends, and Stan had not lost hope he could nudge Cecil back along the path to being a believer.

Cecil rubbed a hand over his whiskered cheek, then opened his guitar case. "I hope we rock the house this afternoon."

"No doubt we will. Are Julia and Charlotte coming?"

"Don't ask me difficult questions," Cecil said after thinking about the question.

"Okay, then." Stan adjusted his songbook on the stand. Looking up, he waved to Layla May who came in with a little flourish of style, swishing a long scarf around her neck. "Afternoon, Layla May. You're looking ravishing, as usual."

"It's my mission," she sweetly replied.

Stan and Cecil both nodded. Layla May was followed by Cordy, Hanni, Millie, and Jayne with her guide dog, Scout. Joe held onto a rail along the wall and with his shoulders hunched, almost crawled to join them. Richard, with his squeak-free walker, brought up the rear. Stan noticed Millie pulled an oxygen tank on wheels, which had the supply tube hooked over her ears. The oxygen tank was one more thing to get in the way of a pack of older adults who didn't see, hear much, or have good balance. Looking up, Stan said a prayer. They found seats without making small talk. He watched Hanni walk with a pronounced slump to her shoulders and moved only a few inches with each step. He thought it was a bad sign.

Skeeter rounded the corner from her office and waved to everyone. "Hello," she began, unsure how Pastor Stan and his Senior Band operated.

She unfolded another metal chair and sat next to Layla May, who looked over at Skeeter after lifting her chin a few inches to give her an air of superiority.

Stan handed out songbooks. When he got to Hanni, he touched her shoulder and quietly said, "We're going to sing some of your favorite songs."

"There are bad people in the attic who leave little specks of dirt everywhere." She looked over his shoulder to the end of the room. "I think it's dangerous for them to do this type of thing when we all should be doing more of that sort."

Stan glanced at Skeeter with a shake of his head. Her nonsense chatter was an indication that Alzheimer's had a stronghold on her today.

A squeal toward the entrance of the building jolted Stan's attention. He looked up to see Charlotte, dressed in a pink tutu with white rubber boots, doing her best to run toward the social room. Julia, holding a kiddie cup with a straw, followed with her aged dog, Bear, lumbering along beside her. Charlotte stopped with great fanfare in the middle of the group of seniors. Squinting, she eyed each senior as if they were creatures from a different universe.

Cecil said, "Hello." When Charlotte didn't answer, he ignored her and began to tune his guitar.

Bear collapsed on the floor with a groan, placing his gray muzzle on his front paws. Julia unfolded a chair and sat behind Cordy, then pulled out her laptop and flipped it open. "Hi, everyone. Hi, Dad," she said. "Don't mind me."

Richard kicked his walker out of the way. It skidded several feet and clanked against Jayne's chair. Scout quickly got to his feet, her service-dog body tense. Jayne turned toward Richard, even though she didn't see him kick the walker. Her ears were better than her eyes at times.

Charlotte spun in a circle to show off her tutu. She ignored her grandfather and went to a collection of children's books which were kept in a basket next to a big television, while she chewed on a cookie and dropped crumbs.

Joe stood. With worry lines across his brow, he looked toward the Center's entrance. "I don't see Mary."

Skeeter stepped to Joe's side, looked at him, and attempted to divert his attention. "I never realized how blue your eyes are," she said.

Joe smiled, his thoughts of Mary fading. "All the girls tell me that."

Taking his hand, Skeeter guided him to his seat. "You are always a gentleman."

Joe sat down, Skeeter returned to her chair, and for the moment, although the room was energized with invisible beams of age and mental confusion, the scene remained calm. She hoped it would last.

Pastor Stan looked at each senior. "All right you singers in the senior band, who wants to suggest a song to start?"

No one offered a suggestion.

Stan patted his guitar. "Okay, let's sing 'The Cat Came Back'. Remember, this is supposed to be a song about a cat who wouldn't die. We're going to play it with a slow tempo, and you guys do your best to make it spooky. Maybe by Halloween, we'll be proficient with this song."

Stan and Cecil began to strum their guitars and sing. Layla May sang along, so did Jayne but Stan didn't see much effort from any of the others. Still, they listened.

Skeeter mumbled words from the songbook. With each verse, more of the audience began to sing. The voices grew with gusto, and then the music suddenly stopped. An eerie, breathless silence followed until Cecil's eyes grew wide, and he sang, "But, the cat came back the very next day, the cat came back, they thought he was a goner, but the cat came back!"

After the cat had been blown into the air, drowned, and lost in the woods, but continued to come back, Cecil would stop to look at everyone, a satisfied gleam in his eyes.

The room grew quiet. Bear snorted. Skeeter decided the scene was one from another reality in her life, but she also noticed Jayne and Cordy and Millie looked perkier. Joe's eyes were closed with his chin on his chest. Layla May removed a bottle of nail polish from her dress pocket and went to work on her left hand. Hanni, however, had a glazed look on her face as if she had been deposited on a foreign planet and the surrounding people were aliens. Skeeter sighed, wondering what it had to be like for Hanni to not realize where she was or who she was or who these people were. It saddened her to think one day her grandmother would feel like this.

Stan suggested "Take Me Home Country Roads" and it was a success. So were "I'll Fly Away" and "Sound of Silence" which didn't go as smoothly as the others, so Stan had them try it two more times before the singers were in sync with the guitar players. "It needs work," Stan said.

Richard said, "Enough of that song. Let's go to 'Home on the Range'. He looked at Stan with a hopeful expression. "It's my favorite song."

Stan turned his music book to the song. He strummed his guitar and then drummed his fingers against the wooden body. "Okay, you singers, this is our song. As you know, 'Home on the Range' is a classic western folk song sometimes called the 'unofficial anthem' of the American West. Dr. Higley of Smith County, Kansas, wrote the lyrics in the poem 'My Western Home' in 1872."

Richard added, "In 1947, it became the Kansas state song."

Stan looked at each person. "Does everyone have it in your songbook?"

Layla May blew on her wet fingernails before flipping songbook pages. Jayne found the page which was in braille. Millie sneezed, her oxygen tube fell off her face, and she fumbled with her fingers to try to find it. She finally got it and attached it with a lopsided result. She and Cordy found the song, and Hanni stared at an artificial arrangement of flowers on the table.

Stan said, "Hanni? Are you with us?"

"They come when you don't want them to besides all the other things that are dangerous."

Again, a nonsense response. Stan pulled a guitar string with a 'twang'. "Okay, then. Let's sing a few verses and the chorus and then let's pause. Ready Cecil?"

"Hit it," Cecil replied.

The rich sounds from the guitars resounded through the building. Jayne sang her heart out, and even Layla May put down her nail polish to sing along, sitting with a straight back and waving her hands, which drew attention to her. Joe opened his eyes and

Cordy and Millie followed in the songbook. Hanni still looked dazed.

"Okay," Stan said as he stopped strumming before the chorus. Today, Stan could tell, the seniors were engaged and ready for more instructions rather than wishing he would quit interrupting and let them sing. He continued, "Today I want you to hold the word 'home' as long as you can. Cecil and I will pause with the guitars." Stan raised his hand. "Homeee," he sang emphasizing the word and holding his hand in the air. "Again, this is hard for you because we all get out of breath, but I want you to take a deep breath and hold the word." He stretched his hand to the ceiling, brought it down, and did it again. "If it helps, hold your hands in the air. Homeeeeeee."

Only Layla May and Cordy did not hold their hands in the air.

Stan said, "Again." He held his hand in the air. The others followed.

Suddenly, Hanni jumped to her feet, extended her right arm to a perfect 45-degree angle, and yelled, "Heil Hitler!"

She sat down.

As if a wet blanket had been thrown over everyone, the seniors sat in stunned silence. Looks turned to Hanni. Her face had turned pallid, her lips pulled tight, her gaze straight ahead. Bear lifted his head and sniffed and snorted. Closing his eyes, his head hit the floor. Skeeter looked at Stan. Stan looked at Cecil. Richard's jaw grew slack. Jayne didn't move. Cordy's lips parted. Joe woke up. Millie gasped and her oxygen tube again fell. Julia stared at Hanni. Charlotte moved to the middle of the group and spun in the circle, fluffing her tutu. Scout, Jayne's guide dog, got up and moved closer to Jayne, collapsing on her feet with a groan.

The silence grew thick, as if a black cloud crept up the valley from the west, covering everything in its wake. Skeeter felt it and knew this was not a good way to end the afternoon of singing. Coughing, she stared at Stan, giving him a little nod of her head. Hanni had regressed to Germany when she was a girl, perhaps fifteen or seventeen. Both of them turned to Hanni to see if she looked alarmed, panicked, out of breath, what?

Hanni met their gazes and said, "Can we sing 'Puff the Magic Dragon?'"

Everyone exhaled a cleansing breath. Tension escaped the room. Skeeter did not have enough experience with dementia to know what had happened, but she realized Hanni's mind wasn't clear when the singing started, and had regressed to earlier times in her life, and now had morphed again to the gentle, amiable silver-haired woman who loved tulips and wanted to sing about a dragon.

Cecil still had a slack jaw when Stan poked him. "Cecil. 'Puff.' Right now."

With a jerk, Cecil blinked. He turned the pages in his music book to find 'Puff, the Magic Dragon.' He didn't look at Hanni but said, "On the key of G."

Stan and Cecil began to strum in unison. Charlotte danced. Layla May went to work on the nails on her right hand. Joe dipped his head and shut his eyes. Bear snorted. Millie tried to find her oxygen line and get it back in place. Cordy, Richard, and Jayne sang about a lonely boy and a dragon. Hanni's lips moved.

For a few moments, everything in the world seemed right.

CHAPTER 7

After the last song was sung, heavy air hung in the room, as if the day already had used too many good hours. Hanni and Millie both looked drained of energy, and it was about all they could do to rise and shuffle down the hall toward their rooms. Richard followed, pushing his well-oiled walker. After chatting with his daughter, Cecil visited with Charlotte for a few minutes, loaded his guitar on top of his walker, and then followed Richard, his walker wheels squeaking. Layla May, Jayne, and Cordy chatted as they followed Richard out of the room, their voices fading. Pastor Stan finished packing his songbook, making sure the pages in his book were in order.

As Skeeter folded the remaining chairs, she stopped next to Joe, who had dozed through the singing and had not made any effort to leave. "Joe, you look rested. Most of the others have gone to their rooms for quiet time before dinner. How about you?"

Despite the late hour in the afternoon, he still looked neat in a long sleeve shirt and a brown sports jacket. He patted the chair she was ready to fold. "Sit for a minute."

Skeeter slid onto the chair next to him. "Did you need to discuss something?"

He put his gnarly hand over hers. "Nothing of too much importance. I wanted to tell you how pretty you are. You remind me of my Mary. When she was younger, she had blond streaks in her hair. Now her hair has turned a silvery gray, but she is still beautiful." He removed his hand from hers.

Cool air covered her hand where Joe's hand had been. "I've seen her picture in your room," she admitted.

With a sigh, he turned his head toward the windows.

She followed his gaze. "I wish I had met Mary."

Joe's eyes brightened. "I'll have you meet her when I see her again." He frowned. "I didn't tell her how much I love her our last night together. It was my mistake. I tell Mary I love her every single night. Except for that last night. I don't understand why she hasn't come home today. I need to tell her."

Skeeter glanced at Stan who joined the conversation. "Why don't you tell me about when you met Mary?" He held Joe's gaze and nodded as if giving Joe the reassurance he needed to tell his story.

Inhaling, Joe's chest expanded. Then he let the air out of his lungs and began, "I was born a long time ago, a long time ago, in nineteen-twenty-three." He leaned forward. "Do you know why the year is important?"

Both Stan and Skeeter shook their heads.

Joe lifted his chin, puffing his chest. "It was the same year Yankee Stadium opened its doors as the home for the New York Yankees....in the Bronx."

Stan leaned closer to Joe. "That makes you ninety-seven years young?"

Joe lifted the corners of his lips. "Yep, although I always claim I am a hundred and two. I like to see the reaction. I was born in

New York. My father was an Italian immigrant. We lived in the Bronx. I followed baseball. I was one of nine children, but none of my brothers loved baseball as I did." He rubbed his thigh. "I wouldn't miss a baseball game even though my dad couldn't give me money for a ticket. So, I sold newspapers on the street to buy a game ticket and for bus fare to the ballpark."

Pastor Stan interjected, "Your mom taught you how to cook? I understand you make a good pasta sauce."

"I make a great pasta sauce, but my mother didn't teach me. She was too busy to teach any of us to cook. Besides, most of the time we ate fish. Fish with noodles, fish with fried rice, fish with brown bread, fish with fish, fish with some green stuff. It wasn't expensive. I had to teach myself to make sauce, many, many years of putting the right things together."

They were getting off track. Skeeter said, "How did you meet Mary?"

"A few years separated me being a kid in the city and the war. When the fighting started, I enlisted. I was a member of the U.S. Army Tank Corps." He sighed. "We suffered tremendous human losses during the war, but I made it. Next thing I knew, it was the summer of nineteen-forty-five, and I boarded a transport ship. The USS *Greeley* was five-hundred-twenty-two feet long and could do seventeen knots. She also rattled enough to make it hard to sleep. I used cotton balls in my ears to blot out the clatter. We steamed toward an American military base in China and boom! It was the middle of the night. The war was over. I was asleep. Someone shook me. I had to take the cotton out of my ears. When I heard the news, I screamed 'I made it!'." He gave Skeeter a broad smile. "'Ain't' that something?"

Skeeter sat back to absorb Joe's emotion. For her, the war was so long ago she couldn't fully comprehend surviving and accepting an end. "I'm glad you made it home."

"Me, too," Joe said, rubbing his thigh as if the muscles were sore. "So, I returned to Fort Meade, Maryland, and then went on leave. I went to Washington, D.C. with a buddy. We stopped at a café to get a drink, and I sat down next to this gorgeous woman who smiled at me. My world started at that moment, the beginning of a wonderful life with Mary. She worked as a seamstress while I worked all those years in the Brooklyn Navy Yards. We've been married for over sixty-five years. Every night when we go to sleep, I tell her I love her, except for that one night." He frowned. "She wasn't feeling so good. She closed her eyes before I could kiss her cheek and tell her that I loved her." He shook his head. "It eats at me something terrible." He took a deep breath. "I am old and used up. I am ready to leave this life, but I can't do it until I tell Mary I love her." As he turned to Pastor Stan, his eyes watered. "Can you help me find her?" He also turned to Skeeter. "Please?" His fingers trembled.

Skeeter glanced at Stan for help.

Pastor Stan covered Joe's hands with his. "How about we bow our heads and say a prayer for Mary. It will help her find her way to you, Joe."

Joe sniffed pending tears. "Mary said her prayers each night. She would also tell me, 'Joe, I have made one human being a little happier today.' And I know she meant it because if it wasn't someone else, it was me."

Skeeter had to look away to gather her feelings.

Pastor Stan closed his eyes and quietly began, "Lord, I ask that You guide Mary to Joe. He is a beloved husband and asks for Your guidance in this situation. Joe and Skeeter and I pray that You open the necessary doors for this to happen, Amen."

"Amen," Joe and Skeeter said together.

Pastor Stan took Joe by his elbow and helped him to his feet. "Do you want me to see you to your room?"

Joe shook his head. "Heh, heh. No. I've slept through singing about a dragon and country roads and other things. I can stay awake long enough to go take a nap. Gad. It's all I do these days."

Skeeter touched his arm. "Thanks for telling us your story, Joe."

"Anytime for a pretty lady like you." Turning, Joe's shoulders slumped, and he began to shamble to the hallway.

Skeeter watched him disappear into his room. "That's hard."

Stan said, "It's real love. Nothing is expected in return."

"How do we get Mary to return to him?"

Stan arranged his music in his songbook. "I'm going to give it some thought. Perhaps through more prayer with Him."

She shook her head. "I don't think that'll work. I'm going to think up something real, to give him a chance to tell Mary he loves her."

Stan arched an eyebrow. "A ghost?"

She shrugged. "Something better, but I'm not sure what."

"You can't hack into heaven, Skeeter."

She laughed. "Maybe not. Maybe yes."

Chuckling, he headed toward the exit. Before he took three steps, he turned. "Skeeter?"

"Yep?"

"It's not only Joe who has a final wish. The others do, too."

She nodded. "Yeah, I know."

"We had better be thinking hard for Hanni and Cordy's sake, and we better be thinking fast."

"Stan, with you, I see your dedication to the older adults. I can feel your belief. How did you find your faith with such an unflinching belief in God and the Bible?"

Stan ran a hand through his thinning hair. "I'm flattered you can feel my relationship with God. I didn't always have such a firm belief. I was tested." He gazed out the doors for several seconds as if gathering his thoughts.

"When I was in my mid-twenties, my family had a singing group. My mother, dad, two brothers, and our sister made up the group. My mother played the keyboard, dad and I played guitars, my brothers played bass and drums, and my sister was learning the keyboard. She was beautiful, musically talented, and a rising star.

"I was the oldest of the four kids. Since childhood, we played music in churches, county and state fairs, school assemblies, nursing homes, and wherever doors opened. We traveled in the summer months and on weekends during school. We played gospel, country, folk, and bluegrass music. One evening we were coming home from a church engagement when a driver ran a red light and broadsided our van. The accident flipped the van, pushed us across four lanes of traffic, and slammed us into a light pole. I heard my mother scream. The band equipment flew inside the van, hitting everyone."

Skeeter inhaled quietly, then slowly exhaled. "I am so sorry. It must have been horrible."

"It was. When I woke in the hospital, my Dad sat on my bed, a cast on his leg and a gash on his forehead. A nurse stood behind him, a grave look on her face. I tried to sit up but I couldn't move. I asked Dad what was wrong with me. He wrapped trembling fingers around my hand. 'You have a broken pelvis', he answered."

"Oh no," Skeeter said.

Stan rubbed his temple. "At the time, I didn't understand. I asked Dad, 'What happened? Where's Mom and the others?'" He paused, having trouble with the story.

Skeeter nodded, urging him to continue.

"He told me that Mom died on the way to the hospital. Dad said, 'I am so sorry.' We wept, holding onto one another as best as we could.

"He also told me that my sister's hand had been crushed, and she would never be able to play the keyboard. My brothers were only bruised."

"That's a blessing," Skeeter offered but it sounded hollow.

Stan nodded. "My mother was gone. I was beside myself with grief and descended into a dark place. Why did God allow the driver to run a red light? Why did my mother die? Why was my sister's musical career ended? I couldn't understand why God would let this happen."

Skeeter took Stan's hand and held it. She let go and said, "Go on."

"When I got out of the hospital, I was in a lot of pain. My anger at God grew. I subsisted on booze and pain pills. I told God I would never do music again. I told him I was finished with him."

Skeeter tried to speak but Stan waved her silent.

"After my physical injuries healed, I became a truck driver. Although I was finished with God, he wouldn't let me go. One day while driving, I yelled out, 'God, I'm finished with you.' I raised my voice even higher, 'Leave me alone and let me go! Get out of my life!'"

"I don't blame you," Skeeter said.

Stan lifted the corners of his lips. "God wasn't finished with me. That night a lady from the church called. She said, 'Stan, I had a dream about you. I saw a horse rearing, its hoofs flashing. Its eyes rolled, its nostrils flared, and it pulled against the bridle reins. The rider pulled the horse to a stop. You were that horse, Stan, trying to run from God, but you couldn't escape.'" I then realized that God was not going to let me go."

Skeeter added, "It's a good thing he didn't."

Stan nodded. "I was amazed that God would answer me so specifically."

Her throat went dry. Skeeter swallowed. She managed to ask, "What did you do?"

"I quit running. Instead, I went toward God, and I thanked Him for leading me back to my faith. Though I still don't have all the answers, I now have faith that God sees the big picture and works for the greater good. After that, I started seminary and began playing music again. While in seminary I met my wife, and we answered the call to pastor a church in Colorado"

"So here you are," Skeeter added.

Stan nodded. "Playing music again was a big part of helping me heal from my anger. My dad suffers from dementia. From him, I learned what music does for those whose memory is fading. Music is one of God's gifts of healing for people. It is powerful, Skeeter. Powerful. That is why I come to the Piney Center and play music for the seniors. It brings me happiness, and it is how I say thanks to God for bringing me back to faith."

"I'm looking forward to going on this journey with you, Stan. I wasn't sure why I needed to be with Beth, but now I know that it was the right thing to do, and she, too, is on a journey without a road map, but I hope to navigate it with her."

"And with God's purpose."

"Yes, I think you're right."

CHAPTER 8

When Skeeter arrived home in the evening, huge cumulus clouds had formed to the east, billowy monoliths of clouds, shooting to the sky. The tops were iced with afternoon sunlight and the bottoms were dark. Behind the clouds, the blue sky stretched to the horizon. Far away, she heard a rumble of thunder. When she inhaled, she smelled something sweet, a mix of sage and grass and ozone. She had to stop for a second to absorb it. San Francisco had its smell, a mixture of ocean breezes and eucalyptus trees together with automobile exhaust, oil, exotic foods, and trash, which mixed into a gut-churning mess. Here in Piney, Colorado, the air was crisp, she felt as though she wanted to inhale it and keep it there.

Beth's car was parked in front of the garage, so she knew she was home. A car she didn't recognize was parked on the street in front of the house. It was an Audi but not a recent model. A small dent was visible on the right front fender. When she went in the side door and to the kitchen, she saw Beth outside on the patio with a man Skeeter didn't know. The man looked about eighty, but he was well-groomed. He had a full head of white hair and wore pressed Bermuda shorts and a polo shirt. She guessed he had transplanted to Colorado from the Eastern seaboard.

Skeeter could go the other way and leave them alone but decided to head to the patio to find out who he was. The patio flagstone deck was in the afternoon shade and was a delightful place to sit, take in the trees, the sound of the river, and the overhead clouds. "Hi," she said as she made her way to her grandmother.

The man rose. After extending a manicured hand, he turned on a mechanical smile. "Hello. I don't believe we've met. I'm Phil."

"Skeeter," she replied and decided he had a nice handshake, not too firm and not a marshmallow. She noticed he had unusually white teeth for someone his age.

Beth looked from Skeeter to Phil. "Roger and Phil play a lot of golf together, and his wife and I volunteer at the museum."

The smile turned off. Phil said, "My wife, unfortunately, died a year ago." He shot a glance at Beth. "I wanted to pay my respects to Beth. I know what it's like to lose a spouse." He glanced around him. "A house can be lonely, even a nice house. I know. I found it's not what I have lost, but what I have left that counts. I wanted to share it with Beth."

She wondered if Phil What's-his-last-name was in the hunt for a new wife. She had no idea about the rules of dating for older adults. "It's nice to meet you. Enjoy the patio. I'm going to duck inside and do some work."

The smile turned on again. "Yes, nice meeting you, too."

Skeeter returned to the house and headed for the upstairs guest room for a shower. When she finished drying her hair and had put on clean comfy clothes, she went to the kitchen. She found Beth there alone with the barbecue lighter flaming and a cigarette hanging from her lips.

Beth inhaled and paused, holding the flame in front of her face.

"Gad, Grandma, you said you would quit smoking and now you look like you're trying to start a forest fire."

Beth puffed smoke. "Dear, I have man problems. It requires a cigarette."

"Man problems?"

"There's Bruce and now there's Phil and I think Hugh McGrath is handsome."

"Who is Hugh McGrath?"

"He volunteers for the park service. He's got a cute trailer up at Sylvan Lake. I met him when I was there with Bruce."

Skeeter pulled out a chair from the slate island counter. "Grandma, Roger died a short time ago. Give it a rest." She watched Beth exhale a cloud of smoke. "Could you at least smoke outside?"

"When I'm through with the cigarette." Beth remained standing near Roger's desk.

Skeeter didn't have the energy to continue. "Did you find your medical records?"

"What medical records?'

"Records that show who your doctor is?"

"Silly you. I don't need a doctor. I am perfectly healthy. Roger died, and I'm fine."

Skeeter counted to ten. She practiced a yoga relaxing breath. "Okay. I'm tired. It's been a long day."

Beth pointed the cigarette at her. "You're young. You should have plenty of energy." With a shrug, she added, "No matter, I'll fix tacos for dinner."

***

The next morning, Skeeter knocked on Harry Chamberlain's office door. She could see him seated at his desk behind his computer but didn't want to enter the office without invitation.

"Come in," Harry said when he saw her.

She sat in a chair opposite his desk and crossed her legs. Today his office was not as sterile as it had been when he interviewed her. A coffee cup with "I Can do it" printed on it was to the left of his keyboard. A stack of unopened mail was to the right. Behind him on a shelf were several family photographs. They made small talk for a few minutes, and she went over what she would do for Hanni's birthday celebration. Then she said, "I have a personal problem and I wondered if you could offer insight?"

Harry smiled as if he had caught her with her hands in the cookie jar. She didn't let his reaction bother her. "It's about my grandmother. I have to admit that for many years I didn't have a lot of direct contact with her, only holiday cards and infrequent phone conversations. I met Roger once. I didn't know much about him and there wasn't time to learn more. She seemed happy and settled here and well...I was starting a career. Since I have been living with her, I have noticed a decline in her memory. I'm worried." She shifted in the seat. "I figured you have seen a lot of folks with memory issues."

Harry pushed back in his office chair, fiddling with a pencil between two fingers. "Almost forty percent of people over the age of sixty-five experience some form of memory loss. With no underlying medical condition causing memory loss, it is known as 'age-associated memory impairment'. It's considered a part of the normal aging process. However, about ten percent of people aged sixty-five or older have a mild cognitive impairment, and nearly fifteen percent of them develop Alzheimer's disease. Due to our excellent medical care professionals, people live longer than ever. Thus, we see a lot more people progress to this dreadful disease."

"Beth is now seventy-seven. She's still active but slowing down. She recently lost her husband, and to me, it appears as though she is moving too fast with another male relationship or relationships. I think there are several guys."

He whirled around in his chair, which almost made the comb-over part of his hair elevate and his tie swung like a pendulum. Harry tapped the pencil on the desktop. "It sounds normal as far as reaction to a recent spouse bereavement, normal because everyone is different, and it's hard to know how someone will react. As a single person, navigating her social life can be complicated. She may not know how to be accepted by her peers. I would give her more time to grieve."

"So, I shouldn't worry about her interest in a new guy?"

He leaned across the top of his desk. "Only if you are a private eye and can discretely find out everything about him." He chuckled. "It may put your mind at ease."

Thanks. I will get on it. By the end of the day, I will have his bank balance, mortgage account, and any court records. "What about her physical condition?"

Harry swung his chair to the right. His hair stayed in place. "She should be seen by her primary physician. I suggest you contact him before her appointment and make him or her aware of the recent mental loss. From there, the doctor can administer a brief memory test, which will give him an idea of her mental capabilities."

"If it is Alzheimer's, what's the progression?"

Harry whirled the pencil in his fingers. "Alzheimer's disease typically progresses slowly in three general stages — mild, moderate, and severe. Since Alzheimer's affects people in different ways, the timing and severity of dementia symptoms vary as each person progresses through the stages. From what you have told me, but without proper testing, I would guess that if it is Alzheimer's, this is the early stage and could last many years."

Skeeter rubbed her temple, unsure if she wanted to hear more. "I need to find my grandmother's medical records. She doesn't remember who her doctor is."

Harry opened his desk drawer and pulled out a business card. He handed it to her. "This is the main number for Piney Medical Center. Call them. Introduce yourself and give them your grandmother's name and birth date. They can tell you her physician's name and her most recent visit."

For the first time, she felt comfortable with Harry as if she might like him as a person. She took the card from him. Looking up, she met his gaze. "Thank you, Mr. Chamberlain," she said, uncomfortable calling him Harry.

Remaining seated, he smiled with his lips pressed together. "No act of kindness, no matter how small, is ever wasted. Remember that."

She jerked. Did he mean she owed him something in return? Was he kidding? Was he serious but she didn't know it? Standing, she said, "I'll have everything ready for Hanni's party."

"Okay, then, thank you." She started to rise but paused when Harry held up a hand.

Turning to his computer, he dropped the pencil. "Oh, one other thing. I have an updated report from Cordy's physician. Her cancer is progressing. We may see some erratic behavior from her. I've notified the staff in the memory unit but I wanted you to be aware"

"Okay." She began to rise.

Harry put up his hand. She sat down. Harry said, "Oh, and one other thing. Lori Martin, from our local library, contacted me about Hanni. They have a connection from when Hanni volunteered at the library. Anyhow, Lori wants to provide the cake for the party." He opened his desk drawer and retrieved another business card. He handed it to Skeeter. "Here's her information. She'll probably drop by to meet you."

She took the card and decided it was safe to stand up. "Okay, thanks." She wondered if she should tell him about Hanni's Heil Hitler event but decided to keep quiet.

Drifting away from Harry's office, she smelled chocolate chip cookies and her stomach rumbled. Besides, thinking about Beth started to give her a headache. She headed in the direction of the kitchen. On her way, she checked her watch. It was only nine-thirty. It didn't matter. Chocolate fixed most ills.

She whirled around the corner of her office and headed toward the dining area and kitchen. In the dining area, one person sat at a table. She took one look and stopped. She inhaled with a gasp.

He had the local Piney Times newspaper opened on the table. What stopped her was his unpardonably good looks, and the ruggedness he eluded. He wore a faded blue and black striped shirt with pearl snap buttons. On the table sat a Western-style hat of some sort. She glanced at his legs and noted worn, sort of dirt-covered jeans with a thick leather belt, and scuffed Western boots, and covered with swatches of what looked like dried manure. He had broad shoulders and brown hair, styled on the top of his head with something to keep it in place, but the hair on the nape of his neck was long and curls lapped over the collar.

He looked up from the newspaper. Their gazes locked. She felt a jolt of heat go through her body. She tried to shake it off but couldn't get enough of him. When he smiled, little indentations appeared in his cheeks.

Skeeter blinked. She almost decided this guy had arrived on earth from another century. Cowboy? Gunslinger? Character actor from a Western movie?

"Hey," he said, and she thought the word came out in a drawl.

Even speaking, he was irresponsibly handsome with a square jaw and perfect cheekbones. He looked as though he worked outside since his face was tan. From her location, he had big brown eyes which grew with intensity as he watched her. "I came for cookies," she blurted.

"Cookies work for me," he replied as he lifted one eyebrow.

She pointed to the kitchen. "I think the aroma is coming from there. I'll check."

"Good idea. Coffee is better with cookies."

Her tongue had swollen in her mouth. She sounded like an idiot and each footstep carried a load of cement. Pushing the door to the kitchen, she tried to shake off the increase in her heartbeat. She stopped for a moment.

Larry, the chef, looked up from mixing chopped chicken, onions, and other things she had no interest in naming. "Cookies," was all she said.

"You've met Bart?"

"The guy in the dining room?"

"Yeah, the guy who can wear authentic cowboy boots without looking silly."

She swallowed to ease a dry throat. "What's he doing here?"

"He's Millie's grandson. He's the ranch manager for a big spread over on the Colorado River."

"Oh."

"He tends to have that effect on women from the city."

"Am I that transparent?"

"Yes," Larry said and heaped a pile of chocolate chip cookies on a plate. "Just remember; cowboys are noisy men with bow legs and iron stomachs who work from the back of a half-broke cow horse. They love the outdoors; hate fences and respect rivers and women; throw one of them into a river, and he'll naturally float upstream. The only way to get rid of one is to shoot him and his horse and bury both deep." He pushed the plate toward her.

She picked up the plate. "Do cowboys like cookies?"

"More than a beautiful woman. You're on safe ground with the cookies."

"Gad. Does he have his horse tied up outside?"

Larry shrugged as he mixed chicken salad fixings. "Go ask him."

Rolling her eyes, she pushed the door open with her backside and headed to the table where the cowboy sat.

"Hi," she said, smiling at him. "Cookies. Still warm, I believe. I'm Skeeter."

Standing, he took her hand. He held it for a long time. She had to lift her chin a few inches to meet his gaze. "I'm Bart. It's nice to meet you."

He held a chair for her.

She slid into the chair, thinking about the last time a guy held a chair for her was when she was at a father-daughter dance in second grade.

He nodded and sat. They each reached for a cookie.

Skeeter bit into the cookie, tasted melted chocolate, looked at the handsome cowboy, and wondered if her day could get any better.

CHAPTER 9

Later in the afternoon, Pastor Stan sat in Skeeter's office. He had a file open with the information about the seniors and what they wanted to accomplish before they died. Skeeter had a word document opened on her computer, and she had listed the seniors with each of their wishes. Both held cell phones. Stan used his phone to call one of the major hotels in Vail to speak with the program director for their bar and lounge, who was a member of his church. Stan chatted about church happenings and hotel occupancy, all the inconsequential preamble to a conversation of more importance. He then inquired if the senior band could play a gig in the lounge.

Skeeter held her fingers above the keyboard when she heard him ask the question. She didn't type, hoping to hear the reply. She couldn't.

"Uh, huh, uh, huh," Stan said as he centered his gaze on the ceiling.

Skeeter waved her hands. "What? Come on?"

Pastor Stan pulled Skeeter's desk calendar toward him. "April thirtieth? A Saturday? Eight o'clock? Sounds perfect. Hold on." Lowering the cell phone, he leaned toward Skeeter. He almost whispered, "The lounge should be vacated by six o'clock after a baptism reception starting at two o'clock."

Skeeter gave him a thumb's up. "Great news," she whispered. She twisted the calendar, so she could see it and flipped the page. "It's about a week away."

With a nod, Stan said his goodbyes. Ending the phone call, he closed his eyes. "Thank you, Lord."

Skeeter made a note on her word document. "Will you and Cecil be ready?"

"We'll practice again at Hanni's birthday party. We'll need the seniors to attend to practice singing. Thank goodness it's what they like to do."

"I hope they can remember the words to the songs."

"Me too." He checked his phone. "Okay, better news. A few months ago, I was invited to a pastor's conference on aging, being held in the Netherlands. At first, I didn't read the particulars since I wasn't planning to attend. Now the church elders would like me to attend. When I checked the details, I discovered the event is not too far from where Hanni lived. I thought about her and the possibility of finding her son—"

"Could you take Richard?"

Stan paused as if in mid-thought. "Wow. I didn't consider him going along."

Skeeter pointed to the computer screen and Richard's wish of traveling again. "This was Richard's one end-of-life wish. If he went to Holland with you, it would satisfy his wish."

Stan frowned. "I have to think about that. My expenses will be covered by the church, and believe me, the church can wrangle good deals on flights and hotel rooms."

"Maybe I can help—"

"What?"

She waved him silent. "Just thinking," she said, then added, "do you need permission from his family to take him from the facility?"

Stan shrugged. "No idea."

"I guess I can check with Harry. What are the dates?"

Stan checked the calendar on his phone. "In three weeks."

They had a lot to do in three weeks. Besides making arrangements for an adaptive van to take them to the hotel in Vail and transport them home after the gig, Stan needed to make sure they all had the correct songs in their songbook, and at least for them to sing each song, again and again, to make sure they didn't add their own flowery words. Then the trip to Europe. His body tightened up when he thought about flying. Moving at five hundred miles an hour at 33,000 feet of elevation left him anxious and nauseous. Stan wasn't sure how far his retreat was from where Hanni's son lived, so he had to arrange transportation, figure out a rental car or driver, get hotels, locate Hanni's son, Finn, and find the location of the tulip fields. He added 'photographer' to his list. He related all these jobs to Skeeter, who typed up a list and then sent it to the printer. A hum and clack, clacking sounded as the printer spit out pages.

She handed Stan a copy and kept a copy. "I think I can help with some of these."

He glared at her. "You cannot use any of your own money for these projects."

She stared back at him. "I wasn't suggesting that."

"Oh," he said. "Don't explain."

***

In the afternoon, Skeeter remained in her office to take care of personal business. She phoned the medical offices and was told

Beth's doctor was a man, Jack Dreyfus. An internist, he had last seen Beth twelve months ago. The medical receptionist could not disclose any more details other than Beth was due for a yearly physical. Skeeter made an appointment with Dr. Dreyfus for a physical. It surprised her that she got Beth an appointment in four days. In California, such an appointment would take weeks. After making a few other calls, she shut her laptop down, gathered her purse, and headed home.

"Hi," she called as she entered the side door, "I'm home." She found Beth on the patio in the lounge chair with her eyes closed and her sunglasses hanging off the tip of her nose. A lap blanket covered her lower half. Her jaw hung ajar. A butterfly flitted behind her head. A glass was on the table beside her with melting ice cubes. Next to the glass was her pack of cigarettes and the flame thrower.

Skeeter tiptoed outside and grabbed the cigarettes and lighter while Beth snoozed. Maybe it wasn't a nice thing to do, but she guessed her grandmother would not remember taking the cigarettes outside with her. In the kitchen, Skeeter put the smokes and lighter in a drawer filled with minor home repair items. In the drawer, she also found a moldy chunk of cheese in a plastic bag. She tossed the cheese in the trash.

After changing into comfy clothes, adding ice to a glass, and then water, Skeeter opened her laptop on the kitchen counter, so she could watch Beth while she napped. Her fingers flew over the keyboard, and soon she had several people search applications opened. She found Bruce Darwin in Piney, Colorado, with no relationship to Charles. He was 73, a retired painter. House painting, not an artist. Originally from Dallas, he was divorced with no children. His life seemed generic. Deeper digging using hacker methods uncovered information that Bruce did not own his home. He rented. He owned a Chevy truck and received Social Security payments of $1400 each month. She guessed Medicare was paid by Social Security, but she couldn't find if he had supplemental insurance. Sitting back, she nibbled on a hangnail. She didn't need to know more about Bruce but something urged her to keep going, so she hacked through the back door of his bank account and found credit card records. She pulled up the latest. It showed nothing out of the norm. He did have charges at a sporting goods store. The biggest expense was at a dental office. *At least he takes care of his teeth.*

So, Bruce Darwin was a single guy with not much financial backing and did enjoy the outdoors. A wealthy wife would fit nicely with his circumstances.

She moved on to Phil. Before he had left yesterday, she had checked the registration on his car and found a last name. She went through the same hoops with Phil as she had done with Bruce. Phil had more resources than Bruce. He owned his home, got close to $2000 a month in Social Security payments, and she found supplemental insurance for him. So, he was covered for physical needs. However, he owned a home with a hefty $345,000 mortgage. He had adult children, one who lived locally, was married with kids, and another son who lived in Los Angeles. She accessed his bank account and found hefty checks made out to the single son in Los Angeles. He had a stock portfolio of $100,000. He also had a membership to the local golf course. She shut down the website and sighed, thinking Phil probably couldn't afford new Polo shirts and was hanging on by his toenails to his golf club membership.

For both of these men, Beth Sutton would be a good catch. Skeeter thought for a few minutes, deciding not to give her grandmother a warning about either man. Besides, she had no idea the value of the house and if Beth would inherit it. Tomorrow, she and her grandmother would meet with Roger's attorney, and she would learn more. She doubted that Beth knew much about Roger's finances.

Her phone chimed. She saw it was Pastor Stan calling. "Hi," she began.

"I'm chatting with Richard right now," he said, his voice full of excitement. "He is thrilled with the idea of going to Holland with me."

She wasn't sure what to say; events were happening too fast. "That's great," she said.

"His mind is a little fuzzy. He tried to turn off his TV with a chocolate bar instead of the remote but I got him squared away. Now he's got my laptop computer open and has pulled up airfare to Holland. Gad, nothing is cheap any longer, but with my plane ticket covered, the cost is doable if we get a few contributions from various charitable organizations."

"Can you do it?"

"I think I can. The power of church affiliations is amazing. Plus, Richard can kick in some. Not a lot but some."

"This is happening so fast. Is Richard fit to travel? How about a passport? Does he need a family member to give him the approval or should we ask someone? Should he check with his doctor?"

"Hmmm. All good questions. I will go over those things you brought up, but Richard wants to confirm the airline ticket. He has found the same flight I'm on, and so we can travel together. We fly to Detroit and then to Amsterdam. We then take a train to Utrecht. Finn lives there. My conference is in Amsterdam, so we'll spend a few days in Utrecht and then go back to Amsterdam for the conference. We should be gone for less than a week."

"Have you found Finn and spoken to him?"

"Ah, no, but I will head to Hanni's room and see if she can give me his information in Utrecht. If she doesn't have it, Harry can give me her son's local phone number, and I can ask him for Finn's information."

"Obviously, you're excited. I think you should have Richard save the reservation and you go talk to Hanni. If you can confirm where Finn lives, then call him. Tell him you are Hanni's Pastor and you will be in Amsterdam for the seminar. See if you two can meet. If it works, then we confirm the plane tickets. Whose credit card will you use for payment?"

"Ah, good question. I guess Richard's. I will pray I can locate funds to pay him back, cover the airfare, and hotel rooms for Richard and any extras for both of us."

"Call me back after you talk to Hanni. Find out where Finn lives. I'll do some internet checking."

"Hold on." She heard Pastor Stan talk with Richard, and heard him tell Richard to check the ticket again. Pastor Stan next told Skeeter, "Richard can only secure the tickets for fifteen minutes. There's only one ticket left for the flight I am taking."

Stan pointed to the computer and told Richard, "Okay. Hold the ticket. I'm going to go see Hanni."

Before Skeeter could reply, his cell phone cut off.

Pastor Stan slipped his cell phone in his pocket, patted Richard on the shoulder, and said, "Be right back."

He hurried out the door and down the hall to find Hanni's door partially closed. He lightly knocked. She didn't answer. Knocking again, he pushed the door open. "Hanni?"

Seated in a chair by the window, she had knitting needles in her hands and a ball of yarn at her feet. A few rows of unmatched stitches were on her needle. She had a confused expression on her face. "Oh, hello." She rocked the chair. "If I rock fast enough it makes me think I am on a roller coaster."

Stan laughed. "I'm glad you get a thrill."

Squinting, she stopped rocking. "Do I know you?"

"It's Pastor Stan."

She gazed out the window. "My son is named Stan, but he lives in Holland. Do you know him?"

Stan guessed this wasn't one of her better days. He stepped inside her room. "I'm Pastor Stan and your son in Holland is named Finn." He smiled. "I was hoping to contact Finn."

"Oh, lovely. He's a good boy. I take him to the park, and he throws sticks in the pond, or is it the canal? Does he still throw sticks?"

Pastor Stan sat in a chair opposite Hanni. Her shoulders were curved and a yellow cardigan sweater was buttoned at her neck. Her eyes were as blue as crystal today, but the lining of her eyes looked red, and he could see her iris jerk as if messages from her brain were shorting out. Deep lines etched her face. It saddened him to see the disease erode her beauty and wonderful mind. "Finn," he said. "He's in Holland. I'd like to talk to him."

"You two can have a beer. He'd like that." Her frown deepened. "I think he's old enough to have a beer. He wears a red sweater."

"Do you know where I can reach him?"

"My mother would know. She is busy, though, with the tulips." Hanni nodded. "Every day she fusses with tulips." She leaned forward. "She should be fixing dinner about now, but you might ask her anyway. Those other things get in the way when there's something there."

Stan checked his watch. Ten minutes until the airline ticket was canceled. He exhaled a lungful of frustration. "Hanni, you look beautiful today. It's nice chatting with you."

She pursed dry lips. "Young man, it was nice of you to visit with me."

With a wave of his fingers, Stan backed out of her room. "Please, Lord," he said as he hurried down the hall, "let Hanni find peace."

He passed Richard's room and fast-stepped to Harry's office. He didn't knock and swung into the office, holding onto the door frame. "Hi Harry," he said as the director looked up, surprised. Pastor Stan bypassed small talk. "I'm on a mission, Harry. I need help and I need it fast."

Harry rocked back in his cushioned office chair. "You look frazzled."

"Yes, yes. Frazzled. I've been working with Richard and now finished visiting with Hanni. It leaves me on the cusp of frazzled."

Harry chuckled. "It's touchy to tangle with Hanni."

"Yes, and it's why I'm standing in front of your desk. I need to locate Hanni's son, Finn, in the Netherlands. I asked Hanni. She recalls when he was a kid tossing a stick into the canal but not much more. That's why I came to you."

"I see." Harry slid his chair three feet to his left to a stack of filing cabinets. He opened the second one, pawed through some files, and removed one. He ran his finger down a page and then stopped. "I have information on Hanni's son, Sven, who lives near here. Her other son, Jon, lives in Denver and I have his number, but I don't have contact information for Finn."

Stan took a deep breath. "I was afraid of that. Could you please give me the contact information for Sven? I can call him and see if he has Finn's information."

Harry sat back. "What's this all about, Stan?"

He didn't want to explain all of it to Harry, not with Richard sitting in his room with the airline ticks being held and the clock ticking. "It's Hanni's birthday soon. I want to chat with Finn. It would mean a lot to Hanni if he'd send a card." He didn't add the rest of it, and wondered if it were considered a lie or simply an omission? He should think about the moral implications and decided on the lie-o-meter scale, what he said was a fib and not an outright lie.

Harry rocked in his chair. He took a piece of scratch paper off a pad, then looked at the paper in the file and started writing.

To Stan, Harry took forever and the noise of his pencil on the pad was irritating. Finally, he slid the paper to Stan. "I've given you both Sven and Jon's phone numbers. You can try both numbers and make sure to invite them to Hanni's party."

Stan took the paper and nodded, backing out of Harry's office. "Okay, fine. Will do. Ah, thanks."

Not quite running but not walking, Stan hurried to Richard's room. A bead of sweat trickled down his temple and his heart thumped against the walls of his chest. He checked his watch to see he had seven minutes before the ticket reservation ended. When he raced into Richard's room, he saw Richard staring at the computer monitor. "Still got the reservation?"

"Yes," Richard said, relieved.

"Okay, pay for it."

"With what?"

"Your credit card. I'll get you reimbursed somehow."

Richard patted his shirt pocket and next pushed himself to his feet and patted his back-pant pocket. "Where's my wallet?"

Stan shrugged, wishing Richard had a different speed other than 'slow'. "I don't know."

"Of course, you don't know where it is, but I usually forget where it is even if I know where it is." Richard pushed away from the computer, found his walker, and shuffled to his dresser.

Pastor Stan checked his watch. "Five minutes."

"Don't rush me. It's the kiss of death." Richard fumbled in the drawer, finally turning with a plastic card between his fingers. "Viola!"

"Get it entered," Stan urged. "Four minutes."

Richard returned to the laptop, shoved his walker aside with a clank, sat down, and began to type. He entered the credit card number and big words flashed on the screen: Credit Card Declined. Richard screeched, "What?"

Pastor Stan grabbed the card. He read it. "Your card is expired."

"Well, double damn. When you are my age, the credit card should not expire until I expire."

Stan pulled his wallet from his pocket. "The cost of the ticket is going to go over my limit."

Richard said, "This is where prayer comes in handy."

Stan gave the card to Richard. "Three minutes."

"I hope I can type that fast."

Stan slowly exhaled and said, "Now I will pray."

CHAPTER 10

After a nighttime rain that left the air crisp, the morning sun covered the dewy grasses with light. Skeeter and Beth arrived at the attorney's office in Avon, a town not far from Piney. On the second floor of a two-story building, the office was tucked behind a large hotel and conference center. Above the town, the ski resort of Beaver Creek was visible through a gap in tree-studded mountainsides. Today, the ski runs were spring-green, lined by groves of aspen trees, pine, and spruce. It wasn't a day to be talking about death.

Paul Murray sat behind a large desk of dark oak. It gleamed under the overhead lights. His desk had a computer monitor, several pictures of kids on the ski slopes, a phone system, stacks of files, and a leather-bound folder in front of him. Paul was about fifty, with a long face and a neatly trimmed mustache. He had a nice handshake, and although Skeeter decided she shouldn't be anxious, her pulse thudded in her temples, and her armpits were damp.

"All right," Paul began in a serious tone of voice, "I'm glad we were able to have you here today. I didn't know Roger as a friend, but I took care of his legal needs the past eight years." He locked his gaze on Beth. "I was happy to learn he had met you, Beth, and the two of you had some wonderful years together. I am sorry for your loss."

Beth nodded.

He turned to Skeeter. "I know Roger has biological children, but I've never met them. It's nice to have you in Piney, Miss Rawleigh." He smiled and his mustache lifted. "I'm glad to know Beth is not alone at this time." He patted the folder in front of him. "So, we are here today to go over Roger's will." He opened the folder. "It is straightforward. Roger's children, Melissa and George, will inherit the majority of Roger's estate, which includes a stock account, savings, and checking accounts. Several months ago, a real estate investment of Roger's paid out a substantial amount, which will go to the children." He looked up from his notes as if to test the waters to see how Beth and Skeeter reacted to the news. He continued, "All of this will be handled by the executor of the estate, who is the president of the American Bank, Sonny Brewster."

"Sonny and Roger play golf together," Beth said with a nod of her head.

Paul smiled at her. "I know Sonny is a scratch player. Roger didn't claim to be as good." He cleared his throat. "To continue, Roger has left you a cash bequest of thirty thousand dollars." He paused. "Then there is the matter of the house. Roger had not made up his mind what he wanted to do with it, so it is not specifically mentioned in his will. Because Beth is the living spouse, this asset will go to her as will the contents of the house and anything else not specified in the will, which means his cars and miscellaneous belongings. I know Roger acquired his real estate in Piney before marriage to you, Beth, so he took care of the expenses. Now you will be responsible for those expenses."

Skeeter rubbed her temple. She had expected the terms of Roger's will, but she also realized taking care of the utility bills, taxes, and such were now Beth's responsibility. Skeeter bet Beth had never even seen one of those bills.

Beth said, "I have my granddaughter here now. She knows how to take care of those things."

But what if I don't want to? Skeeter didn't see any way out of it although Beth could hire a bookkeeper, but with her grandmother's memory slipping, turning money management over to someone unknown was not smart. She felt the start of a headache. "Thirty thousand dollars isn't much for Beth to live on for the remainder of her life."

Paul shrugged. "It's enough for a while. Also, contact Social Security. Whichever payment is bigger, hers or Roger's, Beth is entitled to it. If I were you, I would contact a real estate agent and get an appraisal on the house."

Skeeter's shoulders slumped. All of this sounded like a long-term project. In reality, the thought had been at the back of her mind that Beth had to change her living situation, but she didn't want to admit it. It didn't seem fair her life had been uprooted and forever changed by her grandmother's third husband dying. How could someone who had previously been inconsequential in her life have such a disproportionate impact on her? Life wasn't supposed to dish out stuff like this.

Sighing, Beth pulled her purse closer to her chest. "Is that all?" She checked her watch.

Paul gave her a nod. "I believe so."

Skeeter glanced at Beth, noting her expression hadn't changed. Her grandmother hadn't absorbed the ramifications of being a widow, even if it was the third time. She turned to the attorney.

"You probably have gone through this with other clients. What do most people do in a situation like this?"

He closed the file and tapped his fingers on top of it. "If Beth does not want the upkeep of a large house, the best thing to do is sell it. Downsize. Move into something smaller and invest the remainder of the proceeds."

Meaning I will have to do everything, including preparation for a move. "Yes, I can see it is the best solution."

Beth poked Skeeter. "Let's go."

Standing, Paul handed the file to Skeeter. He turned to Beth. "Would you mind waiting for your granddaughter in the reception room? I have a question for her."

Beth seemed startled by this request.

Skeeter nudged her. "It's okay. Go outside, Gram. I'll be right along."

After Beth left the office, Paul said, "I asked to speak to you because Roger was concerned about Beth's memory. He wanted to set up an executor for her and had discussed changing his will from leaving the house to the kids to Beth." He sighed. "He never got around to making the change, but he had instructed me to remove leaving the house to the children. So, it doesn't change Beth inheriting the house, but his children may petition the court to change it."

"It doesn't sound good."

He waved her quiet. "There's no reason for the court to rule in their favor, but it can drag along, and the house cannot be sold while it is being challenged."

Nodding, she felt little chipmunks thumping inside her head.

Paul continued, "I doubt Beth can handle the legal matters. The state mandates deadlines for probate after a spouse expires. A probate attorney is needed. I can handle this for you."

The chipmunks paused for a moment. "How much will this cost Beth?"

"It will be taken out of the bequeath Roger gave her."

"Is it costly?" Skeeter asked, not wanting to hear the answer.

"Yes."

***

On the drive home from the meeting, Skeeter glanced over at her grandmother who had the window down and a breeze ruffled her gray-streaked hair. She showed no emotion. Skeeter wondered if she truly understood the changes she faced, and for the first time since coming to Colorado, she wished she had friends she could ask for advice. She felt unsure if she could handle everything.

After dropping Beth home, Skeeter headed to the Piney Center and away from problems about money, selling a house, and how her grandmother would live on her own with memory problems. It was close to noon by the time she made it to her office, and her stomach reminded her that she hadn't eaten breakfast. Before diving into her work, she needed fuel. So, she headed to the kitchen via the dining area. When she came out of the kitchen with a leftover breakfast burrito smothered in green chili sauce, she saw Cecil moving his walker so he could safely sit in a chair. He had placed a cup of coffee and doughnut with chocolate icing on the table.

Skeeter placed her plate on the opposite side of the table from Cecil. "Hi," she said.

He glanced up, his smile widening with approval. "Hi, beautiful."

"Mind if I join you?"

Cecil's mouth opened, but he didn't speak for several seconds. If his mind could make noise, it would be cranks and grinds. "It's all right by me. I don't remember your name, though."

When one of the Piney assisted living residents did not know her name, she wasn't surprised. "It's Skeeter."

He pointed a fork at her. "That's right. I tried to remember your name by recalling a mosquito, but it doesn't work."

"Hopefully, something else will jog your memory."

"Hmm." His jaw see-sawed. "Do you know it takes forty times for a person to form a memory?"

She dug into her burrito and shook her head. "No idea." The first bite of burrito confirmed the correct amount of green chili and gravy. The worries of the morning were beginning to fade.

"I learned about memory paths when I was recovering from my head injury."

"How long did it take you to recover?"

"I'm still recovering. I'm seventy-six. I was in a coma for three months after the accident. This was about forty years ago."

"Wow. I guess you're lucky to be alive."

He used a knife and fork to slice his doughnut. "Yep, and chocolate is one of the best things in my life." He popped the wedge into his mouth.

She held a bite of burrito in front of her lips. Green chili dripped from the fork. "Hopefully, you'll hear my name forty times." She pointed to his doughnut. "I see where Charlotte gets a craving for frosting."

"We do have the love of sweets in common."

"Are you all set for Saturday night at the King's Club?"

"Yes. With Hanni's birthday party tomorrow, we'll have one more day for practice." He held the knife and fork in the air while his mind worked on what he wanted to say. "I'm kind of worried about our rendition of 'Sound of Silence'."

"I don't blame you. I think Simon and Garfinkle are hard to beat." Finishing the last bite of her burrito, she commented, "Larry is a wonder in the kitchen."

With a frown on his brow, Cecil asked, "Who is Larry?"

***

Toward the end of the day, her thoughts went back to Beth. Then she thought about Cecil, and how much he had faced in his life, and how a random accident decades ago had left him unable to care for himself. He had to be angry. Yet, he didn't show it. She hoped the night at the King's Club would be everything he hoped it would be, and the night would fulfill his end-of -life wish.

The day finished without much ado. When Skeeter went home, she found a note from her grandmother saying she went to an art guild event with Phil. She wondered if Bruce would be annoyed with Beth for going out with another guy. Then she shook her head, telling herself not to be worried about her grandmother's love life. Beth didn't say when she would be home. The good news was she didn't see the flame thrower or pack of cigarettes anywhere in the house.

The next day was the big event for Hanni and Skeeter decided her head was full of the problems of aging. In San Francisco, she ran in a circle of people who were college-educated and climbing the ladder of success. Women in the corporate world spent most of their paychecks on rent, eating in restaurants, and new clothes. Now she had been transported to a small town in Colorado and was surrounded by elder adults who faced medical problems on top of memory problems. Her life in San Francisco seemed trite.

She thought it was a good time to call her mother who lived on the East Coast. When she hung up with the phone call, she didn't feel more encouraged. Her mother had admitted she had sensed memory problems with Beth the past year, but she hadn't felt it was serious enough to worry about it. Besides, she lived a thousand miles away and had a job she couldn't leave for an extended time.

"I thought Roger would handle it," she had told Skeeter on the phone.

Skeeter now thought to herself: *Roger isn't here anymore.*

All of this would now become her responsibility. She felt cornered and angry about this being her responsibility.

***

The day for Hanni's birthday party arrived. The morning began without a cloud in the sky, the blue so deep it appeared fake. The air smelled sweet with the tang of new grass and blossoming spring trees. Despite being a hub for recreation, Piney had first been a ranching town. To this day, hundreds of acres remained hay operations, herds of cattle, or horses flicking their tails. Already the temperature was in the mid-seventies and climbing and would probably reach close to 80 degrees.

Skeeter arrived at the Center with her arms loaded with party supplies. She had to return to her car for the chocolate sheet cake Lori had ordered which had been decorated with white frosting, and at the bottom, stems of multi-colored flowers. Each bite of the frosting had to contain millions of calories. By the time she had the birthday table set up in the social room with birthday plates and cups and colored confetti, and with the helium balloons tied to either end of the table, she wondered if the sway of the balloons from the air conditioning would leave anyone dizzy. She left the room to go to her office to check on e-mails and phone calls and enjoyed quiet time before the party.

By two o'clock, the social room was a beehive of chatter. The residents had made their way into the room, pushing walkers, using canes, holding onto guide dogs. With Pastor Stan, Julia, Charlotte, and Bear attending, it was a full room with some local friends of Hanni's. Skeeter had attended many birthday parties over the years, a few engagement parties, graduation events, and a few weddings but never with so many elderly attendees.

When Skeeter had asked Hanni to say some words, to explain what it meant to have lived such a long life, Hanni's voice had taken over the entire room. She told her story about living in Holland with a German officer in their house, and she had left the audience stunned with her hellish story of Friedrich Schmidhober living in her house, having his way with her, and then the year of starvation. Then Harry had discovered Joe in the physical therapy room, delivered him to the birthday celebration, and the mood changed. Hanni's memory closed with her view into the years under Hitler's rule and a strange man living in her family's home.

After Hanni's story was left unfinished, expectant vibrations bounced off the walls.

Richard leaned forward on his walker. "Hanni, you finished your story by going home and finding a strange man in your room. Who was he?"

Hanni turned to Richard. She tapped her cane on the floor, one, two, three times. "All of the good things go around to find the happy people and then do what they would rather do."

Richard sighed with resignation. "We've lost her."

Millie, dressed today in a floral dress, white sweater, and tennis shoes, said, "I know who it was." She smiled as attention went to her.

Richard and Cecil both said, "So tell us."

Cordy looked from the men and back to Hanni. Joe dozed. Layla May fiddled with a tube of lipstick. Julia looked up from her laptop computer. Charlotte inched closer to the table with the cake. Bear lifted his head as if he noted Charlotte's intention. Jayne patted Scout, anticipating her guide dog might be tempted by food where it wasn't supposed to be.

Millie adjusted her hips in the chair to find a more comfortable position. "Hanni told me about Holland, and I told her about the good times in Germany when I was growing up. I was hoping to let her know not all Germans were Nazis and not all Germans had been toxic to Jews or others."

"So, who was the man?" Richard anxiously asked.

"I'm getting to that," she quickly added, annoyed because she was pushed to continue faster. "It was two men. One was her brother, Lucas, who encouraged her to come home. He had been injured in the war and spent some time in a hospital in Italy. There he met Francis, who was also recovering from an injury." Millie's eyes twinkled and she laughed. "He was the stranger. Francis Nilsen was a Norwegian born in America who worked in an Embassy in Holland. After a night of drinking, Francis tried to swing from a chandelier, and he missed the attempt. He was taken to the hospital and there he met Lucas."

Richard turned to look at Hanni. So did Cecil and the others. Hanni smiled.

Millie went on, "Hanni then found work at the Ministry of Foreign Affairs and began to regularly see Francis. I've seen pictures of him. He was wonderfully handsome, a tall man with shoulders a yard wide. He had a charming personality and was a world of fun. They emigrated to America, married, and eventually moved to Kansas when Francis bought a ranch. Eventually, he bought a property in Colorado. It was more of a summer place, rather than a permanent home." Millie reached over to Hanni and put her arm around her shoulder. "Hanni was married to Francis for fifty-five years, and although he didn't collide with any other chandeliers, their life together was always filled with adventure. I think Hanni and Francis loved the Colorado Mountains in the summers because it was about as far away from Holland as they could get. Some memories are not easily buried."

Skeeter noticed Charlotte with cake frosting on her fingers, lips, and side of her cheek. "Okay, it's time for refreshments." She nodded to Pastor Stan. "While I serve the cake, how about singing "Happy Birthday" and then passing out the songbooks."

Stan replied, "Good idea. On Saturday, we will be going to the King's Club in Vail to show the world our musical talents."

Layla May added, "Oh, my God. We may be going, but we sure don't have talent."

Jayne glanced in her direction. "You can wear your best lounge dress. I wish I could see it."

Layla May brightened. "I will dazzle. Dressing up is my best talent," she added.

Stan struck chords on his guitar. "Okay, here we go. Time to sing to Hanni."

Skeeter had her back to the group as she smeared frosting over the divot Charlotte had made. Then the group sang "Happy Birthday" to Hanni.

Pausing from cutting the cake, Skeeter thought it was a perfect birthday. She glanced over her shoulder to see Hanni's chin going up and down to the song and a nice smile covered her face. She was quite a woman, Skeeter decided. She thought about the ravages of Alzheimer's disease and how it disappeared at times and memories were sharp, and then other times, the curtain closed and memories were gone and nonsense took their place. For now, Skeeter was glad the memories of Nazi Holland, the German officer, and the starvation had escaped Hanni's mind. It also made her more determined to make her final wishes come true; to see her field of tulips and to know her children had mended their animosity.

When she glanced over her shoulder to see Stan and Cecil strumming their guitars, the other older adults singing as best they could, Skeeter felt an unusual sense of protectiveness for these seniors, people she hadn't even met three weeks ago. It made her smile.

Hanni began clapping before the song was ended but no one cared. Chuckling, Skeeter cut an extra-large piece of cake. She bent down and handed it to Charlotte. "Will you take it to Hanni?"

Charlotte frowned. Skeeter told her, "I'm cutting your piece next."

The toddler looked up at Skeeter. "Can mine be as big as Hanni's?

"Absolutely," she answered and decided tots were not much different from nonagenarians.

Charlotte took the cake to Hanni with Bear following, who hoped that it would not get there successfully and the mess would be his.

CHAPTER 11

Pastor Stan hurried into the Piney Center. The Senior Band would be playing the King's Club in Vail in the evening, and Stan was thankful an adaptive van would transport all the seniors to the event. Although it was only a half-hour drive to Vail Village, he didn't want to be responsible for driving anyone other than Cecil, since he was difficult enough with his shuffling and walker. The van would transport the remainder of the seniors, complete with walkers, oxygen tubes and tanks, dogs, and whatever. Stan and Cecil would load Stan's van with their music equipment and drive into town. Besides worrying about how the gig would unfold, Stan prayed that recent road construction would not close I-70 and leave it impossible to get to town.

For the gig, Stan and the band had selected their ten best numbers for the night. Stan chuckled as he mentally reviewed their chosen songs. They had selected the 1927 Harry M. Woods standard, "Side by Side", but to spice it up, they would add a humorous version, "Senior Side by Side", which talked about a glass eye, missing leg, and hearing aids. They had perfected the right mix of reverb and bass to create a ghostly sound for "The Cat Came Back", the folk song about the cat's nine lives. He hoped they had finalized the correct twang on "Home on the Range" and an Elvis sound for "Peace in the Valley". Cecil's fingerpicking would be featured on "Puff the Magic Dragon" and "Early Morning Rain". Cecil and Stan had finally played in sync on "The Boston MTA" and "The Sound of Silence", but it wasn't always certain they could repeat the feat.

At the end of the night, they would end with their favorite song "All Roads Lead Back to Colorado." If they pulled this evening off the way he hoped, he figured tourists at the King's Club would leave bills in the tip jar. Anything they made would help defray the travel costs for Stan and Richard on their way to Holland. Stan's credit card was now maxed after buying Richard's plane ticket, and although several churches in the area had pledged financial aid to help with expenses for Richard to travel with Stan to finalize a senior's final wish, the money had not arrived, although he didn't doubt he would be reimbursed.

Age and travel and unfamiliar settings could be unsettling with anyone over 70, and their group was a majority of such, plus a decade or two. The King's Club was located in a swank hotel, which specialized in Austrian ambiance complete with blue shutters on the exterior windows, murals inside, flower boxes overflowing with geraniums and pansies, and a wood-paneled interior. Because of usually wealthy, well-dressed clientele, they were accustomed to venues with billboard names. Pastor Stan and the Senior Band were far from a professional group.

As he entered the Piney Center, Stan waved to Charmaine at the reception desk and asked, "How many have signed up for the van?"

Charmaine checked the sign-up sheet. "All of the seniors are going except Hanni. She's not feeling well." She adjusted a floral scarf around her neck. "I'm surprised most of them are going because they think bedtime is right after five o'clock."

"How about Harry? Is he going?"

"No," she said with a shake of her head. "He wasn't happy about this outing, either, but he doesn't need permission for our residents to attend an event away from the Center."

"I had hoped Harry would attend," Stan added with a sigh.

"He said his daughter was having a sleepover, and he wanted to be at home."

Frowning, Stan sat his guitar case on the floor and checked the sign-in sheet. "I don't see your name?"

Charmaine, healthy and active at 63-years-old, shook her head of bottle-blond hair. "I'm going and so is Fritz." She hastily added their names to the list.

Stan ran his finger down the list. "Bart's name is on the list? He's going?"

"Yep. He called after Millie told him she was singing in a band. It is Saturday night, after all."

Stan lifted his shoulders. "Yeah, but Saturday night with a bunch of people who are on the verge of falling asleep or worse?"

Charmaine leaned toward Stan. "I saw him in the dining room the other morning with Skeeter. They looked comfortable together."

"What's that supposed to mean?"

"It means he's a cowboy who chases cows all week or mends fences, and she is a pretty looking filly, and, yeah, it's Saturday night."

"I am getting too old for this."

"Look at me? Too old? Romance is still in the air!"

He sniffed. "I don't' smell it."

"You are too serious; Stan. Life is to be lived."

"Mainly, I look for something to be thankful for."

She leaned closer as if to whisper. "There's always something to be thankful for. Today, I'm thankful the wrinkles on my face don't hurt."

Stan laughed.

Charmaine tapped the sign-up sheet. "Layla May swung by my desk a few minutes ago, dressed to the nines. She wanted to double-check that her name was on the list to attend the gig." She pointed beyond Stan to the meeting room where Cecil stood next to a woman outfitted in a sleeveless gown made of sparkling blue sequins. The dress ended several inches above her knees. For shoes, she wore diamond-studded high-heels. "Take a gander at Layla May."

He followed Charmaine's gaze and a gasp escaped his lips. "Oh, my," he mumbled. He picked up his guitar case and headed to the meeting room.

Layla May stared at Cecil. She had an expression on her face as if she were the cat who lapped the last dollop of cream. Tonight, her eyebrows had been carefully penciled to create a severe arch and colored medium brown, and she loaded turquoise eye shadow on her lids and then added black eyeliner. Her cheeks glowed, and her lips shined with deep rose lipstick. She stood with a straight back and had padded her bra to give her aging body an extra boost.

Cecil, looking handsome in pressed pants and a crisp white shirt, seemed a little taller than his six-foot-three frame. His blue eyes were a good mix with Layla May's dress, and with a little sunburst smile, Stan got a flash of a young man at an earlier time of his life and figured tonight of all nights would be Cecil's night to shine on stage and under the lights.

Stan studied Layla May and thought she looked as smitten as any music groupie. With a smile, he mentally gave a silent prayer of thanks for making this night happen. "Hi, Layla May," Stan began, "you look especially lovely this evening. I love the dress."

She placed her hands under her breasts and said, "I have a dreaded disease: furniture disease. It's when your chest falls into your drawers." She smiled innocently as if she had said a prayer. "Wads of Kleenex fix it."

Stan coughed. "Yep, I guess you women know how to dress."

She cast a glance at Cecil, smiled, and turned her head a fraction to give Cecil her best angle. "You'd think I was twenty-three," she said and ran her hand down the sequins on her hips. "I bought this dress when I was a night hostess at the Cotillion Club."

"Where was it?"

"Oh, on the west side of Wichita." She sighed as if the memory took a lot of energy. "Those were the days of sixty's rock and rollers, and then the seventies and the disco crowds. I introduced the musicians. I saw the Everly Brothers, Paul Revere and the Raiders, Jerry Lee Lewis, the Yardbirds, and some great gals, Bonnie Raitt, and Pat Benatar. I loved working the room and I had a crush on the musicians who played the club, including country singers. Something about a guy and a guitar jangled my chain." She glanced at Cecil. "I still get a thrill."

Cecil cleared his throat and said, "We'd better get our equipment organized."

Charmaine waved to Layla May.

"I'm coming." She smiled at Cecil. "I need to go check on my make-up and change my hearing aid batteries. See you two on stage."

"See you there," Cecil said, happy to see her leaving.

As Stan moved amplifiers, mic stands, and other equipment out of the storage room and began to hand them to him, Stan teased, "Did you see the eyes Layla May had for you?"

Cecil scooted his walker into a mic stand and it fell over. "Damn," he mumbled. Stan held onto Cecil's arm as he bent to right the walker. He pulled it up with sounds of metal on metal.

"Yes, I saw her pout her lips and bat what I think are false eyelashes. She thinks she's twenty."

"Nothing wrong with that," Stan said with a shrug. "The way you play the guitar you think you are sixteen," he said, laughing.

Cecil worked his jaw, the way he did when his brain worked extra hard to produce his thoughts. "See? I'm too young for her. I'm not interested in an older woman."

"Smart Cecil. I appreciate your common sense."

Cecil frowned. "You don't think an atheist or a non-believer can have good morals?"

"It's not that. I appreciate how you aren't willing to lead the ladies on and then hurt them. You're a good man with good values. I wish you could embrace your Christian faith again."

"I'm not blessed with the faith you would like me to have. Truth is, after my accident, I began to lose my faith in God, but I do know this; there is someone upstairs, and he has been watching over me. I used to live on the streets, and now I live with my daughter in a beautiful part of Colorado, and my granddaughter thinks I am the best thing since Gummi Bears."

"Loss of faith is like a wind, it either carries you to a new destination or it traps you in an ocean of stagnation. To me, it sounds as if you are making your way back to finding faith."

"It's a work in progress, Stan."

"Look forward now — and focus on your passion with joyful anticipation."

"Music is my passion, so that will be easy."

Stan rolled up electrical cords. "I hope you aren't disappointed with our show tonight, Cecil. The audience may not appreciate us."

"What's life without risk?" He leaned on his walker. "I take a risk each night when I go to sleep. I'm lucky I wake up." He shook his head. "I'm ready for a new adventure. I've been taking up space for too long. I should have died in the car wreck." He pointed to the ceiling. "If there is a reason I survived the accident, it's because tonight I will play for an audience."

"Or perhaps having a romance with Layla May is another reason you survived?"

Cecil shook his head. "No. Having a romance with her would be the same as another car wreck."

Stan closed the equipment room door. "I guess we will have to put up with her acting like a groupie and appreciate her. We need to start moving this stuff. I have my van parked outside."

Cecil shoved his walker into the amplifier, grunted, and moved forward a few steps. "If I were only younger," he mumbled.

***

With Charmaine checking off names, The Piney Center staff began loading the adapted bus. Besides the seniors in assisted living, others from the rehab facility had signed up to attend the event. The Piney Center bus was better equipped than any of the public transit buses or even the county-funded paratransit buses, which were available to help disabled and mobility-impaired riders. One hour before departure, Charmaine helped twenty-two geriatric adults onto the bus with their wheelchairs, canes, walkers, oxygen machines, backpacks, extra coats, gloves and hats, water bottles, medicine dispensers, and even snack boxes prepared by Chef Larry. Noticeable excitement filled the walkway as they huffed and puffed to move extra-large purses and oxygen packs onto the bus. Charmaine allowed additional time for the 'wheelchair brigade' to individually roll onto the bus's chair lift and to be strapped into place for the slow lift to the floor level and then be unstrapped, rolled into the van, and repeated for the next wheelchair. Oxygen tanks clanked as they were pulled on the bus, walkers banged against metal, a cane goosed someone who yelped, water bottles dropped, and general confusion left an air of excitement.

Skeeter arrived, dressed in a red sleeveless dress and black heels to see Jayne and Scout load the bus and take a seat up front. Then to her surprise, she saw Millie stroll toward the doors with Bart holding her by the elbow. "Room for two more?" he asked.

Skeeter raised an eyebrow. This evening Bart wore new-looking jeans, a light blue button-down shirt, polished boots, and a sexy smile. "You'll be the youngest in attendance by about sixty years," Skeeter teased. "You sure you want to come along?"

He stepped back to appreciate Skeeter and grinned. Guiding Millie to the bus, he whispered to Skeeter, "I wouldn't miss it."

She felt a surge of energy. "Well, let's get going." Bart and Millie found seats. Skeeter began to load the bus when Richard started to disembark. "What?" she asked, confused.

"I need the restroom," Richard announced. "My stomach is making louder sounds than my old coffee maker."

Skeeter backed from the door to give him room. Then she saw Cordy following him. She said, "I may need the incontinence hotline if I don't make it to the restroom."

Charmaine moved beside Skeeter and said, "It always happens like this. Someone always has to use the restroom one last time. I think bladders shrink in conjunction with age and memory loss."

Skeeter and Charmaine waited. The bus motor hummed and so it continued until all of the stars in the planets aligned and the seniors were buckled into their seats, shoulder blankets tucked under their laps, and ready for adventure as if they were a load of kindergarten kids. When the last headcount had been made, everyone loaded, wheelchairs strapped to the floors, oxygen tanks secured under the seats, and backpacks tucked into the overhead compartments, the driver turned off the loading lights and pulled away from the Center.

Skeeter listened while Bart chatted with Joe. They were a strange duo. Tonight, Joe wore pressed pants, a nice shirt, and a brown sport coat with a bow tie. He could have been the poster man for the Best-Looking Guy to hit the century mark. He had to have 70 years on Bart but both men were engaged in conversation.

After a forty-five-minute ride to Vail, made slower by heavy rain, the bus loading scene played in reverse. Finally, the seniors, wheelchairs, and walkers paraded past diners as they headed to their reserved seats at The King's Club.

Bart helped organize the senior's walkers and canes without snagging anyone's pants or someone tripping over a walker or oxygen line. To the right of the bar, was the stage and behind the stage was the equipment room. Stan and Cecil had unloaded their guitars, speakers, and yards of cables. Cecil began to adjust the amplifiers and mics. He studied the electrical connections and volume controls, making changes where necessary. Finally, Stan and Cecil tuned their guitars.

At exactly eight o'clock, the manager of the King's Club gave the nod to begin the show. Stan escorted Layla May to a seat beside Cecil on the stage and next helped Jayne on the stage, closely accompanied by Scout.

Layla May tapped Stan on the shoulder, pointing to the overhead spotlight, which did not center on her. "Can you fix it?" she asked.

Stan fixed it by having Cecil stand up, shuffle five inches to his right, sit down, then had Layla May stand and move to the focus of the light. Stan sat next to Layla May and Jayne would be on his right, close enough so he could hand her the mic on the songs where she excelled. The King's Club now had its entertainment for the evening.

Joe, Millie and Bart, Skeeter, Richard, Cordy, Charmaine, the van driver, and the other residents from the Piney Center watched expectantly, an air of excitement zinging off the walls.

Skeeter held her breath. The musicians on stage looked regal and she hoped the singing would be what they hoped. *So, Layla May is under the spotlight again. Cecil is singing on stage. Jayne is in her element. Their wishes are coming true.*

She glanced at Bart. He had his arm around the back of Millie's chair who sat up straight, her oxygen tank beside her, her back as rigid as the tank. She rested one of her bony hands on Bart's thigh.

Stan began, "Ladies and gentlemen, I am Pastor Stan and I am here with the Senior Band!" Layla waved to the audience and received applause. "Thank you," Stan said sincerely. "It is a privilege to be at the King's Club. Thank you for joining us for what we believe will be a fun evening. To my right is Cecil McFarland and the lovely lady on his right is Layla May." Cecil and Layla bowed. "We also have Jayne and her guide dog, Scout." Jayne smiled, waving in the direction of the applause.

Stan slipped his guitar around his neck. "The first number we'll sing this evening is well-known, 'I'd Like to Teach the World to Sing.'" Stan counted off the timing and strummed his guitar. Cecil followed along with his guitar. Jayne sang the harmony notes. Standing, her sequin dress sparkling under the lights, Layla May swayed and tapped the tambourine. The room was filled with music. Stan and Cecil played together, and the tight vocals caught the diners' attention and soon many joined to sing along. The band finished the song with a flourish, and Stan was pleased.

After the successful execution of their first three songs, Stan took the mic again. "Folks, music fills the world with happiness. Tonight, we can feel it in this room." The diners clapped. Stan continued, "Tonight is special for several of our seniors." He had the diners' attention. "Several seniors have end-of-life wishes." He paused to let the idea sink in with the audience. The room turned quiet. Stan continued, "All of us will face end-of-life, but some of us cannot go peacefully before a final wish is accomplished. At the

Piney Center, we have a beautiful ninety-three-year young woman whose last wish is to see the tulip fields of her homeland in Holland and to have her children with her one last time. Although she could not make the trip tonight, we're raising the money to bring her son to Colorado from Holland. We have a tip jar and hope you'll help bring Hanni's son home, and now Jayne will take the mic and lead us in 'Amazing Grace.'"

Standing, Jayne lifted her chin and sang, her voice strong and clear. Stan and Cecil joined her. The audience remained silent, simply taking in the beauty of the song.

When it ended, Jayne sat down. The room remained silent, as if expectant for something great to happen. Perhaps it did. Perhaps a blind woman singing with friends was beyond special.

Stan said, "Friends, let's pick the tempo up again with 'The Boston MTA!'" Stan set the rhythm and Layla May swayed in time, the sequins on her dress flashing in the light. Cecil had a little trouble keeping up with Stan's tempo, frowning as he played.

The Senior Band played several more songs. Layla May continued to sing and play the tambourine, alternating between tapping the tambourine on her swinging hips or the heel of her hands.

Skeeter watched Layla May. For now, she had been transported back in time to the beautiful lady singers at the Cotillion and imagined herself one of them. As the rhythm of the guitars locked in the solid beats, the crowd sang, clapped, and swayed with the music. Layla's facial expression settled into a soft picture of contentment.

Stan saw a bead of perspiration on Cecil's brow and his jaw worked overtime as if words jumbled in his mouth and needed to escape. Cecil missed a few beats on the guitar. Frowning, Stan wondered if this was too much for him.

When it was time to call it a night, he led the group with the humorous version of "Side by Side", which ended with a marriage between older adults, including teeth on a chair, an eye in a glass, and a spare leg against a wall. When Cecil sang with his dramatic tenor voice, the audience clapped in appreciation. Cocktail waitresses served new drinks.

Cecil lowered his guitar. He appeared on edge as if he needed to accomplish something more, something out of reach but something he had to find.

"And now for our last number," Stan said. "We want to dedicate this song to Hanni. Thank you so much for singing along with us, and we hope you come back soon. Remember, 'All Roads Lead Back to Colorado'."

As the final chorus ended, Stan breathed a sigh of relief. "Thank you, Lord," he quietly whispered.

The evening has been better than he had envisioned. The evening had given smiles to the seniors of Piney Center, and they could return to the Center in a happy mood.

He glanced at Cecil, never expecting what would happen next.

CHAPTER 12

As the last sounds of "All Roads Lead Back to Colorado" faded, Cecil stood, turned up the volume on the electronic amplifier, and began strumming rock riffs on his guitar. He moved his head from side to side and strummed, his lips slightly ajar. The volume increased as he played. Closing his eyes, he stepped on a foot pedal. His acoustic guitar began to scream, the music bouncing off the walls. With closed eyes, Cecil bobbed his head as if he were lost in another world.

"What are you doing?" Stan demanded.

Cecil ignored Stan and stepped on another foot pedal and the volume rose even higher. Sound blasted from the overhead speakers. Stan put his hands over his ears. Cecil pushed a footswitch again and the guitar began to scream with electronic distortion. The noise assaulted ears. The vibration penetrated bodies.

Suddenly, Cecil opened his eyes to see people glaring at him. Layla May beamed at him; her eyes wide. Cecil played louder and harder. Scout howled. Jayne tried to calm Scout but couldn't. By now, the audience stared with annoyance. Several people put their hands over their ears.

Skeeter wanted to leave the room, but she couldn't leave Joe, Cordy, Charmaine, and the others. Bart had a dazed look on his face. Millie winced.

"Cecil! What are you doing?" Stan yelled above the feedback ricocheting from the amplifiers and back through the mics and monitors.

A strange expression blossomed on Cecil's face as if he had found a way to retaliate against the wrongs in his life. He opened his eyes to see hostile stares coming, but he didn't stop playing or lower the volume. Stan guessed what was going on inside his head; pent-up rage brewed over the car wreck, the aborted career due to his brain injury, the frustration at not being able to drive, to walk without a walker, unable to handle his finances, or do anything else without burdening his daughter, son-in-law and ultimately, little Charlotte. Frustration boiled out of his mind and into his fingertips. Sweat poured down his temples.

"Where was God when I needed him!" Cecil shouted.

One of the hotel guests who had too much to drink shook his fist at Cecil. With an angry scowl on his face and with a drunken stagger, he lurched toward the stage, shouting profanities while his face turned red.

Richard spotted him. As the man passed, he stuck out his walker. The man stumbled over the walker and landed on a chair, sliding into a table as he crashed to the floor, cursing and swearing. The chair skidded away and the table fell over, breaking glasses. With a grunt, the man pushed to his knees, wobbling to his feet. Richard leaned forward to nab his walker but missed, sliding off his chair and landing flat. From the floor, all he could see were moving legs. He didn't have the energy to move and for a few seconds wondered what else could he do while on the floor?

Skeeter had reached Layla May and had a hold of her arm. Layla May saw the stumbling man coming toward the stage. In her days at the Cotillion, she had seen her share of drunks. She swung her purse at his head. He tried to grab it and lost his balance and landed on his back. Bart picked up a dining room chair and set the four legs over the man's chest. He grabbed Skeeter and sat her down on the chair.

"Anyone else?" Bart yelled over the noise.

The man struggled to push the chair away, but Skeeter stepped on the man's groin. With a bellow, the man groaned and pulled his knees toward his chest. Layla May continued to hit him in the head with her purse. A nearby diner pushed Richard's walker to him. He grabbed the flimsy frame and pulled it to him. Richard held onto it but had no idea how he would be able to get off the floor.

Another inebriated man decided it was a good time to take a swing at Bart. The cowboy blocked the swing and punched him in the nose. Blood spurted from the broken nose and the man went down with a groan.

One of the hotel guests dialed 911 from their cell phone to report the fiasco. When Stan finally pulled the electrical wire to Cecil's guitar and the horrible sounds stopped, most of the people had moved to the sides of the room or were trying to leave. Hotel security pushed through the door. They saw the drunken man on the floor with a chair on his chest, a woman seated on the chair, and a ninety-pound senior swinging her purse. It didn't take a genius to realize who the bad guy was. Skeeter got up, swiped her palms together, and removed the chair. By this time, several Vail cops pushed through the crowd and took control of the situation. One cop handcuffed the man, stood him up, and deposited him on a chair until he calmed down. The man continued to act belligerently, so the cop dragged him out the door to the squad car and returned inside to get statements from onlookers.

Stan stood, staring at Cecil.

Cecil worked his jaw, his gaze going around the room, looking at the stunned customers and then to members of the senior band. "Okay," he mumbled and began to put his guitar away.

The wait staff straightened the tables and chairs.

Winded, Layla sat down, clearly proud of herself. "I handled guys worse than him at the Cotillion," she puffed and then glared at Cecil.

Bart spotted Richard on the floor. "Kind of tangled," he said as he began to rearrange Richard's limbs.

Richard exhaled a long breath. "It's easy getting down here but impossible to get up."

Taking the walker, Bart set it outside of Richard's reach. Moving behind Richard, he helped him roll onto his stomach, then found a chair. He told Richard to press his palms against the seat. From there, Bart lifted Richard to his feet. Somehow, Richard shook his body as if to make sure everything was in the correct place. Turning to Bart, he said with a nod, "I haven't had so much fun since I was an ornery teenager."

Once assured Richard was okay, Bart joined Millie and Cordy. He found Skeeter. "Nothing but fun on a Saturday night," he commented with a cowboy drawl. "What the hell happened?"

They turned to stare at Cecil.

By now, Cecil's stamina had evaporated, and he collapsed into a chair. He looked tired and confused. "I don't know what happened. I rewired the speakers for more volume to pick up my fingerpicking."

Stan thought there was more to Cecil's story, but in actuality, Stan guessed Cecil would never forget this night. This had been his night to shine, even if it created a bar fight.

Reality found the seniors. Millie had a blank look on her face. Richard found his walker and held onto it with white knuckles.

Layla May's face turned gray and her body looked defeated as if the stuffing had been knocked out of her.

Skeeter moved beside Layla May and asked, "Are you all right?"

She smoothed her sequined dress. "Of course. The best way to forget your trouble is to wear tight shoes." She smiled a smile that dazzled in the lights from the stage. Bending over, she removed her rhinestone-studded shoes. "These things are killers," she mumbled.

Joe looked worn out, along with Millie, Cordy, and the others from the rehab facility. Charmaine helped organize the seniors, and she and Skeeter began to herd walkers, oxygen tanks, spare coats, and backpacks to the waiting bus. Bart and Stan managed to keep Cecil quiet and organized the gear.

Stan helped Cecil from the hotel. Cecil's steps were labored and more of an inching maneuver rather than a step. A valet driver delivered Pastor Stan's car. They loaded Cecil, giving him time to angle himself to the car seat, back up, and sit down, folding his walker when he was seated. He swung his legs into the van, tilted his head back, and sighed.

The bus driver had the vehicle warmed and the loading lights blinking. Bart helped Millie on the bus, then Skeeter and the cowboy made sure walkers and oxygen tanks were in place. Overhead the night sky was a blanket of velvet with twinkling diamonds, a night soft and comforting rather than the atmosphere a little while ago at the King's Club room. With a wave to the bus driver, Bart was the last person to load the bus. The doors closed and the event at The King's Club ended.

Stan watched as the red taillights disappeared into the night. He was ready for silence and a soft bed, but he still had to deal with loading the music equipment in his van. As he returned into the King's Club, he said a silent prayer, telling God about Cecil's guitar picking and the resulting brawl. He needed to communicate with

God and let him know they had good intentions, and they had accomplished Cecil's and Layla May's final wish. He didn't expect God to answer right away but knew God had his way of responding to prayers.

Inside the bus, the seniors remained quiet. The driver turned on soft music. Outside, stars blinked. Somewhere along the drive, Bart found Skeeter's hand and held it, while Millie's head slumped onto her grandson's shoulder.

Sighing, Skeeter whispered to Bart, "Tonight was a success."

He squeezed her hand. "Every project needs a compelling story and you got it tonight." With his free hand, he turned her head toward him, lifted her chin, and kissed her.

Skeeter felt a spark go through her body. "As I said, a success."

***

The following Monday, the dust had settled from the disastrous trip to the King's Club with Pastor Stan and the Senior Band. Cecil had a vague memory of the commotion; Pastor Stan remained embarrassed, and the rest of the older adults thought the evening was a smashing success, and Layla May asked when they could do it again.

When Skeeter reviewed the event in her mind, she tried not to smile, and although the majority of the residents at Piney Center didn't have a good short-term memory, she guessed this was one night that would remain in their memory bank. She thought about Bart. *Gad.* Bart had remained amazingly calm, especially after he decked the guy who threw a punch. While Cecil continued to strum his guitar with screeching sounds, her reaction had been to remove the seniors for their safety. Bart, however, had pushed through the crowd and headed for Cecil. Stan acted first. By pulling electrical cords, he had ended the insanity.

Thank goodness the cowboy had accompanied them. In years to come, if someone were to ask her what was the most memorable date, it would be the night with Pastor Stan and the Senior Band at the King's Club with the electric cowboy coming to the rescue and ending the electrical guitar maniac.

Today, the Piney Center was quiet with only the hum of circulating air interrupting her thoughts. The first thing that morning, she checked her e-mails. Her hacker partner in San Francisco wanted to know when she would be returning home. Steve, the guy who could have been the Billboard poster for Young Professional, wanted to know when she would return. She didn't answer either of them, because she didn't know and because she felt as though she had entered another dimension and was living on another planet.

Two hours later, she had three spreadsheets open on her computer, and her eyes squinted from tracking from one monitor to the other. With her eyes tired, she clicked 'save' on each document and exited the spreadsheets. With a yawn, she arched her neck to exercise it, glancing at the sepia-toned walls. She needed to stretch her legs and left her office. She spotted Charmaine at the reception desk, chatting with a person who needed to log into the visitor's book. She glanced at Harry's office. His door was slightly ajar.

Her phone chimed. She clicked the accept button and heard Pastor Stan's voice. He asked how things were going at the Center. She replied that she hadn't seen Cecil today. "I wonder if he will remember the brawl?"

He laughed and said, "I guarantee it. He will never forget Saturday night and probably is reveling in the success. He meant no harm, even if he had a momentary lack of judgment." Stan chuckled. "I can still hear Cecil's scream about God. It was probably about time he expressed himself. He has a lot of suppressed anger. I hope he will be willing to talk about it. I understand what it is to have to work with God through one's anger."

"It's been an eye-opening experience."

"Overall, the success of the evening far outweighed any negativity. The evening was a small slice of time in the seniors' long lives. Everyone has a 'bucket list'. By the way, I called the airlines to see if Richard and I can upgrade to Business Class seats for our trip to Holland. I wish Richard didn't have to travel so far in economy class. It's going to be difficult on his knees. I should hear back from them."

They discussed other plans and both ended the call with a feeling they had done something positive for the seniors. Layla May and Cecil had fulfilled their wishes. If tomorrow were their last day to live, they could go on the next adventure with a life fulfilled.

After ending the call, Skeeter sat back and thought of how far she had come in the past few weeks. It was a journey she hadn't planned, but she would not erase it if she could. Grabbing the thermos off her desk, she needed to reload on coffee and get the cobwebs out of her brain. She headed for the kitchen, spotting Cordy ambling down the corridor, her back hunched, her shuffling steps measured in inches. Dressed in polyester pants in sage green color, a patterned top, and a scarf around her shoulders, she looked like an old woman wearing pale colors. She held a book of some sort and something else in her hands.

In her few weeks at the Piney Center, Skeeter had learned that each resident in assisted living had a life story worth telling, and what she first assumed did not define their lives. Picking up her step, she hurried to the kitchen, filled her thermos with coffee, and made a cup of tea for Cordy. Backing through the swinging door to the kitchen, she saw Cordy struggling with her arms full and working to pull out a chair at a table.

Skeeter took several steps to Cordy's side, put the drinks down, and grabbed the chair. "Let me get it for you."

Cordy smiled at her, which created big divots in her wrinkled face. "Oh, thank you, dear.'

Sitting, she slid her possessions on the table.

Skeeter sat across from her. "I thought you might like tea. I'm going to join you."

Cordy patted both ears. "Just checking to see if I have my hearing aids today. It never ceases to amaze me how sometimes they take a vacation and I don't see them for days."

Skeeter nodded, happy to know today was a good day for Cordy. "What have you brought with you?" she asked, pointing to the things on the table.

Cordy moved what looked like a towel aside and showed Skeeter a coloring book, plus a pack of crayons, and the stuffed bear she kept with her. "I thought I'd color. There's nothing better than bright colors to break up the monotony of brown walls and beige carpets."

She was surprised that Cordy felt the smothering sameness of the décor. "I agree."

Cordy held up the box of crayons. "Neon colors, besides."

"Nice."

Grabbing the wedge of material next to the coloring book, Cordy placed it on her head. "That should do it."

Skeeter wasn't sure what it was or what the purpose was. "Is it a hat?"

"Not a hat. It's a safety towel."

Skeeter had to look closer. It looked like a remnant of fabric. "What's the purpose?'

She adjusted the material on her head. "It's to keep the kangaroos away."

Biting her lip to keep herself from laughing, Skeeter sipped her coffee, taking a second or two to decide how to comment. "Hmm. I wouldn't think it would be a problem in Colorado."

"It's more of a problem in other countries but I like to take precautions," Cordy said with staid seriousness.

"Have you traveled a lot?"

Cordy fingered the edge of the coloring book. "Honey, I've been on all continents. I've flown in every conveyance which takes to the skies. I've been on ocean liners and river barges. I've ridden on elephants and ostriches. It started when I was younger and began and ended with balloons."

"Balloons?" She wondered if this went along with neon-colored crayons and kangaroos.

Pointing a bony finger at Skeeter, she said, "I like you. It's frustrating when I know all the answers but nobody asks the correct questions." Cordy thought for a few seconds. "It was the nineteen fifties and I met a man who was experimenting with hot-air balloons. I liked the science of lighter-than-air-flight and had him show me how the balloon worked. The first day I rode in a balloon, I never wanted to come down. I followed him to Australia to crew on his balloon. Australia is where I learned to be wary of kangaroos. They look cute but are mean. They kick hard." She tapped the top of the pack of crayons.

Skeeter ignored her finger tapping. "Tell me more about balloons."

"Not much to tell. I followed Ed around the world to various ballooning events — and I met my future husband in England during a festival." She sipped from her tea and paused as if memories had taken her a long way away. "Over the years, I juggled marriage, children, and piloting balloons." She sniffed. "The marriage ended but not my love of balloons. I became a pilot in the United States and flew out of Albuquerque. My kids were raised there." She adjusted the material on her head as it began to slide sideways. "I retired here a few weeks ago."

Skeeter knew it wasn't true; Cordy had been a resident of Piney Center for more than five months, but she was amazed Cordy's memory was as good as it was today, even if she thought she had to scare off kangaroos. "You have a daughter living close to you?"

"No, she lives a million miles from me but she has a condo here for vacations. She sells expensive real estate and she doesn't particularly care for hot-air balloons, which is a shame. Everyone should experience flying a balloon. Flying an aerostat is a unique sensation." Closing her eyes, she waved a hand. "It's like floating freely through the air. The burner fires a six-meter flame to heat the huge balloon." She circled her hand above her head. "The craft goes higher and higher. From up above, the landscape is amazing and looks so tiny. It is quiet. Because the balloon goes with the wind, a passenger cannot feel the air. It's a sensation like no other."

Skeeter admitted, "I've never flown in a balloon."

"Each ride is different," Cordy continued. "As a pilot, control over the balloon's direction is absent, other than going up and down so you have to let the winds take you. I never knew for certain where I was going to land, and I could only control the direction to a small degree. Getting where I wanted to go and landing where I planned was exciting. I've been waiting to fly again."

"Here? In Colorado?"

"I don't care where it is. My end is coming, and I want to savor the weightlessness of flying." She tapped the box of crayons. "It makes me anxious, this waiting for the end. It gives the cancer power over my body, which I hate. I need to fly one more time before I die. I'm in a hurry, too." She stared at Skeeter and pointed a bony finger. "People say old folks don't know anything, but I'll tell you something. When you have lived as many years as I have," she paused and leaned forward on her arms, "you know what lies ahead, clear as a big old movie picture in the theater."

"You can see death?"

"I can't see much of anything because my eyes are so bad but I know things. I know the cancer is taking away my chance of going up in a balloon. It's the only thing I am afraid of — cancer winning. It shouldn't be my last memories, of pain and medication."

Skeeter felt Cordy's words, could sense her feeling of loss, and a speck of anger tossed in to add to the mix. "I agree. Perhaps we can help you with your wish."

Cordy grinned. "It gives me hope."

Skeeter checked her watch. She should be getting back to her office, but she didn't want to end her discussion with Cordy; she wanted to hold on to the good day with Cordy and her flying memories. Her cell phone rang. Skeeter checked her phone. "I have to take this call." Pushing herself to her feet, she grabbed her thermos. "Loved chatting with you, Cordy." She headed down the hall to her office, returning to beige walls and tan carpets.

The phone call was from Beth's doctor, reminding Skeeter about Beth's scheduled appointment the next morning. "Thanks," she said and ended the call. She checked her messages. One was from Stan who said the airline had confirmed his and Richard's reservation from Denver to Amsterdam, but he could not upgrade to Business Class.

She glanced over her shoulder at Cordy, her shoulders slumped, her knobby fingers opening the coloring book, and then she spotted Millie shuffling down the hall and knew she would be a good companion. Funny, she thought, but thinking about everything Cordy told her made her feel as if she were missing something in life. Although statistics said Skeeter's life had a long haul in front of it, she wondered if she reached Cordy's age, if she would have something as interesting to tell her friends or grandchildren? Would she be as determined to accomplish something before she died? A passion? Or would the end be as blah as the tan walls and beige carpets in the Piney Center?

Back in her office, Skeeter called her grandmother who answered on the third ring. She reminded Beth of the doctor's appointment tomorrow morning and was set to see the doctor. Relieved with the chore accomplished, Skeeter answered a few e-mails from friends in San Francisco, and her pal in the hacking business, who wanted to know when she would return to the Bay Area. She honestly replied she had no idea. However, after she e-mailed him, she sat back and thought, while staring at the brown-on brown picture on the wall. She had to admit she missed the thrill of hacking.

Opening her computer, she let her fingers rest on the keyboard while she thought about what to do. It didn't take long for her to make a decision. Her fingers flew as she opened certain websites and found what she wanted. Occasionally, she glanced out her office door to make sure Harry wasn't on his way to speak with her. One website was especially slow to open. She knew it had to do with the internet service at the Center. *Small towns,* she thought. Finally, she found the key to the back door to the airline, and then entered the general system. She found Stan and Richard's reservation which would take them to Amsterdam. She had their confirmation number and seat assignment — 33 D and E, in the back of the plane. *That has to change.* She canceled their seat assignments and located the seating chart. Then she added new seat assignments. They were now reserved in 8 A and B in Business Class. *Drinks and a meal would be served.* Scrolling on the website, she added the option for their luggage to travel without charge.

Satisfied she had done as much as she could do from her computer, she exited the pages and closed the computer.

CHAPTER 13

The next day, Skeeter was awake and dressed and had a cup of coffee while standing at the kitchen island. The house was silent. The outside air remained still, the tall cottonwood trees near the river motionless in the early sunlight. Blackbirds fluttered in the trees, squawking when a red-tailed hawk entered their space. Spring grass, its colors a mix of lime and emerald green contrasted with the browns of the cottonwoods. In California, other than fall coloring, the foliage remained similar all year long. Springtime in the Rockies meant a mix of sunshine, spitting snow, rain, sleet, and warm temperatures. For Skeeter, it was refreshing to see the seasonal changes.

Sliding into a counter seat, she ate a bowl of yogurt with fruit and scanned her e-mails and text messages. When she finished her coffee, she checked her watch. "Gram," she yelled, "we have to go in fifteen minutes."

As Skeeter washed her dishes and cleaned the counter, her grandmother came into the kitchen and yawned. "Where are we going?"

Turning, she saw Beth wearing a nightgown and bathrobe. "You're not ready? We're headed for your doctor's appointment."

Beth scratched the side of her head, mussing her already messy gray-streaked hair. "I'm not sick." From the cupboard, she found a coffee cup.

Drums began to beat inside Skeeter's skull. "We talked about this. You agreed to go to the doctor for a checkup."

Beth poured coffee. "I don't recall agreeing to a doctor's appointment." She shook her head. "I'm feeling fine. I'm not going to see my doctor."

Cymbals clanged in Skeeter's skull. "You promised."

Beth stirred sugar into the coffee. "I'm going with Bruce on a tour of Leadville's Mining Museum."

"No! You have a doctor's appointment."

Beth frowned. "I'm not sick," she said, enunciating each word. "I don't have a sore throat or fever or a body ache. I am fine and I *am* going on the tour with Bruce. I'll pour my coffee and then get dressed. He's supposed to pick me up at nine or ten, I'm not sure which."

Skeeter saw the look of determination on her grandmother's face. Whether it was fear, denial, thriftiness, distrust, or embarrassment, Beth had dug her heels in and was not going to go to the appointment. Her grandmother could not perceive the changes in her cognitive function, and Skeeter knew dementia was to blame for her being unable to reach a sensible decision about a yearly checkup.

Feeling at a loss of action, Skeeter slid off the kitchen chair and picked up her laptop computer and purse. "I'll see you tonight," she said, trying hard to keep her voice light, her anger in check, and a tear from escaping her eye.

Beth headed to the master bedroom. "It'll be nice, dear. We'll have something simple for dinner."

Not tacos. "How about we go out for a hamburger?"

"Okay. If Bruce is here, he'll have to come along."

"Sounds good." She headed for the door.

"Skeeter?"

Stopping, she turned toward her grandmother.

"I love you very much. You are a dear granddaughter. Thank you for being here with me."

The words made Skeeter's eyes fill with tears. "I love you too," she said and hoped her day would go better than it had so far.

On the drive to work, she mentally went over what she needed to do before she was able to start her day of work. She needed to cancel today's doctor appointment for Beth and had no idea if there would be a cancellation fee, and she had to call Social Security to change Beth's benefits. Next, she needed a list of utility companies to call to change the billing name from Roger to her grandmother. She rubbed her temple with her fingers as she thought about Roger's cars, his clothes, his sporting equipment, and the damn house. She wondered who carried the insurance on the house? She hit the steering wheel with her palm. Somehow, she needed her grandmother to help with decisions, but how? Maybe Pastor Stan would have a suggestion?

When she walked into the Piney Center, Harry waited for her. From the look on his face, she felt as though she were the kid who had been sent to the principal's office. She hadn't talked with him since the fiasco at the King's Club so, she had an idea of what was on his mind. "Hi, Harry," she said, put her purse and water bottle on her desk, and slid into her chair.

Harry stood in the doorway with one hand on his hip. "I spoke with the manager at the King's Club. Saturday night our seniors started a brawl."

Skeeter couldn't deny it. "Someone was drunk and didn't like Cecil's electric guitar playing."

"Millie's grandson left a guest with a bloody nose."

Skeeter nodded. "It was self-defense."

Harry moved both hands to his hips. "We need to keep a good image of the older adult population in our county. We can't let this happen again."

She bit her lip, deciding she should not reply with a quip or be smart with Harry. "I agree," she said, giving him a practiced smile.

"Good." He leaned against the door frame. "So, if any other event is scheduled away from the Center, I want a notice two days in advance. If necessary, I can have one of our security people go with the group, but I also suggest you do not encourage our assisted living people to choose entertainment at a nightclub or bar. Furthermore, I don't want any of our residents to leave Piney Center without prior approval from me."

It sounds like being quarantined. "That's fine," she chimed but thought it was anything but fine.

She would like to ask Harry how best to handle her grandmother, but she didn't think this was the time. Instead, she decided to enlighten him about Richard and his upcoming travel. "Under those guidelines," she began, "you should be aware that Richard and Pastor Stan have planned an extended trip."

Harry raised an eyebrow. "Where? Denver?"

Skeeter coughed. "Ah, no. Actually, to Amsterdam."

Harry pushed off the door frame. He shot laser beams with his eyes. "What? It's a million miles from here!"

"Harry, this is important to Richard and more important to Hanni. Stan is facilitating the trip. It coincides with a church retreat for Stan, so Richard will be escorted."

"Richard is not going to Europe!"

"He and Stan have confirmed Business Class tickets, non-refundable." She didn't want to be aggressive but decided she had to be more assertive. "Richard's family is supportive of the trip, and if successful, it will make a difference to Hanni as she becomes closer to the end-of-life."

"Did you plan this?" he asked, his tone accusatory.

She felt little hairs go up on the back of her neck. "I had nothing to do with it. Why would you suggest it?"

He bent toward her. "You're from the city. You think differently from those of us who live in a small town." He took a deep breath, exhaling hard. "I didn't think you would fit in here."

Those familiar cymbals began to clang inside her head. "I fit," she refuted. "I am here."

I've become friends with every senior, and I am aware of Hanni's, Cordy's, and Cecil's desire to finish something in their lives, so they can die peacefully. How about you? Do you know Richard wants to travel in a jet before he dies? He can't let go unless he does this."

"Baloney, it's not like people choose a time to die."

"Perhaps, but they can choose a time not to die."

Harry glared at her. "So, you believe something is holding Richard back from death?"

"Yes, I do, and I believe Richard will be happier after this trip is completed. Besides, after this trip, Richard will smile again, and he'll not complain about his knees hurting as much, and Hanni's children will surround her before she dies. Tell me it's not important?"

Harry's jaw went slack. "Skeeter —"

She interrupted, "I have learned more about the needs of seniors in the past month than I thought I would ever know, and Richard has not had this much excitement in his life for years. Don't deny him this."

Harry stepped back, his breathing coming in controlled breaths. "I don't like this. I have a feeling you have something to do with the trip. I'm giving you the warning to do your job —"

She interrupted again, "Interacting socially was part of the job description you gave me."

"And no more," he added. He rubbed his neck. "Okay, okay, I'm probably overreacting. I'll talk to Pastor Stan, and I'll have a chat with Richard." He paused as if thinking hard. "Really? Amsterdam? Usually, a big trip here is to go to the Ski Museum in Vail."

She realized he had softened with his attitude, but she still got the feeling he didn't trust her, and she may be on thin ice where her job was concerned. "Okay," she managed.

"When do they go?"

"In five days."

"Good grief. Do they fly from Denver?"

"Yes, Denver to Amsterdam and then by train to Hanni's town of Utrecht."

"Denver International Airport. The terminal is monstrous. I doubt Richard can navigate it. If he fails, it's going to be a blow to his emotional state. Have you thought about the consequences?"

"I haven't thought of failure being an option."

Harry tapped the door frame, thinking. "How are they getting to Denver? This time of the year, those Vail van companies are overbooked to Denver International Airport. The mountain passes can close with spring snowstorms. Lots of stuff can go wrong."

Lots of stuff can go right, she thought. Skeeter said, "Thanks for telling me. I'll have Pastor Stan make van reservations for himself and Richard."

Harry pointed a finger at her. "I don't want to be asked to drive them over two mountain passes when spring conditions may bring two feet of snow."

"I'll note that," she said without sounding snippy.

His attitude left her feeling as though she had sat on a cactus. Feeling angry with Harry's knee-jerk reactions to everything, she decided to ignore the work she needed to do on a spreadsheet of Piney Center potential donors. She felt as if it were a tiny payback to Harry. Childish, she decided, but necessary. Besides, she had to hack into a website and reserve two seats on a van going to Denver International Airport for Richard and Pastor Stan.

CHAPTER 14

On the departure day, Pastor Stan patted his jacket pocket. He had to make sure he had the confirmation for the airline tickets, his and Richard's passports, and his cell phone. His briefcase held a packet of information about the church seminar in Amsterdam, scheduled for two days after their return from Utrecht. It also had a printout of their hotel reservations in Amsterdam. The van ride from the Vail Transportation Center started smoothly although the driver had to exit the van to place a stool on the ground so Richard could manage the steps. Stan also tipped the driver an extra five bucks because he had to wrangle Richard's walker besides their luggage.

At the Eisenhower Tunnel approach at almost 12,000 feet of elevation spitting snow turned to a whiteout on the east side of the tunnel. Stan's fingers ached from gripping the armrest, while Richard gazed out the window with a dopey expression on his face as if he enjoyed watching every snowflake. When they began the descent into Denver, the snow turned to sleet and by the time they arrived at the airport, the skies had cleared.

Stan and Richard stepped off the van with stiff bodies. They wrangled their bags and navigated their way through the airport terminal that was thick with hurried passengers, luggage, backpacks, snowboards, golf clubs, and strollers. Many of the travelers wore earbuds and had wires attached to hidden phones. Pushing his walker, Richard remained bright-eyed with a thin line of perspiration on his brow.

Richard pointed to escalators that would take them to the check-in counter. "Up there," he said.

Stan headed in the correct direction. "It's a good thing you know where you're going."

Talking slowly, so he could inhale between words, Richard said, "Have the tickets and your driver's license ready. We'll get rid of the luggage and head for security."

Twenty minutes later, they had checked the luggage, passed through security without much ado, although a TSA employee did a body scan on Richard after they detected metal in his hip. Richard grumbled to Stan, "I wish I could get a copy of my body scans. It would save me a lot of money the next time I go to the doctor."

Stan chuckled as he sat on a bench and put on his shoes. Richard groaned as he sat next to Stan, wiped his brow with a handkerchief, and took some deep breaths. On his feet again, Stan helped Richard stand, and they headed for the terminal trains to the concourses. Someone shoved Richard as they stepped off of the train, and Stan luckily caught Richard's elbow before he went down. "Whoa," Stan said.

Richard smiled in his humble sort of way but then stopped, taking deep breaths. Stan pointed to a long concourse. "We have a bit more to go."

Squinting to see better, Richard groaned. "Boy, it's a long way. I think I've lost my touch. When I was a tour leader with an elderly person with a walker, I would reserve a wheelchair for them. I should've done that for myself."

Stan led the way, using his body to block a path for Richard and his walker which had developed an annoying scratchy-sounding squeak. Relaxing his grip on his walker for a brief moment, Richard leaned against the walkway walls, resting his tired arms. Pastor Stan stepped to the side of the walkway and waited.

When he was ready, Richard grasped his walker and began to make his way toward the plane's gate, now with a little limp in his step. Stan matched his pace and walked beside him. With frustration in his voice, Richard panted, "Twenty years ago, I could've walked this concourse in two minutes. Now it's taking me twenty minutes!"

"It's okay," Stan said. "We're doing okay on our time."

They made steady progress. They passed gates 18 and 20, onto gate 26 and 28, and finally arrived at gate 32. The seating area overflowed with passengers.

Stan spotted two seats in the middle of a row of seats. He pointed.

As a line of sweat dripped down his temple, Richard edged his walker to the seats, knocking into a trash container. A little boy sat on the floor with a baggie of crackers while he watched a show on a Kindle. Richard couldn't navigate around the child.

Bending, Stan tapped the kid on the shoulder. "Can you move a little?"

Without looking at Stan and without moving, the boy shook his head negatively as he picked a fish-shaped cracker from his kiddie cup. The child's mother pretended not to see or hear what was happening.

The airline boarding attendant announced early boarding for their flight.

Richard pointed to the door to the plane's sky bridge. "That way. Now!"

He quickly spun around and with a final burst of energy, pushed the walker to the loading door. Stan handed the attendant their tickets, and she smiled at both of them and said, "Welcome aboard."

As they made their way down the sky bridge, Richard said, "I used to be super at anticipating everyone's needs on these trips."

"You're doing great," Stan replied.

They reached the cabin of the big jet. Stan pointed to the coach seats while he handed the flight attendant their tickets. Frowning, she pointed to Business Class. "Your seats are to the left."

When Stan stopped, Richard's walker crashed into the back of his legs. "Business Class?" Stan asked.

The attendant smiled with glossy red lips. "Yes, where the seats are bigger."

Richard nudged Stan with his walker. "Just go," he said. He handed his walker to the attendants who folded it and slid it into a storage compartment.

Richard led the way, holding onto the back of each seat, carefully making his way down the aisle until they reached their seats. With a groan, Richard moved aside. Stan slid into the window seat, Richard took the aisle, and they buckled up for the flight.

Stan stretched his legs, his body comfortably fitting in the seat. "How did we end up with these seats?"

Richard shrugged, sighing with exhaustion. "I think Skeeter had something to do with it. She also made our van reservations, and I asked her to make several hotel and restaurant reservations." He didn't look at Stan. "I should have done it, but she is so fast on the computer. My eyes and fingers don't always match up."

"Did she use your credit card? Mine is maxed out."

"I never got a new one. I have no idea how she paid for the reservations."

Stan chuckled, closing his eyes. "Skeeter," he mumbled. "I don't know if I should be praying for her soul or her good work." He did pray, as he always did when traveling by car or by air. "Lord," he began, "this plane was built by the cheapest bidder. Please don't let it fall out of the sky, and Lord, I thank you for allowing us to fly in comfort, and I am sorry for whoever was supposed to have these seats." He crossed his hands over his stomach and sighed. Turning to Richard he added, "I hate to fly, especially long trips."

Richard said, "Flying is safe. The odds of dying in a plane crash is only one death for every three million flights."

Before Stan knew it, the captain gave full power to the engines and the plane leaped down the runway, gliding into the air at160 miles per hour. Stan felt pressure on his body and was pushed back in the seat. He looked at Richard who had a huge smile on his face, his eyes wide with delight. He had never seen Richard happier. With a sigh, Stan looked out his window as the plane cut through the clouds and higher in the sky, silently thanking God for their safety.

After landing in Detroit, they joined the stampede of travelers to a new gate for their flight to Amsterdam. Again, they were directed to Business Class seats. Stan now had to wrestle with his conscience, but he asked for forgiveness and reminded himself the result would be life-changing for Richard and Hanni. Leaning back, Stan felt less anxiety than he had in previous flights. He closed his eyes and thanked God for having the seniors in his life, and for listening to his prayers. He smiled, too, knowing God had brought Skeeter into his life for a reason. It made him rest easier.

Three hours later, after they read the flight magazines front to back and did the Sudoku, they watched the flight monitor on the back of the seat. Stan noticed Richard rubbing his knees. "Legs bothering you?"

Richard nodded. "At my age, a balanced lifestyle means fifty percent aches and fifty percent pains."

"Imagine what your knees would feel like if we were seated in coach."

"On fire."

"It's a good thing the plane's door is locked because people like me would be tempted to open the doors and jump. I'm tired of sitting. How much longer?"

Richard checked his watch. "Four hours."

Stan groaned. "I don't got this!"

"I think Johnny Carson said that on a Saturday night skit about a hundred years ago."

"It's still pertinent."

"Let's go over the itinerary for when we hit the ground."

"Don't say hit."

"I mean 'land'. Anyhow, after we land, we take a train to Utrecht. It's about twenty-five minutes. We'll head to the hotel. Then tomorrow I've arranged to meet with my college friend, Lars, and he'll bring his grandson, who is an excellent photographer. Lars uses a walker, too, so the grandson can wrangle our extra legs and mollify our aged temperaments. I'll go search for Hanni's tulip fields, and you will go talk with Finn."

Stan checked his watch. "We still have almost four hours?"

"Yep, but we'll be halfway around the world." Richard closed his eyes. "Take a little snooze. Dream about Hanni's tulips fields, and thank God for being able to make this trip. He needs to know. I'll be ready when He calls me home."

CHAPTER 15

Once the plane landed, Stan and Richard found their luggage, passed through customs, and took a taxi to the train station. Richard's knees ached, his stomach rumbled, and he had to hold onto his walker to remain standing. At the train depot, they changed dollars to Euros, and they purchased train tickets from an automated system. The train took them to Utrecht on schedule. When they arrived in Utrecht, they took a taxi to their hotel. It was almost nine o'clock but the bar remained open, and they ordered sandwiches. Stan wasn't sure whether the food was good or bad he was so tired. The men retired to a comfortable room with twin beds.

The next morning, Stan checked his cell phone to see a text from Hanni's son. They agreed to meet at 11:00 a.m. at Finn's townhome. After a breakfast of excellent coffee, rolls, and cheeses, Richard took Stan on a taxi tour of the town. Built around the Dom Tower, the tallest church tower in the Netherlands, the tower could be seen from anywhere in Utrecht. The town had beautiful canals with extraordinary wharf cellars housing cafés and terraces by the water. After several stops, Richard managed his walker on the rough sidewalks, but at times he grated his teeth against the pain.

Stan tried to imagine Hanni here as a young girl in a town taken by the Germans. He visualized Nazi soldiers in their uniforms and heard the rumble of tanks as they came through town. When they passed a market, Stan envisioned Hanni's mother trying to buy food with vouchers and having no success. A stab of anger grated in his stomach.

When they returned to the hotel, Lars was there to meet them. A tall man with snow-white hair nicely groomed, Lars pushed a walker which was a testament to European design because it did not squeak. After the introductions were made, including Lars' grandson, Jason, the group split, Richard going with Lars to see if they could locate Hanni's family farm, including her field of tulips.

Stan waved goodbye and hailed a taxi. After a five-minute ride along canal-lined streets, he arrived at a brick townhome covered with climbing ivy. After paying the taxi driver, he stood for a few seconds, inhaling a tangy aroma that came from the canals. He closed his eyes and let Hanni come into his memory, her blue eyes and wrinkled smile giving him courage for the meeting with her son. Opening his eyes, he knocked on the heavy wooden door.

Finn answered. He was a medium-tall man with brown hair, kind gray eyes, and black-framed glasses. He wore wool slacks, a long-sleeved white shirt, and a brown vest. He extended his hand. "Pastor Stan?"

Stan's heart thumped in his chest. "Yes. You must be Finn."

The two men entered a cozy sitting room lined with shelves showing porcelain vases, shoes, and other shapes. To his right, Stan saw a door to a kitchen, and he heard running water and the clash of dishes. The air smelled of cinnamon. Stan guessed Finn's wife was in the kitchen, baking something sweet. Finn asked if Stan wanted coffee or tea, and Stan declined.

After chatting about the town and the weather and the state of travel, Stan came to the point. "Thank you for seeing me, Finn." Stan chose each word with care. "Your mother sends her love. She is still a beautiful woman but she is declining. Some days her memory fails, some days she is clear-headed. She feels something is unfinished between you and your brothers, and she cannot let go of it and wants her children with her before she dies. As a man of God, I know Hanni is waiting for this to happen before leaving her earthly body."

Finn sighed. "I'm sure my mother told you the whole story of my father's death and the disposal of the family property in Vail. It was done without my knowledge or agreement. Sven and Jon cheated me, and I'm still angry. The wounds are old and deep." He gazed out the window as if reminiscing years of hurt. "I'd like to visit my mother. I've missed her, and I know she is reaching the end of her life, but I don't want to face my brothers for fear I'll explode. It won't make Mom happy and will leave me feeling worse."

Stan calmly said, "I see your dilemma." He kept steady eye contact with Finn. "Would you be willing to let me help you make peace with your siblings? Amends are always possible and should bring relief to everyone concerned."

Finn's chin trembled ever so slightly. "It would be a great thing, but I don't know how you can bring us all together." He shook his head. "Everyone has open wounds."

"You are the oldest sibling, and I think your influence could start the ball rolling."

Finn looked surprised. "How?"

Reaching into his briefcase, Stan removed a magazine article. "I'd like to leave this with you. It's the true story of a woman who ultimately forgave the man who murdered her seven-year-old child."

Finn inhaled sharply.

Stan nodded. "It's a short read but the insightful story of Marietta Jaeger. You can find more about it online. Please read it. The woman's journey to forgiveness came in steps, and these can apply to anyone. I hope we can find a solution to find forgiveness for your entire family." He set the article on the table in front of them. "So, I'd like to return tomorrow after you have read the article."

Finn took the pages, glancing at them while his glasses slipped down his nose. "I'll read it, Pastor, but no guarantees."

"The only guarantee we have in life is death. Let's see if we can make your mother's end-of-life a happy one."

Finn's jaw dropped an inch, but he gave Stan a little nod. The two men lightly chatted until Finn checked his watch. "I have to drive my wife to town."

Standing, Pastor Stan held Finn's gaze. "It was a pleasure to meet you, Finn. I'll see myself out." With light steps in his feet and heart, Stan turned and left Finn's house.

The spring day was lovely. Stan was in no hurry, so he chose to walk to the hotel. Following a town map, he strolled along canals and past quaint Dutch homes. Then he came to Holy Trinity Church. The edifice was delightful, created out of brick and wood with dressed stonework. Wandering inside, he found a seat. The interior design followed the traditional form of a nave, chancel, and sanctuary. Prominent features were the stained-glass windows. They illustrated important moments in the life of Christ, following the church seasons and main festivals from Christmas to Ascension. As he sat in a pew and gazed at the colorful stained-glass windows, he prayed for Finn and Hanni, and Finn's siblings. He prayed for Richard, thanking God for bringing them safely so far from home. Letting his thoughts clear, he decided it was a perfect way to finish his visit with Finn.

***

When Skeeter returned home from work, she found Bruce's car parked in the driveway. She nibbled on her lower lip and stared at the car. With no plan in place on how to proceed with her grandmother, she hoped she would find a solution. Gathering her purse, laptop, and water bottle, she got out of the car and headed inside.

When she entered the house, the first thing which hit her was the smell of cigarette smoke and something burning, perhaps hair? Several bags of groceries sat on the counter.

Bruce saw Skeeter and said, "I hope you don't mind. I bought makings for hamburgers to put on the grill."

Skeeter looked at her grandmother and back to Bruce. She tossed her belongings on the counter. Then she stared at Beth. Immediately, she knew what had happened. "Gram, I thought you gave up cigarettes!"

Beth tilted her head. "I did."

"You've been smoking."

"No, I haven't!"

Skeeter's cheeks grew hot with anger. She moved to her grandmother and pointed to her bangs. "If you haven't been using the flame thrower on your cigarette, then you have a bad hairdresser because your bangs are singed!"

Beth touched the frizzled hair on her forehead. "Oh, dear."

Skeeter tossed her hands in the air. "I give up!"

Turning on her heels, Beth started for the master bedroom. "I'd better go see if I can fix this."

"Yes, you had better." Skeeter glared at Bruce. "I'm sorry for erupting. I've had a long day and I thought my grandmother had thrown away her cigarettes."

Bruce continued to organize the groceries from the shopping bag. "No need to apologize. I left Beth here while I went shopping. Her hair looked burned when I got back."

Skeeter collapsed in one of the island chairs. "She uses a barbecue lighter and it has a huge flame."

"I see," he said.

"I'm frustrated. You've become a friend to my grandmother, and I appreciate it." She tapped the marble counter with her fingernails. "She has memory problems. I didn't realize how bad it was until I spent time with Beth."

"I've noticed," he said as he took a head of lettuce to the sink and washed it.

She sighed with relief. "I don't know how to get her to do what she needs to do, regarding her health and also making decisions about this house. I've been dumped with a lot."

Bruce patted the head of lettuce dry with paper towels and set it on a chopping block. "My father had similar issues. He lived at home with me until he moved to a memory care facility. He had Alzheimer's."

Skeeter's jaw sagged open. "You went through this with your father? And you have noticed Beth's memory issues but continue to see her?"

Bruce's eyebrows narrowed. "She is a lovely woman and has many good years ahead of her. It's only friendship."

She rested her head in her hand, her elbow on the counter. "Can you give me some advice?"

Bruce removed the packaged hamburger from the bag. "Do you have a bowl?"

She pointed to the cupboard behind him. He found the bowl and dumped the hamburger in it. "Seasonings?"

"Drawer to your left."

Bruce found the seasonings. "Life with my father had its ups and downs. After getting his diagnosis, we sold his house and he moved in with me. Some friends pulled away when they learned he had memory issues. For both of us, it was hurtful to realize certain family and friends weren't available for support. I think it stirred up fears about *their* future. For Beth, people who can't be a part of her support circle may later reappear once they have time to adjust."

"That would be nice for Beth. Did you struggle with your dad going to his doctor?"

He sprinkled seasonings with the hamburger. "Dad didn't particularly like doctors, so with my father, I never told him he had a doctor's appointment. I made the appointment for the morning, steered him out the door, and told him we were going for a ride." Bruce worked seasonings into the meat. "Sometimes he would ask where we were going, but not always. We'd drive to the doctor's office, and I'd put my arm around him and chat with him while we went inside. I didn't have any further problems."

"Wow. Sounds simple."

"It may not go as smoothly at first, but it's better than the head against the wall when a loved one refuses medical care."

Skeeter went to the refrigerator and found a bottle of wine. "Do you want some?"

"No, thank you. It's better if Beth doesn't have alcohol, and she'll want to do what I am doing."

Feeling as though a weight had come off her shoulders, Skeeter poured herself a glass of wine. "How about all the stuff she has to do since Roger died? It's as if she is pretending it isn't there. I don't know how to get her to make decisions or pay attention."

He formed hamburger patties. "Don't ask her to make decisions. You are her lifeline. You make the decisions for her to the best of your ability. Perhaps tell her you are going to do so-and-so. Asking her opinion or for her to do it herself is, right now, too much to ask. Maybe her memory will stabilize after more time from Roger's death."

She took a sip of wine and let the chilled liquid slide down her throat. "She hasn't organized a memorial service."

"Beth said Roger has adult children." He pointed toward Roger's desk. "Most likely he has their e-mail address and phone numbers on his computer. Contact them. Ask what they would like to do. Perhaps a small, private celebration of life with his children or nothing at all would be their preference. I am certain Beth will be happy with whatever is decided as long as she does not have to make decisions."

"So, it means I have to make all decisions?"

At first, he didn't meet her gaze. Then he lifted his head and locked stares with her. "You became her caregiver by default. There it is. Down the road you will need to see a lawyer who specializes in elder care. You will need to have a power of attorney in place, so that you can make decisions for her, but that is further down the road. Yes, you need to make the decisions for her, but you also have to take stock of yourself and figure out your situation."

"It doesn't seem fair."

"Life throws curveballs," he said simply. "You need to put the legal and financial matters in place for yourself, research options for future long-term care needs for Beth, and seek advice which will help you maintain your sanity as a caregiver. You should also be prepared for Beth to go to assisted living when the time is right for both of you."

"When will I know?'

"It's different for everyone, but my dad did go into a memory care facility in Grand Junction when he no longer knew who I was, and I needed to resume my life. Dad was happier once he adjusted to his new home. He smiled more. He had missed socialization while living with me, and they dispensed his medicines better than I could do, and I never regretted the decision to place him there."

"How did you pay for it?"

"We sold dad's home before he moved in with me. It was three years before he moved to the memory center. I felt a huge relief when the house was sold. None of us siblings would have to worry about paying for his care."

"Hmm, I'm thinking Beth needs to do the same thing with this house."

"In this locale, several developers have built nice homes with attached apartments. Beth's home is well-built and the property alone is valuable. I'd advise Beth to sell it, buy something smaller with the attached apartment, and you move into the apartment. She could put a chunk of money away and have it invested until she needs it for assisted living care. Or you could live together and rent the apartment if you wanted. It opens up lots of possibilities for the changes coming for Beth." He sliced onions and tomatoes for the burgers. "Shall I put them on the grill?"

Skeeter didn't have the correct words to tell Bruce how much it meant to her that he had experience with memory loss and could share his experience. She had figured him as a gold-digger but now decided otherwise. She was relieved to know another person would be available to talk about her grandmother's issues and perhaps help. "Yes," she answered Bruce, "but I have no idea where Beth put the flame thrower."

CHAPTER 16

In Utrecht, Stan and Richard dined on steaming plates of sauerkraut stamppot and Rookworst while they discussed the events of the day.

"How did it go today?" Stan asked.

Richard replied, "I went to Town Hall and researched family properties. During the war, documents were lost or destroyed, but I had a general idea of where the farm was located from what Hanni described, and Lars was a great help." He leaned across the table as if letting Stan in on a big secret. "His knees and hips are awful. The man needs all-new body parts." Richard chuckled and speared a hunk of worst. "I found the family's farm and the tulip fields."

"On the maps?"

Richard's blue eyes sparkled. "I went to see them for myself. The family house is gone, and a company has taken over the fields, but the tulips remain the way Hanni described them. Rows and rows and rows of tulips. As far as the eye can see, yellows, reds, pinks, oranges, purples, whites, candy cane, zebra-striped." Richard wagged his head. "Glorious, simply glorious."

"Do you think we can capture realistic pictures of these fields, enough to convince her she is there?"

"Yes, I think so. Technology with photographs is so much more advanced today than when I had a Brownie camera, cranked the lever, and it went 'click'."

"I have a disposable camera," Stan admitted.

"Lars took me to the media room at his library. I tried the virtual reality headset. Wow. I thought I was in Africa, looking down the dust of a charging elephant. I went down on my knees to escape being trampled. I thought I would never get up again."

"How do we use the photos?"

"By the miracle of digital photography. Lars will give me the memory chip, and we'll take it to our library." Richard waved his hands. "We'll create a huge picture of the tulip fields. I know Hanni will recognize them as her fields. We'll have a fan going for a breeze, and we'll import enough tulips to plant a small plot for her. She can sit or stand among the tulips. If all goes right, she'll believe she is home." Richard paused for a few seconds as if savoring the day's memories. "This is such a satisfying feeling. It's the best I have felt in years. How did your meeting go with Finn?"

Stan gave Richard an update and finished by saying, "I appreciate how you are a man of faith. Please say a prayer Finn will find forgiveness."

After a dessert of ice cream and apple tart, it was time to call it a day — and what a day it had been. After Richard pushed his walker down the hall with squeaks and rattles, Stan turned the key into the hotel room, and with a sigh, Richard collapsed on the bed and didn't move. Stan looked at him and smiled. He removed Richard's shoes and covered him with a spare blanket.

Opening his laptop, Stan checked his e-mails and then shot off a message to Skeeter. He told her about their day and asked her to check with the Piney library to see if they, indeed, did have a media room. He pushed 'send' and decided today had been a good day.

After turning off the lights and allowing his brain to slow down, Stan thought about the gorgeous stained-glass windows he had seen today and the power of prayer. He prayed, "Lord, help Finn grasp the importance of forgiveness and reconciliation. Help me accurately explain the journey of forgiveness he needs to take." He looked over at Richard and could only see a lump on the bed. "Bless Richard and let his discovery of the tulip fields be what is needed to give Hanni a smooth passage to You, and please give Richard's hips and knees the ability to take him home."

***

With Pastor Stan gone, Skeeter had to manage social time at the Piney Center by herself. For one of the days, she asked Lori to bring the best books of the year to show the seniors. Cecil gravitated to the non-fiction books, and Millie and Layla May went for the who-done-it genre, and Cordy and Hanni enjoyed the children's picture books. Joe admitted his eyes were so bad he couldn't read the print in most books. Jayne held books on tape Lori brought for her.

Lori, a slim blond-haired woman in her fifties, told Joe, "Any book you like I can order in large print."

Joe smiled at her and said, "I think it would still be impossible to read. These hundred-and-two-year-old eyes are not good for much."

Lori didn't give up. "How about an audiobook?"

"How does it work?"

"I'll bring you a recorder. The book will be on tape. It's easy to use."

As Skeeter listened, she decided the Piney Library made it possible for anyone with disabilities to enjoy books. She glanced over Cecil's shoulder. "What book interests you?"

Cecil turned, adjusting the book in his hands so she could see the title. "Anything by Neal Stephenson is good. This book, *Snow Crash*, presents the Sumerian language as the firmware programming language for the brain stem."

She didn't understand any of it. "Maybe what Layla May is reading would be better for me."

Cecil nodded. Skeeter moved to sit by Layla May. "What are you thinking of reading?"

Layla May showed her the cover of a book with a red three-inch high heel. "*The Devil Wears Prada.* It's about a horrible boss." Layla smoothed out the wrinkles on her linen pants. "I had one or two like her."

"What was your profession?"

"After college, I served drinks in nightclubs and tried a stint as a singer. I did enjoy my time at the Cotillion Club but after we married, we moved around the country for my husband's job. I couldn't always find a suitable job that involved singing. At one time, I decided to become a model. I had the figure and flare for showing it off. In the beginning, it was fun. I enjoyed it except the boss was difficult, if not impossible. I learned two things from my time there: one, don't die with vacation time on the books, and two, don't try to control a bad boss although you can control how you react to them." She leaned forward. "The lesson served me well throughout my life."

Skeeter took it all in. "How did you end up in Piney, Colorado?"

"My husband wanted to retire here, so we did. It was fifteen years ago. We had good years and met a lot of friends, and then the docs told him he had cancer. It was a long progression with many setbacks. Toward the end, we sold our home and moved into a rental. Now I have heart disease. I couldn't manage even a small home on my own, so here I am."

Skeeter squeezed Layla May's hand. "I think you would like my grandmother. Let's get together for coffee."

Layla May agreed and Skeeter then moved on to Lori as the librarian began to pack up books and shoved them into a fabric bag. "Thanks for coming, Lori."

"My pleasure." She pointed at Cecil. "What an excellent mind he has. I'm happy to have found something he'll enjoy reading. I'm sorry Stan and Richard aren't here today."

"They're having their fun," Skeeter told her. "Stan e-mailed me and asked me to talk to you about the media department at the library." Skeeter told Lori about the quest of placing Hanni in a field of tulips and about Richard bringing back pictures of Hanni's flowers.

Lori responded with enthusiasm and suggested that Skeeter come to the library to see the media room for herself. She ended by saying, "This will be a wonderful project."

Fiddling with a hangnail, Skeeter also told Lori, "We need to put Cordy in a hot-air balloon and Jayne in an ocean and somehow bring Mary to Joe."

"That's why you have Pastor Stan. He can make miracles."

***

The next morning in Utrecht, Stan arrived as agreed at Finn's house at 11:00 a.m. Finn was warmer with his greeting, but not by much. Stan could tell from Finn's body language and hear in his voice a greater receptivity to him than yesterday.

Once they were settled and the small talk was over, Stan asked, "What did you think of the Marietta Jaeger story?"

"It is truly powerful," Finn replied. "But I don't see how she could forgive the person who murdered her daughter. However, one passage made sense to me; the killer would have two victims if Marietta continued with her rage. I can see I've been victimized at least twice, myself; once when I was cheated out of the money and again while carrying the anger for years. It has also kept me away from my mother. So, she is a victim, too."

"I'm glad you can understand the concept, Finn." Stan continued, "I suspect your siblings have suffered through this. I'd like to explore how to move forward toward forgiveness and ultimately reconciliation with your siblings."

"Okay by me," Finn replied.

Stan could hear the skepticism and reservation in his voice permission but felt he had to continue. "With your permission, I'd like to read Matthew 5:44, the passage which guided Marietta Jaeger with how to forgive."

Finn nodded approval.

Reaching into his briefcase, Stan found a New Testament with a brown cover. Turning to the scripture, Stan said, "These are the words of Jesus, 'But I say to you, love your enemies, bless those who curse you, do good to those who hate you, and pray for those who spitefully use you and persecute you.'"

Stan finished the passage, placing the Bible on the coffee table. He held Finn's attention by meeting his gaze. "How many steps do you count in this verse?"

Finn picked up the Bible, read the verse silently, and then counted out loud, "One — Love your enemies. Two — bless those who curse you. Three — do good to those who hate you, and Four — pray for those who spitefully use and persecute you. I see four commands."

"Great. That's the way I read it. I'd like you to do something which may be hard at first, but as you practice it, it will become easier. This will be the first step toward your ultimate goal of seeing your mother, along with your siblings in Colorado." Stan paused a moment, cleared his throat, and continued. "I want you to pray for your brothers."

Shifting uncomfortably in his seat, Finn looked to the floor and then back up at Stan with his eyes narrowed and his hand raised in protest. "Whoa, I'm not a religious man. I'm not sure I believe in God, much less believe in praying for my siblings."

"I understand," Stan replied. "I'd like you to go along with me and see what happens."

Finn continued to look at Stan as if he had asked him to jump out the top window of a thirty-story office building and fly. "I... I... I don't know," he stuttered. "I'm not sure I know how to pray," he continued. "I don't know how to do it. I don't think I believe." Finn finished his objection with impatient frustration in his voice.

"Okay, here is how you pray. Simply say, 'God, I would like to see my mother again and I'd like to be free from the anger and bitterness in my heart.'"

"I don't believe it will do any good."

Stan replied, "The nature of prayer is such that if you start with only a sincere wish in your heart to see things change, you will begin to see it happen. Your deeply held wishes and desires can become a focused hope, and hope can become faith, and faith can move mountains."

Finn protested, "I'm not sure I believe in God."

"It's okay," Stan said. "When you begin to pray, I want you to imagine you're coming to a powerful friend who wants to help you. The Bible teaches God loves us and wants to help us. When you pray, make your wish from the deepest place of your heart. When you sense the slightest presence of hope and faith, embrace it. Go with it, and, Finn, I believe if you'll do these things, as Marietta did, you'll begin to see some changes and don't forget to include your brothers with your prayers."

Finn laughed a mocking laugh, "If I can fake prayer, I guess I can include prayers for my brothers, but all of this will be fake. I don't believe in any of it."

"As I've said, go along with me and let's see what happens. We'll stay in touch by phone and I'll coach you on this. You're not alone in this."

With a shrug of his shoulders, Finn said, "Okay. If this works...I'll see you in Colorado."

When Stan left Finn's house, he took one last look over his shoulder. If he were a betting man, he would place money on seeing Finn in Colorado.

***

As the days progressed, Skeeter began to feel her job at the Piney Center had become her refuge, and she had found Colorado's weather, which varied from days in the seventies to spitting snow, allowed her to take the bike from the garage in the late afternoon and ride as many miles as she wanted along Brush Creek. It was a lovely valley studded with hay fields, cows, horses, and ranch buildings of varying ages. After a brief trip to the local museum, Skeeter learned about gold in the local creeks. When gold was discovered in the Eagle River, it had started a flurry of prospecting high on the peaks above Brush Creek. Come summer, she promised herself to visit the mining camps.

At home, Skeeter made a list of things that needed to be accomplished since Roger died. She printed the list in 22-font letters and taped it to the kitchen island. She had 15 items on the list. As jobs were accomplished, she put a check by each number. Before Skeeter left for work, she would point out a job for her grandmother to think about. Sometimes it worked, sometimes it didn't. One of the first things on the list was to contact Roger's son and daughter and ask them what they would like to do for a service for their dad. She coached Beth on leaving phone messages for Roger's children.

One afternoon when Skeeter was home for lunch, Roger's son called. He introduced himself and explained that as the oldest child, he and his sister would like to bury their dad's ashes with their mother in the family grave. Skeeter told him she would contact the mortuary and could have them send the ashes to the son.

Then he said, "It won't be necessary. My sister and I would like to come to Piney and collect the ashes, also to go through dad's belongings."

Skeeter felt a little tick of her pulse in her temple. She wasn't sure how it would go if George and Melissa came to the house and told Beth they would sue the estate over the house. "It sounds like a plan," she said, thinking she wished they wouldn't come at all.

George went over the calendar and gave dates when he thought he and Melissa could arrive. Skeeter asked, "Will you be planning to stay at the house?"

"Not this trip. We want to see the house, figure out what dad's garage looks like, and come back again with a trailer to haul some of dad's things home to my house. Then there are his cars to consider."

Skeeter didn't know what to say. "Keep us posted as to when you will arrive."

Skeeter was convinced all had gone as well as they hoped, when George next said, "My dad said he would leave his house to me and my sister. We're not happy that Beth had him change his mind."

Little hairs went up on the back of her neck. She knew Beth had done no such thing but had no ammunition to support her knowledge. She sighed wearily. "My grandmother was his wife. They had a lovely marriage. She has no income except Social Security—"

He interrupted, "My attorney is reviewing dad's will. Beth will be hearing from us."

Civility was gone. "Beth's attorney is also reviewing it."

"Fighting us will cost her everything dad left her."

She hated the tone of his voice, hated that he thought Beth had something to do with changing Roger's mind about the house. She nibbled on a hangnail. However, she didn't want to further anger him. "It was nice chatting with you, and I'll contact the mortuary for you and have your dad's ashes held there until you pick them up." She didn't wait for him to comment and ended the conversation.

When she hung up, she glanced out the window at the fluttering leaves on the cottonwood trees, to the grass growing tall, and through the trees, she could see bits of Brush Creek in the twilight. She wondered how it could be such a beautiful day with a phone conversation that left her depressed.

She thought about going back to the Center and chatting with someone, anyone who would make her day brighter.

CHAPTER 17

Grabbing her purse, Skeeter left her grandmother a note to expect her home for dinner and since it was a warm day, she rode Roger's road bike to the Piney Center. The ride helped clear her head from her conversation with George.

She thought about her life in San Francisco. The worst stress was city traffic, and next was coordinating the right skirt with the correct top for work and how to change from work clothes to looking great. Now she had to contend with a relative she didn't know who wanted to sue her grandmother, and it was only the start of problems.

Entering the Piney Center, she left her bike next to Charmaine's desk since she had no idea about the safety of a bike without a lock. She headed to the kitchen to see if Larry had cookies leftover from lunch. When she ventured into the kitchen, she found the chef seasoning a pan of chickens that were going to be roasted for dinner. Larry had a cell phone wedged against the ear held in place with his shoulder. "Cookies?" she asked.

He pointed to a plate on the counter behind him.

"Thanks," she whispered, grabbed a few cookies, put them on a paper plate, and headed for her office, stopping when she saw Millie on the patio with Bart. It wasn't hard to change her direction, and she pushed through the patio door.

When Bart looked up to see Skeeter, he broke into a smile. "Hey," he said and stood. Millie turned to Skeeter and smiled. Bart brushed leaves off a chair. "Come join us."

She didn't have to be asked twice. "It's beautiful here," she commented, glancing at flowering columbines mixed with poppies in tones of orange and reds. In the afternoon sunlight, his lanky body moved with easy grace, and she could have been describing him, rather than the garden. She wondered how he mixed looking great with ranch work. Then he smiled at her, and she saw touches of humor around his mouth and near his eyes, an expression she liked seeing. "Cookie anyone?" she asked, holding the extras in a napkin.

Both Bart and Millie nodded their heads. She held the plate for them.

Each took a cookie. A half dozen cookies remained. Skeeter pointed to the framed photograph that Millie held. "A new picture?"

Millie turned the frame for Skeeter to see. She gasped. It was Millie, take away seventy years. She sat on a handsome horse whose coat glistened in the light. Millie wore riding pants and shiny black boots. She looked at the sun. Rosy cheeks blended with green eyes; her head held high with pride.

"It's me," she said to Skeeter. "I was thirteen. We were living in Warendorf, Germany. My father trained horses. He was invited to work for the German Olympic Committee for Equestrian Sports." She glanced at the photograph and sighed. "I loved that horse."

Bart pointed to the shiny-coated animal with a flowing black mane. "She was a Bavarian Warmblood, highly prized in Germany, a big horse but solid on her feet."

Skeeter looked at Millie's green eyes flecked with gold. "Were you an Olympian?"

She laughed. "Oh no. I was only allowed to ride because my father was a trainer. We lived there for five years. I rode all over the country." She rubbed her temple. "I hated to leave but I wanted to finish my education in America and dad was ready to come home." She looked away and squinted. "It was difficult in Germany after the war. Feelings were hard. We were ready to return to America."

Bart, looking good in jeans with a few layers of dust, a blue shirt, and scuffed boots, pointed to the picture. "It's the best picture I have of Grandma. I thought she should have it."

Millie held the picture to her chest. "I never rode a horse like her again."

Skeeter asked, "Did you do a lot of riding in America?"

"I rarely got the chance. I was off to college when we came home and then I married and then kids came along and work of some sort or the other. Life got in the way." She turned to Bart. "My grandson has horses—"

He interrupted, "I manage a ranch and the owner has horses. There's a difference."

Skeeter saw a black Stetson on the chair next to Bart. "Are you a modern cowboy?"

He laughed. "Cowboys have been fictionalized to the point of disbelief. No, I am not a cowboy." He pointed to the wide-brimmed hat. "I wear it to keep the sun off my neck. Yeah, I ride horses and wear jeans but I also spend half the day on the phone, the rest of the day moving equipment, doctoring animals, and working with a shovel in irrigation ditches. I manage a large chunk of land for a guy who thought he wanted to be a rancher and found out it's a lot of hard work, but he fell in love with the land, and he hired me to do the stuff he doesn't want to do."

Skeeter noticed scars on one hand, and he had a bit of five o'clock shadow which gave him a sexy appeal. The closest she had ever come to meeting a cowboy was a guy who worked for a vintner in Napa. That guy wrangled grapes, not cows or horses. "How do you know so much about ranching?"

He pointed to Millie. "She married my Grandfather who was a cattle brand inspector, and who also bought and sold ranch properties. He owned various ranches. I learned by doing."

Millie adjusted her oxygen line around her ears. "My father always landed somewhere where horses were concerned: training, trading, transporting. I miss them so. I don't have long to live in this life, but I want to ride a horse one more time."

Bart darted a nervous glance at Skeeter. "We've been over this, Grandma."

Millie waved him silent. "Young folks don't know everything, but you think you do. I need to sit in a saddle, period. I don't have to run a race or climb a mountain, but I need to sit — plain sit in a saddle on the back of a horse — and preferably a big horse before I die. If I can do it one more time, my life will be complete."

Bart's expression was of pained tolerance. "I know."

Gathering her oxygen line, Millie adjusted the oxygen tubing in her nose and began to push herself to her feet. "It's been lovely, but I am an old woman with bad lungs, a failing memory, and aching bones. I need a nap."

Bart stood and held her elbow.

"I can manage to walk to my room," she told him as she balanced herself, tilting her head to Skeeter. "You've got a pretty little filly here to keep you company." Smiling at Skeeter, Millie pulled her portable oxygen tank alongside her and shuffled toward the patio door. She punched a square plate on the wall and the door opened.

Nodding, Skeeter almost had to pinch herself to make sure she wasn't dreaming. Millie's history and Bart's story were so far removed from her reality that she had to shake her head.

After the patio door closed, Bart's expression softened. "She doesn't have anyone else but me, and when I landed this job in Colorado, I brought her along. She couldn't live on her own and thankfully, she can afford to live here, and they take good care of her. Although she has bad arthritis and emphysema, she won't stop nagging me about getting on a horse before she dies. She usually means what she says. Somehow I want to do it for her."

Skeeter handed him the plate of cookies. "Chocolate usually helps when the situation is stressful."

Bart reached for another cookie. He took a bite. "Hmm. Good. It does help."

She suddenly felt like a school girl when she had a crush on a guy.

His smile relaxed. "I stopped by to see Millie today because I was in town but I also wanted to see you."

Her heartbeat thudded in her temples. She fumbled for the correct reply. "Anything I can do for Millie?"

"No. But there is something you can do for me. My boss, Mark Malone, is throwing an engagement party at the ranch on Saturday for his niece. I'm invited, I think to be there in case something needs fixing, but I wondered if you would accompany me?"

She was too startled by his invitation to offer any objection. "I'm not sure what to say?"

"Say yes. It's as simple as that."

"Okay, yes," she replied without wanting to sound too excited. "It sounds like a nice event." Tilting her head, she asked, "What do I wear to an engagement party on a ranch?"

With a smirk, he answered, "I suggest clothes."

***

Stan and Richard caught the train to Amsterdam. As the train zipped along smooth tracks, Stan wondered if Finn was successful with his prayers. He knew it was not an easy thing for Finn to do, but he hoped for Hanni's sake that he, at least, was trying. As the countryside flashed outside the windows, Stan pondered the question of Finn's ability to reconcile with his siblings and came up with no answers.

Richard looked rested and had not complained about his knees or hip bothering him. Stan asked, "How did the photographs come out at the tulip field?"

Richard pointed to his suitcase. "I have the media card in my luggage. Jason said he shot many good photographs. We'll let Lori and her crew at the library decide which one is the best."

Stan folded his hands across his chest, enjoying the speed of the train. "I hope Finn will come to Colorado to visit Hanni."

Richard said, "If he wants something bad enough, he has to do something he has never done before."

Stan let the words sink in and wished he had said the words himself. Closing his eyes, he thanked God for being allowed to be Richard's friend.

Once they arrived in Amsterdam, they checked in to a hotel located on a picturesque canal. Once settled, Richard told Stan, "I've made reservations for us at the d'Vijff Vlieghen, or the Five Flies restaurant. Long ago, I brought our tour groups to the restaurant. It's over three hundred years old and is almost a museum. It's in the old part of the city with individual dining rooms which have been cobbled together from five different canal houses. Each room has a different name and ambiance."

Stan frowned at Richard. "Why do they call it the Five Flies? It doesn't sound appetizing!"

Richard laughed. He explained it was about the sanitary conditions of the huge place. "The way the restaurant is laid out, you might think it would have been fly-infested before windows. The nine dining rooms ramble over five seventeenth-century townhouses. It's a reference to the absence of flies in the seventeenth century when the restaurant opened in the Dutch Golden Age, before the advent of screens to keep flies out. The place was clean, even back then. You might find one fly in each of the five dining rooms. Thus, the Five Flies. Believe me," Richard added, "it is sanitary and delightful."

"I guess we will find out," Stan commented.

On the taxi ride to the restaurant, Richard gazed out the window. "Skeeter made the restaurant reservations for me. I wonder what credit card she used to make it."

Pastor Stan didn't answer.

At the restaurant, the hostess led Stan through the restaurant's maze-like interior. Room after room of old-world charm greeted Stan. Each intimate dining area had its own unique character and collection of antique objects. Plenty of exposed beams and dark wood gave a feeling of age; the rooms were filled with locals and tourists talking in languages Stan had never heard. Decorated with beautiful gold-plated leather from the 17th and 19th centuries, the antiques seemed endless. Each room was small and seated only a few patrons. Several stories of narrow staircases finally led to the reserved room where Richard waited, having taken the elevator.

They were seated at a table made of hand-crafted wood. Linen placemats looked too pristine to touch. Wonderful aromas drifted from the kitchen: roasted meats, onions, and cinnamon, all blending to entice the salivary glands. A buxom woman wearing traditional Dutch clothing took their order. Stan ordered the soup of Jerusalem artichoke, button mushrooms, and hazelnut oil to start with and a main course of cod with spring pearl onions, leek, and a dash of potato and poultry gravy.

Richard took a long time reading the menu. He finally settled on veal sweetbreads for a starter and followed by the pan-fried Dutch beef served with lemon beans.

When Stan's cod dish arrived, he looked down at glazed onions and he thought about Hanni, subsisting on tulip bulbs for an entire winter. He had to push the vision of Hanni eating tulips from his mind to be able to enjoy the onions, and he wondered if Richard felt the same about the shallots, which cradled the beef.

They finished their dinner with a selection of Dutch cheeses. When the final dishes were removed, Stan felt a pang of guilt, knowing that Hanni and her family had starved during the war. He wondered if Friedrich Schmidhober had dined in this restaurant. He tried to erase Nazi soldiers from his mind but it was difficult.

The following morning after a light breakfast in the hotel, Stan and Richard headed for the Mecure Hotel to attend The Faithful Aging Conference. The conference was held for persons of all faith traditions to share the best ministry practices and knowledge related to aging congregations and meeting the needs of older adults, inside and outside the walls of faith communities. Stan and Richard checked in and received a schedule of the day's events. The men separated to attend different seminars on various subjects. They met for lunch and again attended information classes in the afternoon. Tired by the end of the day, they had dinner and went to bed. The next day was a repeat of the day before. On the third day in Amsterdam, long hours of sitting and lectures had left them drained, they were happy to head to the airport for their trip home. Richard shuffled through the terminal and a bead of sweat lined his brow.

Stan finally called a halt to their progress and told Richard, "I am going to get a wheelchair for you. No protests."

Richard didn't squabble.

Once in Colorado, Stan pushed Richard through the airport in a wheelchair. Richard later said it didn't hurt his ego to use the wheelchair because he was too tired to think about his ego. They arrived in Piney in the evening, and the cool air and familiar aromas of the mountains welcomed them home.

***

At home, Skeeter had made progress on her list of things to do for Beth. She'd checked several items off the list, and had printed out Beth's most recent bank statements. She also had the bank close Roger's accounts and directed them to contact Roger's attorney to find out where to send the balance in the accounts, if any. She had also contacted the electric company, the gas company, the water district, the Direct TV people, and the trash service. All providers changed the name on the accounts and monthly statements would now be sent to Beth. By doing some internet searching, Skeeter determined a ballpark value of the house. The property was more valuable than others in the area since it was close to town and on the river. Also, the house was only eight years old. She placed calls to two real estate agents with inquiries about the possibility of them listing the house for sale. All of this was foreign ground to Skeeter, so she wanted to take it slow. Some days, she wanted to bash her head against the wall because she had to take care of all of this but felt unprepared, overloaded, incapable, and only wished Beth's memory was better to help with decisions. Wondering if she would ever return to her life in San Francisco, she didn't see how. She had no one to lean on and no one to suggest an alternative solution. She felt alone, stuck, unappreciated, and angry.

The question remained on her mind late Saturday afternoon when she drove along the Colorado River Road to the Lone Pine Ranch. The drive itself soothed her nerves with the river twisting along steep sage-covered hills in shades of tan to tinted pink, to meadows dotted with cottonwood trees, and in the distance snow-covered peaks. Driving under a log entrance sign for the ranch, she joined other invitees and parked in an area next to a large brown barn. A party tent took up half of the front lawn outside of a log home with a wrap-around shaded porch. Pots of spring pansies and other red flowers were a happy contrast to the vibrant green of spring lawn and pasture grasses.

Bart spotted her. He raised his hand and soon joined her.

When Skeeter saw him, she decided he looked devilishly handsome in clean jeans, a white shirt, silver-buckled belt, and polished black boots with red inlays. She also noticed several of the other women in the crowd looking their way when Bart greeted her. She took in his attractive male physique and decided all the other women who looked at him with interest would have to survive with him being eye candy.

Tonight, this cowboy was hers.

The event at the ranch along the Colorado River was delightful. The engagement party included many people about Skeeter's age, and they came from all over the country. She guessed which guests came from the East Coast with their accents, including a's instead of o's and the Southern accent where people drawled the words. For the New Yorkers, they talked too fast, and from the West Coast, they spoke with an air as if they knew more than anyone else.

She had a fun time with Bart and learned more about ranching than she needed to know. One of the highlights was taking a flute of champagne on a tour of the horse barn. Located at the end of a rock path about a hundred yards from the house, the barn smelled of sawdust and oiled leather and animals. Bart introduced her to the horses, each hanging its head over the stall door. He stopped at the last stall and ran his hand along the cheek of a horse with a black coat and white blaze on its head. "This is Misty," he told her. "She's twenty-five years old and with a gait as smooth as a limousine. This is the horse I think Millie could ride."

Skeeter sipped the champagne while visualizing Millie pulling her oxygen tank and struggling to walk the length of the Piney Center. "Ah, how do you plan to do it?"

"When Millie says she wants to sit in the saddle, it's exactly what she means. She is not going to go on a trail or trot in an arena. I only want her to sit on Misty. Hold the reins. Stroke her neck. Feel the heat from the horse."

"Still. I don't see how she can climb in the saddle."

Bart rubbed the back of his neck. "I know, I know. Misty is a big horse. Mark has a nephew who is handicapped, so Mark's truck is equipped with a hydraulic lift to get him in and out of the truck's passenger seat. I'm thinking of using it for Millie."

"Lifting her onto Misty?"

A flash of humor crossed his face. "Yes. Swing her up, let her sit, swing her down. Simple."

"It's a long drive to the ranch," Skeeter said as she envisioned Millie tired from the drive and then making the walk to the barn.

The beginning of a smile tipped the corners of his mouth. "I'm thinking of bringing Misty to Millie."

"At the Piney Center?"

"Exactly." He rubbed Misty's ear and the animal rubbed its head against his chest.

She laughed. "We had better make sure you do it while Harry is at lunch."

"Yes, ma'am." He pointed to her empty champagne glass. "Let's go join the party."

She had no objection.

CHAPTER 18

In the town of Utrecht, Finn climbed the carpeted stairs to his upper-floor office. Finn sat in his easy chair in the large bay window and looked out at the other houses in the upper-middle-class neighborhood. He tried to pray as Stan had instructed him.

Today, he watched his neighbor as he tinkered under the hood of a vintage Ruska. Finn grumbled to himself, "Working on a Ruska would be easier than this damned mental and emotional work. I'm a practical guy; I don't do emotions."

Finn hoped there was some kind of master mechanic in the universe who could help him get his emotions repaired. When he thought about his siblings, his chest hurt. It made him wonder if his anger clogged his arteries and weakened his heart. He knew it wasn't healthy, physically, or mentally. Since something had to change, he decided to pray.

At first, he felt awkward and foolish. *How to pray? Is there a wrong way?* He didn't know if he should close his eyes, fold his hands or kneel or what, but Stan had told him no particular physical posture was required, merely a mental attitude open to the possibility of a God who wanted to help his desire to see his mother again and be free from the anger toward his siblings.

He remained in his chair. The outside world faced him. He did not close his eyes. "God," he said out loud, "this is Finn. I'm back again. I feel so weird, even foolish, talking to no one. I'm glad no one can see me or hear me, but I am trying to find my faith, and I want to believe someone is listening. I am praying." Finn paused a moment to see if he could sense any sort of response, but he felt nothing. Doggedly, he continued his prayer. "God, if you are real, please help me visit with mom before she dies, and God," he paused, needing time to find the correct words, "I need to have the courage to face my siblings. Please help me to forgive them. One last thing. God, I should bless them so, here goes: I send wishes for happiness and the hope they will forgive me for being absent for so many years. Amen."

Glancing over his shoulder, he checked to make sure he was alone. This start of praying was to be between him and God and no one else. Getting up with a muted groan, Finn moved closer to the window. The world continued as before. His prayer had not changed anything and he felt worse as if he had faked praying. He wondered about the wisdom of letting Pastor Stan suggest he find God again. Rolling his fingers into tight balls, a new anger brewed. He wanted to see his mother, and to do so he needed to make amends with his siblings, but he wasn't sure how.

***

Skeeter tapped the top of the marble island, anxiously wondering how the morning would go. While Stan and Richard were away, Beth had taken a trip to Denver with Phil, and it had not turned out as expected. Phil drove a sporty BMW, and the drive through the mountains was delightful. After a tiring day of sightseeing and visiting with Phil's extended family, he woke the following morning with an anxiety attack. His daughter took him to her doctor, who prescribed Valium. The medication left Phil with his eyes closed and mumbling his words, swearing that he could drive the car to Piney. Because he couldn't keep his eyes open, Beth took over the driving duties. Over two mountain passes it rained, which turned to sleet, and she admitted that the drive had left her anxious and exhausted.

Beth had recovered from the drive home from Denver. Today would be the second attempt for an appointment with her primary care doctor. Determined to have Beth seen by her physician, Skeeter made the appointment for mid-morning and now waited for Beth to finish her coffee and get dressed, finish fiddling with whatever, and be ready to go. When Beth breezed into the kitchen with an empty coffee cup and a paper plate with muffin crumbs, Skeeter was glad to see she was dressed. Skeeter slid off the stool, took her purse, and said, "Grandma, you look nice. We're going out."

Beth's expression changed to surprise. "Oh, lovely. Where are we going?"

"You'll see," Skeeter said and grabbed her purse, moving to Beth and putting her arm around her waist. She guided her through the door and to her car. "Hop in," Skeeter said as she held the car door. She didn't look directly at her grandmother when she closed the car door.

"This will be fun," Beth said and adjusted a colorful scarf around her neck.

As they drove to the doctor's office, Skeeter asked Beth to point out which businesses she liked. One was a flower shop; another was a small café which advertised to-die-for pastries. Skeeter pointed to the café. "Let's stop for a cinnamon roll on our way home."

Beth agreed.

Skeeter nibbled on her lip. *So far, so good.*

When Skeeter pulled into the parking lot of the medical center, she parked the car but did not look at her grandmother. "We're getting out here," she told Beth and added nothing more. Agreeable, Beth slid out of the car. Skeeter saw her frown and pointed to the building. "We're going in there."

They entered the medical building and found the doctor's office. Inside, Skeeter pointed to an aquarium, and Beth stood next to it while Skeeter checked in with the receptionist. Then they both watched colorful bettas and a clownfish.

"Beth?" a nurse in scrubs called.

Skeeter nudged her grandmother. "Let's see what that is all about." They followed the nurse to an exam room, where the nurse introduced herself and made small talk while Beth's blood pressure and other vitals were taken.

"That's a nice service," Beth commented.

The nurse left the room. The door was barely closed before the doctor entered with a big smile and introduced himself. He locked eyes with Beth and said, "I was happy to see you on the schedule today." Moving to the sink, he washed his hands. Over his shoulder, he said to Skeeter, "I'm going to chat with Beth. She'll meet you in the outer room in a bit."

Skeeter didn't give Beth a chance to protest. "Okay. I need to check my e-mails." Leaving her grandmother was both difficult but a relief. She sat in the waiting room and nervously tapped the floor with the heel of her right shoe.

Close to an hour later, Beth swung through the door to the exam rooms, chatting with the doctor. If Skeeter didn't know the doctor was thirty years younger than her grandmother, she would have thought Beth flirted with him. "Thanks for bringing Beth to see me," he said to Skeeter. "When is a good time to call you?"

Skeeter answered and gave him her cell phone number. The doctor knew how to work with Skeeter without ignoring Beth, which made her sigh with relief. With a nod, the doctor left them.

Beth moved against Skeeter and both headed for the front door. Beth whispered, "He's such a nice man." She looked over her shoulder. "It's too bad; he is way too young for me."

On the drive from the doctor's office, Skeeter purposely did not ask questions about the appointment. If Beth wanted Skeeter to know how it went, she would tell her. Stopping at the pastry café, they chatted while they splurged on a giant cinnamon roll. The rolls were rich with tender dough, the cinnamon filling warm, the icing enough to coat their tongues, the treat a perfect ending to a successful trip to the doctor.

***

Anxious to hear how Stan and Richard did on their trip, Skeeter also knew jet lag would put them out of commission for a day or so. After dropping off Beth at home, Skeeter headed to the Piney Center. Waving to Charmaine who was on the phone, Skeeter peeked toward the dining area but didn't see anyone. She retreated to her office and turned on her computer. Suddenly, Harry appeared in her doorway.

"Skeeter," he said with a worried tone to his voice, "glad you're here."

"What's up?"

Harry frowned. "It wasn't such a good weekend. Hanni had a mild stroke and Joe fell and bruised both his hip and his ribs. Joe is in bad shape. Hanni is not eating and taking little fluids. I'm afraid her body is shutting down. Both of them are in the rehab facility."

The news took her breath away. "Are they okay?" She got up. "I should go see them."

Harry waved her to stop. "In a minute you can go visit. Hanni will be okay, but it means her days are numbered." He frowned. "As to Joe. Anyone who is his age and has a broken hip will face problems."

"Problems?"

"Generally, pneumonia and blood clots."

She felt the air whoosh out of her lungs. "I knew both of them were old, but I thought they would go on and on like the Energizer Bunny."

"I know you and Pastor Stan plan to do something for them, as far as the end-of-life wishes."

Skeeter saw a genuine look of concern on Harry's face. "It's true."

He ran his hand through his hair. "Make sure you don't do anything to jeopardize their health."

"They have end-of-life wishes, Harry."

Pointing a pencil at her, he then began to twirl it between two fingers. "Just don't break my rules or worsen their health issues."

Hairs on her arms stood up. She wanted to grab his pencil and run it through his nose. "Stan and I only want to help Joe and Hanni make a smooth transition to death."

He flicked a lock of hair off his forehead. "You'd better hurry up."

She nodded as her chin trembled. Unable to look at Harry, she stared at her computer. "I know."

Turning, she watched Harry as he retreated from her office. Skeeter gathered her emotions and allowed herself time to quiet her heartbeat by breathing in through her mouth and out through her nose. When she felt ready, she put on fresh lipstick and ran her fingers through her hair. With a wave, she passed Charmaine and headed into the rehab area.

She found Hanni in a single room where the curtains were drawn, allowing in little light. Hanni looked like she had been swallowed by the bed. She lay still, with her head only slightly inclined and the light covers drawn to her neck. One sheet was crumpled, so Skeeter straightened it, then stroked Hanni's cheek with the back of her fingers. Her skin felt cool, her eyes closed, her breathing coming in shallow breaths, her skin the color of cement. Skeeter covered her hand and squeezed; it was the best she could do. She sat beside Hanni, letting the silence calm the pace of her pulse thudding in her temples. She wished Stan were with them. Bowing her head, she said a prayer for Hanni, not asking for healing but comfort and peace. With a sigh, Skeeter opened her eyes, withdrew her hand, and left.

She found Joe in his shared room. However, the second bed was empty. Joe's blue eyes brightened when he saw her. "Skeeter," he gushed, "you made my day."

Seated in the chair next to his bed, she found his hand, which felt cold and skeletal. "So, you wanted more individual attention?" she chided.

He pointed to the empty bed. "I had a roommate, but he checked out."

"Did you know him?"

"Nah. He was still wet behind the ears, but he had a real problem. Yeah. They had to open him up and redo some of his wirings. He got a pacemaker for his heart. When he spotted a pretty girl, his heart went crazy, the pacemaker malfunctioned, and opened the garage door."

Skeeter nearly fell off her chair. "Joe!"

He grinned at her and winked. "I'll be on my feet in no time."

She wondered how much in life she had missed by not having a relationship with either of her grandfathers. "I know you will, Joe."

"Yes, and I expect Mary to be here any minute. Ain't that something?"

She nodded. "It is." She saw Joe had a different picture of Mary on his bedside table. In this photograph, she was older, perhaps in her seventies. Her hair had turned silvery gray which curled around her face. She had a slight figure and the photograph was grainy as if not a perfect exposure. Picking up the picture, she studied it.

Joe leaned toward Skeeter, squinted, and then groaned. A shaky finger pointed to Mary. "I can barely see anymore, but I think she is holding a book or a pie."

Skeeter looked closer. "It's a pie."

"She makes the best peach pie. Maybe she'll bring me one today." He again groaned.

"Maybe you shouldn't move."

He barely lifted his shoulders. "It's a new hurt."

She rubbed the back of his hand with her thumb and felt a connection to him, reaching beyond friendship. "I want you to get better," she whispered.

With his hand that had an IV line connected to a blue vein, he patted their joined hands. "Me too, but I'll tell you something. This place keeps my mind occupied. I get enjoyment from hearing about other people's operations, and the nurses flirt with me. Don't tell Mary."

Skeeter's mind whirled. Her head was full of her grandmother's problems, her risky date with anxiety-prone Phil, Hanni, and Joe's situation, her job, a non-existent family, a life away from San Francisco, and her infatuation with a cowboy.

"I wouldn't dream of telling Mary." She stroked Joe's hand. "Do you pray, Joe?"

"In my fashion."

"Let's pray together. For Mary."

Joe smiled, that smile that lighted an entire room.

***

For afternoon social time, the tone in the social room turned somber. Cecil, Cordy, Jayne, Millie, Layla May, and a sleepy Richard attended. Julia and Charlotte were absent. The group missed Joe and Hanni. Jayne's dog, Scout, seemed out of sorts and was not eager to settle. Skeeter tried to cheer them up but found it was hard to keep a smile on her face and a light tone to her voice. They shared news of the Nation and discussed the latest political scandals. The discussion turned to books, and Richard bored them with a review of a non-fiction book about plastic trash in the Bermuda Triangle. Cecil tried to one-up him about a Mechanical Engineering article concerning artificial intelligence in breast implants. Nobody believed him. With Cecil, Skeeter decided it was hard to tell if he had read such an article or was having fun with them. That afternoon everyone wanted to end early to take a nap. Skeeter decided it was more that they didn't want to have a good time without Hanni and Joe joining them.

Returning to her office, she remained listless. Although she never knew when it would strike, today was one of those times at work when productivity had vanished. Sneaking by Harry's office, Skeeter left the Center and drove to the Piney Library. A lovely building along the Eagle River, the Piney Library was a mix of glass and wood with generous windows facing the sloping lawn to the river. Big comfy chairs circled a fireplace and expansive windows. Today sunlight filtered through the trees in spears of light to hit the river. Skeeter had to forgo the setting and head downstairs to the lower level. She found Lori in the media room and broke the news to her that both Hanni and Joe were in the rehab facility with a poor prognosis.

Swinging around to face her computer, Lori said, "I'm sorry to hear this." She pointed to the screen. "I picked up the memory chip from Richard this morning. I was uploading the photographs from the Netherlands."

Skeeter glanced over Lori's shoulder. The large computer monitor was bright and filled with rows of tulip blossoms. In the foreground, the sky went from dark to light blue. Tulip colors ranging from red to pink or orange to purple to black to mottled burst in front of her. The photos were stunningly clear. She could see drops of moisture on the buds. "Oh my," she commented.

Lori scrolled through several other photographs but came back to the one she had first shown Skeeter. "I think it's the best one. I sent a copy of it to Pastor Stan."

"How do we put Hanni in the picture?"

Lori drummed her fingers on the tabletop. "I think with Hanni now in a rehab room, we will have to come up with a new plan. I'm not sure what it will be, but it has to be surprising and something which shows off the vividness of the tulips."

If they could not send Hanni to rows of tulips with earthy soil under her feet, perhaps this field of tulips would be enough to put her there in her mind. "I need to talk to Stan. Hopefully, he has progressed with Hanni's children."

Lori sat back. "Okay. Do that." She whirled around and pointed to another table with some strange equipment on it. "I've found a program for our virtual reality system. We can put Jayne at the beach with frothy white waves coming up and curling around her toes. "

"Except she'll be standing on the floor."

Lori let her glasses slide down her nose, and she glanced over them at Skeeter. "Ah, no. We'll bring in a kiddie pool, add some bags of sand, and put in five inches of water. She is going to think she is at the beach."

She will know in a heartbeat that she is not at the ocean. "I'd like to figure out how to take her to a real beach."

Lori shrugged. "That's a tough one. She doesn't have a family."

Skeeter sighed. "Maybe we'll have to accept virtual reality for her."

"Same with Cordy. I have a hot-air balloon program. It's shot in Monument Valley and the balloon rises against red rock towers and sails over the desert. Gad, it is breathtaking."

"You make it sound so simple."

"It's a type of magic. Pictures are magic. People disappear when they die and eventually, all memory of them ceases, but through technology, we can rediscover them. A picture can return us to them and their moods. Most of all, a picture of a loved one can comfort us, and by the miracle of photography, our loved ones are preserved forever. Yes, we have to accept Hanni and Joe will not be with us for much longer, we can keep them close to us through pictures, and we can give them the gift of wishes through technology. It is magic."

Skeeter swallowed to ease a lump in her throat. "If I bring my grandmother to the library, can you do some magic for me? Maybe a picture of her with all those tulips?"

Lori said, "Sure."

"What about Joe? How do we bring Mary to him?"

Lori frowned. "That's a tough question."

The room grew quiet. Skeeter thought about all the hack jobs she had done and felt a morsel of guilt, something she had never felt previously. As hard as she thought, she couldn't come up with a way, by magic, pictures, or hacking to bring Mary to Joe.

Somehow, they had to find an answer.

CHAPTER 19

Stan's first day back at the Piney Center was met by the news that Hanni and Joe were in the rehab facility and not in assisted living. He hustled to both of their rooms, got updates from the nurses, sat with Hanni who was weak and only managed a short visit, and then spent time with Joe, who was on a long road to recovery and had not lost his sense of humor.

Despite having an oxygen tube in his nose, Joe made the sound of a race car engine, then said, "My doctor says I'm going to need a walker. Dang! I'm going to have to join Richard and Cecil with the box-car-walker brigade race series."

"I imagine you'll find a way to speed."

Joe looked over Stan's shoulder toward the door. "I'm waiting for Mary. She's a little late today."

Joe's awareness was clear on any subject except Mary. Stan didn't want to remind Joe that Mary had died but also didn't want to perpetuate the delusion that Mary would arrive today. Standing, Stan said, "I'll check in with you again. Mind the nurses, Joe. I have some calls to make. I'm also going to visit Richard. I'll tell him to grease his walker wheels."

Joe waved Stan silent and said, "I'll still beat him."

Stan left Joe, saying a silent prayer, asking God to heal him and allow Joe to challenge Richard and Cecil with his new walker. Only twenty-five percent of people with hip fractures would experience a full recovery and return to a semblance of their pre-fall life. The odds of someone aged 97 doing that were slim. Joe had a pasty look to his skin and the oxygen monitor flashed, indicating he was not getting enough. Worry lines creased Stan's brow, and he hated to leave Joe. However, he knew rest was the best medicine for Joe.

In Skeeter's office, Stan went over with her all that transpired in Utrecht and Amsterdam. Time was of the essence for Hanni to have her family together. He checked his watch. "I need to call Finn to see how he feels about coming to visit his mother and reconnecting with his siblings."

"You call Finn and I'll go see Hanni and Joe. I want to check on something with Harry, too."

Stan sat back in his chair, took out his cell phone, and dialed Finn. It felt strange to know the call traveled halfway around the world. Finn answered on the fourth ring. They made small talk, and then he told Finn about his mother's stroke. After that, he asked, "How are you progressing with prayer?"

Finn breathed heavily into the phone. "I feel like such a hypocrite. Nothing is happening. I'm afraid I'll let you down, and I won't be able to see mom. I'm frustrated."

Stan could hear the despair in his voice. "Finn," Stan said gently, "this isn't surprising. When people start to pray, they feel God isn't listening. The key is to persevere. God in his wisdom seemingly delays his response to our prayers. You've been at this for only a week. Trust me, you must persevere with prayer."

Finn snarled. "What kind of a Heavenly Father is God to make someone wait when they pray?"

Stan winced at the anger and sarcasm in his voice. *Ouch,* Stan thought to himself, *that hurts.* "Because of reasons we may not understand, God knows what he is doing and the delays are necessary. When God is working on things behind the scenes that we know nothing about, we can't judge when the time is right for the prayer to be answered. At times, God delays His answer to deepen our desire for his best answer, rather than His quickest answer."

"I guess it's true for a lot of things in life," Finn admitted, his voice now gentle.

"God may delay a quick answer to give a better answer. Let's not give up, let's persevere and see what He may have in store for us."

Finn didn't answer right away. Stan could tell Finn thought hard. "Okay," he replied. "I'll give it a little more time, but God better not delay much longer or I'm going to throw in the towel."

Stan gently replied, "I do understand."

Finn sighed; his point of view had been heard. "I'm glad you see how troubling this is for me."

"I do," Stan continued. "I have been a pastor for thirty years. I've prayed for you. I know God is already working behind the scenes, and I am going to talk with your brothers today. I hope to get them to agree to a reconciliation."

Stan ended the call. He checked his watch. It wasn't eleven a.m., and he was already tired. However, he needed to talk to Sven and Jon. He reached Sven right away. He was the second oldest brother and lived in the Avon area, which was between Piney and the Vail ski area. When Stan introduced himself, Sven sounded cool but became interested when Stan told him he had recently returned from the Netherlands and had gone to Utrecht to see Finn.

"Ha! I haven't talked to my brother in years. He ended communication with me and my brother a few years ago. He thought we cheated him."

"Hanni told me." Stan softened his voice and was careful with each word. "Hanni is failing, Sven."

"I know about her stroke. Harry called me."

"Before she dies, she wants her boys together. Here in Colorado. Soon."

"Finn won't come. He hates us. He thinks we stole his inheritance."

Stan closed his eyes, "He is working through his animosity and differences with you and Jon so he can come to Colorado and see Hanni." He didn't wait for a reply and continued, "He wants to let bygones be bygones."

Sven snorted, "Good luck with that."

Stan crossed one ankle over the other, nervously bouncing the top foot. "This animosity between you boys," he said quietly, "it's a wound which won't heal, not unless all three of you mend it. If you would let me, I would like to help you make peace so you can be with Hanni."

"I don't know how it would be possible."

Stan said, "If you have a festering wound, do you forget about it? This wound in Finn's heart has not healed, and I don't think it has begun to mend for you or Jon either. If you let me, I'd like to help the three of you."

"I don't believe it's possible," he said curtly. "My brother and I will probably never see one another again. Speaking for myself, I don't trust Finn."

"Why is that?" Stan tapped his fingers on the tabletop. "He said you and Jon disposed of the family property in Vail without consulting him. He feels you are the perpetrators and he is the victim." Out on a limb here, Stan felt he needed to take the chance of airing the disagreement between brothers.

Sven said, "That's his side of the story, but I have mine."

Stan said, "Tell me your side of the story? Help me to understand? My objective is to fulfill your mother's wish to have her children around her and to heal the pain you and your brothers share."

Sven said, "Dad loved his property. He bought it long before Vail became a huge resort. For college, Finn followed his roots to the Netherlands and he stayed. Jon and I made our life in the United States. Jon took a job in Chicago. Mom and Dad retired to Arizona. The house in Vail was too big for me, so we rented it, and I managed it. Jon was able to help with decisions, but I had to handle all the details about the house, especially after Dad's health began to fail. After Dad died, Mom moved into the house and that ended the rental income. For many years, things were fine until Mom could no longer take care of herself. So, the only solution was to move her to assisted living and rent the house again. Great. However, the house was now over forty years old and needed repairs. I wrote to Finn, asking him to help financially with Mom's care. He said he couldn't help us. He thought the rent should cover her living expenses. It didn't. Taxes and repairs ate up most of the income. Her care ran between six to eight thousand dollars per month. No way could Jon and I handle the expense. So, we had to sell the property. We had to prepare the house for sale and had to put money into a new driveway, fix the roof, and replace most of the windows. It cost a lot. The property finally sold. We put most of the money in a trust for mom. Jon took a share and we sent what we thought was fair to Finn, considering he has done nothing over the years. I admit; it wasn't much. After the Piney Center was built, we were able to move Mom there. All these years, Finn left Mom's care on our shoulders. I don't trust him to help with Mom."

Stan rubbed his temple. "I'm beginning to see how this looks from both sides. I think the solution is the same for you and Jon as it is for Finn. There has to be forgiveness and an agreement on what is a fair disposition of the money."

Sven asked, "How would you go about it? Finn is stubborn. I don't think any of us know how to begin to make it right."

Stan nodded, "I am a man of faith. I believe where there is a will, there is a way, and God can show us the way."

"I'd like to be over the resentment I've had for Finn and I do want to grant Mom's wish in her last days. I'd like to have peace between the three of us. We are brothers, after all. We had good times growing up."

Stan said, "I was happy to meet with Finn while I was in Hanni's hometown. We found her tulip fields. With the help of technology, we are going to put Hanni among those tulips." He sighed. "Finn wants healing and reconciliation. I think he has started on his journey. I left him with an article about Marietta Jaegger. The article tells the story of a woman who forgives when it looks impossible. I'll send you a copy via e-mail We can learn from her. I'd appreciate it if you would forward the article to Jon. Then all of us will be on the same page."

"I'll read it, and send it on to Jon. No promises, though. Did you see Hanni today? Is she doing okay? I plan on seeing her soon."

Stan wondered what his definition of 'soon' was, but he wouldn't press. "Hanni is doing as expected. She looks comfortable and is in no pain. She is surrounded by caregivers who do care."

"That's great. I always thought she was a fighter."

If you only knew, Stan thought. "It was good talking to you, Sven. Take care."

After he ended the call, Stan phoned Jon in Denver and went through the same dialog as he had done with Sven. The result remained the same. Stan ended the call and leaned his head back.

He had both of the boy's e-mail addresses and sent both a quick e-mail with the Jaegger article attached.

Skeeter swung into the office, looking a lot fresher and brighter than she felt. "Hanni is better today, and Joe is remarkable. He can barely move his toes, much less get up and walk, but he is already talking about what model of walker he wants." She poked Stan's arm. "It's lunchtime. Cordy and Cecil and Layla May and Jayne and Millie are together in the dining area. I saw Richard shuffling down the hall. They want to hear about the tulip fields."

Pushing himself to his feet, Stan said, "What smells so good?"

"Larry cooked lasagna for lunch. Oh, and don't ask Cordy why she has a piece of strange material on her head."

He tossed his hands in the air. "Okay, but I doubt my day could get any stranger."

Skeeter peeked out of her office and saw Julia, Charlotte, and Bear ambling inside from the parking lot. She smiled, "Trust me. It can."

***

After lunch, Skeeter and Stan worked in their office. Stan worked on correcting lyrics in Cecil's music book and Skeeter updated the resident information files. As she scanned the names and worked on their files, her mind drifted to the details of health problems, successes, and failures of the aged people she had come to care about in the Piney Center. As she entered the information, she learned who paid how much per month. The prices varied depending on the type of care, with those in the memory unit paying the most per month. The amount shocked her. As she thought about her grandmother, her pulse thudded in her temples.

Skeeter had not planned on living in Colorado with her; the idea had been for her to help Beth with the transition to becoming a widow, but now Skeeter was faced with the realization that plans had to be made, changes would come, Beth would not be able to live on her own in the future. *How to pay for it? Will I have to use my savings to fund her care?*

For the first time, the idea turned frightening. She shoved the thought away and went back to the files in front of her. Cordy's file was next. Cordy had followed her heart's dream of ballooning and traveling around the world. She had chosen a professional life as a balloon pilot over a strong family unit. She had kept herself afloat with her dreams. Her adult children were now adrift. Skeeter smiled to herself as she hummed the 60s song by the Fifth Dimension, 'Up, Up and Away, in my beautiful balloon.' It should be Cordy's theme song. Layla May also had been a butterfly, but she had missed out on having children. The files with Cordy and Layla May's lives felt lightweight, Skeeter thought. She didn't want to end up old and infirm, living in assisted care, while her family lived thousands of miles away and who she rarely saw. Jayne's file was next. She was an inspiration. After having lost her eyesight in her twenties, she had overcome depression and anger and now lived a productive life. Skeeter asked herself, *Would I have the strength to do what Jayne has done?*

Tapping Jayne's file, Skeeter thought this was one woman who deserved to have her end-of-life wish fulfilled. *She needs to put her feet in the ocean and smell the salt air.* Somehow, she and Stan would figure out how to let Jayne experience waves on her feet, sand in her toes, even though Skeeter had no idea how they could do it.

One by one she worked on each resident's file. Their data created a detailed landscape of their lives. Her mind cataloged her grandmother's long life. Beth had a big heart but was perhaps a little too naive. She had given her heart to many men, too much wine and song, not enough savings for her future, and now dementia had begun to ravage her mind. *Grandma. You are an inspiration*

*but I don't want to end up with my world so confusing that I don't
know how to care for myself.*

How can I avoid being broke? She couldn't answer the
question. Mixed emotions filled her mind, a befuddling mixture of
love and irritation.

She turned to Stan at his desk, "Stan," she said as she waved
the files at him, "how can I avoid the mistakes these seniors have
made? Their lives are outlined in these files. What will I have on
my file when I'm their age? Notes in a file? A spreadsheet of how
much money it takes to live? A 'do not resuscitate clause'? A log
of who comes to visit me? Being alone? How can I make correct
choices for the rest of my life?" She piled the files next to her
computer.

Stan looked up from the lyric sheets, "You've already started."

"How?" she asked arching her eyebrows.

"Because asking these kinds of questions is the starting place.
Do you want me to give you the latest scientific research shared
with us at the Amsterdam Conference on aging or give you Biblical
wisdom?"

Skeeter hesitated only briefly. She admitted, "I can Google any
of the latest scientific data, and I can listen to the recordings of the
conference speakers online, but I wouldn't know where to start to
gain a Biblical perspective."

The corners of his lips lifted, satisfied that Skeeter had enough
intelligence and curiosity to ask questions. "I like that you are
asking for Biblical answers. Let me start with your knowledge of
the scriptures," Stan told her. "The reverence for the Lord is the
beginning of wisdom we need for skillful living. Honoring God
helps us make better choices and avoid pitfalls in life. It will help
us reach the end of life prepared and at peace."

Skeeter didn't reply. It sounded generic but gave her no sound principles. She stood as Stan closed his computer and slipped on his jacket.

As they locked the office door to leave for the night, Stan said, "Why don't you read the Bible books of Ecclesiastes and Proverbs? They are among the books of the Bible known as the wisdom literature. If you read approximately one chapter per night, it will take you through the next forty-five days. You'll begin to gain some time-spanning biblical perspectives and values which can serve as the foundation for your decision-making."

Skeeter said, "Okay, I know it can't hurt."

They waved to Charmaine as they passed her desk. Skeeter glanced down the hall to where Hanni and Joe's rooms were. Pastor Stan remained silent, and words stuck in Skeeter's throat; she didn't want to share what was on both of their minds.

Skeeter slipped into her car, wondering what she would find at home with her grandmother, and Stan got into his car, deciding life traveled a wandering path, one bringing new people to him, also taking people away.

As he drove away from the Piney Center, Stan prayed, "Father, thank you for bringing this beautiful young lady into our lives. Guide her as she seeks wisdom for the many years of life that lie ahead of her." Then, he smiled to himself and thought, *Oh, I forgot to ask her if she had anything to do with our seats in Business Class?*

CHAPTER 20

On Wednesday, Skeeter was happy to be home. Then she realized that she had mentally called Roger's house, 'home'. For the time being it was home, she admitted to herself. Going in through the garage and passing between Roger's trendy BMW Coupe and an older model Jeep Grand Cherokee he had kept in excellent shape, she went inside.

It hit her; the smell of smoke and burning hair. *She's done it again!*

In the kitchen, she saw her grandmother waving her arms.

Once Beth saw Skeeter, she stopped fluttering her hands.

Skeeter glared at Beth. The time had come to take firmer actions. "Grandma!" She swiped the pack of cigarettes off the counter. "That's it. These are going in a dumpster far from here." She stood in front of Beth with her hands on her hips. Beth's bangs were singed and her eyebrows, too. "Where's the lighter?"

Beth waved the last wisp of smoke from her face. She smashed the cigarette in the sink and ran water over it until it was soggy. "I put it someplace."

"Put the cigarette in the trash." Skeeter pointed to her grandmother's hair. "You need a new hairdresser right away." She looked around the kitchen for the lighter. "Where is it?"

After tossing the cigarette, Beth looked confused. "It was here a minute ago."

Skeeter checked the counter and then saw the barbecue lighter sticking out of Beth's purse. She took it. "This is going in the trash, too."

Her cell phone rang. She grabbed her phone. She wasn't sure she recognized the number but answered. It was George, Roger's son. George told Skeeter that he and his sister would arrive in Colorado over the weekend to go through their father's belongings. They would remain for a few days. Frustrated with her grandmother, and with no idea how this should be handled, Skeeter mumbled something and mentally put Roger's children's arrival on her calendar.

As soon as she hung up, her cell phone chimed again. She hit 'accept' and snapped, "What?"

Doctor Dreyfus said, "Is this a bad time? I have the test results with Beth and would like you to see me to discuss these with me."

She felt bad for snapping and glanced at her grandmother who was pulling strands of her burned bangs down on her forehead as if she could hide the frizzled ends. Moving to the patio door, she told herself to calm down and said, "Yes, I can do that. When?"

"I have time this afternoon. How about in an hour?"

After agreeing to meet him, she ended the call. She had thought her day was finished but it was far from over, and now on top of everything else, Roger's children would be coming for the weekend. She realized she didn't ask if they planned on staying at the house or a hotel. Glancing back at Beth, the anger dissolved. Despite what was happening to Beth, Skeeter loved her. It was not

Beth's fault she had something going on with her memory. "Gram, who is your hairdresser?"

Beth nibbled on her lower lip. "Sandy some-one-or-other. She brings her dog with her to work."

"Sounds fun. Where does she work?"

Beth took some herb cream cheese from the refrigerator, put it on a plate, and added crackers and a knife. "Oh, the place on Third Street, next to the place that smells really good."

"The flower store?"

Beth smiled. "Yeah, that one."

Moving to Beth, Skeeter ran her fingers through the ends of her grandmother's burned hair. "It's not too bad. I think a new cut and highlights to bring out the silver in the gray would be fun."

Beth smiled. "That'll shock Bruce." She spread cheese on a cracker and handed it to her granddaughter.

Skeeter let go of her anger. "Yep, and Roger's kids are coming this weekend to decide what they want of his belongings."

"A party. Lovely."

Skeeter nodded, grabbed her purse, and put her arm around her grandmother for a hug. "I've got to run a few errands. I'll make a hair appointment for you. I'll stop at the store for something for dinner." *It won't be tacos.*

Beth padded to the pantry and found a bottle of sparkling water. "It's lovely outside. I have a new gardening magazine I want to read." She picked up the plate with the cheese and crackers. "I'll see you when you get home."

Skeeter squeezed her grandmother's shoulders and headed for the car, wishing every day would end on a good note like this one.

Forty minutes later, Skeeter was seated in the doctor's office. Doctor Dreyfus sat behind his desk with a medical file open in front of him. She nervously tapped the heel of her right shoe on the floor. The sound calmed her nerves but she knew it was annoying.

Doctor Dreyfus, looking professional in a white coat with his name monogrammed over the breast pocket, began, "I have done a neurological exam on your grandmother. This evaluates her for problems that may signal brain disorders."

Skeeter inhaled sharply. "Oh, no."

Dreyfus glanced over his glasses resting on his nose. He put a hand on her bouncing knee. "Take a deep breath. Don't let the term scare you." He continued, "During the exam, I checked for signs of small or large strokes, Parkinson's disease, brain tumors, fluid accumulation on the brain, and other diseases which may impair memory. I found none."

Skeeter's heart thudded against the walls of her chest. "I see."

He went on, "Next, I administered The Mini-Mental State Examination or Folstein test, a thirty-point questionnaire that is used extensively in clinical and research settings to measure cognitive impairment. Your grandmother scored a twenty-five, which is mild impairment."

Skeeter wasn't sure if she felt good or bad about the score. "What does it mean for Beth?"

He closed her file without answering Skeeter's question. "I can schedule an MRI of her brain to detect for other disorders if you would like, but it could be upsetting for Beth, and the tests that I have done give ninety-percent accuracy." He paused. In a gentle voice, he told Skeeter, "She has early Alzheimer's disease. She may have clinically significant but mild deficits, likely to affect only the most demanding activities of daily living. That's the good news. The bad news is that the average score for a person with Alzheimer's disease declines two to four points each year."

Skeeter had to swallow a dry lump in her throat. She felt pressure on her chest and wanted to breathe fresh air. When she stood, she wasn't sure she could speak. "Thank you," she managed as her chin trembled. "Is there any medication she should be taking?"

He handed her a prescription. "Although there is no cure, this medication has proven successful with slowing the progression of the disease. Also, if you find she is easily upset, I can order a mild anti-anxiety medication."

Skeeter slipped the prescription in her purse. "Not much upsets her."

"I'm glad to hear it. As her physician, I believe it is a right for my patients to be informed of their condition. However, it has been my finding not to inform patients if they have confirmed dementia. Most physicians feel the same way. For example, most geriatric doctors believe the information would be too traumatic or confusing for certain patients. At this point in Beth's journey, I don't think she would fully accept the diagnosis, and it would be perplexing for her and difficult for you. Right now, you are Beth's only caregiver, and for her health as well as yours, I believe withholding her diagnosis is beneficial for both of you." He looked up from the file on his desk. "I will, however, tell her in broad terms about her memory loss if you want me to do so."

Skeeter's mind whirled. So, he had dumped the decision of telling her grandmother that she had Alzheimer's disease. Would Beth be impacted when receiving the news of her diagnosis because she was at a stage of the disease that left her too forgetful to retain it or unable to understand it? Would that do her any good? Or if Beth were capable of understanding, would it be best for the doctor to present the information? She envisioned Beth hearing the news, saw the confusion in her grandmother's eyes, wondered how many questions she would ask and what she wouldn't remember. Would she stay angry at Skeeter after being informed? She lowered her head, shaking it. "For now, I don't want you to tell my grandmother."

He nodded. "All right. We'll leave it this way for now. Let me know if you change your mind. I'd like to see her again in six months."

Six months. Where will I be? Where will she live? How is this going to work? Am I her caregiver? Is this my responsibility? How did this happen? In the past half hour, my entire world has changed.

On her way home, she questioned who she could call. She needed to vent, needed to calm down, needed to hear a sane voice. She thought about her mother, or a friend, Steve, or a co-worker. She hit speed dial on her phone and after the third ring, Pastor Stan answered.

She reviewed what the doctor had told her.

He made a few comments but let her complain about how this wasn't fair, this wasn't her life, and the decisions should not be on her shoulders.

Pastor Stan agreed with everything she said. Then he added, "Talking about it helps. So is finding online support and articles, joining online conversations, and getting counseling for yourself. It can help get you through these times. Talking about the guilt of feeling trapped is helpful. Putting into words how you feel - without shame or guilt - can substantially lower stress levels."

"What do I do about right now? I never thought I would be here permanently or even for a few months. Damn! I can't believe this is happening to me."

"Skeeter, you aren't alone although it appears that way. You also have to trust that God will be with you through this. Take some deep breaths. Let your mind settle. Think about what you need to know to help Beth. To begin with, you'll need to figure out how much money Beth has at her disposal for, say, the next ten years. Then figure out a primary caregiver, you or someone hired, or a facility such as Piney Center. Perhaps reach out to your mother and ask her to help her mother?"

Skeeter squeezed her eyes shut for a second. She couldn't imagine her mother giving up her life or interrupt her busy schedule to do this for her family. "No, my mom was never the nurturing type."

"How about your grandfather? I've known estranged spouses who have become caregivers."

"He has been deceased for many years."

"Siblings?"

"None."

"I'm sorry. Take it one day at a time right now. Have faith."

"Thanks. On top of this, I received a call from George. He and his sister will arrive this weekend to decide what they want from their father's stuff."

Stan added, "On top of that, Harry talked to Hanni's doctor this afternoon, and he called me into his office. Hanni is fading. We need to hurry up with her last wishes."

Skeeter groaned. "I'll hit the library tomorrow to see Lori."

"I'll join you. I'm going to call Finn and his brothers. I'm going to tell them they need to see their mother. Now."

"Talk about stress,"

"Yes. I need to pray hard."

***

Thursday morning, Skeeter and Pastor Stan arrived at the library. Outside the library windows, new leaves had budded on the aspen and cottonwood trees. Robins picked worms from the sloping lawn. People walked along a recreation path next to the library, enjoying the sunshine. Spring was in the air.

Pastor Stan and Skeeter found Lori in her office, and she greeted them and chatted about all the events the library had planned for the off-season time in the ski resort. Then they headed downstairs to the media center.

Lori flicked on the lights. In front of them, stretching at least twelve feet long and eight feet tall was a sheet of canvas. It was white and blank. "Ta, da," she said, outstretching her arms to the fabric.

Pastor Stan and Skeeter stared at nothing. "I see a blank sheet of something," Stan said without emotion.

Lori smiled. "Right. But watch." She moved to a projector at the rear of the room. When she turned it on, they heard a whirring sound that quieted after a few seconds. "Ready?"

She turned off the lights, plunging the room into darkness. Suddenly, a field of tulips appeared on the canvas, brilliant rows of every color tulip imaginable- reds, pinks, yellows, oranges, so clear and perfect, it felt as though a person could reach out and touch each petal.

The natural reaction caused Skeeter to inhale, expecting to smell fertile dirt and expectant flowers. She had to tell herself to exhale. Pastor Stan mumbled.

Lori said, "That's Hanni's field in Holland. Now we'll bring her here. I'm thinking about next week. We will let her stand in front of the canvas. She's going to feel immersed in tulips."

Pastor Stan rubbed the back of his neck. "We may have a problem. Hanni had a stroke. She's failing and she's probably not going to be able to leave the Piney Center."

Lori didn't comment.

"We're so close to making her wishes come true," Skeeter said as she wrapped a strand of blond hair behind her ear.

Standing in front of the tulip canvas. Lori put her hands on her hips. "Damn and double damn. This shouldn't be happening to Hanni or us." Tulips blossomed on her torso, mingling with colors on a blue-striped shirt.

"All this for Hanni," Skeeter whispered. "We have to make it happen."

Lori opened her arms as if to embrace the tulips. "I had this built for Hanni to come here. I envisioned how perfect it would be; she would be wrapped in tulips. That's a lot of canvas. I borrowed the uprights from the high school volleyball team to hold it up. Now I'm not sure what to do."

Pastor Stan said, "If I can get Finn on a plane to come here, plus his brothers, then Hanni's field of tulips are going to go to her room at the rehab facility."

Neither Lori nor Skeeter argued. Pastor Stan had an inside edge with God, and in this case, he would use it.

***

Skeeter left Pastor Stan in their office while he called Finn and the other brothers. First, she went to visit Hanni in the rehab facility. The halls were quiet, and she found herself almost tiptoeing into Hanni's room. The curtains were partially closed, only allowing a little sunshine. Lights were dim. Hanni reclined in a semi-sitting position with a cup and straw on the rolling bed table along with an uneaten package of Graham Crackers. An oxygen tube went from a wall supply to her nose. It looked crooked. The whoosh, whoosh noise of oxygen passing through the tube was the only sound Skeeter heard. An aqua hospital gown had slipped down on one of Hanni's bony shoulders. Today, her face was the color of fine china. Skeeter adjusted the cannula so it was comfortable.

She wished Hanni would vent about the German officer who had stolen her childhood and her dreams. She wanted Hanni to open her eyes and spit venom. Seeing her so still and fighting for each breath made Skeeter wipe tears from her cheeks. She mumbled swear words, thinking Finn should be here, as should Sven and Jon. Reaching for her hand, Skeeter covered Hanni's with her own. She massaged her fingers and the palm of her hand, bringing more warmth to her skin. "Hanni," she whispered.

Transparent eyelids fluttered open. Blinking, Hanni turned her head toward Skeeter. "Hello, dear," she said, her voice weak.

"I'm glad to see you," Skeeter answered.

"Yeah, and look at me. I always knew I would get old, but it's surprising how fast it happened."

Skeeter swiped moisture off her cheek. "I think I can find a better nightgown for you to wear than this hospital one. It may help."

Hanni looked away, toward the window. "I'm ready, Skeeter. I know it's going to be good. I want to go, but I need those boys with me."

Skeeter squeezed Hanni's hand. "Pastor Stan is working on it."

"Tell him to hurry up." She closed her eyes and lay still.

From Hanni's room, Skeeter went to Joe's room. Sleeping, he looked calm and had color in his cheeks. On his bedside table, he had a picture of himself with Mary. She could see that the glass over the picture was marred with fingerprints. Not wanting to wake him, she quietly backed out of the room.

She needed something to cheer her up, so she headed into the assisted living wing and found Cecil shuffling down the hall. She waved, "Hi Cecil!"

"Hello, sweetheart!" The tennis balls on his walker caught on the carpet. He had to jerk it to get it to move forward. "I'm as smooth as always! Ready to visit with a cute little thing like you."

"Do you want coffee?"

"Sure, as long as you can find something to go along with it."

"I think I can," she said and felt better than she had in hours. Cecil could make others happy. He'd had a terrible misfortune with his accident, but he continued with life and made others feel good. She felt privileged to call him 'friend' and was damn proud of his misbehaving at the King's Club. "Be back in a flash," she said and disappeared into the kitchen.

Cecil yelled after her, "Whatever you find, make sure it's chocolate!"

***

On a warm afternoon, Skeeter sat out on the patio by herself. After a full day at the Piney Center, sitting quietly and hearing the birds' twitter, left her relaxed. She closed her eyes for a moment, listening to the sound of the creek as it grew in proportion to high country snowmelt. Her phone chirped. She answered and heard Bart's voice, although the communication was sketchy. He said he was on his way to town and wanted to meet her for a casual dinner.

A note on the counter had been from her grandmother who said she was going with Bruce to a presentation at the library. Skeeter agreed to meet Bart and ended the call. Inhaling deeply, she leaned her head back and looked at the fluffy clouds sailing overhead. She thought about Bart and how easy it was to be with him, and she momentarily compared him to Steve, the guy she was dating in San Francisco. *Two guys couldn't be more different.*

The thought made her smile, and her heart began to pound a little harder against the walls of her chest. Whatever it was between her and Bart had been there from the first moment they met. People who are attracted to each other had their way of communication. It's not something they intentionally did, she decided; it's them sharing something they can't share with others, and they had shared an immediate reaction between the chemistry of their bodies. They couldn't hide it, and when they were together the surrounding energy seemed to zing off millions of atoms. She could still remember the feel of his hand holding hers, a tingling sensation that warmed her entire body. At the ranch after the engagement party, he had lightly kissed her good night, and he might as well have given her a deep kiss because rockets went off. She guessed the saying was true; opposites did attract.

As much as she was excited to see him again, she had to protect her heart and not let this develop into a doomed relationship. Skeeter wasn't good at committing herself to a man. She didn't know herself well enough to allow a man into her heart. In high school, she'd been too smart for boys to pay attention to her, and in college, she hadn't learned how to successfully flirt and tease. Uncomfortable around good-looking guys who ogled her, she preferred impersonal relationships in chat rooms with her computer buddies. When she had given her heart away the first time, the guy had decided he wasn't ready for a serious relationship. It stung, and she was humiliated and embarrassed. On the next try, she decided to be proactive and not allow that person close enough to leave her heart bruised. It was like hitting first in a school fight or hacking an account before the other guy. It was the smart thing to do. Although one other guy had bent her heart, she didn't allow him to break it. It had been the pattern of her survival up until this point.

Besides, Skeeter was in Piney on a short-term basis. She did not need to complicate matters by a handsome guy with slim hips and manure-encrusted boots.

Tossing her work outfit on the bed, she pawed through the clothes she had brought to Colorado and chose a loose-necked aqua blue short-sleeved shirt and pair of high-waisted black pants. She added closed-toed sandals and a pair of dangling earrings. She washed and blow-dried her hair, running her fingers through it to give it enough fluff. She added a dab of mascara and frosted deep-pink lipstick. As she went out the door, she tossed a short leather jacket over her arm. She guessed her outfit was about right to meet a cowboy after he got out of his truck and sauntered into a hamburger joint.

When she walked into the restaurant, she spotted him at once. Leaning against the bar with one ankle over the other, he seemed to have gold sparklers shooting from his boots. The air around him appeared energized with an aura of neon particles. He stood there, devilishly handsome, turned, and smiled when he saw her. Her heart skipped a beat. After he pointed to a table by a window, she nodded, and he carried two frothy glasses of beer to the table.

She felt awkward, which was a strange feeling for her.

He put the glasses of beer down and held a chair for her. "Good to see you."

Sitting, she ran her hands through her hair, then tossed it back over her shoulder. It was a flirty and nervous flick of her hand and she had not intended to do it. "You too."

The evening lapsed into easy chatter. Somehow a waitress took their order and Skeeter noted the way the woman stared at Bart a little too long. Hamburgers and French fries appeared and then were eaten. After the last dollop of catsup was scooped by a French fry, Bart said, "I want to bring Misty over for Millie to ride the first part of the week."

Skeeter let a mental spreadsheet run in front of her eyes. Hanni's family might be in town. George and Melissa could still be here. Hanni was going downhill. She didn't know if she should tell Harry about Millie riding Misty. "Ah, sure. Perhaps Tuesday is better than Monday or Wednesday or Thursday. Can we confirm on Monday? Hanni is declining and I am not sure how I can handle it if…if she leaves us."

Bart touched Skeeter's hand. It was only a tap but it was enough to convey his feelings. He finished the last of his beer. "Okay." He clicked on his cell phone. "Looks like the weather should be good on Tuesday."

She asked, "Are you sure the lift in the truck is going to work? Millie is under my supervision when I am with her at the Center. I can't have her injured."

He covered her hands with his. "Yep. I got this, and she is my grandma. I know what she can do with a horse, and I wouldn't want anything to happen to her, either."

Skeeter nodded. "Things happen. Look at what Cecil did at the nightclub."

Bart laughed, his lips forming a smile that carried a little mischief. "I remember. Lucky for us, Millie doesn't play the guitar."

CHAPTER 21

Pastor Stan sat in the Piney Center office with his cell phone pressed to his ear and the fingers on his free hand rubbing his temple. Skeeter sat in her chair with the computer screen open to Skype. Stan and Skeeter both heard Harry's voice in the hallway. Stan lowered his phone. Skeeter turned off the computer monitor screen.

Harry stopped in the doorway to their office. Skeeter and Stan turned to their boss.

"What's up with you two?" Harry rested one hand on his hip. "You look like you're planning another music night at the King's Club. I hope not. It's quiet today, and I want to keep it that way. No funny business." He looked at both of them as if they were sheep, and he was the wily coyote.

Harry's attitude toward them grated like fingernails on a chalkboard. He had his rules but neither Stan nor Skeeter wanted to see how far they would bend them. Stan managed a smile. Skeeter grabbed a file on Piney Center's list of contributors, a long and boring list. She held the file in her hand. "Work."

Stan said, "Going over the week's events."

Harry flipped errant hair off his forehead. It stayed in place for three seconds. "Make sure you check on Hanni today. She needs visitors, but she's fragile. No music in her room and no excitement."

After a glance at Stan, Skeeter gave Harry her championship smile, the same one she gave math contest judges when she was thirteen. "Will do," she said and waited for Harry to leave.

Harry shrugged. "Then, carry on." Turning, he headed for his office.

"At times I think he has the sensitivity of a speed bump." Skeeter turned on her monitor. The home page for *Skype* came up. She turned to Stan. "You all set for this?"

"I've been on the phone for two days, and praying each day." He checked his watch. "It's four o'clock in the afternoon in Utrecht. We arranged to call right now."

Skeeter turned to her desktop computer. "Okay, give me the numbers. I'm ready."

Stan's fingers shook ever so slightly as he held his phone and pulled up numbers for Finn, Sven, and Jon. He gave the numbers to Skeeter, and her fingers flew over the keyboard. They heard pings and chimes and more pings. The screen fluttered and suddenly Finn appeared. Next, the screen blinked and Sven appeared. After a short pause, Jon showed up, his face in more of a shadow than his brothers. Stan's face was in a small box at the bottom of the computer. He could join the discussion but hoped he wouldn't need to. However, he wasn't sure how the conversation would go.

Finn broke the ice. "Hello, everyone. Unbelievable I am half the world away and I can see you, Sven, and you too, Jon. Both of you look healthy and fit."

Sven commented and so did Jon.

Finn said, "I know our mother is in the twilight days of her life. It's time as brothers we come together and be with her." He paused. The tension on the brothers' faces softened. "We are family and need to remember it, especially now for mom." Finn's eyes watered. "I'm coming to Colorado."

Sven's lips turned upwards at the corners. "It's the best news I've had in years."

Finn paused for another moment and continued, "I truly apologize for my lack of involvement with our family home, and my failure to participate in contributing to Mom's care. I was selfish. All it did was hurt me and you, Sven, and Jon. Worst, I lost valuable time with mom." He let his breath out in a long whoosh and added, "A house is only a house. Money is not important. Mom is important and so are both of you. Will both of you please forgive me? It's what mom wants and what I want."

Jon spoke first, "I need to make it right with you, too. You've been far away and I let distance become an excuse that you didn't care about us. I've harbored resentment, and I know it's only made things worse. Hearing your voice makes me realize what I have missed. I want to rekindle our relationship, not only for mom, but for me, for you, and Sven. You will always be my brother. We need to move forward with no more resentment."

Sven said, "None of us have the market on bad behavior. I, too, should have reached out to you, Finn. I felt a tremendous burden by making the decisions on the house. As I reflect, I could have explained my feelings to you. Instead, I withheld and grew angry. I hope you will understand and forgive me."

Finn began to speak again, his voice trembling. "We need to remember the good times we had at the house growing up, the magical experience of the mountains, playing in the creek, taking hikes, a campfire in the back yard, picking raspberries for mom, overnights under the stars, hiking to remote lakes. Do you remember when we panned for gold and were sure we would find a fortune? All those days Dad had us work on the house; painting the outside, mowing grass, cutting firewood for winter, and winters building snow caves and sledding. Thank you, brothers, for giving me good memories and now understanding. When I think about it this moment, I feel a weight has been lifted from my shoulders, and when I get to Colorado, I don't want anything to stand between us." He inhaled, then slowly exhaled, and said, "I'll be on the plane to Colorado in the morning."

When the call ended, Skeeter felt her eyes water. She didn't look at Stan. She had to move. Getting up, she figured this was a good time to go to the kitchen and find something sweet to eat. If Larry had something with chocolate in it, she'd take two of whatever and hike down the hall to Cecil's room and sit with him for a few minutes and simply enjoy the creamy taste of chocolate in her mouth and the feeling of knowing she and Stan had accomplished something good. Somehow, despite the hard life Cecil had been handed, he was always a comfort and made Skeeter feel better. *Such a gift.*

***

Twenty-four hours later, Finn's plane began its descent through the clouds, circled the DIA runway, and landed in the Mile-High City. As the plane came to a stop and the door opened, Finn could feel the loss of oxygen and the difference in pressure from where he lived. Being from sea level, he couldn't get enough air. He inhaled deeply and took it slow. However, he wanted to exit the plane but disembarking went along at a snail's pace.

Finally, he headed for baggage claim. The concourse was jammed with people going in both directions. He dodged passengers pulling suitcases and looked for the signs to luggage pick up. He wondered if American airports were less efficient than those in the Netherlands. Then he heard an announcement: the bags would be delayed. He groaned. The thin air, slow passengers, and baggage delays caused his pulse to thud in his temples.

He damned himself for being bullheaded, refusing to reconcile with his brothers before this. Closing his eyes, he thought of his mom. He could smell the Dutch apple cake she would bake, recalled how she laughed, remembered the ragged pink slippers she always wore, and how she had raised him and his two brothers. He recalled the few times she spoke about the war in Holland. She had mentioned eating tulips to survive. *Why didn't I listen more? Did I even ask how she survived?* Now it wouldn't be long before his mother was gone. Finally, his suitcase arrived, and he found the local van service that would take him to Piney. Once onboard the van, he glanced at his watch; he had been traveling for twelve hours. Tired, he leaned his head against the window and dozed, barely awake to view Loveland Pass with Eisenhower Tunnel and then Vail Pass. Finally, the van rolled to a stop in the Piney Center parking lot. Finn gave the driver a tip and headed into the building.

Inside, it was quiet and cool. The colors of walls and floors were blah and unimaginative. It smelled of lemon oil and an antiseptic cleaning solution. He signed in at the reception desk with a lady with a name tag that said, Charmaine. As his heart drummed inside his chest, he asked for directions to his mother's room. The receptionist pointed to her right.

Before he reached her room, he spotted Sven. His brother had aged, his hair thinning and gray at the temples. He had put on weight and looked tired, but he raised a hand with a greeting. This was Finn's bothersome brother, the kid who could never do anything right and always was in trouble but came out of it with a grin. Now he looked vulnerable, and it gnawed at Finn's heart. With a wave, he closed the distance to his brother. After a brotherly hug, they smiled and stepped toward their mother's room. Jon, the youngest brother who was good in school, gave him quick hugs and stepped back, so he could move to his mother's bed.

Hanni lay still, her features pale, her breathing shallow. He was surprised at her body, now a shell of what she had been, her face wrinkled, her hands a road map of blue veins on cellophane skin. Her white hair with curls on her forehead had been neatly brushed. Blue lines on pale eyelids made him gasp, shocked to see his strong mother so compromised. As he realized how wrong he had been to hold a grudge and not see his mother in her later years, he sniffed back emotions he didn't want to erupt.

Finn sat in the chair beside her bed and picked up her left hand. It felt limp and was cool to the touch, but not cold. *No, his mother had never been cold.* He held her hand in his. Folding his fingers over hers, he began to talk to her in a quiet voice, a voice he was sure she would recognize. "Mom," he said, "it's Finn. It's your son. I hope you can hear me. I am so happy to be with you."

Gently squeezing her hand, he rubbed her arm. He felt a connection, something deep inside his body. Without looking toward Sven and Jon, he shut his eyes because he didn't want to try to explain it. The only thing he heard was his heartbeat, but he recalled the times their souls smiled together, reached out invisibly, and touched. Opening his eyes, he whispered, "I've missed you, but you have always been in my thoughts, every single day." He held in a chuckle. "You always told me how to be happy, but nothing compares to what I feel now that I am with you, and with Sven and Jon."

She gave no sign that she was aware of Finn holding her hand, much less a sign of recognition that all her boys were together. Her slow, halting, shallow breathing didn't change.

Finn looked to his brothers. They nodded back at him.

Sven said, "She fades in and out of consciousness."

Finn glanced around the room, which had white walls and pale curtains over Venetian blinds. "There should be a big photograph of mother's tulip fields."

Pastor Stan walked into Hanni's room. Finn turned and asked, "Where are mother's tulips?"

Stan ran his hand through his hair. "Yes, the tulips. We have them. Lots of them. A whole room full of them. Just not here."

Finn frowned. "Where are they?"

Stan's shoulders sagged. "At the Piney Library on a big canvas, too big for one person to move."

Finn put his palms up. "Well? Where is the library? What can we do?"

Stan's eyes grew big. "We need Skeeter and Lori for this."

Finn repeated, "Skeeter, Lori?'

Stan waved to Finn, Sven, and Jon. "Let's go. First, we need to find Skeeter."

***

In the afternoon, Melissa and George arrived at the house in a car they had rented at the Denver airport. George was a stocky man with a full head of brown hair with gray at the temples. To Skeeter, he looked like the kind of guy who wouldn't take orders but never needed to; whatever he was supposed to do, he did. It left her worried. Though he had been traveling all day, his attire was crisp. He wore a long-sleeve polo shirt, dark khaki pants, loafers, and an expensive-looking leather belt, and it told her that he knew how to dress and had class. He offered a hand to Skeeter. Taking it, she felt a muscular hand which she guessed had worked with wood and hammers. With an inherent strength in his face, Skeeter got the impression whatever game he played, he was unaccustomed to losing. She tried to see behind his eyes to know if he would sue Beth to get the house. If so, he wasn't giving anything away.

Melissa, younger than George, had curly brown hair with a face that had inherited good genes and created smooth skin with few wrinkles. Casually dressed in jeans, a pale blue tank top, short linen jacket, and a neck scarf, she wore the appropriate makeup for someone her age, and her hair had been recently brushed and had a nice fly-away look to it. Between the two of them, Skeeter guessed George would be harder to deal with.

"I'm happy to see you again," Beth said after her in-laws had moseyed into the den and had a seat. Thankfully Beth had done a nice introduction for Skeeter and now sat with her hands on her thighs, waiting to see how this would play out.

George angled his head to glance into the kitchen, to the outdoor patio and yard, visually inspecting the house. "I wish it were on different circumstances," he said as he cleared his throat. He stared at Roger's desk with its computer and files.

Skeeter said, "You must be tired. It's a long day. Can I get you something to drink? Wine? Soft drink? We have iced tea."

Melissa smiled. "Some iced tea would be nice." With a glance at Beth, she frowned. "Your hair looks burned."

Beth pulled at the frizzled ends of the hair around her face. "I hoped it wouldn't be too noticeable."

"A good haircut will fix it," Melissa said. She looked at the patio. "You have a beautiful view of the river."

George turned to Skeeter. "Dad always had good whiskey. How about a drink on the rocks?"

Beth frowned. "Roger likes his whiskey without ice."

Skeeter nodded to Melissa and George. "Let me get those drinks. It's nice out on the patio this afternoon if you'd like fresh air. We like to take advantage of it; in Colorado, climate can change in a matter of minutes." She felt her knees wobble when she stood; this was way out of her league. She didn't know either of these people except what she hacked and learned about them. It didn't tell the whole story, though, and she had no idea how Beth would converse with them. She wondered if they would demand Beth turn the house over to them or if they would sue, or would they concede Beth should have the house?

She hated the unknown.

While Skeeter got the drinks, she checked her cell phone. Cordy had suffered a fainting spell on Friday and had been moved to the rehab unit for observation. Her doctor said it was due to brain cancer. Skeeter was worried about her and happy to see she had no message updating bad news about her condition. She poured the whiskey into a highball glass with ice when her cell phone chirped. She checked the text.

It was from Bart. It said: "I have your jacket. You left it in the restaurant. I'm going to bring it to the house."

She overfilled the highball glass with whiskey and it splashed on her hand. "Damn," she swore and had to redo the glass. *Look what that guy does to me.*

Bing! Her phone chirped another text. She glared at it, again afraid it was news about Cordy or Hanni. It was from Stan. It simply said: "We're on our way to your house. Stan, Finn, Sven, Jon. Be there in a few minutes."

Taking the glass of whiskey, she turned her back to the patio, gulped booze from the glass, prayed George didn't see her, and squinted as it burned her throat. She delivered the glass to George, plus a glass of iced tea to Melissa, and hoped they couldn't tell her nerves were shot.

George thanked her for the drink, then kicked a loose flagstone on the patio. "You need to redo this courtyard. These stones are uneven."

She appreciated his observation. "I don't know anything about remodeling."

George toed the loose stone. "I'm a contractor. I've done every type of home project imaginable."

The side door opened and someone yelled, "Hello?"

She yelled back, "Whoever it is, come in."

She looked to see a parade: Pastor Stan, Finn, Sven, Jon, and Bart. They walked to the patio and saw two strangers who looked out-of-place in Piney, Colorado. Skeeter's gaze went to Bart. When her world was about to turn upside down, he was the man she wanted next to her. He's the guy who felt shock waves but stayed on his feet. Right now, Skeeter felt as if her world was wobbling. Hastily, she made the introductions, but afterward, she wasn't sure everyone understood who and where they were connected.

Stan decided he had to take charge. He held up his arm in the air as if leading a rousing rendition of "Home on the Range." He announced, "Folks, we have a problem."

Melissa, George, and Beth had a blank look on their faces. Skeeter was aware they knew nothing about tulips and a dying woman. Finn and his siblings traded anxious glances. Stan pointed to Finn and his brothers. "We have a wonderful woman at the Piney Center. She is ready to be with God, but she needs her tulips." He heard murmurs and waved his hands. "It sounds stupid. Not real tulips, anyhow. She's from Holland and her dying wish is to see tulip fields. We have a big, and I mean a giant canvas. We planned to transpose a picture of her tulip fields from Holland to this canvas. She was supposed to sit on a chair, surrounded by flowers. This was to be a final gift for her before she dies. However, she is dying **now**. The canvas is at the library. We need help with moving it to the Piney Center." He paused for emphasis. "Like right now."

Silence fell over the room. Stan's information needed to settle on brains ready for an afternoon of socializing and gazing at spring grass and wild iris and hearing the Eagle River in the distance.

George drained the last of his whiskey. "Let's go," he said without hesitation.

Finn, Sven, and Jon started for the door.

Melissa took Beth by the hand and said, "I've been sitting all day. I'm happy to have something to do."

Skeeter glanced at Bart who shrugged and pointed to the door. "I've got a truck."

Stan punched phone numbers on his phone, "I'll call Lori and tell her we're coming."

Nine people tramped out of the house through the garage, nobody remembering to shut the garage door. No one cared.

Fifteen minutes later, in a hail of chatter among strangers, the group herded themselves into the library and tramped down the stairs to the media room. Lori looked frazzled when they entered, and Skeeter didn't blame her. It was a small room for all her equipment and a large canvas held up at each end by volleyball uprights. The room had a pungent odor common to the new canvas.

As everyone jammed into the room, Lori said, "Don't mind the smell. It's the result of petroleum byproducts that are found in water repellent agents. It fades with time

Now the room was jammed with tired people. Stan asked, "What do you want us to do?"

Lori swiped hair off her cheek and said, "All of this is so sudden. Okay, then. We'll roll up the canvas. Who has a truck?"

With a grin, Bart waved his Stetson at her.

Lori pointed to him. "We'll put the canvas in the truck first. Someone carry the projector. It's already loaded with the correct photograph. We'll put the projector on Hanni's bedside table. Then we need the two volleyball uprights loaded in the truck."

Finn said to his brothers and Bart, "We get the uprights, lads." He pointed to the women. "You ladies handle the canvas." Last, he nodded to George, "Can you bring the projector?"

George nodded. "I got it. I'll put it in my car and bring the women."

With grunts and groans, the uprights, the canvas, the projector, and electrical cords were carried up the stairwell and to Bart's truck. As they loaded, Skeeter nudged Stan. "What are the chances of Harry not letting us do this?"

Stan frowned. "Probably good. He may consider this 'funny business." He pulled out his phone. He dialed the Center. Charmaine answered on the second ring. Stan inquired, "Is Harry in the building?"

The receptionist said, "Yes. We had a new intake in rehab. It was someone Harry knew, so he wanted to be here."

Stan whispered to Skeeter, "He's still there."

With a frown, Skeeter snapped the phone from Stan's hand and turned to the Pastor. "I'm sorry but someone other than you must do this." She turned her back to Stan. "Charmaine, call Harry. Get him out of the building. Lie to him if you have to."

Stan cringed.

Skeeter continued. "Tell him his daughter needs a pick up at school. He'll buy it, even if it is Saturday."

Charmaine ended the call.

Sheepishly, Skeeter handed the Pastor his phone. "Sorry about this, Stan."

Stan glanced at the sky. "The lies I know God forgives are the ones close enough to the truth to pass under the radar, or else the ones so big you'd never dream a person could make it up. I think we're safe."

Bart closed the truck's tailgate. "Let's go."

Sven yelled, "Shotgun!"

Bart backed his black truck to the front entrance and revved the engine before shutting it down. Two other cars parked close to the truck and a slew of people climbed out, talking and making too much noise. The parade into the Piney Center should have been recorded on video.

First, Skeeter went inside and found Charmaine. "Did you get rid of Harry?"

Charmaine nodded. "I lied, but it was more like a fib."

Skeeter used her two forefingers to rub her forehead as if she could fend off a guilty headache. "Sorry I made you do that."

Charmaine smiled. "The fib slipped off my tongue smoothly and easily like melted butter running down toast. It was my pleasure."

Skeeter waved to the crew outside. "All clear," she told them.

After they unloaded the truck, Bart and Sven carried one upright, Jon and Finn the other. They bowled through the reception area, turned wide, and headed down the corridor, narrowly gouging a chunk out of the right-side wall on the next turn. Slowing, they lowered their voices, shortened their steps, and calmly entered Hanni's room. The men set the uprights up at the foot of her bed, almost touching either wall. The top of the uprights skimmed the ceiling.

With muted groans, the women dragged the rolled-up canvas into Hanni's room. They unrolled the canvas, stretched it out, and tied it to the uprights. George meanwhile set up the projector on Hanni's bedside table. He found an outlet and plugged it in. Awake, Hanni stared at them with a confused look on her face.

Everyone stood still and tried to catch their breath. Hanni's oxygen supply continued to emit a soothing whoosh-whoosh sound.

Stepping back, Finn turned the lights off in his mother's room. George flicked the switch on the projector.

Nine people gasped. The room exploded in color. It radiated off the ceiling and slithered across the bedspread. It bounced off the walls and shined off the floor. A rainbow of tulips; reds, yellows, oranges, pinks, purples, whites, stripes, mottled, feathered. Silence filled the room after the gasps. The canvas was so beautiful no one wanted to take away from the enjoyment. The reds were so vibrant they sang, the yellows deep and creamy, the pinks a riot of color, the purples dark and foreboding, the whites pristine, the flowers nestled in loving arms of green foliage.

Hanni lifted a bony hand and pointed. "My tulips," she whispered and closed her eyes.

The sound of scraping interrupted any further words from Hanni. Bodies turned and a path opened. Richard pushed his walker through the crowd.

He looked at the tulips. As his jaw sagged open, a crooked smile broke on his face. He had to remember to breathe. Looking around him, he found Stan and Skeeter, and Finn. Then he smiled at Hanni. Turning his head back to the canvas, he sighed with pleasure and said, "We did it."

CHAPTER 22

As the sun slipped behind the mountains to the west, weary people trailed out of the Piney Center. Finn, Sven, and Jon retreated to Sven's house. Stan rode with Bart back to Beth's house. Skeeter, Beth, Melissa, and George went together in the rental car. It was a strange group of people. However, a sense of camaraderie brought them together. Bart easily chatted with George, and Skeeter found Melissa to be a gentle soul who realized Beth had memory issues. George, Melissa, and Beth shared memories of Roger, recalling his sense of humor and his delight in fishing and frustration with golf. Afterward, Skeeter wondered how it would have happened had they not all been involved with the delivery of Hanni's tulips.

Pizzas were delivered along with two huge salads. Paper plates came out of the pantry, and Beth thrived on making sure everyone had what they needed. Skeeter observed her grandmother's social skills and also was thankful that today was a good day for Beth. It made her giddy to see George and Melissa glimpse the joy that Beth had brought to their father.

It was close to ten o'clock when George and Melissa left for their reserved hotel rooms, and Bart left soon after. Exhausted, Skeeter collapsed into bed.

***

The next morning Finn, Sven, and Jon arrived at the Piney Center at 9:00 a.m. They anxiously walked into the lobby together.

Charmaine looked up and smiled. "She's still with us!" she reported.

Relieved, the three walked the hall to their mother's room. To their surprise, Hanni was sitting up, sipping apple juice through a straw. The projector had been turned on, the curtains drawn, and now the tulips brightened the room.

Jon stepped forward. Finn and Sven held back. "Mom," Jon cried. "It's wonderful to see you're awake."

Hanni looked at her son, and with a smile and a weak voice said, "Yes, Jon. And look at you. Handsome as ever."

He moved aside, pointing to his brother. "Sven is here too."

Stepping forward, Sven bent down and hugged his mother. He placed his hands on her shoulders, leaning close to kiss her cheek.

Hanni patted Sven's face as he straightened up. "It's good to see you." Hanni weakly turned her head toward her other son. A questioning look filled her face.

"Yes, mother, I'm here too." Finn stepped into Hanni's line of sight and held her gaze. Her eyes were bright with recognition, eyes he hadn't seen in many years.

Hanni's worn face brightened. Her blue eyes sparkled. Energy flowed into her body, and she reached for Finn. He bent over and let his mother hug him, gently holding her shoulders and inhaling her scent. She kissed his forehead and then his cheeks. Salty tears blurred his vision and dropped onto his mother's arm. Then, he fell to his knees beside her bed and buried his face in the blankets. He pulled her close as if gathering her would let some of his strength and size go to her. With his arms across her body, Hanni rested her hand on his shoulder, her fingers lightly tapping to let him know she understood all of his emotions, a way of allowing the past to fade, and letting her son know her future was short. Her oldest son had made her journey to the next adventure possible, and she was ready to accept it.

He freely wept. Sven and Jon stood in reverent silence with misty eyes as they watched the miracle of repentance, love, and forgiveness unfold before their eyes.

Finn wiped a tear from his cheek. He held her hand. "I have missed you so much." He paused and let the words fill the room. Then he continued, "I am so sorry I didn't come to see you before this. To be angry at my brothers was childish; I wish you had scolded me."

"We all retain childish ways. It's in the past." She caressed his cheek. "My boy. Such memories flash in front of my eyes. Oh, Finn, I remember your first steps, and when you fell off a bike which was too big for you, and I remember when you caught your first fish."

Sven piped in, "He was always a better fisherman than me."

"Yes." Hanni ran her knobby fingers through his hair. "Finn, I'm so happy to see you." Her shoulders lifted as she inhaled deeply. "You came all this way. You were my firstborn. Such love is hard to explain. A mother's love never dies, and how could I hold a grudge? I knew you boys hurt in different ways and because you were brothers, you would find a way to let go of it." She smiled.

Jon and Sven stepped forward. They moved behind Finn who still knelt beside the bed. Hanni looked at Sven and Jon, and then to Finn's upturned face. She brought Finn's hand up to her cheek and reached out to his brothers. They extended their hands to her, and she placed them on Finn's hand. "Boys," she said, her voice gaining strength, "fulfill my final prayer before I die. Forgive one another so I can hear you."

Finn spoke first. "Mom, as you said, 'All is forgiven.' We have talked. We have made amends."

Sven and Jon nodded in agreement. "All is good," Finn whispered.

Hanni relaxed and let her head settle into her pillow while she talked with her sons. She told them about her tulip fields, how the family planted the rows by color and size, how they weeded the fields, and how she had dreamed her heavenly home would be surrounded by tulips.

Opening her arms, she nodded. "Here I have my tulips. I can almost smell them. I can remember walking among those flowers, recall when the fields were planted, the moisture in the soil, how it ran through my fingers. Sometimes fog twined through the rows, turning the field into a mysterious place. When we were starving, the tulips fed us. God had a way of letting nature take care of us even under clouds and fog. Then the sun would shine and change it again. Oh, my." A tear slipped down her cheek "For me, the tulips erased all the ugliness of the war. It was healing for me. Thank you, boys, for coming and bringing me my flowers."

The boys stayed beside their mother for almost an hour, but then they could tell she became tired. After each kissed her forehead, they excused themselves to let her rest. Hanni fell into a peaceful sleep.

Outside, cumulus clouds reared into the sky. The hills surrounding the Center were dotted with dark green foliage while cottonwood and aspen trees budded with spring leaves, sprinkling the day with lighter colors of green. The brothers walked three blocks from the Center to the Dusty Corral Café. They had a light lunch and then strolled back to the Piney Center and Hanni's room.

She was still sleeping when they checked on her. They left her room and retreated to the garden adjacent to the social room.

It had been years since the three boys had been together. Finn's eyes began to water again as he told them how he was sorry he had added to their pain. He explained why he felt hurt and his brothers listened without retribution. "I am looking forward to making up for the lost time." Sven and Jon relaxed with their older brother. A deep sense of bonding settled around them like a soft blanket as they shared childhood memories.

After an hour, a nurse leaned outside to the garden. "Your mother is awake and is asking for you."

The brothers filed into their mother's room. A nurse finished brushing Hanni's hair, patted her on the shoulder, and quietly left the room. Hanni reached out to her three sons. They stood beside her bed.

"At last," she whispered, her voice weak, "I can go in peace. My children are together with me." The prospect of death appeared more comfortable than it had been in weeks. She took shallow breaths and looked away as if she had entered another room. Then she returned to her sons, to this place with her family and tulips. "My soul is contented." Her breathing turned ragged. She closed her eyes. "I see Francis. He is pulling me toward him." She mumbled something indistinguishable. "Now I see angels and Francis has to move aside." Her breath became a whisper and her face relaxed. Finn, Sven, and Jon stood quietly together and joined hands. Her breathing stopped.

The three men lingered at their mother's bed, saying their final goodbye to their mother, and then quietly slipped from the room. They left the projector on with the field of tulips brilliantly filling the room.

CHAPTER 23

A hasty memorial service was orchestrated so that Hanni's sons could attend. Her urn of ashes had been placed on the altar at the Center's chapel. A bouquet in front of the podium brightened the room. Her boys sat in the front row. Pastor Stan looked sharp in the dark suit he wore for funerals. Cecil and Richard were also nicely dressed. Cecil wore dark brown suit pants and a tweed jacket, and Richard a navy-blue suit which showed age. Layla May looked stunning in a fitted black dress with flashy scarf, and the others gathered in their best attire. Cordy could not attend, nor did Joe, although he said he could and tried to get out of bed but was given a stern lecture by one of the nurses. Harry arrived with a stoic expression on his face. Bart sat next to Skeeter and on the other side of her sat Layla May. Charmaine, Larry, and numerous other staff members were on hand to pay their respects to a favorite patient. Accompanied by Bear, Julia brought Charlotte who was dressed in her frilliest dress with pink berets in her hair and gleaming white patent leather shoes.

Pastor Stan said an opening prayer, read the Twenty Third Psalm, and gave a brief eulogy for their departed friend. Cecil, steadied by Julia, stood and shuffled his way to the front of the chapel, his walker squeaking. With one hand still on his walker, he picked up his guitar. He stood at the podium, his back straight. Charlotte wandered to him, pulled on his pant leg, peeking around the corner of the pulpit. Bear followed her and collapsed. Julia stood nearby to steady her father if he needed help. Cecil fingerpicked his guitar and sang an old spiritual song, "All My Trials Lord Will Soon Be Over." Then he, Julia, Charlotte, and Bear returned to their row of chairs. Charlotte, being a toddler, had to twirl and make her skirt flare before she sat down. Bear slumped to the floor with a groan.

Pastor Stan continued the ceremony and offered the opportunity for anyone to comment with their memories of Hanni. Skeeter held her breath, fearful Jayne, Millie, or Layla May would bring up Hanni's story of the Winter of Starvation and the German Soldier. This would ruin everything.

Layla May stood, lifted her head, and walked to the podium. She flicked a floral scarf over her shoulder. A string of pearls dangled around her neck.

Skeeter felt her eyes fill with liquid, thinking of this lovely woman who was past her prime and ventured now into the shadow of memory loss and loneliness and did so with the utmost grace. Perhaps performing had been what she matured with, but now it was friendship and the loss of a friend.

Layla May tapped her finger on the podium. "So, here we are." She nodded to Finn, Sven, and Jon. "Children from a gracious woman. Hello to all three of you." She sighed and shifted her weight from hi-heel to hi-heel. "Hanni," she whispered. She gazed at the ceiling. "I know you are with God and watching over us. You are with your tulips and your beloved Francis." She smiled. "We grieve your loss but cheer your passing to where you belong. Let the years reflect they have brought the wisdom of the mother and the love of the wife. Remember the good arms you have fallen into, and remember those who sought your arms. We know your heart and it was open and warm." She glanced at Hanni's sons. "You will always be the shoulder your children seek, wherever they might be. We love you so, Hanni. God's speed."

Lifting her head one inch higher, she pushed the hair off her cheek and took a moment to look at every person in the chapel. Then she slowly and queenly returned to her seat.

Millie stood, swayed, and said, "I am too emotional to be the focus of attention." She turned in a circle and looked dazed. "Hanni became a friend in my twilight years." She blew her nose. "She was a good friend." Sitting down, she wiped a tear from her cheek.

Standing, Richard pushed his walker to the podium. Turning, he took a deep breath and exhaled, as if letting the air inside of him escape. "Although we are here to honor Hanni and her life, I would like to tell you about her sons." He pointed a shaky finger at Finn, Sven, and Jon. "Her sons came to be with her, and it took a lot of prayers, several thousand miles of travel, and the determination to heal old wounds. I have been proud of many things in my life, but not much can top what a few of us accomplished in a short time to make Hanni's next journey successful, surrounded by her three sons." He paused for emphasis "And her tulips." He nodded with a deep sigh. "We have glimpsed Hanni's tulips and have seen them as a photograph on canvas. Today, I assure you, Hanni walks among those tulips. Thank you to Pastor Stan and Skeeter, to Lori, and to Finn, Sven, and Jon for making this happen for all of us." Holding onto his walker, he shuffled to his seat.

Skeeter wiped tears from her cheek. Moving closer to Bart, she took his hand. He gently closed his fingers over hers.

Pastor Stan returned to the podium. After clearing his throat, he said, "Joe could not be here today with us, but for someone who is ninety-seven, even though he fibs and says he's one-hundred-and-two, he is working on recovery from a broken hip. He sent these words: 'Hanni, your forehead was wrinkled by many peaks and trenches caused by too many events in your life to review, but your eyes always sparkled and remained steadfast with a unique shade of blue. It was pure love coming through your eyes. I will never forget.' Thank you, Joe."

To everyone's surprise, Harry stood and in a steady stride, arrived at the podium. He opened a folded paper. "Thank you all for being here. We are saying goodbye to Hanni, who was with us since we opened the Piney Center." For a second, he was at a loss for words. He tapped the paper and then brushed it aside. "Some of you knew Hanni better than I did. I wish it were different. She left me with a lesson on how to know someone." He shook his head. "I didn't know her, but as I look out at all you who did know her and did love her, I feel her presence, and I am humbled." He chuckled. "One of our rooms in rehab is now filled with a big canvas. A projector sits against the wall. The projector seems hard, only pieces of plastic and metal parts. Against the wall, the canvas gives the room a strange smell. The nurses trip on the volleyball uprights. Sanitizing it is questionable." His gaze landed on Skeeter, and Lori who sat behind her. "But the room is filled with love and memories." He shook his head. "I don't know how we will handle it, but I want her field of tulips to stay with us forever."

Finn poked Sven, who nudged Jon.

Harry's gaze landed on Skeeter. "Thank you all for coming. The Piney Center is a better place because of you and Hanni." He folded his paper, stuffed it in his jacket pocket, nodded, and left the podium, looking straight ahead, daring not to meet anyone's glance.

Pastor Stan again stood at the podium and said, "Mourn not the passing of a life well-lived, rather celebrate. Hanni would want that. Count the times your lives smiled together and touched. Death is only the end of a chapter, friends, and for Hanni, it is the beginning of a new adventure. Let us pray."

The service ended with hugs and handshakes. A reception of cookies, cheese and crackers, and drinks followed in the social hall. Voices were subdued.

The silence left Cecil tapping his fingers on his thigh, so he brought out his guitar, and Pastor Stan joined him. Jayne nudged Scout toward the guitar players, and Layla May elbowed Jayne to her right, so she could take the mic first. They decided to sing "I'll Fly Away." Called the most recorded gospel song by many denominations, it was a joyful song about going to God. Richard kicked his walker out of the way. Skeeter held hands with Bart. Bear snorted. Charlotte danced in the middle of the room, her patent leather shoes tossed aside, her skirts twirling. Cecil worked his jaw extra hard, and Richard rubbed his knees. Harry sauntered into the room and smiled.

Finn, Sven, and Jon somehow fit in.

It was as it should be.

CHAPTER 24

A spring storm rushed over the Great Basin, pushing into Colorado with strong winds and loaded with moisture. After lovely days along Brush Creek in Piney, the sleet came in sideways and then softened to big white flakes of snow drifting from the sky. After Hanni's memorial service, it was fitting; the green growth of spring turning dismal and gloomy.

At the Piney Center, life continued but the social room appeared empty without Hanni. Joe continued to recover in rehab, but he had several setbacks with his blood pressure and oxygen levels. The staff worried about pneumonia and the constant threat of pulmonary thrombosis. Cordy returned to the assisted living section of the Piney Center when her vitals stabilized. Although weak, she used a new *Nova Rollator* walker with a purple frame, which Cecil called, "Sporty."

Finn helped his brothers sort through their mother's belongings at the Piney Center. The last box to leave was filled with letters and miscellaneous items from her life in Holland to America and later

Colorado. As the snow from the spring storm piled up outside, Hanni's sons met with Harry in his office.

Harry, wearing a short-sleeved shirt and khaki pants, was a creature of routine and wore a short-sleeved shirt to work when the calendar turned to April. Hanni's sons crowded into three seats opposite Harry's desk. After they settled, Harry opened a file on his desk. "I want to start by saying it was a pleasure to have had Hanni with us. There are a few details to finalize now that she is gone." He slid some papers across the desk. "These are release papers because Hanni is no longer in assisted living."

Next, he pushed an envelope in their direction. "This is a check for the residue of her account with us."

No one reached for the envelope.

Harry cleared his throat. "The last order of business is Hanni's tulips."

Finn let out a long breath. "I guess you can't keep a giant canvas in a hospital room."

Harry found a pencil and began to roll it between two fingers. "I'd like to but it's not safe, especially for the nurses in a small room with the steel uprights."

Jon pointed to the envelope on the table. "I have an idea." He paused to look at his brothers. "I have a friend in Denver, David Fields, who is an artist. He produces original photo prints under acrylic glass produced with Lumachrome HD and Super Gloss photographic papers. I've seen his work in a gallery." Jon continued to tap the envelope. "The print is then mounted behind a sheet of crystal-clear acrylic glass." He shook his head. "It's hard to explain the result. Prints show incredible visual depth and an almost three-D quality with astonishing vibrant colors. With proper lighting, the work appears to be backlit."

Jon looked out the door of the office and scanned the inside of the beige room. "I don't want to forget about Mom's last wish and her tulips. I noticed one wall in the dining area is blank and uninspiring." Picking up the envelope, he tapped the edge on the table. "To remember our mother, I'd like to contact David and have him turn the wall into a piece of art with her tulips." He waved the envelope. "We could pay for it from this." Before anyone commented, he locked gazes with Finn and pushed the envelope toward him. "This should be your decision, Finn. Sven and I discussed what should happen to the remainder of Mom's estate. This check should go to you."

Finn laughed. "I think it's funny. After all this, after the hard feelings over money, and now this check is shuffled on the table."

Tension threatened to zing off the walls but Finn laughed harder. "For me, taking the check is impossible." He gave a close-fisted bump to Jon's upper arm. "Your idea is the best thing I've heard."

Jon turned his attention to Harry. "What do you think?"

Harry put the pencil down. "Good news all around. We can remove the volleyball uprights from the rehab facility. Piney Center will have its first piece of art. Finally, a bright color will liven this place, and the final news is that I will present your offer to our Board of Directors at our next meeting." He grinned. "I think we can get this done."

***

The spring snow continued to fall in giant flakes. Skeeter sipped morning coffee in the kitchen. The remains of poppy seed muffins littered the counter, along with empty water bottles, a bowl of cantaloupe chunks, and coffee cups. She heard voices and the shuffling of boxes from the direction of the garage. George and Melissa had remained in Piney after Hanni's memorial service to go through their father's belongings, but they were due to leave later in the day. They had been agreeable while at the house and had included Beth in sorting Roger's items. But every time George glanced at Skeeter, she thought he was inspecting her as if he could see inside her head or her heart to see what her intentions were as to the house.

So far George had not brought up the omission in his father's will about who should inherit the house. It left a pall over their relationship. She felt the time had to come to discuss it, and since she had found George to be a decision-maker, she figured he would be the one to have an opinion on what should happen. Skeeter hoped it would not end up with a lawsuit, which would strap Beth for cash and end with raw feelings.

Looking at the snow falling on grass growing tall and green, she thought about her life in San Francisco. It had only been a little while, but it felt as though she had lived in Piney for a long time. The town had a settled feeling to it. People weren't in such a rush; things got done but tomorrow was okay rather than a quick phone call and action today. Local women didn't need boutiques for shopping; they wore sensible shoes rather than high heels with arch-killing height. Sports talk was more frequent than a discussion of dinner reservations or the newest dot com company. Skeeter found herself sleeping better at night, especially when she cracked the bedroom window to let in the cool mountain air.

Her cell phone chirped a new text message. It was from Steve. *Are you ever coming back?* Was it asked in jest or was there some anger between the lines? She didn't have an answer for him. She had a hard time pulling up his face in her memory bank and tried to think of the reasons she had dated him. Looking outside at the falling snow, her mind felt adrift, swirling with indecision and changeable as the snowflakes.

Her cell phone chirped again. She found a text from Bart. *Going to New Mexico this week. Back Friday. It's not a good week to put Millie on a horse. Hope to see you over the weekend.*

She answered this text. *Travel safe. Hope to see you too.*

Beth came into the kitchen from the garage. "We're getting a load to take to the recycle store, and another load for the dump. There's a set of women's golf clubs in the garage. I don't play. Do you want them?"

Skeeter shook her head.

Beth sighed. "How about Phil's wife?"

"She died about a year ago, Gram."

"It's a shame. Okay, those clubs go to the community auction." Beth disappeared into the garage.

Grabbing her purse, Skeeter slid off the kitchen chair. It was a relief to know George and Melissa would spend the day at the house, going through Roger's things. It meant she didn't have to worry about her grandmother. Heading through the garage, she chatted a few moments with Roger's children and then waved goodbye. She ducked her head against the snow and hurried to her car.

Pausing at the reception desk at the Center, she found Charmaine doing a crossword puzzle but looking nice in a black print dress with a bright yellow scarf. "Morning," Skeeter said as she placed an elbow on the reception desk. "All quiet this morning?"

"Yes. No rumbles from the walkers down the hall."

She detoured when she decided she wanted to visit Joe. Veering past Harry's office, she navigated toward Joe's room, nodding at nurses, and listening to the low voices from the central nursing station. When she arrived at his room, she found a nameplate outside his room. *Joe Sabattini.* Smiling, she rapped at the door and entered his room. He sat up in bed with something in his hand and looked up at the television, which played a rerun of the *Bridge Over the River Kwai.* His oxygen tubing sagged off his face. The picture of Mary was under his left hand. Although he needed a shave, his hair was neat, and although he looked pale, he grinned when he saw her.

He pressed whatever was in his hand. "I can't turn the television off."

Setting her purse down, she went to Joe's side. "Let me see it," she said, pointing to the remote control.

He handed it to her. She put it aside since it was a battery-powered shaver. She found the remote and turned the TV to local news and turned down the volume. "Better?"

Joe ran his fingers over Mary's picture as if to make sure it was in place. "Much better," he said.

She adjusted his oxygen cannula and would offer to help him shave but felt Joe's dignity would be better served if she chatted with him and let a nurse's aide help with his hygiene. She pulled a chair close to his bed. Shifting slightly, Joe groaned while a pained look covered his face. His aches were constant companions, Skeeter decided, and his wife was not here to ease those pains. "You're looking good," she commented, wishing she could do more for him besides fixing the TV and his oxygen tube.

"Good is hardly a word to describe me," he said, speaking the words with care. He tapped the picture under his fingers. "When Mary comes, I'm going to kiss the most beautiful girl in the world."

"You are a lucky man," she said.

"Mary made me the luckiest man the day we got married."

"How's the hip coming along?"

Coughing, he adjusted the plastic tubing which had drifted under his chin. "Awful. Hurts all the time. Can't sleep. Can't sit. Can't do anything. The nurses try to move me. It hurts. So, I lay still. Then they come and move me. Mary will make it better."

Skeeter picked up the photograph. Still trim, Mary was not the young girl in the other photograph Joe had in his room. This Mary had gray hair curled around her face. She wore a pale blue dress and a string of pearls around her neck with pearl earrings. She held a pie and wore a broad smile. Something about both Joe and Mary was the way they lit up a room with their smiles. It must have been something to be together with them, as if sparklers sent shooting rays of happiness into the air. He lay back and closed his eyes. Despite what he said, she could tell he was tired in the way an old man grew tired; suddenly with strength escaping each pore. He closed his eyes. Skeeter adjusted the oxygen tube around his left ear and under his nose.

As he took several breaths, he smiled. "Thank you, Skeeter."

Getting up, she bent over and brushed her lips against his forehead. "I'll be back," she whispered, straightened, sniffed, and left his room.

She found Pastor Stan in their office, sorting through music sheets and rearranging his master songbook. She peeked down the hall before sitting at her desk. "Looks like everything is calm here."

"Too calm. It grates on my nerves. I expect something to happen."

Skeeter woke up her computer. "No news is good news?

Pastor Stan put up one finger. "Check your e-mails. Harry sent good news. Finn and the boys are going to use the remainder of Hanni's funds to have an artist — David Fields I think is his name — create a wall in the dining area with a picture of Hanni's tulips. Harry sounds excited."

She pulled up her Outlook account and scrolled through her e-mails. She found Harry's message and quickly read it. The following e-mail from Harry gave an update on Cordy and Joe. As she read this e-mail, she frowned. "Sounds like neither Joe nor Cordy is recovering as well as can be expected although Cordy has returned to assisted living."

"Yes," he said with a sigh. "If we want to help both on their way to fulfilling their final wishes, we had better hurry."

"I think Lori has an idea for Cordy. I'll check with her. Do we need to inform Harry?"

Pastor Stan squinted as if he were in deep thought. "Harry spoke with a light heart at Hanni's memorial service. I'm a trusting man but also intuitive. Harry's job is to keep the rooms filled in assisted living. Our job or 'goal' is to help our friends to find their way to heaven and to eliminate those things standing in their way. I'm not sure Harry and our views are copacetic."

"I'm thinking the same thing, yet I don't want to antagonize him any more than we already have. By virtual reality, I think we can accomplish Cordy's wish to be in a balloon."

Stan frowned. "Of all people, she would know it's fake. I'd like to see her climb into a balloon basket and rise."

"With her health issues, I don't think we can leave the Center, travel several hours, and have her go up in a balloon. It would probably kill her."

"Not go high, anyhow, but maybe we could find a local company, someone who has a hot-air balloon for a festival."

Skeeter thought about it and nodded. "If we could get her in a balloon, she'd only need to go up fifty feet or so."

Pastor Stan frowned. "I'm not sure about the ethics of what we are doing. On one hand, these seniors have final wishes but when we make these wishes happen, then the person dies sooner. Look at Hanni. It only took her a few days to pass after her sons joined her."

"You once reminded me of the one absolute truism of life. We all die. We can't change it for them, Stan. What I believe we are doing is granting these final wishes so death can be acceptable, rather than miserable with regrets of things left undone."

Stan rubbed his chin with his thumb and forefinger. "I don't know. In some ways, we are creating fake reality to hasten death."

"Do you think we should ignore these wishes? To deny them? Lie to them? Tell them we can't help achieve their final wish?"

Stan exhaled hard. "I need to pray about this. It's not lying, but it's in the shadows of being correct."

Skeeter pulled her hair into a tighter ponytail. "Stan, what we want to do for Cordy is a blessing. For goodness' sake, she is being consumed by cancer. Her mind is full of plaque which takes away the memories of her life, and you are worried about whether she remains alive longer to suffer or allows herself to let go and drift to heaven in her balloon?"

Stan mumbled something more to himself than to Skeeter. He checked his watch. "I'm going to practice music with Cecil. I'll think about what you've said and I'll pray." He shuffled his song pages together. "I'm going to do research on upcoming events and see if any organization has hot-air balloons as part of their activity. You go talk with Lori to see what she can set up at the library."

"And schedule it for when?"

"Soon," he said as he picked up his guitar and left the office, adding "and schedule it when Harry is away from the Center."

Skeeter grinned. *Will do.*

CHAPTER 25

That night when Skeeter returned home, she saw the message machine blinking. When she turned it on, she heard a message from Sandy, Beth's hairdresser. She scheduled an appointment with Beth for tomorrow for a cut and color. Skeeter made a note in her cell phone and jotted it down on a notepad beside the phone.

Outside, car doors closed. She glanced out the side door through the garage to the driveway. George, Melissa, and Beth got out of George's rental car. Roger's children had spent all of Monday, going through their father's belongings. They had finished sorting his clothes and had now started in the garage, which had been Roger's man-cave. The garage had bays for three vehicles. His BMW and Jeep took up two of the spaces with the extra bay going to his recreational equipment, which included fishing gear, golf equipment, some old tennis equipment, hiking stuff, cross-country ski gear, bicycle, and a workbench for Roger's do-at-home projects. As they walked into the house, Skeeter decided they looked tired as they dashed through the last of spitting snow into the house. George carried a bag of groceries, which he deposited on the counter.

Beth and Melissa disappeared into the powder room to wash their hands; George did the same in the kitchen sink. "Recycle store, county dump, and grocery store. Phew. We'll have an early dinner then be on our way to Denver. Our flights leave early tomorrow morning."

Skeeter checked her watch. "It's been a long day."

He began to unload the grocery bag. "Melissa claims she can cook, but the claim stretches the truth from here to the East Coast." He had a package of pork ribs, a bottle of teriyaki sauce, some russet potatoes, and a prepackaged salad. "This should do." He pulled out a new flame thrower. "I know you need this."

"How about a glass of whiskey?"

He grinned. "Sounds good. With ice."

"Gotcha. I'll have wine." She paused and met his gaze. "George, thank you for doing all of this. I know it hasn't been easy for you."

"First of all, pour the whiskey. Then we'll talk about what is easy and what isn't."

Skeeter poured the drinks. Melissa and Beth had disappeared into the den with the local weather on the television. "Cheers," she said as they held their libation.

George nodded. "To good health and happiness."

"To that," she said.

George looked over his shoulder at his sister with Beth. "We're about done here for this first visit. My dad was never a keeper of junk, but he did have a lifetime of stuff in the garage."

She raised her glass. "Here's to stuff."

He ran his finger around the rim of the glass. "The house."

Skeeter felt her pulse tick in her temple. "Yes, the house."

"I wasn't happy when dad decided to retire and move to Piney, but he was alone when my mother died, and it was his dream to retire to the mountains. Then he met Beth. When an adult child learns his dad, at age seventy-four, is getting married, it takes some adjustment. I didn't like the idea. Perhaps I was stubborn, and we didn't often visit. I never got to know Beth." He looked in the den at his sister chatting with his step-mother. "After these days visiting, I see the gentleness in Beth, the lovely soul she has, and I am happy dad had those years with her. Dad loved the outdoors, and Beth shared it with him."

Skeeter nodded agreeably.

"However, Dad told me this house would someday be ours. He never mentioned changing his mind. I don't know what he was thinking."

She attempted to speak, but he put up his hand in the sign of 'stop'.

"I have an excellent lawyer. He thinks he can file suit and have an agreeable judge agree with us."

Skeeter exhaled a deep breath. "I don't know what to say. I hoped this wouldn't happen. You must know Beth doesn't have much of an estate."

He leaned forward. "It's not my problem."

The little hairs on the back of her head stood up.

He went on, "Beth has memory problems. I don't know how severe."

"She has Alzheimer's disease."

"I am sorry. Dad loved Beth. She brought joy into his world. So, I am not sure how I want to proceed with the house."

Skeeter nearly choked. "By rights, Beth inherits it."

He sipped his whiskey. "I like this town, Piney. Who would have thought? I like you." He glanced at the den. "I like Beth, too, so does Melissa. Our mother died a long time ago, and she misses a mentor in her life."

"So, what are you saying?"

"By legal rights, Beth inherits the house. I get it. I can fight Beth in court, but it will cost us both a lot of money. This was my dad's last hurrah. When Beth dies, her daughter would rightfully inherit the house, who I understand is financially stable on the East Coast, or you, who is," he shrugged, "stable."

"Stable is not in my vocabulary."

"You're not flattering yourself. You'll always land on your feet but Beth won't. So, I have not decided one way or the other about filing a suit against the will. I need to think about it for a few days."

She didn't like the sound of it. "I had hoped you would not want to challenge your dad's will."

"I was thinking the same thing." He didn't continue.

"What? Not challenge Beth as to the house?"

He took a quick sip of whiskey. "If we go to court, she and I can wrangle it out with our attorneys and probably pay thousands of dollars for a judge's decision, or we could agree we've wasted time not getting to know one another and propose we consolidate our family relationship? Perhaps we spend more time together?" He glanced outside at a few flakes of snow. "I bet this is a marvelous place in the winter."

"You won't sue?"

He found the bottle of whiskey and poured another inch in his glass. "Skeeter, I don't know what I want anymore." He chuckled. "I came here determined to convince Beth that dad intended for Melissa and me to own this house, but it was...what...a week ago? Before Hanni's tulip experience and getting to know you. I also know something about you. You may be pretty and look sweet, but I paid a PI to take a look at your background."

Shocked, she inhaled sharply. "You hired a private detective?"

He stared through her. "My attorney knows a guy."

Heat filled her cheeks. She thought about throwing her wine glass at him but then realized she, in a way, had done the same thing to him. She swallowed a sip of wine. "I do have talents." She locked stares with him. "I am not someone you want to cross."

He chuckled. "So, I found out."

She had to give him credit. "What'd the PI say?"

George ran his finger around the rim of his glass of whiskey. "Don't tangle with her."

"I'm glad he got accurate information." Skeeter looked around the room, upstairs, and to the den. "This house is more than Beth can manage."

George nodded. "I agree. The best plan for her future is to get her into something smaller, a place where she can live for several years, and then when the time comes, have her move to the Piney Center."

Since moving in with her grandmother and realizing that she had memory problems, Skeeter felt surrounded by people who understood the path Beth was on. *I'm not alone in this.*

George added, "We've almost finished with the garage. I'm coming back in two weeks to take care of the things we want and get rid of the stuff we don't want. I don't know how you want to handle Roger's cars."

"Beth's attorney said they would be included with the house as belonging to her."

He pointed to the garage. "Do you want to advertise and sell those cars? Do you know their worth?"

Skeeter's shoulders slumped. "I haven't thought that far."

"Both have a high value. I've checked the Blue Book on each. If you want, I can place an ad in the local paper advertising the cars for sale. People may call to arrange for a visual inspection over the next few weeks. When I return, I can facilitate the sale of cars. The proceeds from the sale of the cars will go to Beth. When someone facilitates a car sale, a commission or percentage of the sale price is usually paid to the facilitator. If you would agree to let me stay here, rather than the expense of a hotel, I would call it even."

She thought quickly but didn't see any reason this wasn't a good idea.

He then added, "When I return in two weeks, I will have a decision made then about the house."

She wished he would say he wouldn't consider a lawsuit. "If Beth wants to sell the house, how do you feel about it?"

He didn't answer right away. He glanced over his shoulder to the view across the patio and the river. "Piney has many beautiful views. I don't see how she can keep *this* house. The value is in selling it and investing wisely."

Skeeter had pushed the reality of getting the house ready to sell, then moving and setting up a new home to the back of her mind. "I think you're right."

"It's what I'll do if the judge decides in our favor."

Skeeter wanted to punch him, but also knew he spoke the truth.

***

George and Melissa were gone. The clouds were gone, giving way to Colorado Bluebird skies. The following day Beth had her appointment with the hairdresser in the morning. Skeeter went to work and checked on Joe. She found him out of sorts and grumpy, which was unusual for him. The on-duty nurse reported that he had trouble clearing his lungs, which was not good news. She next went to the assisted living wing of the building and poked her head in on Millie, Cordy, Cecil, Layla May, and Richard. Everyone acted a little off-kilter as if Hanni's passing and Joe's accident had left a pall over everyone.

The bright spot in her day was when she got a call from Bart. He had returned to town and asked her to come to the ranch in the afternoon. "Wear jeans," he told her.

She agreed and happily slipped on her jacket, heading to her car with a skip in her steps. The drive west gave her a glimpse of spring in the Rockies with snow-capped peaks in each direction and cottonwood and aspen trees dotting the Eagle and Colorado Rivers. The recent rain and spitting snow had cleared the air and the skies were brilliantly blue. The tan and gray high desert gave way to vibrant grass and lime-colored leaves on the trees. As she passed ranches along the Colorado River, she saw cows in the pastures with new calves. A rebirth was everywhere she looked.

Bart came out to greet her as she got out of her car, smiling as he moved toward her. He had the kind of face that stopped women in their tracks. She wondered if he got used to it, but guessed he wasn't driven by his ego and probably didn't realize what he did to females. Waving to her, his grin pulled at her heartstrings.

"Hey, good to see you."

She wondered if he'd kiss her briefly but then guessed he wouldn't. She liked that about him. "Hi, to you, too. How was New Mexico?"

"Busy, dirty, taking care of calves." He pointed toward the barn and handed her a pair of supple leather gloves. "I thought we'd take Misty out for a spin today."

Her lips parted with surprise. "Me? Riding a horse?"

He turned in a circle, then started for the barn. "Not a cloud in the sky, spring is in the air, it's a great day for a ride."

As she fell in step with him, she worked the soft leather of the gloves. "You promised Millie won't fall off Misty. Can you do the same for me?"

"First time on a horse?" he said with mischief in his eyes.

"First and only."

He put his arm around her. "I won't let anything happen to you, and I will show you the magic of Colorado in the spring."

He did show her and it was magic.

***

Skeeter arrived home with a fresh outlook and sore muscles. She had left worrying about Beth, the house, what George would do, Joe, Cordy, and Millie. Being on the back of a horse with a commanding view of green sagebrush and yellow cowslip, the river in the distance, and the snowcapped peaks of the Sawatch Range, left her in awe of the beauty of the terrain. While Misty climbed a narrow ridge, carefully picking her way around shrubs and rocks, they reached the top of the hill. Skeeter thought about an adventure in San Francisco being riding the cable cars. Her life had dramatically changed. As she looked ahead at Bart's straight back in the saddle of a big black and white paint horse, muscles rippled beneath his shirt. A man who sported a day-old beard and Italian suit used to give her goosebumps, now it was a cowboy with strong hands, a straight back, a Stetson hat, thighs packed in Levi's, and a man who let her be herself.

She had to watch herself with Bart. This man could reach inside her chest and manhandle her heart. With him, it was dangerous territory.

Riding a horse, feeling the power of the animal, and trusting it to carry her safely, caused her heart to thud against the walls of her chest. It left her exhilarated and wanting to explore more territory from a saddle. She wondered what her grandmother would say about it?

When she came inside the house after her ride with Bart, she spotted Beth in the den, standing with a table lamp beside her. She held a book in her hand. The light caught her, bathing her upper body and face. She was outfitted in a light blue dress with a string of pearls around her neck. There was something in the way she held herself, as if she were in another time and place, as if unsure of where her limbs should be arranged to be comfortable. For a few seconds, Skeeter stared at her. That hair! Shorter, curled around her face. Soft. Caressing her.

Skeeter gasped. For a moment, it was as if time stood still. *Déjà vu.* She had seen this sight previously, somewhere, at some time. Her heart drummed in her temples, and she had to swallow because her throat grew suddenly dry. She took a step forward to make sure she was seeing what she thought she saw.

That's it. I've previously seen this setting. I need to tell Pastor Stan.

***

Still shaken by the sight of Beth standing by the lamp, Skeeter nibbled on her lower lip. She tapped a fingernail on the granite counter while switching screens on her laptop computer. She glanced up several times toward her grandmother, who watched the news on television. Bits of information rattled in her mind as if marbles on a roulette wheel. One minute, she knew what she needed to do and the next minute she felt she shouldn't do it. Right and wrong were at war with her principles. If she had found herself in this situation two months ago, she would not have hesitated to make a 'yes' decision, but with Pastor Stan her co-worker, and the expert on ethics, she wasn't sure it was so easy to move forward.

As she mulled it over in her mind, she heard Pastor Stan's voice at the door leading to the garage, "Hello? Skeeter? Are you home?"

She sighed, happy to know Stan had arrived to help with clarity to the problem. "Yes, come on in."

He waved, "You look like you've been outside. Your nose is sunburned."

"It's because I spent the afternoon on the back of a horse, following Bart up and down hills on his boss's ranch."

Stan grinned. "It agrees with you." He scratched the back of his neck, noticing color had blossomed on her cheeks. "Oh my. The cowboy wins the damsel's hand."

"The cowboy knows how to impress a damsel new to Colorado, and the damsel was left charmed."

"How are the legs?"

"I discovered muscles I never knew I had."

"It's a good way to leave a lasting impression." He chuckled. "Still, I like him."

She smiled. "Me too."

Stan pulled out a chair beside her. "What's up? Anything new?"

"Yes." She held up a hand. "Don't sit yet. Nothing earth-shattering is new except we are one day closer to death."

"Yikes, Skeeter, you know how to end the day with a chill."

"Forget I said it. A lot is on my mind. It's good to see you."

Tilting his head, he looked to see Beth in the den. "You had something you wanted to discuss?"

Skeeter sipped from a glass of ice water. "Yes. I'm glad you're here, but before you get comfortable, go in the den, turn on a light, and take a look at Beth."

He shrugged. "Okay."

Watching him, she noted the way his body was relaxed until he stood directly in front of Beth and turned on the table lamp next to her. He stiffened. Skeeter couldn't hear what was said, but after Stan turned off the lamp and returned to the kitchen, he had a serious look on his face. Standing at the kitchen island, he placed his hands on the counter. "It's as if I have seen a ghost."

With a nod, Skeeter glanced toward Beth. "She finally ruined her hair with the flame thrower and had to have it styled. Her hairdresser did some highlights."

"She's beautiful," Stan said slowly. "She's Mary."

"It shocked me, too."

Pastor Stan locked gazes with Skeeter. They didn't speak for several seconds. With a nod, he said, "What are you thinking?"

"I think you know what I am thinking. We can give Joe his Mary, if only for a one-time visit."

Stan cocked his head as if wanting to listen carefully. "I'm not sure I want to know your thoughts, but tell me."

Skeeter did.

When she was finished, worry lines creased his brow. "I don't know, Skeeter. This is farther in left field than taking Cordy on a fake hot-air balloon ride."

She and Stan may not agree on this, and she believed she was correct, but she would not go against Stan's ethics or religious beliefs to satisfy what she thought was right. However, she needed to convince him that they had a chance to make a difference. "I realize this is a stretch, but I also have seen the look of sadness on Joe's face. He's ninety-seven or one-hundred-and-two, depending on who's telling the story. He can't get out of bed, is in constant pain, and the chances for him living another twelve months after a broken hip are slim at best." She pointed to her open computer screen. "I've read lots of reports."

Stan rubbed the back of his neck. "It's close to outright lying."

Skeeter flipped to a fresh computer screen. She pointed to it. "Lying to someone who has dementia may be justified when it's necessary to promote well-being." She scrolled to another screen. "Lies that reduce suffering and stress in patients unable to fully appreciate the cause of distress can be beneficial." She nodded. "That clearly defines Joe's present state. His distress is daily. The photograph of Mary is marred by his fingerprints; he lovingly holds the photograph, thinking Mary will show up at any minute, so he can tell her the words he forgot. He truly believes he didn't say he loved her the last night they were together. I can't imagine the torment he has."

Stan grimaced. "I don't know. It's outright deceit."

"It's not the truth but then what is truth? Truth has to rely on perspective. Love is truth; it's a truth that brings us to a certain understanding. We both love Joe, and Joe loves Mary. Is it wrong to bring an abridged truth to the one love of Joe's life, a life without a long future?"

Stan chuckled. "You are getting better at mixing words to make everything sound good."

"I've read the chapters in the Bible you asked me to read. Most of them anyhow. Those chapters talk about right and wrong, about loving others."

Stan rubbed the back of his neck. "I'm still not sure—"

She interrupted, leaning forward. "I learned a few things from the chapters in the Bible. Love unconditionally. Seek to understand and to show compassion. What I give out I will expect to receive the same. Learn forgiveness. Seek to show peace and love and to ease suffering." She reached out to touch Stan's hand. "By bringing Mary to Joe, we will be doing all of those things. We need to do this for him." She sniffed back her emotions. "Stan, you know he doesn't have long in this world. This will make his passing a blessing."

"It's not deception?"

"In this case it's love."

He glanced over Skeeter's shoulder to Beth. She resembled Mary, the way she looked in the photograph Joe cradled in his knobby hands. "Love takes many forms," he commented. "Love is what makes us who we are; it is the energy which brings us to life, and it is the peace that can let us go to be with God."

She squeezed his hand. "You're the one who taught me that."

Pastor Stan smiled.

CHAPTER 26

The following morning, Skeeter rose early to work on a hacking project. When finished, she refilled her coffee cup, toasted a bagel, and ate it with cherry jelly. She answered e-mails, ignoring a text from Steve.

She placed a call to Joe's son, asking if they could meet for coffee late in the afternoon. Tony replied that they could meet. She next texted Pastor Stan and told him to join her and Joe's son at a coffee shop on Main Street.

Outside, the day was a perfect hint of all the lazy summer days ahead. The rays of sun fluttered through the cottonwood trees as blackbirds hopped between branches. Through the grass, she could see the sun sparkle off the river. The whole effect was enough to slow her pulse and calm her nerves.

"Good morning," Beth said as she emerged from the master bedroom, already dressed in light pants, a long-sleeve print shirt, and a pair of sneakers.

"Hi Grandma," Skeeter said and her heart increased in tempo. "You're looking good this morning."

Beth found a mug and poured herself coffee, adding sugar and stirring. "It's going to be a gorgeous day. Look at the view."

Glancing outside, Skeeter slid off the chair at the island counter. "Let's take our coffee out on the patio and enjoy the morning sun."

Beth smiled. "It sounds lovely."

On the way out the patio door, Skeeter commented, "Your hair looks great. It gives you a new flair."

"Thanks. I have to admit I was feeling dowdy." She fluffed her hair with her left hand. "I feel like a different person." Beth sat on the lounger, facing the rocky peak called Castle Peak. She stretched her legs and sighed. "I love this place."

Skeeter scooted a patio chair closer to her grandmother. "I know you do and I understand why." She swirled her coffee and then held the mug between both hands. "Grandma, I have a favor to ask."

Beth turned, shading her eyes with her hand. "Whatever, dear." With a frown, she paused. "You look serious. It's not like you."

Skeeter managed a half-smile. "I met a man at the Piney Center."

"A new boyfriend? I thought you had caught that cowboy's attention?"

Laughing, Skeeter waved her grandmother silent. "I hope so, and the man at the Piney Center is almost a hundred years old. He has become a friend."

Beth beamed. "It's lovely."

"He's dying, Grandma."

A frown marred her brow. "That's terrible."

"Not when you think about it. He's had a long happy life. They say a man who lives fully is not afraid of death. Because I know the type of man he is, I know he will meet death as a new challenge."

Reaching out, Beth patted Skeeter's thigh. "It's nice he has you as a friend."

"I'm a friend because he is the type of person who lives the way people should live, and because I want to help him."

"It sounds like you. What's wrong with him that he needs help?"

Skeeter took a deep breath and exhaled. "He's sad and it makes me sad, too."

Beth lowered her voice and asked, "How can you help him?"

Skeeter stroked the back of her grandmother's hand. "Joe's wife, Mary, died a little while ago, and the night before she died, he forgot to tell her that he loved her. This wears on him, Grandma, something terrible. He is ready to die but he can't do it until he tells Mary he loves her."

"It's not good," she said, her voice close to a whisper.

Nodding, Skeeter touched the hair on her grandmother's cheek. "She looks a lot like you, especially with your new haircut. When I saw you last night in your blue dress and wearing the pearls around your neck, you looked exactly like the picture Joe has of his wife."

A stagnant moment filled the air. A blackbird screeched in the trees. Beth studied her granddaughter. "I see the look on your face, Skeeter. You are up to something and it has to do with me. I have a feeling it has something to do with Joe, too."

Smiling, she met her grandmother's stare. "You're right, and I think you can do it."

Beth leaned forward as if wanting to make sure she heard every word. "So, tell me what you want me to do."

Skeeter also leaned forward until they were only inches apart. "This is what I want."

When she was finished telling her, Beth straightened her back. "It's easy. The one thing I do is charm men. It doesn't matter how old they are. I don't remember if you told me if he's handsome or not?"

Skeeter sighed like a slight spring breeze, soft and gentle. "He is handsome, and a gentleman, and he loves baseball."

"I watched the San Francisco Giants in Candlestick Park. Your father was a fan."

"I know you went to many ball games, and I remember Dad knew all the players."

"Is Joe a fan of the Giants?"

"No, he lived in New York and was a Yankees fan."

"Hmm. San Francisco got the Giants from New York in 1958. I remember seeing them at Seals Stadium. Then they moved to Candlestick Park, and we had to dress for sub-zero temperatures when we went to the games. I never did go to a game after the Giants moved to Oracle Park. I don't think I was living near the city then."

It amazed Skeeter how her grandmother's mind could remember details but not recall which of her friends had recently passed away. "If Joe talks baseball, you won't be lost."

Beth sipped her coffee, gazing toward the pinnacle of rocks far off in the distance. A smile crept across her face, warming her face with the morning sunshine. "When should I plan to visit Joe?"

"Soon," she answered. She added, "I need you to wear your pale blue dress with the string of pearls and fix your hair like it looks today."

"Lovely. I will be playing a part. Simply lovely."

***

Pastor Stan and Skeeter met with Joe's son, Tony, at the deli on Main Street. Although Tony was taller than his father, the resemblance was apparent. He looked like Joe thirty years ago with dark hair and a hint of gray at the temples. His shoulders were broad, his body still filled with muscle. He wore tan shorts and a polo shirt. He had the same lips and nose as his father. A scar ran over his right eyebrow. Skeeter didn't see a resemblance to Mary in him. He greeted them with a nod and a handshake and pointed to a table by the window overlooking the street. Next door was a bike shop, and the view outside was a blur of riders in colored bike shirts as they rode by.

"Beer, wine, soft drink?" Tony asked.

They settled on what to drink, and he and Pastor Stan made small talk, while Skeeter bounced her foot under the table and felt a bead of sweat run down her temple. Finally, Pastor Stan ended the chit-chat and related to Tony Joe's sadness about forgetting to tell Mary that he loved her the last night they were together.

Tony didn't look surprised. "He's told me how it happened and it's left him feeling awful. He loved my mom. I've always been envious of a love like that." He shook his head. "He hasn't been the same since she died."

Pastor Stan sipped iced tea. He nodded toward Skeeter. "We've become friends with Joe and feel the same as you do about your dad. As a man of God, I cherish life, but we all must face the end. For Joe, it only means an end to a chapter. If he could tell Mary he loves her, we think he won't suffer the guilt hounding him. Every time we visit him, he asks for Mary and wishes he could find her. It's holding back Joe from leaving here and joining her."

Tony nodded. "I wish I could fix it."

Pastor Stan smiled. He proceeded to tell Tony about Beth and the strange resemblance. Then Skeeter picked up the conversation and related to Tony their idea of bringing Mary to Joe one last time. She ended with, "We did not want to proceed with this idea unless we talked with you to see how you feel about it."

Frowning, Tony looked at his hands. "I don't know. It feels deceitful. What if dad realizes it's not Mary?"

Skeeter expected this. "Joe can hardly understand an eighteen-font menu from the dining room. He can't read a book. He isn't sure about colors and tries to turn the television off with his razor. His eyesight is failing along with other body parts. Now he has a broken hip with a lot of pain. My grandmother is a dead ringer for Mary. I wouldn't suggest this if I wasn't sure she could become Mary for the short time it takes for your dad to see her, become emotional, tell her he loves her, and my grandmother will nod and leave. It's simple."

Tony leaned forward. "I spent time in China. They have a proverb: 'Some simple things aren't.'"

Pastor Stan cast a nervous glance at Skeeter, who sighed, then added, "Yes, it could go wrong. I admit it, but this is a love we're talking about — love Joe has for Mary, and your dad wants to be with Mary but is struggling to get there. Let's help him — you, me, Pastor Stan, and my grandmother. Have you heard him gasp for breath the past day or two? Or seen the look in his eyes, like he is seeing someone far away but can't reach them? I have. So has Pastor Stan."

Stan added, "I believe the angels have surrounded Joe. They want him."

Tony fiddled with the paper label on his bottle of beer. "I haven't visited Dad since they called me about his broken hip," he admitted. "I never thought he would live this long, especially after Mom died. I have such good memories of him when they were together, and Dad was spry and able to do more than nap and look for Mom. Now, it's too much for me."

Pushing herself back, Skeeter's chair hit the wall with a thud. "Let's help your dad." She looked across the table to see Tony's eyes pool with liquid.

"If Dad thinks it's Mary, it will give him the greatest joy he has had in months," Tony said as the realization came to him that this would release his dad from torment over losing Mary.

"My grandmother could have been a successful actress. She's had three husbands, and I don't know how many boyfriends, who all think she is the greatest thing since sliced bread, and she likes nothing better than a handsome man, and Joe is handsome even if he is almost a hundred."

Pastor Stan and Skeeter exchanged worried glances. "What?" Tony asked as he realized they were not telling him something.

Skeeter ran her finger around the bottom of her glass of cold tea. "My grandmother has Alzheimer's disease. We thought you should know. Sometimes she forgets things. Other times her mind is clear. I told her about Joe, and she has agreed to be Mary. However, I can't guarantee she won't slip up and say the wrong thing, only because she won't remember what she is supposed to say. On the other hand, she could be the best actress ever."

Pastor Stan added, "When the memory is dim, it is hard to know exactly how a person will act. Beth's recent hairstyle has come as a blessing, and when we acknowledge our blessings, it ignites passion and creative solutions."

Tony sighed. He studied both Skeeter and Stan. "I think it's worth a chance. You wouldn't have come to me if you didn't think it would work. I don't want Dad to go on like this."

Stan nodded in agreement. "Either do we. I have prayed about this, Tony, and believe God has put myself and Skeeter in place to help alleviate Joe's suffering. It's a kind and loving thing to do. At times, God asks for our help, at times he asks us to be His hands and feet and eyes. I believe this is one of those times."

Tony remained silent for a few seconds before slapping his thigh. "I hope this works." He looked up. "My mother took chances. She took one when she married Dad and it lasted fifty-eight years. I think she would like this plan. Okay, you have my blessing."

Pastor Stan turned to Skeeter and the two of them smiled.

CHAPTER 27

At home, Skeeter began to check off things that had to be done at the house. George had listed the cars for sale in the local newspaper and several people had come by to look at them. Two different real estate agents met with Skeeter and Beth and toured the property, leaving with assurances they would get back with an estimate of the value of the property. One real estate agent was a woman with brunette hair who seemed as if she had been transplanted from a big city, either New York or Chicago. Tall and willowy, she wore expensive pants and a designer jacket. Her makeup was heavy and her accent jewelry flashy. She reeked upscale chicness. She was so slick, Skeeter thought she would slide off the kitchen chair. The other agent was a man about fifty with a balding head and mustache who had stopped by the house and gave the impression that he tried to fit in Piney, Colorado, and didn't quite make it. Skeeter knew she didn't want to work with him and turned her mind off to everything he said. Both Realtors guessed the appraisal for the house would come in around one and a half million dollars. It made Skeeter's head swim. *Is that enough to make George sue?*

At the Piney Center, Cordy spent more time sleeping. Cecil worked on the timing of "Sound of Silence", Richard read a biography of George S. Patton, Jayne sang along with Cecil, Layla May ordered several new facial clarifying wash kits, and Millie decided to write her life history. Joe remained weak; the nurses said he didn't eat much and had quit complaining about pain, which they said was not a good sign.

The day had come for Beth to transform into Mary and arrive at Joe's side. For the event, Pastor Stan would meet them at the Center at 3 p.m. Before it could happen, though, Skeeter had to make some adjustments on her computer. Feeling only a tinge of remorse, she hacked into Harry's Piney Center calendar, and also his cell phone; she couldn't chance Harry would interrupt the plan.

She opened his calendar. It was clear. Sitting back in her chair, she tapped her foot, wondering where she should send Harry this afternoon which wouldn't raise suspicion. When it came to her, she started typing. Finished, she closed Harry's calendar and decided she had better learn what Larry had in the way of something chocolate. She needed her mid-morning fix and figured Cecil did, too.

Before heading to the kitchen, she checked her text messages. One was from Bart: *Two things. I miss you. Are you free this weekend? Next Tuesday would be a good day to bring Misty to the Center for Millie?*

"Tuesday," she muttered and first answered Bart. Next, she reopened her laptop and went back to Harry's Piney Center schedule for Tuesday. "Tuesday. Let's send you to Vail to the hospital for a joint meeting of medical personnel who deal with older adults." She typed in the information, closed Harry's calendar, shut down her computer, and headed to the kitchen with a spring in her step.

After lunch, Skeeter chatted with Charmaine and Joe's nurse and then headed home, where she found Beth on the patio with a bag of potting soil and several flats of annual flowers in a riot of color. "Hi Grandma," she said after sitting on a chair, enjoying the feel of the high-altitude sun on her shoulders.

Beth glanced up from the empty pots. She pointed her garden trowel at the flowers. "I like this time of the year. Spring blossoms make me feel good inside, the type of feeling that warms me all over." She bent her head, almost touching the blossoms in the flat. "The smell of flowers cuts through the tangy sweetness of the pasture grass."

Smiling, Skeeter was happy to know her grandmother had a clear mind today and did agree with her about the power of flowers. One garden glove covered Beth's left hand but her right hand was glove-free and smudged with dirt. "Looks like you enjoy this."

"Yes." She pointed to purple and yellow pansies. "Those were Roger's favorites."

Skeeter fingered a delicate blossom. "I'm glad you are doing something for Roger. This afternoon, I'd like you to do what we talked about for Joe." She crossed her fingers, hoping that her grandmother would remember their discussion.

Beth dropped the trowel "Today? Was Joe the nice man we talked to about Roger's will?"

Skeeter's shoulders slumped. "No, Grandma. Joe is my friend at the Piney Center whose wife, Mary, died. I asked you to go visit with Joe and pretend to be his wife for one afternoon."

She snapped her fingers. "Oh, right. He's the Yankee's fan."

Skeeter almost cried. "Yes, grandma. The Yankees."

***

A little before three p.m., Skeeter escorted Beth into the Piney Center. Outfitted in a pale blue dress and a string of pearls around her neck, and with her hair freshly washed and curling on her forehead and cheeks, and with a fresh dab of pale pink lipstick, she looked like Joe's Mary.

When Charmaine saw her, she gasped. "Oh, my."

Pastor Stan joined Skeeter and Beth. He gazed at her from head to toe and shook his head with disbelief. "If I didn't know better, I'd say Mary has joined us."

Beth extended her hand to Pastor Stan. "I'm Mary. Today I like the Yankees, but only for today." She swung in a circle. "Do I pass the test?"

Pastor Stan nodded, then turned to Charmaine. "Has Harry left?"

Charmaine gave him a thumb's up. "Meeting with the senior group in Summit County." She checked her watch. "He won't be back for a few hours."

With her nerves stretched thin, Skeeter did not look at Charmaine or Pastor Stan. Clearing her throat, she touched Beth's elbow. "Let's do this. Remember Grandma, pretend to be Mary. Let him lead the conversation. Grandma, he'll want to say he loves you. After that is when you leave."

Beth raised her chin an inch and straightened her shoulders. "I am Mary. Show me his room. I can talk baseball with him, despite him being a Red Sox fan."

Skeeter gritted her teeth. "It was Yankees for him."

"I got it," Beth said and followed Pastor Stan to Joe's room.

Mentally counting to ten, Skeeter walked behind her grandmother and said a quiet prayer this day would be all right. She imagined Pastor Stan prayed harder than she did.

At Joe's door, Beth ran her hands down the sides of her skirt to press out any wrinkles.

Pastor Stan whispered to her, "We'll be right outside."

Beth nodded and entered the room, where the blinds were lowered halfway to the windowsill. The television was silent. Joe's head reclined on a pillow, his eyes closed, his lower jaw slightly ajar. His oxygen machine emitted a low whoosh-whoosh sound. His bedside table held his water and an uneaten carton of vanilla pudding. She approached the bed, looking down at the man who held a picture of a woman who looked exactly like herself. Pausing at his bed, she inhaled and held it, slowly letting her breath escape her lips. Bending closer to him, her pearls swung from her body. She curled her fingers and ran them down his cheek. "Joe," she whispered with a smile.

His body jerked. He opened his eyes and blinked. "Mary," he gasped, his voice a raspy quiver.

She smiled. "Yes, it's me. I'm here." She watched his lips turn into a smile and saw how it came from deep inside to light his eyes and spread across his face.

Finding her hand, he squeezed. "I've been waiting."

"I know, Joe. I'm here now." She wound her fingers around his hand.

"Sit with me," he said, reaching up and pulling his oxygen tube away from his face. "I hate that thing." He leaned toward Mary. "Now I can see you better. Oh, you are so beautiful. I've missed you so."

Pulling a chair closer to the bed with one hand, Beth sat down and scooted the chair closer to his bed. "Me, too, Joe."

Joe wrapped his arms around Mary, and she let her head rest on his chest. He stroked her head, allowing his fingers to twine in her curls. "I knew you would come. I told them, Skeeter and Pastor Stan, and Layla May, and Hanni."

From the corridor, Skeeter closed her eyes, praying her grandmother would not ask Joe who the people were who he mentioned. Next to her, she could hear Stan's whispered prayers.

Beth sat up, still letting Joe hold her hand. "You have always been my everything."

Joe fumbled to reach for the picture of Mary. He brought it to his chest. "You have been with me every day."

Beth brushed a wisp of hair from the side of Joe's face. "I didn't want to go but it was my time, but even when I was gone, I've always loved you."

Closing his eyes for a second, Joe nodded, lifted her hand to his lips, and kissed it. "I forgot to tell you how much I love you the last time we were together."

Beth leaned closer to him. "You didn't need to tell me. I always knew."

Joe gasped as if shocked to the core. "But I told you every night."

"I listened. Even though I didn't need to hear the words, I knew it in my heart."

In the hall, Skeeter brushed a tear off her cheek.

Joe smiled a smile lighting up the room. "Oh, my Mary, my dear Mary. I shouldn't have worried, but I did, but here you are. Now I can…. I don't have to worry any longer." He coughed and struggled to take a deep breath.

Skeeter poked Pastor Stan. Whispering, she said, "She did it. Should I try to get her out of there?"

Pastor Stan shrugged. "I think these are some beautiful moments. Perhaps you shouldn't interrupt?"

"What if Grandma suddenly asks who he is?"

Pastor Stan put a comforting hand on Skeeter's shoulder. "I think, my dear, that your grandmother has this scene under control. She has a way with men. Let Joe enjoy the time with Mary."

Skeeter bit on a ragged hangnail, while turning back to Joe and Beth.

Joe's voice grew softer. "I remember when I gave those pearls to you," he said as he lifted a shaky hand to feel the pearls.

Skeeter grew rigid. *Uh, oh.*

Beth fingered the pearls. "They're my favorites," she purred.

Joe added, "You used to wear them with a sweatshirt to the ball games."

Double uh, oh.

"I always wanted to look pretty for you, Joe."

With a deep sigh, Joe closed his eyes, still holding tightly to Beth's hand. He closed his eyes and sighed, his breath a rattle in his throat. "I am tired," he said, each word spoken with an effort.

Beth slipped her hand from his. "I'm going to let you sleep now."

He didn't open his eyes. "I love you."

"I know. I love you, too." Rising, she walked to the door and sailed past Skeeter and Pastor Stan.

CHAPTER 28

The weekend passed in a blaze of outdoor activities for Skeeter with Bart. Even though the ranch was spread over hundreds of acres, activity went on daily. Bart was not supposed to be working on the weekends, but something or other came up at the ranch which needed doing. Skeeter didn't mind, because she enjoyed watching him work, the way his shirt stretched across his back, the way his hands managed a calf or a fence post, or a piece of equipment. His boss didn't order Bart to do things, he asked because it was obvious Bart was the best one to do the job.

They rode horses again in the afternoon on a trail along the Colorado River. Cottonwood leaves dangled in the breeze, while ponderosa pines soared into the sky with warm brown bark to hold up stately limbs. The river, swollen with snowmelt, surged down the canyon, giving off a sense of power. Skeeter rode behind Bart's large paint horse, admiring how his butt fit the saddle, his long legs moving in subtle ways to tell his horse which direction to go. She began to trust Misty with making the right decisions about where to go and figured Millie would be about as safe as she could be in the saddle for her end-of-life ride. Skeeter had no idea how to guide Misty but also asked questions about riding, and Bart answered without intimidation. It made her like him more than she wanted to admit.

They veered off the river and headed up a steep hillside to the east. Over his shoulder, Bart told her, "Lean forward in the saddle to help Misty. Move your weight to her shoulders, not her haunches. If it's steep, almost lay on her mane."

Skeeter did as he suggested and felt Misty's power beneath her, felt her dig in with her front legs, and lunge with her rear legs. At the top of the ridge, Misty stopped beside Bart's gelding, her sides heaving, tossing her head.

Bart laughed. "For an older horse, Misty does not want to stop. She has a huge heart and big capacity with her lungs."

Skeeter stroked Misty's neck while she looked at the trail going down the backside of the hill. It looked steep, dotted with gray rocks and jade-colored sagebrush, the grasses green with spring growth. "How about going downhill? Maybe I should walk her down?"

He tipped his Stetson off his head to let the sun cover his face. "I don't want you to walk. There's a greater chance she'll slide and plow into you. You are safer in the saddle. This is where you lean back and put your weight on her haunches. Push forward in the stirrups and hold on with your knees. With Misty, you won't have to neck rein. She'll find the best path down." He pointed to his gelding. "With this one, I have to guide him around every shrub, otherwise he'll plod over the top. Some horses are like that."

She turned in the saddle, gazing up toward the rock castle formation in the distance and down to the river, surging brown with silty runoff. The hills had a daytime hue of pale tan and pink. Here and there juniper trees slanted toward the sky.

Bart pointed in a northerly direction. "The Ute came this way because they couldn't get through Glenwood Canyon." He turned and pointed west. "Years ago, the early settlers found an Indian graveyard over there."

She squinted to where he pointed. The country was breathtaking. Misty pawed at the ground. "What's she doing?"

He slid out of his saddle, moving to Misty. "She's anxious to go down the hill. I'm going to tighten your cinch." Looking up, he smiled at her. "There's nothing worse than having the saddle ride her neck on the way down."

He moved close enough so that his shoulder rubbed against her leg. She felt a spark of heat race through her body. When he finished, he offered her a drink from a water bottle. "Drink?"

She let her fingers trail over his when she took the water bottle from him. Guys she had known had treated her to drinks in skyscraper buildings or on decks at a marina, but she couldn't remember anything as special as cold water sliding down her throat at the top of a mountain while on a horse and with this cowboy by her side. "Thank you," she said and added, "for everything."

He climbed in his saddle, easily swinging one leg over the horse's side. With the heel of his boot, he nudged his mount forward. His gelding tossed his head and began to prance down the steep face. Bart pulled him in and talked to him, and within a few steps, the horse quieted and found his way down the hill. Misty started down the slope. To Skeeter, she felt as though she were at the top of a roller coaster, looking down the steep plunge. Misty's rear end swayed and a few times slid as the soft dirt gave way, but Skeeter trusted the horse. When they reached the bottom of the hill, she smiled at Bart and leaned forward to stroke Misty's neck. "That was fun," she said and was almost surprised to hear herself say so.

She found Bart handsome from the depth of his eyes to the expressions in his voice. She liked watching his eyes sparkle with a new idea, or when he listened to one of hers, he enjoyed it so much he lost himself while staring at her. By the end of the day, she had given him a chunk of her heart, which she knew he would keep safe.

When he kissed her goodbye, the sun slipped over the mountains to the west, and she held on to him as if she never wanted to let him go. And then her thoughts went to Joe. *Was this the type of love he and Mary had shared?*

Sunday night Skeeter dragged into the house close to midnight. Her body was tired, her mind at ease. It was the way it should be after spending the day with a man who held her heart.

On Monday, Skeeter slept later than usual and when she padded into the kitchen to get her morning cup of coffee, Beth greeted her with a perky tone to her voice. Dressed in the blue dress and with the pearl necklace swinging around her neck, Skeeter didn't know whether to question or compliment her. "Grandma," she said, "the blue dress? What's up?"

Beth brushed a curl off her cheek. "Bruce wanted me to go with him to Denver to look at a new refrigerator, but I told him I wanted to visit with Joe."

"What?"

With a nod, Beth said, "He's a sweetheart." She locked eyes with Skeeter. "His son was with him most of yesterday."

Skeeter swallowed to ease a dry throat. "You met Tony?"

Beth beamed. "A lovely man." Her tone of voice turned serious. "I met him yesterday. Joe's dying, Skeeter. He's ready to leave this life. He told me we won't have any more walks in the park, no more birthday celebrations with Tony, and we won't see another snow season."

Skeeter sat at the counter, placed her head on her palm. "Grandma, you don't have to do this."

Beth moved to her granddaughter. "I'm not being forced to do this, dear. Please, give me the credit for understanding some things about growing old, because I am old, and I know my memory is going to hell, and I can't do anything about it, but you have given me a chance to make a difference in this man's life." She put a hand on Skeeter's shoulder. "In the end, I couldn't do that for Roger. It was too sudden, too permanent, too unexpected."

For a moment, Skeeter closed her eyes and felt the warmth of her grandmother's touch on her shoulder. *So, Pastor Stan was right. Beth hasn't grieved the way I expected her to but she has grieved.*

Skeeter took her grandmother's hand and kissed it. "Thank you," she said as a tear slipped down her cheek.

Beth gave her a gentle pat on the back. "I love you, too." With a swish of her blue dress, she grabbed her purse and headed out the door.

Exhausted from her emotions, Skeeter took her coffee out on the patio, slipped into the lounger, and gazed off at the mountain called Castle Peak.

***

Joe died peacefully in his sleep on Tuesday afternoon. Earlier he had been visited by Tony, Mary (Beth), and Pastor Stan. While those who knew Joe tried to show a glimmer of sadness when he died, in reality those who knew Joe were happy that he had found Mary and was now on a new adventure. The tone in the Piney Center was part loss and part celebration.

Pastor Stan simply said, "It is as it should be."

Skeeter decided he was the wisest man she knew.

Tony wanted time to write an obituary for the newspaper and to arrange for a memorial service for his dad at a later time in the summer. The service would be at the top of Vail Mountain at the wedding deck, which overlooked Mount of the Holy Cross. With

Hanni leaving them only a month earlier, everyone decided it was a good decision. Cecil, Layla May, and Jayne practiced songs they would sing at his service. As each day went by, the residents of the Piney Center looked forward to Joe's memorial service as a celebration of life.

During the week, Skeeter planned fun activities with the seniors in assisted living, and Julia made a special effort to visit, bringing Charlotte and Bear. Cordy dozed off in the afternoons more than usual and sometimes she didn't show up for socializing. Richard gave updates on his Skype meetings with Finn. Layla May arrived with a smile and with some sort of important fashion information, and Millie talked about her son who lived in Texas and who was busy, but also sparkled with bright eyes when she talked about her grandson, Bart.

Millie offhandedly said, "My Bart has a new girl. He won't tell me much about her but if blushing were possible by a cowboy, I think it would explain the way his face reacts when he talks about her."

Skeeter had to put a hand over her lips when Millie said such things.

Pastor Stan had been working on the problem of Cordy and her balloon experience. He continued to say a solution was coming, but Skeeter wondered if it would be soon enough.

On a Wednesday, Harry breezed into their social time and stood with his hands on his hips. "Hi, everyone," he announced. "I have good news. We will be having a new addition to assisted living. Her name is Doris, and she grew up in Leadville, which is south of us." He glanced at Layla May. "She was the curator of the museum at Leadville for many years, specializing in fashion styles during the heyday of mining, so if anyone is a history buff, this is your opportunity to learn or challenge her, whichever seems to fit."

Skeeter rolled her eyes toward Pastor Stan.

Harry added, "She'll join us in about a week. I hope everyone will welcome her."

With a new resident an expert on fashion style, Layla May looked as though someone had poked her in the eye. Millie smiled. Cordy dozed. Cecil and Richard traded glances. Pastor Stan nodded.

Harry shifted his weight from foot to foot. "Another thing. I've had some difficulties with the calendar on my computer and on my phone, too. I've checked with my internet provider, and they can't figure out what has gone wrong." He found Skeeter and stared at her.

Purposely, she sat with a rigid back, did not blink, and lifted the corners of her lips ever so slightly. She strummed her fingers on the back of Cecil's chair.

"So, if you are planning any special event, I want to know." Harry pointed to Pastor Stan and ended with a laser shot of guilt directed at Skeeter. "You two. Follow my rules. They are in place for the safety of our residents. You approved these rules when you signed the volunteer and employment agreements. Understand?"

Pastor Stan nodded. Skeeter looked through Harry and lifted her lips one-eighth of an inch higher. Those from assisted living remained quiet, wondering why Harry spoke in such a stiff manner.

Harry tossed his hands in the air. "That's it. Carry on."

***

Skeeter communicated with Bart daily. She looked forward to his phone calls and when he came to town, they met for a quick bite to eat or something quick at the house Skeeter fixed for them, and they were able to take outside and enjoy the last rays of sunlight. They went over the plans for Millie to ride Misty outside the Piney Center on the following Tuesday, having postponed it a week due to Joe's passing. Pastor Stan would alert the staff at the rehab facility and assisted living. The only one they didn't tell was Harry. She toyed with the idea of sending him somewhere by placing an appointment on his calendar, but she was savvy enough to know Harry had figured out someone had altered his calendar, and he had looked directly at her. By Friday, she didn't have an answer to the problem of what to do with Harry.

George arrived from the East Coast. Skeeter was happy to pick him up at the Piney County Airport. Although she couldn't read his emotional condition when she met him, she decided that by the end of his stay, she would know one way or the other whether Beth would have a legal battle with him. The problem was, Skeeter liked George. At the house, he took over the extra bedroom in the lower level and therefore could have as much privacy as he wanted. Bart came over in the late afternoon with pork loin for the grill and mixings for a salad. Skeeter poured a whiskey for George, a beer for Bart, and wine for herself. Beth arranged appetizers and brought out colorful cocktail napkins and small paper plates. They shared their drinks on the patio, while the twilight filtered through the cottonwood trees and meadow birds flitted through the grass. Off in the distance, Castle Peak glimmered under late day sun while thunderheads reared in the background.

If the cloud of uncertainty over the house didn't hang over her, she could have relaxed a little more, but the cloud remained as though a miasma layer, keeping Skeeter on edge. When she glanced at Bart with his handsome profile and the muscles in his shoulders pushing against his shirt, she wanted his arms around her to take away the tension. She had to take her mind off of him, however, chastising herself for having such strong feelings.

George got up to start the grill. Beth said, "I'll fix the salad and I have baked beans."

Bart leaned closer to Skeeter. "Are we all set for Millie's ride next Tuesday?"

Skeeter nibbled on a hangnail. "Millie is all set. Very perky. Her hips give her trouble, so I'm glad you can get her in the saddle. She showed me riding pants. They must be fifty years old and fit!" She paused, sighing. "I'm only concerned about Harry."

George adjusted the temperature on the grill. "Harry from the Piney Center?"

Bart answered, "Yeah. I guess you met him at Hanni's memorial."

"Yes." He angled the grill scrapper at Bart. "He was okay."

A frown marred Skeeter's brow. "Sometimes," she mumbled.

"What? Another emergency?"

She wound an errant strand of blond hair behind her ear. "You could say so." She then told him about Millie's wish to sit on a horse before she dies, and the plan for Bart to bring Misty to the Center on Tuesday. "The only problem is getting Harry out of the way. I know he won't approve of us doing this for her. We need him to be away from the Center for a couple of hours, tops." She thought again about hacking his calendar and her frown deepened. "I can't send him on a false errand."

George shrugged. "Hey, I can help. I can invite him to go to lunch with me. I'll tell him I'm interested in information about assisted living for Beth. I think he'll accept."

Skeeter looked at Bart and raised an eyebrow. He held her gaze. "Why not?" he asked with enough mischief in his eyes to make her believe it would work.

George tipped his glass to his lips, then raised. "Okay then, I will call him on Monday and make plans to pick him up to go to lunch in Vail. It should take several hours, and I like strolling Vail Village in the early summer. All those flowers and the gondola running and I bet you can still see snow on the highest ski runs."

Although Skeeter didn't want to be in George's debt, she had to admit this was a good plan. With a nod, she said, "Okay." She nudged Bart. "We're on. You have Misty at the Center at noon on Tuesday. George will have whisked Harry away, and we should have plenty of time to give Millie her ride."

He leaned over and kissed Skeeter quickly. "I can't thank you enough."

She whispered next to his ear, "I can think of a few ways you can show me."

The rest of the weekend passed in a blur of activity. George organized more of his dad's belongings and also disappeared to fish the Piney River for a few hours. Beth hiked with Bruce, Skeeter accompanied Bart to Meeker, Colorado for a Border Collie Sheep Herding exhibition. If one of her friends from San Francisco knew she had spent her Sunday at a dog show, they would have burst with laughter. However, the scenery on the way to Meeker was of stunning rock formations capped with snow, spring grass so green it looked fake, and expansive meadows speckled with dandelions. Rivers gleamed under the sun as if diamond chips had been strewn from above. Crab apple trees in bloom looked more like popcorn, and the air smelled sweet with the nectar of everything spring. She wished Beth and Bruce had joined them, and thought of George and guessed he would have loved it.

With a smile, Skeeter decided her life had taken a strange turn. Then her thoughts went to Millie and her ride. She wondered what would happen if Harry found out about it? Would he fire her? Then she sighed, deciding their plan for George to take Harry to lunch should work and there was no need to worry. *Except I do worry.*

CHAPTER 29

Monday afternoon, Stan knocked on Cordy's door, hoping she wasn't napping and the intrusion wouldn't wake her.

A shaky voice replied, "Come in."

Stan turned the doorknob, stepped across the threshold, and into the brightly lit room.

"Hi, Cordy."

"Welcome, Pastor Stan," Cordy said with an attempt at being upbeat. "It's nice to see you. Did we have a date?"

"No, Cordy. I'm here for music and singing with your friends. I arrived early and thought I would check to see if you planned on joining us?

"Do I like singing?"

Stan glanced around Cordy's room. He noticed numerous photographs of hot-air balloons on the walls and smaller ones in picture frames, sitting on the table against the left wall. "Perhaps not as much fun as going up in a balloon but you usually say singing is fun."

She slapped her knee, then adjusted the piece of cloth on her head. "If it's fun, I'll be there."

Unlike so many of the residents in the Piney Center, Cordy kept her curtains open during the day to let in the sunlight. The view looked onto a busy street with an intersection overlooking downtown Piney. From Cordy's room, he could barely make out the neon sign of the Dusty Corral Café. Stan checked his watch. "We have a little time."

Cordy pointed a shaky finger at a chair at the end of the table. "Have a seat, take a load off."

Stan sat, still glancing at the colorful pictures of hot-air balloons and ended by a glance at the strange-looking patch of cloth on Cordy's head. He kept quiet, knowing better than to ask her about it. Skeeter had filled him in on Cordy's fixation with kangaroos.

Stan shifted his focus from the patch of cloth. "Skeeter told me you loved to go ballooning."

She nodded with a smile. "It's one of the passions of my life. It's been too long though since I flew in a balloon."

"How long has it been?"

She rubbed her chin with thumb and finger while a frown split her forehead. "My brain is fuzzy. But I think it's been about six years. Or is it sixteen? My memory isn't good. Anyhow, it was at a festival in Albuquerque, New Mexico. Did you know the Albuquerque International Balloon Fiesta is the biggest balloon festival in the world? That much I remember."

Stan nodded. "Sounds interesting."

Cordy continued, "It's a nine-day festival in early October featuring over five hundred balloons from all over the world. It's amazing. I can recall so much about it because I attended for many years." Cordy dropped her head and said in a whisper, "I miss it so much." Her voice brightened again, "One of the most awe-inspiring events is the Mass Ascensions when hundreds of balloons launch into the sky all at once. Zebras help coordinate the launch so the balloons rise without crashing into each other."

"Oh, no," Stan thought to himself. *She also has an obsession with Zebras.* "Zebra's?" Stan asked cautiously.

"Oh, I'm sorry," Cordy said with a chuckle. "They are the launch directors. We call the men and women who help launch the balloons 'zebras" because of their black-and-white-striped outfits. They serve as 'traffic cops,' making sure safety is observed."

Moving to the table, Stan picked up a photograph of a yellow and orange striped balloon rising. "It looks exciting, although heights make my heart flutter."

"It's not only the flying. The festivals are a big part of what makes ballooning fun. They are family-friendly. The festivals include face painting for the children, clowns bouncing around making mayhem, people laughing, always something to do. Food of every sort is available, music everywhere, and happy and laughing people having fun. Camaraderie is built around the love of ballooning, and," Cordy said, lowering her voice, "they don't let kangaroos onto the festival grounds."

It was all Stan could do not to laugh. Cordy was as colorful as the balloon pictures on her walls. *How can such a sweet, smart woman imagine kangaroos in Colorado?*

Stan stared at the floor, trying to gain his composure. He hoped Cordy couldn't see his shoulders shaking with amusement. To hide his laughter, he glanced to his right and saw a magazine lying on a small table. Bold words in black proclaimed the name of the magazine; *Ballooning.* In smaller type were the words, "Journal of the Balloon Federation of America." The picture on the cover was an aerial view of brightly-colored hot-air balloons rising into the air. This rescued Stan from his laughing spell, and he picked up the magazine and pointed to it. "What is this all about?" he managed to ask with a straight face.

Cordy's eyes brightened, and when she smiled the lines in her face deepened, a testament to many hours in the sun. "Oh, my favorite magazine! Did you bring it?"

Stan shook his head. "It was here on the table."

"Wonderful. It's all about new products for ballooning, technical tips, and interviews with pilots. But my favorite part is to read about the balloon festivals all over the world."

Stan thumbed through the magazine. Over 50 pages of eye-popping, full-color pictures of balloons in every size and shape drew him in like a magnet. As he looked at the pictures and read the captions, Stan began to feel a little of Cordy's enthusiasm for flight, although he wasn't sure his anxiety with heights would diminish.

Stan and Cordy continued chatting. Stan found himself amazed at how her mind grew sharper as she talked about the past and her ballooning. She told Stan, "The average height a balloon rises is one thousand to three thousand feet."

Too high, Stan thought.

"The record for the highest balloon flight was recorded in 2005 by a businessman from India. The man piloted his balloon to 69,852 feet."

Way too high. Stan shuddered. "It's higher than a passenger plane."

Cordy waved him silent. "For people like you at the festivals, the balloon rides are tied to the ground with strong ropes or cables and ascend only fifty to a hundred feet into the air. It's a good spitting distance."

Stan's stomach lurched.

Cordy told him, "The average balloon ride without tethers is about four hours, but the longest amount of time spent up in a balloon was almost twenty days."

Stan cringed. "What was the longest time you were in the air?"

"While at a festival in France, I flew for about ten hours. I can remember with clarity. My partner and I launched before sunrise and landed around 4:00 p.m. Oh, it was wonderful, hours of silence broken only by the intermittent roar of propane burners and quiet conversation. The feeling of weightlessness and freedom. Nothing is like it in the world." Cordy's face softened as she floated in memories. Then with a reverent voice, she said a prayer Stan had never heard: "May the winds welcome you with softness. May the sun bless you with its warm hands. May you fly so high God joins you in laughter and sets you gently back again into the loving arms of Mother Earth."

"It's beautiful," Stan whispered, thinking Alzheimer's disease stole some memories but not all.

"It's the Balloonist's Prayer," Cordy replied. "I say it each night if I can remember to say it. I also pray I can go in a balloon one more time before I die. I need to feel the air on my cheek, hear the hiss of the gas, and feel the fiber of the basket. I've been praying for the chance to do it. I'm not long for this world." She leaned closer to Stan. "I'm ready to go, Pastor, and some days the pain in my head screams for me to let go, but it's like those tie-downs on the balloons. One is tied to my soul and won't let me launch until I fly one more time." She sat back with a sigh. "At times, it's hard to let go of life."

Stan rubbed the back of his neck and wondered how he could help Cordy fulfill her end-of-life wish, but he was the last person to be able to help with a big flight, although if he prayed enough, he might be able to drift fifty feet in a balloon tethered to solid ground. He and Cordy continued to talk for a while longer as Stan absently turned pages in the hot-air balloon magazine. As he glanced through the magazine and saw the brightly colored pear shapes rising into the sky, it occurred to him that hot-air balloons, looking like inverted teardrops, represented the tears, prayers, and petitions of people around the world ascending to God, and as he heard Cordy speak of her longing for a lighter-than air-flight, he thought, *Doesn't this represent the dreams of people everywhere, the hope of rising above the mortal and mundane realities of life and death, and to have a transcendent experience with God?*

Stan thought of the World War II pilot John Gillespie Magee, Jr.'s poem, *High Flight.* He had used the inspiring poem in sermons, and President Reagan had referred to it on January 28, 1986, when America's space shuttle exploded. The President had quoted it to comfort a grieving nation after the loss of all seven astronauts on board the Challenger. As Stan thought on the words of the poem, he knew they were the cry of the human heart: "Oh! I have slipped the surly bonds of earth…Put out my hand, and touched the face of God."

Somehow Stan had to help Cordy fulfill her wish to fly one more time. But how? Could Lori help them with a virtual reality experience? Despite cancer eating at her brain and memory loss, was Cordy too mentally alert to appreciate anything less than a real flight?

Cordy's shaky voice snapped him out of his reverie. "Pastor, Skeeter said she would try to help me fulfill my wish to fly again before I die."

Stan shrugged, "I wish we could help you go up again, Cordy, but I don't know how."

With a firm voice she admonished Stan, "Pastor, you are a man of faith. I, too, have faith, and where there is a will there is a way. I have the will. If you and Skeeter and I pray, God will find a way."

Stan chided himself and mumbled, "Oh ye of little faith."

"If you help me fly in a balloon, I'd like you to go with me."

Stan looked at her, clearly surprised at her request. "Cordy," he said, "I don't like to fly in an airplane, but I could manage a balloon ride with you."

"Yes," answered Cordy. I not only *want* you to go with me, but I'll *need* you to go with me. I'm getting feeble. I'll need help in and out of the basket and help to stand. I'd like one other person to have with us."

"Who?"

"I would like Skeeter with us."

"I think she would love it," Stan said with a nod. "But I'll let you tell her. I don't want to spoil the surprise."

***

Stan knew big questions were on the horizon to get Cordy in a balloon. Would her health permit it? Would Cordy's doctor permit it? Would Harry permit it? Were there any balloon companies in the area? And what were the things he couldn't anticipate? Stan groaned, "Lord, how do I get myself into these situations?" Then he thought about Cordy's gloomy face and her urgent words, "Where there is a will there is a way." Stan breathed a prayer, "Okay, Lord, here we go again. Cordy has the will, you will have to make the way."

Stan began to look for a balloon company that could help with a special-needs client. He called several companies in Denver and on the front range, but, as soon as they heard he was in Piney, over two hours away, and over two mountain passes, they wanted to charge an extra one thousand dollars for the travel time and expense. Several companies didn't want to work with such an elderly and sick individual. Stan was understanding but frustrated.

He turned his attention to the largest town on the Western Slope of Colorado. Grand Junction was also about two hours from Piney, but to the west and with no passes to cross. The few companies in Grand Junction also wanted additional money for an elderly client, or flat out refused to consider it. Finally, Stan called a small company in Glenwood Springs, thirty minutes to the west of Piney.

He had put off a call to them thinking the larger cities would have more competitive prices than a small-town operator with no competition. Their company name was *Magic Carpet Balloon Rides* and their advertisement read, 'Let us Spirit You Away on a Magic Adventure'. Stan gave them a call. He was greeted by a pleasant voice and Bill Stevens, the owner of the balloon company, introduced himself.

After Stan explained what he wanted, Bill, confidently replied, "No problem. We have helped older adults on balloon rides. We can provide a small bench in the balloon basket where your senior can sit."

"Great. Our senior is short of breath and needs to carry a portable oxygen tank. Would it be a problem?" He didn't get a reply. He shook the phone, wondering if the phone had disconnected. "Are you there?"

"Yes, I'm here," he replied. "The seniors we've taken up have been active and healthy. I was thinking about your senior's shortness of breath and going up to a higher altitude. I'm not sure it would be a wise decision for the senior."

Stan checked his watch, thinking the phone call would end soon with a negative result. "I agree, but this is a special person. She has flown balloons all over the world, but she has a terminal disease, and this is her wish before her time is over. She insists she can't die until she has her last balloon ride. I need to make it happen for her."

Bill mumbled something, then said, "How high?"

"If we could get her into the air above the Piney Center, maybe fifty to a hundred feet, it should be sufficient," Stan explained. "I want this to be a tethered ride so there's no chance of going higher, and besides, we can take Cordy's oxygen tank with her. It's small about the size of a handbag."

"Yes, that might work," Bill said. "Except that brings me to our biggest problem."

"What's that?" Stan asked.

"Taking an oxygen tank up with our propane burners. Oxygen tanks and fires don't mix."

Stan felt his heart sink. *Cordy's wish isn't going to happen.*

"I wish I could make this happen for you and your gal."

"I hadn't thought of oxygen and fire," Stan said flatly. "I guess it's a deal-breaker. Thank you for your time, Bill. It's been nice talking with you and dreaming of taking our Cordy for a final ride."

Bill made final comments and ended the call. Stan closed his phone and rubbed his temples, wondering if he prayed harder it would help.

Later in the day, Stan's phone rang. He answered.

A familiar voice sounded on the other end of the line. "This is Bill from *Magic Carpet Balloon Rides* in Glenwood Springs. We spoke earlier."

"Hi," Stan said, surprised to hear from him.

Bill continued, "I've been thinking about how we could get your senior into one of our balloons. I believe I have the solution to our biggest problem — the problem of the oxygen tank and our propane burners."

"That's wonderful," Stan replied. "What are you thinking?"

"We can use a material called Nomex, which is a flame-resistant material used in other industries such as race car drivers' suits and also in firefighters' apparel." Bill went on to explain how they would seal off the bottom of the balloon and create an impenetrable skirt around the propane burners so there was no chance of a sudden gust of wind blowing a spark from the burners in the wrong direction. Stan followed Bill's explanation closely, knowing he would have to explain it to others.

"When do you want to arrange this for your senior?"

"Soon," Stan answered.

"How soon and where?"

A headache ticked on the side of his head. This was happening fast. He picked up a community calendar and scanned it. He pointed to an event in ten days at the Piney Fairgrounds. "Amazing," he mumbled. "Ah, Bill, I think I have the perfect solution. Our town is having a festival the weekend after next at the fairgrounds. It's a celebration of spring. I know there's plenty of room for a balloon and many people will attend. You would have free advertising and we could let Cordy have her ride."

"We took a balloon to the event a few years ago," Bill explained. "Great idea. I'm checking my calendar to see if we have a crew who can be there. Yep. We do. We'll provide a 75'-85' tall balloon that carries passengers up to 100' above the ground. The tether site should be a grassy or paved area, relatively level in slope. The balloon requires a minimum of 150 ft radius of unobstructed tether space. We will only fly in the morning hours. The cost is one thousand dollars plus any tips you want to give the crew."

Stan cringed at the price. He doubted Skeeter could hack this and adjust the price. He asked a few more questions, then thanked Bill for getting back to him. "Let's plan on that weekend."

"I'll need a credit card for a down payment."

Stan closed his eyes and reached for his wallet, wondering how he would explain this charge to his wife, and still wondering if he could convince the Council of Pastors to help pay for it. Then he smiled: *going up in a balloon is getting closer to God. Yes. Every pastor can let their seniors know it is a heavenly experience.*

Bill thanked Stan for his business. He finalized with billing and e-mail contact information and closed the call.

Sitting back, Stan's sweaty hand lowered his cell phone. He did a fist pump, "Yes!" he exclaimed. Once again, faith, patience, and prayer had paid off. Now to tackle the other challenges: money and Harry. Transportation for all seniors? Maybe Pastor Stan and the

Senior Band to perform on stage? Perhaps Larry for chocolate chip cookies? Local TV coverage? Permission from the Piney events committee?

Now, what have I gotten myself into?

CHAPTER 30

Tuesday, Skeeter left home after George departed for an early golf match. She met Pastor Stan at the Piney Center. Because the plan for Millie's ride depended on a lot of scenarios working, her nerves were shot. Stan wasn't much better, considering he was on the fence about the ethics involved with thwarting Harry's knowledge of Millie's horse adventure.

In their office, Stan and Skeeter again went over the plan. She touched base with Bart with her cell phone, and he assured her it would go smoothly.

After she hung up with Bart, she headed to Charmaine's desk and to get her portable radio. She took it back to their office. "The nursing rehab staff has radios, so do the janitors," she informed Stan as she waved the radio in the air. "Harry has a radio, too. You and I and Bart will connect via cell phone." She held the radio in her hand. "The staff will communicate by radio. I've set Charmaine's radio to channel nineteen. We'll have the others set their radio to channel nineteen. I want the staff to have a code word if Harry shows up unexpectedly or something goes wrong. Any suggestions?"

Stan said, "I like 'Praise God', but I think 'Code Red' would make them more aware we have a problem."

She handed him Charmaine's radio. "Okay, go to channel nineteen. Will you check with the nurses in rehab and the janitorial staff? 'Code Red' will mean Harry is coming, change of plan."

Stan nibbled on the side of his lip. "This is getting to sound more like a James Bond stunt rather than an activity for older adults."

"I don't want you to compromise your ethics, Stan."

"This is on the fringe."

Skeeter pointed to the radio. "I'd think of this as being the bad guy in a movie who ends up innocent and everyone rejoices."

"I don't feel like a bad guy, but as a guy trying to weigh the right from the wrong, and with what we want to do, the right outweighs the wrong. It still leaves me feeling off-kilter, but as I wobble the line, I know God is wobbling with me."

"Okay, I got it. At least we aren't fibbing to Harry to get him away from the Center."

Stan smiled. "Yep. It's a good thing." Standing, he shoved the radio into his pocket. "I want to tell everyone in person, so I'll go tell the rehab nurses what to expect and track down Carmen who should be doing housekeeping chores today, and then I'll return the radio to Charmaine."

"Okay. I think I will 'borrow' Harry's radio today so there is no chance he will be alerted." She would have to wait until Harry left for lunch with George to snatch his radio. The thought of her being caught made her blood thud in her temples.

Stan nodded. Heading to the rehab wing, he spoke with Sherry, the head nurse on duty. She had her radio on her station desk and turned it to channel nineteen. Next, he found Carmen in the social room, where she vacuumed the floors and straightened the chairs. Her radio sat on her supply cart and she switched the channel as well. He swung by the reception desk to return the radio to Charmaine, making sure it was tuned to channel nineteen. Everything was set.

Stan and Skeeter worked in the office until they expected George to arrive. Neither Skeeter nor Stan could concentrate on constructive work, so they discussed social games and activities they could do with the seniors. At 11:30 p.m., Stan peeked outside the office and saw George stroll through the front door.

He signed in at the reception desk with Charmaine.

Charmaine welcomed George and commented, "You look sunburned."

"I was on the golf course at nine a.m. today. I forgot about the high-altitude sunburn." He ran a hand across his brow. "Next time I'll remember."

She recommended a good sunscreen and then added, "I have new golf clubs. I hope the driver gives me an extra ten yards off the tee." She checked her watch. "Harry will be right along. It's not like him to be late."

Leaning over the reception desk, George whispered, "He can't be late. I'm the secret plan to get Harry away so Millie can ride her horse."

Charmaine waved him silent. "I know," she whispered. "Pastor Stan and Skeeter have planned this for a long time. Millie suffers from emphysema and congenital heart disease. She's lived longer than her doctors thought. It's awful to hear her fight to breathe."

"Perhaps after today, life won't be such a struggle for her."

"Millie told me that happiness is sitting on a horse, waiting for a moment, and letting that gift of happiness soak in. She intends to find happiness, if only for a few moments, and then she can die in peace."

George commented, "It's comforting." Then he gazed beyond Charmaine and waved. He saw Harry approaching the reception desk with a scowl on his face and one wedge of hair falling across his forehead.

"Hello George," Harry said, his tone harried. The men shook hands. "Sorry to keep you. I had an important phone call."

George managed a relaxed smile and pointed to the front doors. "No problem. Shall we go?" He turned to leave.

Harry shook his head while he swiped the wedge of hair off his forehead. "I apologize again, George, but I need to stay here. I have another call I have to take. Again, I'm sorry, but it can't be helped. We can have lunch in our dining room. Larry has a creole dish on the menu for today. It sounds authentic."

George stammered, flustered, unable to speak. He glared at Charmaine. "Ah, sure, having lunch here is fine, but could you show me your office? I'd like to see the information you have on residential living for older adults." He figured it sounded awkward but he had no other idea and knew Bart would be pulling the trailer to the entrance at any moment.

While George and Harry exchanged a few words, Charmaine picked up the radio, hit talk, bent over, and whispered, "Code Red". She snapped the radio away from her lips, managing a crooked smile, hoping Carmen heard the message.

From their office, Pastor Stan watched the interaction between Charmaine, George, and Harry. "Uh, oh," Stan mumbled. He strained to hear but couldn't make out everything said. The best he got was the word 'phone call' and 'sorry'.

"What?" Skeeter asked.

"I think we might have 'Code Red' before the gig gets started."

Skeeter held her breath, wishing that she had Harry's radio. Before she could exhale, her desk phone rang. She grabbed it.

"Code Red," Charmaine whispered into her phone. "Harry can't leave. He wants to eat lunch with George in the dining room." Ending the call, she managed to smile at Harry.

The corner of Harry's mouth twisted. "We'll be in the dining area if you need us after we finish in my office." He patted his radio clipped to his belt. "You can reach me by radio if you need me. We'll be about fifteen minutes."

George moved around the reception desk without looking at Charmaine. His palms grew sweaty. He hoped Harry couldn't hear his heartbeat. They started for Harry's office.

Skeeter swore under her breath. Chipmunks began to beat drums in her brain. Ending the call from Charmaine, she glared at Stan. "Code Red."

He stiffened.

Grabbing her cell phone, she speed-dialed Bart. He didn't answer. "I can't reach Bart. He must be on his way."

Stan said, "Now what?"

Skeeter didn't have an answer.

Charmaine checked her watch. She figured George and Harry would spend ten minutes or so in Harry's office. If luck were with them, Harry would disappear with George to the dining room before Bart arrived. Her fingers shook. Staring out the front door, praying Bart wouldn't arrive anytime soon, Charmaine gasped when she saw Bart drive into the Piney Center, pulling a horse trailer behind his Ford F150 truck. He stopped in the porte-cochere. Charmaine speed-dialed Skeeter and Stan. "Definite Code Red. Bart just pulled into the entrance." She hung up and glared at the truck with the horse trailer.

Bart slowed the truck into the Piney Center entrance, downshifting with a rumble from the powerful engine and slowed the horse trailer to a stop. When he heard Misty kick the trailer, he knew she was anxious to unload. Checking his watch, it was almost noon. Confident Harry had left the building with George, Bart slid out of his truck and walked to the back of the trailer. He spoke quietly to Misty, trusting that his voice would calm her, and she'd quit kicking the side of the trailer. Tied with a short lead, Misty tossed her head and again thumped the side of the trailer with her front hoof. Reaching his hand through the side rails, he gave Misty a horse treat. Tossing her head, she neighed and banged her head against the trailer's roof.

Bart opened up a storage compartment behind the front seat of the truck and pulled out a set of bars, clamps, chains, and something resembling a children's heavy-duty plastic swing seat with safety belts. He slid a five-foot-long, steel bar into a pipe welded to the inside of the passenger door frame. He fastened a horizontal bar to the steel upright and attached the chains to it and finally added the swing with the safety belts. Then, he plugged an electric winch box into the truck's power plug. He hit the power button, heard a buzzing sound, and pushed the toggle control button. A whirring sound let him know everything was working properly. His boss had a nephew who had limited use of his legs. This hoist was modified from a *Milford Life* lift, which was designed to move people from wheelchairs to vehicle seats. His boss used the lift to seat his nephew on Misty or the truck's passenger seat. Satisfied everything was ready, he moved to the rear of the trailer to unload Misty.

From Charmaine's desk, the hall to the east wing led to the rehab facility. Assisted living veered to the west wing with the social hall, dining area, and kitchen in the middle of the V-shaped facility. Directly behind her was Harry's office and the central nursing station, with Stan and Skeeter's office adjacent to the kitchen. Her heart beat against the walls of her chest. She tapped her fingers on her desk. Glancing over her shoulder, she gasped. Harry and George walked toward Charmaine's desk; they had not veered to the dining area. With Bart and the horse trailer outside the front doors, Harry would be able to see the horse trailer at the entrance to the Center. With only a second to decide what to do, Charmaine pitched out of her chair and stumbled toward Harry, coughing, doubling over, gasping for air.

Harry realized Charmaine was in trouble, increased his steps, grabbed her, and held her as she continued to stagger farther down the hall where he lowered her to the floor. George remained a few feet behind Harry, his pulse racing, unsure what to do.

"Water!" Charmaine gasped pointing toward the water fountain at the end of the hall.

Hearing loud voices with Charmaine coughing, Skeeter and Pastor Stan left their office. When Skeeter saw their receptionist on the floor, she realized disaster was taking place and speed-dialed Bart on her cell phone.

He answered. "I'm here. I'm about to unload Misty."

Skeeter talked fast, "We may have a problem. I'll meet you at the front door."

Sherry, the head of the nursing staff, heard Charmaine's distress and hurried to the commotion. She knelt next to Harry with George standing behind them. "What's going on?" Sherry asked.

Harry looked over his shoulder to see Stan coming toward them with Skeeter veering to the front doors. "Charmaine had some sort of allergy attack." He pointed to the water fountain. "She asked for water."

Standing, Sherry placed a hand on her hip. "I think she's okay. Take her to the dining area and give her another glass of water. Have her take deep breaths."

Charmaine propped up on her elbow with her face turned from Harry.

Skeeter saw the little smile on Charmaine's face and hurried to the front doors. She glared at Harry who had his radio clipped to his belt. *He's supposed to be in Vail with George.*

Charmaine cleared her throat, placing a hand on her neck. "I think I'm good now," she said.

Definitely Code Red, Skeeter thought.

Charmaine feigned another coughing episode, pausing to point to the door to the garden. "I need fresh air," she rasped.

Stan looked toward Harry, Charmaine, George, and Sherry, and then to the front entrance. Skeeter was about to push through the doors to meet Bart. His pulse raced. If they didn't divert Harry, he would see Bart's trailer. Skeeter paused and whispered to Stan. "We've got this. You get Millie."

Turning, Stan moved away from Skeeter, heading for assisted living. He needed to guide Millie outside the building by exit doors at the end of the west wing. They could then walk to the front of the building and meet Bart.

Outside the front doors, Skeeter ran to Bart. "Stay here. Harry is headed to the dining hall where he will be out of view. Pastor Stan will bring Millie to you on the outside of the building."

Harry helped Charmaine to a sitting position and then to her feet. To George he said, "We'll go through the garden area which connects with the social and dining rooms."

Leaving Bart, Skeeter pushed through the doors to the Center. She speed-dialed Stan on her phone. "Do you copy?"

A garbled reply came, "Copy that. I'm on my way to Millie."

Skeeter turned in circles, wondering if they should call this off or dare to go ahead. "Roger that. Take Millie outside by the west end exit." Skeeter peeked around the door to the dining area. She saw Charmaine comfortably seated in a dining room chair with Harry standing next to her. Carrying a glass of water, George arrived from the kitchen. Larry followed George and all three of the men bent down beside Charmaine as if crowding would help.

A moment of stagnant silence followed until a rattled squeaking noise made them look down the hall to assisted living. Cecil pushed his stroller into the dining area, stopping his walker next to Charmaine, Harry, and George.

Cecil worked his jaw, paused with his steps, and tilted his head. "You guys having a party without me?"

Harry rested a hand on his hip while he studied Charmaine. "Hi Cecil, and no, it is not a party. She had an allergy attack."

"She should choose another day for an attack," Cecil dryly commented.

Harry moved back from Charmaine and tripped over Cecil's walker. He swore and caught himself before he went down. "What next?"

Hurrying to the reception desk, Skeeter grabbed Charmaine's radio while glancing out the front doors. Bart had Misty tied to the trailer. Skeeter waved to Bart, then raced through the front doors, nearly crashing into him. "Don't go inside. Harry is there. Stan will bring Millie to you. We're still good to go."

Bart nodded, turned, and grabbed Misty's reins. He brought her up alongside the truck's passenger door.

Holding onto Millie, Stan guided her around the outside of the building. "We're ready for the ride," he said as he met Skeeter and Bart.

Millie wore sharp-looking riding pants, a soft wrist-length shirt, riding boots, and had her portable oxygen canister slung over her shoulder. Stan guided Millie to Bart. "You'd better get her in the saddle and disappear."

Millie beamed. Bart took his grandmother's hand, bent to her ear, and said, "Let's go riding."

Using the radio in one hand, while holding her phone in the other, Skeeter radioed housekeeping and explained the situation while heading inside the Center. "Millie is in the saddle. You've got to create a diversion. Harry has his radio. Radio him. Tell him to come to the east wing."

"Tell him what?" Carmen queried.

"I don't know," Skeeter replied, her voice holding back panic. "Anything. Stop up a toilet with a towel. Tell him someone died. Something to get Harry to the east wing. He's in the dining room. Tell Harry to come through the garden and over to one of the rooms in the rehab wing."

"I'm in rehab now," Carmen said in her thick Jamaican accent. "I'll manage a problem and will radio Harry, but I'm not telling him anyone died."

Skeeter rubbed her temple. "Okay. Create the diversion. Call him on your radio."

Outside Millie swung in the air as the hoist raised her to the saddle, while her portable oxygen canister bumped along her back. She banged into Misty's side. Misty turned her head toward the direction of the bump. Bart continued to raise the seat, Millie kicked her legs, smiled as big as a barn, and squealed with delight. When she was high enough, Bart swung the top bar over Misty's saddle and toggled the button to lower her down. "Success," he mumbled and tipped his Stetson off his forehead. He looked at his grandmother and handed her Misty's reins. "How does it feel?"

She slipped her riding boots in the stirrups and adjusted her balance. "Seems like old times." The excitement caused her to breathe in gasps. When her breathing settled, she leaned forward, sniffed Misty's mane, stroked her neck, and struggled to inhale a deep breath. Tears pooled in the corners of her eyes. "There's nothing better than the smell of a horse."

Bart pointed through the parking lot to the sage-covered ground. "Take her west. I'll walk beside you."

Millie worked the reins between her fingers. "What? You don't think I can handle this horse?"

He patted her thigh. "I know you can, Grandma, but I would like to share this experience with you."

She smiled. "That's my boy." She adjusted the oxygen canister on her back and then nudged Misty with her heels. "Get up," she said.

In the dining room, Harry tried to quiet his nerves after helping Charmaine recover from the asthma attack. Things had to be in control, he decided. Then his radio squawked. "What is it?" he snarled with impatience. He listened for several seconds and said, "I'll be right there. I'm in the dining area. It will only take me a moment to get there. Unit 113? Okay."

Harry smacked his thigh with his palm. His day wasn't going as planned, and he had a lot to do, and still needed to give George a tour of the facility. He didn't have time to help an employee through a coughing attack and now oversee a plumbing problem in the east wing.

While Bart and Stan walked beside Misty with Millie securely seated in the saddle and her feet in the stirrups, Skeeter was on the radio with Sherry and with Carmen. "I know we all love Millie and want to see this last wish of hers fulfilled." Her cell phone chimed. "Hold on." She accepted the call. She had the radio pressed to one ear and the phone to the other. Stan said, "Keep Harry occupied so he can't see the truck out front."

"Gad, the man has legs. I don't know which direction he will go."

"You'd better get out front and move the truck to the parking lot beyond the buildings."

"Me? The biggest truck I've ever driven was a *Tonka* truck, which I could assemble and disassemble when I was five years old."

She heard Bart's voice next and knew he had taken the phone from Stan, "Pull up your pantyhose, cowgirl. Put the truck in drive. Give it gas. You can't hurt anything."

"Code Red,", was all she could mumble and looked to the front doors and the truck and trailer with the hoist dangling in the breeze.

"Sherry!" Carmen urgently whispered into her radio from room 113 where she had staged a toilet overflow. "Sherry, can you hear me?" Static squawked from the radio.

"What's up?" Sherry whispered.

"Harry is heading in your direction. He's coming toward me, and I'm in suite one-thirteen. He's heading to the east wing. If Harry looks out the windows, he is bound to see Millie."

"Got it!" Sherry whispered and swung into action. She headed to the rooms where Harry would pass, bulldozed her way into each room, and shut the curtains. If anyone objected, she said, "Code Red. Don't argue."

Carmen told Sherry, "Intercept him when he gets to room one-thirteen. Tell him I fixed the problem. I'm headed to the entry to recreate the Red Sea, only I don't want Harry or Moses to part it."

Sherry had no idea what Carmen meant but didn't ask.

From the supply closet, Carmen wheeled her yellow mop bucket and orange 'Caution! Wet Floor' cones toward the main entrance. At Charmaine's desk, she swung sharply around the corner, sloshing soapy water from her bucket. Down the hall, she saw Harry rush around a corner, head down, and walk quickly toward her. From this angle, Harry would not be able to see outside the double doors, but once he walked another twenty feet, he should be able to see the truck and trailer. Carmen quickly pulled her mop from her bucket and began to swing the mop across the hall, directly in Harry's path. Soapy water flowed out in every direction, hitting the walls of the corridor and then crashing back into the pathway. "Mister Harry!" she cried out. "Stop! You'll slip on this wet floor."

Pausing, Harry raised his head in time to see Carmen and her mop. "I think I can manage a wet floor."

As he looked down, Skeeter hurried out the front doors and climbed into the truck. She had no time to shut the tailgate or secure the hoist. Finding the key in the ignition, she turned it, and the truck roared to life. She jammed the gear lever into *drive.* With a glance, she checked the rear-view mirrors but couldn't see anything. "Damn," she swore and pushed her foot to the floor.

The truck leaped to life, zinging from the entry, side-swiping a newspaper box with a crunch. The hoist's arm swung from the open passenger door and clipped the American flag. The red, white, and blue flag wrapped around the arm of the hoist and fluttered in the breeze as she drove away. The truck created a mushroom cloud of dust when it jumped the parking lot curb and careened across the sage-covered lot behind the Piney Center.

Inside the Center, Carmen smiled and said, "Mister Harry, could you please go down to the rehabilitation wing. I've got water and soap backed up to Charmaine's desk."

"I came from that direction," Harry grumbled. He started to step around her, but Carmen stood firmly in front of him. The stern expression on her face, the muscles in her toned arms, and her mop, raised like a weapon, indicated it wouldn't be wise to disobey her.

"What the hell?" he said as he angrily jerked away from Carmen and headed to the east wing to cut through the outdoor garden to arrive in the dining hall. He turned to George, "Sorry about all this. I'm hungry. How about you?"

Behind Harry, George got a glimpse of a woman on a horse doing a lively canter, her oxygen canister slapping against her body, and two men running after her.

"Starved," George replied and had to cover his face to hide his laughter.

CHAPTER 31

Pastor Stan and Skeeter decided Millie's ride was successful, despite it not going smoothly. The fallout, though, came with repercussions. Harry found a pile of horse manure at the entrance to Piney Center and he couldn't explain how it got there. Suspicious, he reviewed the security tapes and discovered a big truck and horse trailer at the Center. He also saw Millie's grandson unloading a horse from the trailer. From there, the cowboy loaded Millie on the horse, much like raising a bale of hay to the upper story of a barn. Millie rode the horse off into the sunset, as best as Harry could determine. Although he couldn't determine who it was for sure, a person climbed in the driver's seat of the truck, drove away, while crashing into the newspaper stand and snagging the American flag off the building.

He also reviewed more security footage and discovered a woman entering the Piney Center who was a dead ringer for Joe's wife, Mary, who supposedly was deceased and buried. As he viewed the tapes, he felt his blood tic in his temples and he ground his teeth together. He immediately knew who was to blame for these antics.

When he called Skeeter into his office and showed her the tapes, she admitted to the schemes with Millie and Joe, saying, "Harry, we gave these seniors their final wishes. Joe died a happy man, believing he had not failed Mary. How is it wrong?"

"Because you broke my rules," he snapped. He pushed a document toward her. "This is your employment termination agreement. You are no longer employed here."

Skeeter refused to look at the paper or sign it. "Harry, I agree I have broken your rules, but please do the seniors a favor and don't make me sign that termination agreement until after the Piney Festival this coming weekend."

"What? Another escapade at the festival?"

She didn't answer him.

Harry stood. Being a big man, he was intimidating with his size and expression. With a frown of stacked worms on his forehead, Harry nervously played with a pencil, leaning across his desk, glaring at Skeeter. "And who has been changing my calendar?"

Skeeter decided she had no reason to lie. She shrugged. "Me. Do you need any parking tickets fixed? Plane seats adjusted? Maybe your daughter's grades adjusted? No, probably not, but I can discreetly do almost anything." She thought she saw steam coming from Harry's ears.

His voice was sharp with frustration. "Millie riding a horse across our lawn? By the way, she is in the rehab facility. She can barely breathe."

Skeeter was sorry to hear Millie was failing but didn't feel they should have ignored her last wish. She told Harry, "Although the last wishes of the dying are unique to every person, many involve something they need to do before they die. It could be as simple as food, music, atmosphere, relatives, a field of tulips, or reconnecting with those they loved. Millie may be near the end, but I know life is no longer a struggle. Take a look at the security film. Take a look at her face when she rode Misty. See the pure happiness filling her body, and you can tell she felt the best she has in many years. It was a gift, Harry."

Harry didn't comment. With a sigh, he sat down.

Skeeter added, "Bart ran beside her the entire ride. Pastor Stan tried to keep up but he almost passed out. Both men sacrificed a lot to do this for Millie."

Harry tossed his pencil in the air and let it drop on his desk. "How about Mary? How did you pull it off?"

"It was my grandmother. She recently had to have her hair redone due to memory loss and a barbecue lighter—"

He interrupted, "I don't want to know more." He inhaled, closed his eyes, and exhaled. "How about the trip to Amsterdam?"

"Harry," Skeeter said and let his name slide off her tongue as if it was something sweet, "was there anything more beautiful than seeing Hanni's sons with her at the end? She died a happy, fulfilled woman. After the horrors of World War II, can't you see that as a blessing?"

He lifted one shoulder as if unsure how to respond negatively but unwilling to concede her point. "You had no idea her end would turn out as it did."

"None of us did. Pastor Stan has a way with people." Skeeter met Harry's hard glare. "I'll sign the termination papers but not until after the festival." She rose. "I care for every older adult in the Piney Center." She sniffed back emotions. "You can fill my shoes with someone else, but no one will care as much as I do. This job is the greatest privilege given by one human being to another; the seniors trust us to care for them at their most vulnerable time. Pastor Stan and I have been a mere speck in their lives, timewise, but at those moments, we're the most important people in their world."

Lifting her chin an inch, she turned but stopped. Over her shoulder, she added, "Pastor Stan cares more than I do. Please, please, please do not eliminate his volunteering here. It would be a giant disservice to the seniors."

Harry scowled. "No more trips to Europe," he mumbled.

"I'll see you Saturday at the festival."

"I hadn't planned on going but I see my calendar has changed. Did you do it?"

She held his glare with one of her own. "Yes. You need to be there."

He was the first to look away. "No surprises," Harry added.

Skeeter didn't answer.

***

Skeeter left the Piney Center that afternoon with a heavy heart and without talking to any of the seniors or Pastor Stan. She felt as her lifeline to living in Piney had been severed. Wiping a tear off her cheek, she mumbled words she didn't try to understand. Nobody but herself had brought this upon her, and although being fired was the worst thing that happened to her, she still believed what she had done was the correct thing.

At home, she poured out her soul to Beth and George. Beth nodded as if she understood everything, but Skeeter could tell by the vacant look in her eyes that she didn't completely comprehend. George understood and he tried to get her to see the silver lining on this dark cloud but it didn't help. Then he said, "About the house."

Exhaling, Skeeter said, "I think I need a glass of wine to go with this discussion."

Beth offered to get it and also George a splash of whiskey. To Skeeter, it was amazing how her grandmother could tune in on the small things, especially at the right time.

She brought Skeeter a long-stemmed glass with chilled chardonnay. Sipping cold wine was a start to finish the day, and now with George ready to tell her his decision, she figured it would be further bad news. She tipped her glass to George. "So, what have you decided? Does Beth call her attorney? Does she have to fight you and Melissa for the house?"

His expression went from bland to serious.

Skeeter anticipated bad news.

George looked at the whiskey. "As you know, I am divorced. I've been alone now for two years. I've figured it out, sort of; perhaps not how to keep up with laundry or how to make a nourishing meal, but for the most part, I can clean a bathroom."

"I can't cook," Skeeter admitted. "Maybe since I won't have a job, I'll have to survive on Ramen Noodles."

George chuckled. "I have a proposal."

She almost gagged on her sip of wine. "Marriage?"

"That's a good one. No, I'm not marrying again and you could be my daughter, but I like Piney. I'd like to transition here."

"Move here?"

"Yes. I need to sell my house, get rid of a lot of junk, and make the move. I propose you allow me to move in with you and Beth after I sell my house." He shrugged and then pointed to the patio. "I'll make permanent plans after that, perhaps after a year or so. You need new flagstone on the patio and some tiered planter beds would look great." He pointed toward the patio. "You need some aspen trees against the west wall and the yard needs landscaping and the master bath needs a remodel. That's what I do: I build things. I can also add a mini-kitchen to the downstairs area. It will add value to the house. I'll pay some rent or expenses. We can work that out." He gazed toward Beth who had moved into the den. "Down the road, you're going to need help with Beth, perhaps a shoulder to cry on."

305

She was barely able to control her gasp of surprise. For weeks, she had expected George to fight Beth over ownership of the house. The stress had been more than she wanted to admit, and now George had tossed this suggestion her way. Wordless, she stared at him with her mouth slightly ajar. For the second time today, she felt her emotions about to deteriorate. "George," she managed, sniffing back tears, "I'm speechless."

He held his glass to hers. "Don't be. Piney is a wonderful place. You and Beth are special. I feel as though I have a new family. I've been involved now with events at the Piney Center and I want to continue the connection. Harry has a few finishing-touch jobs he wants to be done at the Center and I'll give him a competitive bid. I'm confident I can land the job."

She had to breathe through her nose and out of her mouth to bring her emotions under control. "I've had a horrible day, and now you have changed it to a bright day. I need to explain this to Beth but you have made me very happy."

He raised his glass. "I'll drink to that."

"To family," she said and smiled.

CHAPTER 32

Harry had grown frustrated with things at the Piney Center. So much that happened was out of his control, like Millie riding a horse outside the Center. The potential liability made his head hurt. He had to fire Skeeter and had chastised Stan but he also knew housekeeping and nursing employees were involved and who knew who else? And now he was left feeling off-balance after firing Skeeter. Yeah, she'd broken his rules and had been warned, but was she incorrect in doing so? It grated on his sense of what was correct and couldn't get a clear view of what was right or wrong.

The issues with his online calendars remained a problem. He would enter an event or appointment on his calendar and then the next time he looked at it, the dates were gone. Just like today. He could've sworn he had scheduled this Saturday for a trip to Denver. He had told his wife and daughter they would be going to the city but when he checked his calendar before leaving the Center, it told him he was scheduled to be with the seniors at the Piney fairgrounds. *I work with them all day*, he thought to himself. *Now I have to socialize with them on my day off?*

When he tried to beg off from going to the festival, Skeeter had narrowed her eyes to slits and glared at him, and said, "You need to be at the festival, Harry. It's your job. The seniors expect to see you." Anxiety and guilt hit him when she said those words. *Now what?* he wondered.

He would find out. His family was headed to Piney's celebration of spring.

The Piney Festival was a party to welcome spring, and today was a poster day for the town; blue skies, no wind, and temperatures in the mid-seventies. Harry and his wife, Rose, and daughter, Brianna, who was a spunky eleven-year-old, arrived at the fairgrounds and parked next to the Piney Center's bus. Harry knew the seniors had loaded the transport van over an hour ago, and it took that much time to safely load their walkers, oxygen tanks, and cool weather clothing. Several made final trips inside to use the bathroom before leaving. With all of the delays, the walkers rumbled across the gravel parking lot, and the white-haired seniors padded to the entrance. Harry spotted Cecil and Richard, Layla May, and Jayne with her guide dog, Carmen, Larry, and other employees. With their bus now parked in the fairgrounds parking lot, they made their way toward the carny booths, bandstand, Ferris wheel, and other rides, which were a long walk over a rough dirt parking lot. *"This is handicapped parking?"* Harry thought. *It looks like a mile away from the entrance. He would have to talk to the County Commissioners about it.*

Rose and Brianna piled out of the car and quickly made their way to the line of seniors now strung out across the park with walkers, and wheelchairs and hunched backs, and oxygen tanks on wheels. Jayne's service dog had to stop to check numerous spots. Cecil had trouble with the tennis balls on the front legs of his walker, and Harry noticed a hint of glee on Richard's face since his walker buzzed along as if it had newly-oiled wheels. Along with several staff members, everyone inched their way to the festival, and the crowd absorbed them until heads and faces blurred.

Harry watched as Brianna ran up to Carmen and hugged her, and he could hear Carmen fuss over his golden-haired daughter. Harry recalled Carmen blocking his way down the hall to the rehab Center. She'd been part of Stan and Skeeter's scam to divert him from seeing Millie's horse adventure. Harry took his wife's hand and whispered, "Why can't life be simple?"

Rose squeezed his hand. "Life is messy. You can't change it."

As they passed the entrance to the festival grounds, Harry spotted a hot-air balloon, rearing into the air on the far side of the bandstand. "Balloon ride?" he asked as if testing the idea.

To his right, he spotted Bart and Skeeter, holding hands and walking toward the rising balloon. Pastor Stan followed behind them, helping Cordy with a new walker and an extra sweater. Harry asked himself how he could be so angry with Bart, Skeeter, and Stan. They had helped terminal residents at the Piney Center enjoy their final days, even if it meant risking their jobs and working around him to help them. A spike of guilt filled his body for feeling resentful toward the Piney team.

The band of weary, aging warriors, with the help of Rose, Carmen, Sherry, Charmaine, and others from the Center, arrived at the fringe of trees and picnic tables. Carny music played and an atmosphere of excitement filled the air as children chased each other through the trees and around the vendor booths. Richard and Cecil quickly found a bench in the shade and settled back to enjoy the scene. Larry had prepared chocolate chip cookies that he piled on plates. Layla May sashayed around the tables and gave Cecil a smile meant to tease. On the bandstand, a country trio sang about a truck driver and love gone wrong.

Stan sat on the bench with Richard and Cecil, and Jayne sang along with the band while Layla May disappeared into the swirling crowd of gaily dressed people, pink cotton candy, smoke from turkey legs grilling, a carousel with prancing horses, and little children getting in the way. The event was the exact way Cordy had described hot-air balloon festivals. Stan found Cordy a seat near Cecil and Richard, while Bart and Skeeter visited the giant balloon for a visual inspection. Stan sat across from Cordy, chatting, and was relieved to find that Cordy's mind was clear. She did not wear the piece of green material on her head for repelling kangaroos.

Stan asked, "Cordy are you comfortable?"

Winded from the hike across the park, she managed to gasp, "Pastor Stan, this is so exciting. The music, the families, children, and the balloon take me back to the festivals. This is a dream come true." Wheezing, she adjusted the oxygen cannula in her nostrils. "I can't tell you how much this means to me."

A conversation wasn't necessary since people-watching was an activity. Bart and Skeeter moseyed toward them and gave Cordy and Stan thumbs up. Pastor Stan watched Bart and Skeeter and what he saw was love. He saw how they gave of themselves to each other and others, and the energy they created was the gift of love.

Bart stopped and told Stan, "They'll be ready for Cordy in about half an hour. They're selling a lot of balloon ride tickets and want to take care of those people first. With no wind, the balloon rides should be able to keep going into the afternoon." Holding Skeeter's hand, he and Skeeter sat on a bench near Cordy and the others.

Julia and her husband, Nick, and Charlotte arrived. Charlotte held a cone of pink cotton candy and it matched the frilly rosy-colored tutu she wore. Her fingers were sticky with cotton candy and her tongue was red. All her attention concentrated on the cotton candy. When Charlotte saw Skeeter, she pushed the wad of cotton candy toward her and said, "Do you want a bite?"

With a laugh, Skeeter declined, but smiled at Charlotte, especially her sticky fingers and cotton candy stuck to her cheek. Bart put his arm around Skeeter and smiled.

Bart introduced himself to Nick and asked, "Want to head to the shooting range?"

Nick nodded. "Let's go."

Nick and Bart competed with each other at the shooting booth for stuffed toys for Charlotte. Skeeter and Julia cheered for them and welcomed Beth and Bruce as spectators, and to her surprise, Sven and Jon arrived. Bart began to pull ahead of Nick and won several stuffed toys for Charlotte. Skeeter kept her eye on the line to the hot-air balloon ride, wishing it would become smaller.

Harry and Rose wandered over to the balloon. Brianna had diverted her attention to a castle bouncy house and bounced while her parents took a balloon ride. When Harry and Rose went up in the balloon, Harry had an overview of the festival, and it surprised him to look down and see many of his staff and seniors from the Piney Center enjoying themselves. After their ride, Harry bought tickets for Brianna and Rose to take a ride together and he had the simple pleasure of watching the joy on his daughter's face when the pilot released propane gas and the fire flared and the balloon tugged to rise in the sky. When the big balloon settled to earth, Brianna hopped out and ran to her daddy, grinning from ear to ear. "Oh daddy, it was super awesome!" she exclaimed as she gave her dad a big hug. Harry felt like a kid again himself.

As the country and western band announced they would take a break, the man in charge of the balloon rides took the microphone and introduced himself. He pointed to the balloon, where one of his employees worked to attach a plastic-looking fabric around the area that held the propane. "Ladies and Gentlemen," he said, "I am Bill Singleton with *Magic Carpet Balloon Rides*. Today, we have a special guest who will ride in our balloon. This lady has traveled the world in balloons. She has piloted many crafts, both experimental and classic, and has set an altitude record for her age. She has covered more than two thousand miles in one hot-air balloon trip when she was sixty-six years old. She is now ninety-three. She is fighting a terminal disease and has one last wish."

Harry turned his head toward the speaker. His lips parted and he frowned. Bill continued, "Ladies and Gentlemen, tonight we are privileged to fulfill Miss Cordelia Johnson's wish to fly one more time in a hot-air balloon! Today, for Cordy we will double the extensions, and Cordy will fly to a hundred feet!"

Harry staggered, taken completely by surprise. *Cordy? My Cordy at the Piney Center? She's too old! A hundred feet! It's too high! It'll kill her!*

He turned to find Cordy with the other seniors and saw Pastor Stan leading Cordy to the balloon's basket, while Bart and Skeeter carried her oxygen tank and coat. Bill opened a newly customized half-door made into the side of the basket and set in place a wooden ramp. Bart helped Cordy slip into her coat and get steady in her walker. To Harry, Cordy stood a little straighter, her chin a little higher, her lips upturned in a smile, her eyes sparkling brightly as if diamonds fell from them. Skeeter held onto Cordy as she struggled to walk up the sloped ramp to the basket floor. Bart followed with her oxygen tank and a throw blanket. Skeeter helped Cordy sit on a wicker stool. The seat raised Cordy's shrunken body high enough to see over the edge of the basket. Stan joined Cordy in the basket. Skeeter kissed Cordy on the cheek, Bill shut the basket half-door, and Bart pulled the ramp away from the basket.

Cordy put up a hand and said, "Wait!"

Bill looked puzzled. "What?"

Cordy pointed to Skeeter. "I need her with me."

Skeeter shook her head. Bart gave her a little push toward the basket door. "She wants you with her. Be brave." He kissed her cheek. "See you when you land."

Skeeter reluctantly loaded into the basket and stood next to Cordy, placing her arm around her shoulder. "Let's do this."

Bill waved to the pilot and a gush of flame leaped into the balloon. The giant craft began to rise.

Before Harry could fully comprehend what had happened, horrible guitar music blared from speakers at the bandstand. He spun to see Layla May swaying next to Cecil, with Cecil strumming his acoustic guitar off-tempo. Layla May bounced her tambourine on her hip and Richard and Jayne sang "I'll fly away." Julia and Charlotte danced in circles, with Charlotte's new tutu swinging, and the crowd sang along in several different keys.

Harry watched as the balloon began to rise with Cordy in it. He'd heard nothing about this happening. He clenched his mouth tighter. *This is a walking lawsuit. Who had approved of this? Why had he not been told about it?*

All of his resolve to be pleasant disappeared like ice under the fiery heat of anger. He lunged forward to stop the events but was seconds too late to grab the side of the rising balloon basket. He grabbed one of the tethers, thinking he could stop the balloon. He held onto the tether and felt his feet rise off of the ground. He heard someone yell. The balloon continued to gain elevation. Suddenly, Harry realized he had better let go of the tether or risk being taken a hundred feet into the air. Letting the tether slip through his fingers, he began a fast fall. In a split second, Harry knew he was in serious trouble and screamed.

Nick and Bart heard the scream and looked above them. They saw Harry falling. They tried to catch him. The impact of Harry's two hundred- and twenty-five-pound body falling from twenty feet sent them sprawling. They landed in a heap with Bart rolling off

Nick and Harry groaning as he came to a stop. The music stopped. The men lay on the ground in a cloud of dust, catching their breath as Rose, Brianna, and Julia rushed to them. Charlotte moved closer, her eyes big and her cheeks covered with cotton candy.

Leaning over the side of the basket, Skeeter shook her head and yelled, "What happened?"

Bart and Nick turned their heads to stare at Harry.

CHAPTER 33

On a spectacular day in mid-June, friends of Joe sat on wooden benches in an amphitheater that overlooked jagged mountain peaks. Pastor Stan stood at a pulpit with his back to a stunning view of the northern Sawatch Mountains with Mount of the Holy Cross rearing in the middle of the range. The amphitheater was called the Wedding Deck and was accessible by a gondola ride out of Vail Village.

To view the Mount of the Holy Cross was something close to holiness. At 14,001-feet, the mountain soared from the valley, harsh black granite naked of vegetation. The snowy cross in the mountain reared some 1,500 feet high with horizontal arms almost 750 feet across. Ravines fifty to eighty feet in depth held the vast tons of snow in place during the winter.

A mining theory claimed the vertical staff of the cross contained gold. If not true, it didn't matter. The Mount of the Holy Cross was a religious symbol, natural feature, and inspiration for love, marriage, life, and death. To behold it on a glorious summer day was close to a heavenly experience. The Wedding Deck was like nothing on earth.

Pastor Stan felt a slight breeze on his cheek. It reminded him that he was alive and thankful for this day and the people who were seated on the benches in the amphitheater. He looked at many faces he knew: Tony Sabattini, Harry and Rose, Skeeter and Bart, Beth and Bruce, George, Lori from the Library, Richard with Finn, Sven and Jon next to him, Jayne, Layla May, Julia and Nick, and Charlotte, Charmaine, Sherry, Carmen with her husband and children, other staff from the Piney Center, and family friends of Joe's, plus those who did not know Joe but came anyhow to honor the other residents of the Piney Center who were no longer on earth. Beth sat with Bruce, who wore a starched shirt and pressed pants. A few new residents of the Piney Center sat in the crowd: Doris whose body shook from Parkinson's Disease and whose daughter was an Olympic ski racer, and Brad, a gentleman with dementia who had fought in World War II and survived being a POW. A moment of sadness trilled through Stan's body when he acknowledged Joe was missing from the group, as were Hanni, Cordy, and Millie. Cordy had slipped into a coma and died. Millie had passed away from heart failure with Bart by her side.

Cecil sat on a stool beside Pastor Stan and sang John Denver's song, "Country Roads". When the last word crossed his lips, he lifted his head and smiled. Every person seated in view of the mountain with the cross knew Cecil had given his best to Joe and the others.

Pastor Stan began, "Thank you, Cecil, for the beautiful rendition of a song we all love." He looked to his left to see Charlotte swinging a bright pink coat in a circle while creating a cloud of dust. "We are here today to honor Joseph Sabattini who we came to know, admire, and love while he lived and thrived at the Piney Center. Joe was born in Brooklyn, New York, and depending on who was telling the story, he was either ninety-seven or one-hundred-and-two years young when he passed away." Stan saw smiles from most of those in attendance. For the next twenty minutes, Pastor Stan related the long and storied life of Joe Sabattini and his happy marriage to Mary. When he mentioned Mary, he found Beth and smiled. He also glanced a few times to Harry who did not change expression although Stan was aware Harry knew the story of the fake Mary who gave Joe peace and allowed Joe to let go of life.

Bart, handsomely outfitted in a starched black shirt, pressed Levi's, a leather belt with silver buckle, and polished black cowboy boots, slipped his hand into Skeeter's. She turned toward his profile and almost had to pinch her arm to jolt herself. She was loved by this man and had given him her heart. Pastor Stan's words floated into her brain but didn't stick; no one had to tell her about Joe or Mary or the others who had become such a part of her and now were gone.

From the valley below the Mount of the Holy Cross, a large bird swooped up the ridge and sailed over the amphitheater. All eyes went to the bird as it glided away, his wings only flapping once.

Cecil blurted, "A bald eagle. By golly, that's Joe giving us a sign everything is okay."

Pastor Stan watched the eagle soar off into the distance. "I think you're correct, Cecil. Let the eagle be a lesson to us not to mourn the passing of a life well-lived. Celebrate. Soar with the eagles. Count the times our souls smiled together, especially Joe's smile. He reached out invisibly, yet tangibly, and touched each of us. Death is not final but only an end of a chapter, and I believe Joe and his Mary are journeying together in a new chapter."

Charlotte skipped alongside the seated audience, paused at the bottom of seats, turned to see if anyone noticed her, assumed not, and hurried to her granddad. She wiggled between his legs, facing the audience. Sunshine glistened off of a big white ribbon pinned in her hair. She smiled, the beam of childhood and innocence.

Pastor Stan finished his words about Joe and the new adventure which Joe, Cordy, Hanni, and Millie had begun. He then opened up the stage for anyone to say words about Joe. Dressed much like Joe always did in a polo shirt, khaki pants, and plaid sports coat, his son, Tony, walked to the podium and spoke in a firm voice, reminiscing about a dad who loved baseball, loved his wife, and when he smiled it lighted the entire room. Harry also spoke, as did Richard, and Layla May. Then Beth got up and stepped to the podium.

Skeeter began to rise to go to her grandmother to bring her back to her seat, but Bart squeezed her hand and held her back. "It's okay," he said.

Beth stood at the podium. She fidgeted with a Kleenex. Today Beth's hair brushed her cheeks, the curls a little longer than they were several months ago. Some days, her memory was fine, while other days her mind felt clogged with lint or clay or a haze of film. A breeze lifted her hair and she brushed it out of her eyes. "Joe," she said in almost a whisper. "I knew him for only a few days, but I realized that in the first moment he saw me, he was aware of what was inside of my heart. He whispered 'Mary'. Then Joe gave me the smile that lighted the whole room." She sighed. "A smile can last forever, and for me it has. I gave him Mary and it enabled him to smile once again." With a nod, she left the podium and sat down. Some whispers came from the crowd, questions about what Beth had meant. Those from the Piney Center understood. Harry grinned.

Pastor Stan thanked everyone for their comments and turned to Cecil. "Will you end our service with another song?"

Cecil worked his jaw. "Delighted," he said, adjusted his guitar, and began to sing "I'll Fly Away." With Mount of the Holy Cross at his back, Cecil serenaded the mountaintop and valley below. It was a fitting send-off for Joe.

Refreshments were served on the deck at the top of the gondola. Once again, Skeeter had a policeman's eye on the sheet cake while Charlotte circled the table, casting a glance at Skeeter to check to see if she was watching. Richard's walker got stuck in the deck planking and he grumbled, while Cecil's tennis balls kept his walker from sticking. Layla May flirted with any willing male, and Jayne nudged Scout to a safe spot to sit and chat with Carmen and her family.

Bart and Nick nursed bottles of beer and talked about fishing the Eagle River now that the high water had receded for the spring and bugs had hatched for trout to snatch. Skeeter visited with Hanni's sons and thanked Finn for returning to Colorado for Joe's service. She also met many people who had come to pay their respects to Joe and the others.

With a glass of iced tea in his hand, Harry joined Skeeter and Pastor Stan by the refreshment table. "You two," Harry began, which was his way of starting a conversation awkwardly.

Pastor Stan nodded. "That's us."

Harry looked around to see if anyone could overhear him. "When I am with you two, I always feel an energy that leaves me nervous."

"I think it's God's love," Stan said.

Harry nodded. "Yes, perhaps." He looked hard at Skeeter. "I still wonder if I did the correct thing when I tore up your termination papers."

"Some things are not easily answered," she said and took a sip from a glass of lemonade, while she watched Charlotte slip around the end of the table toward the cake.

Harry laughed. "I know. However, the Piney Center is a better place because of both of you, and I am a better person because you are there." He shrugged. "This once, I want to say thank you."

Skeeter and Pastor Stan glanced at each other, turned to Harry, and in unison said, "You're welcome."

From across the deck, Bart moved to Skeeter, placed his hand on her waist, pulled her close, and landed a quick kiss on her lips. Then he pulled away, leaving her with a smile…. perhaps a glimpse of what was to come.

Pastor Stan saw the love leap between Skeeter and Bart and guessed the next ceremony here would be a wedding.

"Well, then," Harry added, turning to find Jayne and pointing to her, "what about her last wish?"

Skeeter and Pastor Stan shared glances. Stan stammered; Skeeter bit her lip.

Harry frowned. "What? Something dangerous? Something I won't approve of? No? What?"

Stan shook his head. "Nothing dangerous. Jayne wants to put her feet in the ocean."

Harry's lower lip sagged open. "We live a thousand miles from an ocean."

Watching Charlotte's white hair ribbon move farther toward the cake, Skeeter tuned Harry out, mainly because she knew he would react the way he was reacting.

"There are logistic problems," Stan admitted.

"All solvable," Skeeter interjected while she followed Charlotte's line of travel and saw her hand reach over the edge of the table.

"How?" Harry asked as his eyebrows pinched together.

Stan said, "We thought—"

Skeeter interrupted, "With some planning, we thought you could take her to California."

Harry's eyes grew big. "Me?"

Skeeter smiled. "It should be simple."

Harry mumbled, "Jayne and Scout on a plane, transportation in another state, hotel rooms, meals, a blind person with a dog—"

Stan interrupted, "Not insurmountable."

Skeeter tapped Charlotte on the head. The white ribbon bobbed up and big blue eyes looked guilty although her fingers were free of cake frosting. "Not yet," Skeeter said to Charlotte, and then said to Harry, "Anything is possible, Harry. Trust me."

Harry didn't answer.

Skeeter grinned.

With a knowing look, Pastor Stan thought, *it is as it should be.*

The End

Shirley Welch is the author of The Eagle River Valley (Arcadia Publishing), Vail, the First 50 Years (Arcadia Publishing), Mister Fahrenheit, Dark Horse, Sammy Little, The Sexy U Girl, and Tracking Cat from Amazon Publishing. Shirley lives in Colorado and can be reached at swelch1810@hotmail.com

Dan Matney has been a pastor for twenty-five years and leads a senior adult ministry. He lives in Colorado and can be reached at pastordanmatney@hotmail.com